At Scotland Yard, DI Timothy Stoker is no better than a ghost. A master of arcane documents and niggling details who, unlike his celebrity-chasing colleagues, prefers hard work to headlines. But an invisible man is needed to unmask the city's newest amateur detective, Hieronymus Bash. A bon vivant long on flash and style but short on personal history, Bash just may be a Cheapside rogue in Savile Row finery.

When the four fangs of the Demon Cats of Scavo—trophies that protect the hunters who killed the two vicious beasts—disappear one by one, Stoker's forced to team with the very man he was sent to investigate to maintain his cover. He finds himself thrust into a world of wailing mediums, spiritualist societies, man-eating lions, and a consulting detective with more ambition than sense. Will this case be the end of his career, or the start of an unexpected liaison? Or will the mysterious forces at play be the death of them both?

And just who is Hieronymus Bash?

STOKER & BASH:

The Fangs of Scavo

SELINA KRAY

Stoker & Bash: The Fangs of Scavo

Copyright © 2017 by Selina Kray
Cover Art: Tiferet Design (www.TiferetDesign.com)
Editor: Nancy-Anne Davies
ISBN: 978-0-9959925-1-1

First Edition
June 2017

Dedication

To my friends, Nancy-Anne, Marya,
Astrid, Isabelle, and Colette,
who carried me when I wanted to give up
and loved me when I couldn't love myself.
This book would not exist without you.

Dramatis Personae

THE DETECTIVES
Detective Inspector Timothy Kipling Stoker, Scotland Yard
Hieronymus Bash, a consulting detective of growing renown
Calliope "Callie" Pankhurst, Bash's ward and apprentice
Han Tak Hai, manservant, confidant, sculptor

Superintendent Julian Quayle, Stoker's boss at the Yard
DS Littlejohn, Stoker's nemesis at the Yard
DS Parker, a sergeant at the Yard
DS Small, a sergeant who works at A division
DC Croke, a constable who works at A division
PC Hobbs, a constable who once worked with Stoker

THE MEMBERS OF THE BELGRAVE SPIRITUALISTS' SOCIETY, AKA THE SUSPECTS
Commodore Abyndon "Goldie" Goldenplover, a long-time friend of Bash's
Stephen Tiquin, Earl Blackwood, self-imposed leader
Landgrave Valentine Vandenberg, a German noble
Landgravine Millicent Vandenberg, his wife
Lady Thomasina Stang-Helion, widow
Dahlia Nightingale, a medium
Johann Whicher, her associate

BASH'S HOUSEHOLD
Aldridge, the butler
Minnie, the cook
Angus, the chauffeur
Jie, the ladies' maid
Ting, their daughter
Monsieur Henri, Bash's tailor
also Admiral The Viscount Apollonius "Apollo" Pankhurst, Callie's uncle
and Bash's former lover, deceased.

Chapter 1

*T*he woman hovered in the air above them, mewling in ecstasy.

Hieronymus Bash had never seen anything like it, and he had seen a great many peculiar things. She thrashed her limbs as she swam through the ether. The frills of her cuffs and the billows of her dress rippled like a mermaid's scales. The black cascade of her hair whipped to and fro with the force of a slaver's lash. As she rose toward the shadowy void of the ceiling, her pallid skin took on a spectral cast. All the while she cooed to her spirit guide in that shrill cockatoo's voice that pecked at Hiero's temple.

He needed a drink, preferably something amber and throat searing. He settled for a peek at the other séance participants, mouths agape in rapture. Dahlia Nightingale was one of the rare mediums whose showmanship rivaled P.T. Barnum's. Even Calliope, firm lipped and hawkeyed beside him, leaned forward in her seat. It took more than simple cabinet tricks to impress her.

Not that they had been deprived of the usual theatrics. Once the party had assembled around the sacred circle—Miss Nightingale trussed to her chair with more rope than a goose for roasting—they had shut her into a cabinet. Every element of her imprisonment was inspected by Commodore Goldenplover, their host and master of ceremonies, prior to her enclosure. Her assistant, Mr. Whicher, had led them in the typical incantations, "Come, O spirit, and bless us with your light" and so forth, as the lights dimmed. The clank of the door had startled them; they were locked in.

A tense silence overswept the drawing room. Whorls of smoke misted the air. Whicher snuffed candle after candle until there were only five flickering points of light. Not a shuffle or a rattle could be heard from the cabinet in the long minutes before the doors creaked open to reveal Miss Nightingale, the pale moon of her face hung above them.

With a shrieking moan, her eyes rolled white in their sockets. Her lashes flickered in otherworldly semaphore. Another shriek and her features contorted into the maniacal grin of her spirit guide.

Hiero would not have thought such a plain and slight girl the equal of Brutus Aurelius, Roman gladiator, but she played him with a stunning conviction. Once Miss Nightingale descended from her perch, her stature imposed and her swagger impressed—the mark of a gifted performer. Only the voice gave her trouble. It would have been a feat if she managed a tenor, let alone the deep bass of a career warrior after all that shrieking. As she growled out commands and bickered with the men in the audience—going so far as to strike one—Hiero suffered a twinge of jealousy, the highest compliment he bestowed upon a fellow actor.

Then she levitated, astounding and confounding them all.

"How the devil is she doing this?" Hiero threw his whisper in Callie's direction without turning his head, an old ventriloquists' trick.

"I rather thought you'd know. I deal in logic and reason, not illusion."

"Well, you'd best think fast. Her climax is imminent."

Callie poorly masked a snigger. She loved a double entendre almost as well as a challenge. "Wires, surely, but from where?"

Whicher, armed with an enormous steel hoop, threaded Miss Nightingale's floating body through this makeshift eye with the deftness of a seamstress. Gasps erupted along with a chorus of cheers.

Hiero groaned.

"You do realize," he hissed at Callie, "that there is more than just my reputation at stake? This enterprise of ours—"

"Stop your prattling that I might concentrate!"

Hiero grunted in protest but did as she wished. There was certainly no shortage of spectacle to behold. Brutus, in the form of Miss Nightingale, reenacted the moment of his death, mauled by a lion before a savage Colosseum crowd. The medium clutched her "wounds" with such force she tore rivets in the fabric of her dress. Hiero was surprised she didn't dig her nails into her skin for her audience of aristocrats, famously as bloodthirsty as the Romans.

A booming pop and a burst of flame caught his attention. When Hiero looked back, Miss Nightingale had dropped on the rug like a discarded doll. Commodore Goldenplover and a few others rushed to attend her; the rest burst into applause.

He shifted toward a shamefaced Callie. "Well?"

"I've no earthly notion."

"You think her authentic?"

"I think her... clever."

"More clever than you?"

"Yes, at the moment. But then she does have the advantage of knowing how she's deceiving us."

"But you are confident you can disprove her?"

Callie let out a long, impatient breath. "Given time, I have no doubt. She is no more the vessel of a Roman gladiator than I am the reincarnation of Boudicca."

"You are no less towering a figure, my dear."

This earned him a faint smile. "Your flattery, though kind, isn't very helpful."

"In but one sentence, you have distilled the essence of my character."

"Don't I well know it." By this time the crowd at the center had dispersed. Miss Nightingale, swaddled like a newborn babe, sank into a fat-cushioned armchair across from them. "What will you do, Hiero? I'll not come to any solid conclusions in the next few minutes."

"Why, my dear, what I do best." He leaned in to whisper into the shell of her ear. "Stall."

The drawing room doors whooshed open, and a fleet of footmen swooped in, bearing trays of after-dinner cocktails and mignardises. No sooner had Hiero snatched himself a brandy than Callie stole it out of his hand with a censorious look.

"You'll do this sober, or you won't do it at all."

"A few spirits never hurt the cause of disproving... well, spirits. I'll have you know—"

Commodore Goldenplover stood to address them. Hiero shut his eyes, took a moment to ready himself, then swung around to face his rival.

If by "rival" one meant "old friend." Commodore Abyndon "Goldie" Goldenplover had served in the Royal Navy with Calliope's uncle and guardian, Admiral The Viscount Apollonius "Apollo" Pankhurst, since their boyhood. Their friendship, forged on the high seas, solidified through cannon fire and toil, spanned four decades and three marriages with no issue. While Apollo and Goldie never shared a bed out of more than necessity, they did share certain proclivities, and thus became the keepers of each other's secret. Hiero had come to know Goldie through his prolonged and very special relationship with Apollo, his lover of many years. Their acquaintance intensified into true comradeship upon the admiral's death and Hiero's inheritance of his lover's fortune. So was born their long-time debate over all things supernatural.

Goldie was a believer, one of the four founding members of the Belgrave Spiritualists' Society, a group dedicated to proving the existence of the spirit realm. To this end this first of four soirees had been organized to showcase the so-called talents of Dahlia Nightingale, a rising star in spiritualist circles, with each of the founding members taking their turn as host. After years of decrying his friend's hobby, Hiero had been invited to Goldie's showcase for the express purpose of playing devil's advocate. He endeavored not to disappoint.

"Ladies and gentlemen," Goldie barked as if he commanded a motley group of seamen rather than guests. "I am pleased to announce Miss Nightingale's communion with the beyond is not the only course of entertainment on our menu this evening. As you know, the Belgrave Spiritualists' Society has never turned away the doubting Thomases who seek to infiltrate our ranks. Rather we welcome them with open minds and avid ears. Speculation is an essential part of our investigations and, as no less an authority than Milton said, 'I cannot praise a fugitive and cloistered virtue, unexercised and unbreathed, that never sallies out and sees her adversary.'

"In attendance tonight is a man who has caused something of a sensation in our circles. His most recent exploits include the return of Lady Windermere's prized collection of antique fans, the resolution of that gruesome incident in Morgue Road, and the events that led to the arrest of the thief who nabbed Lord Collins's moonstone. He is also, despite his purpose here tonight, a gentleman I am proud to call friend. I give you Mr. Hieronymus Bash!"

The applause was polite, but then Hiero had faced his share of hostile crowds. With a twirl of his cape, he leapt to his feet, striding to the center of the room. The circle of chairs had stretched into a demented oval; some guests had fled to the fireplace or the drinks trolley. For a long, silent moment, he surveyed his audience, allowing them to take his measure. He met each person's eyes with his most penetrating look—a technique that revealed very little about one's guilt or innocence but served to unnerve the faint of heart. A few nervous nellies, he had learned, could often sway the mob in his direction.

Hiero spared his most thorough examinations for the other

members of the Belgrave Spiritualists' Society. The twinkle in Landgrave Valentine Vandenberg's ice-blue eyes belied the sternness of his Teutonic features. When his father's landgraviate, Hesse-Kassel, was annexed by Prussia, he was permitted to keep his meaningless title, but robbed of its lands and power. A shrewd marriage transplanted him to London and blessed him with a Dutch surname. The trace of a smirk he spared Hiero hinted at mischief.

Lady Thomasina Stang-Helion may have been dressed in mourning hues, but her smile could not have been brighter. Though she had lost her husband several years earlier, she remained as faithful to him as their sovereign to her Albert, and just as determined not to let this shadow over her heart darken her disposition. As they locked gazes, Hiero sensed her mentally matchmaking him with a suitable list of lady friends.

Stephen Tiquin, Earl Blackwood's face was as seamless as a Chinese box and, despite Hiero's best efforts, as unlikely to crack. A chilly personality who ruled the Society with an usurper's stealth, he had few intimates. The three-foot circle of space around him at all times spoke for itself. In the dark fathoms of Lord Blackwood's eyes lurked the gleam of a zealot.

A fizzy undercurrent of tension buoyed the atmosphere in the room. Hiero straightened his back, cleared his throat, and began.

"'All the world's a stage, and we are its players.'" The last of the conversations hushed in the wake of his pronouncement. "Some of us actors play fair. Some do not. I could waste valuable breath disproving Miss Nightingale's methods, but I feel it more effective to prove to you that anyone, with a little help and a little practice, can reproduce them." A delicious ripple of disbelief and intrigue sped through the crowd. "I've identified three stages to her performance—and apologies to the lady, but it *was* a performance."

"So you say." Lord Blackwood scoffed.

"Yes, well, I *am* the one tasked with disproving her. I would gladly pass you the baton, if you cared to... grasp it." Hiero relished the resulting titters almost as much as the reddening of Blackwood's face. Zealots. So easily provoked. "I judge you to have a firm hand."

"You'll see the back of it before the evening's done."

"I look forward to that singular pleasure, my lord."

"Perhaps we should proceed?" Goldie interjected with a meaningful look.

Hiero waved him off. "As I said, three distinct stages: the enclosure in the cabinet, the transformation into Brutus, and the grand finale." A subtle gesture invited his manservant and bodyguard, Han, to bring the ropes. "Stage one."

With a magician's flair, he stripped down to his sleeves, entrusting Han with each successive layer of garment. Hiero then sat in the very same chair used by Miss Nightingale for the trick, permitting himself to be roped and chained in the same manner, but outside the cabinet. Once Han completed the preparations, Hiero invited his audience to test the strength of the binding.

To no one's surprise, Lord Blackwood was elected. He pulled and prodded far more than strictly necessary, even going so far as to slip a finger between Hiero's wrists and the twine to check for slack.

"If only he was so thorough in his spiritual investigations," Hiero muttered to Han as he shoved the chair to the side to improve the audience's view.

"We should forget about this disproving nonsense and keep you there," Goldie chuckled. Hiero heard Callie second his laughter. "If this goes wrong, you've every right."

"You could display him in your gallery, Abyndon," Lady Stang-Helion suggested. "An avant-garde display called..."

"*The Court Jester!*" Landgrave Vandenberg supplied to the amusement of all.

They recovered from their hysterics to discover Hiero free of his shackles and standing atop his chair. He answered their universal shock with a neat little bow.

"Stage two. Do clear the space."

Han shooed away those too dumbfounded to respond. They all stood, wide-eyed and slack-mouthed, on the outskirts of the circle. Hiero swiftly made the rounds, another glare for each one in turn. He'd convinced some, but others redoubled their defiance.

Three guesses as to whom.

"Stop gaping like fish!" Lord Blackwood admonished. "The medium clearly managed to escape her bonds—he has done nothing but prove her capable. Let us see him replicate Brutus!"

"In time. But first..." Hiero revolved once more around the crowd, then selected the snobbiest-looking of the lot. "You, madam. Name the first animal that comes to mind. Quick!"

"An orangutan."

"Wonderful! An ape. Hmm... Not much of a transformation required, some would say, but I'll let you be the judge."

Hiero convulsed. The ladies gasped. He swung his head from side to side in a slow rhythm, hunching his shoulders, crouching down until his fists dragged on the floor. Hiero scrabbled up to the very same woman, chittering and hopping, frenzied in his primitive gestures. He loped over to a portly man, who patted him on the head as he played with his pocket watch. He latched himself to a footman's leg and gibbered until he won himself a sprig of grapes, which he proceeded to pluck off and pop in his mouth. The grapes weren't the only thing Hiero had in the palm of his hand.

"You!" Han pointed to a young bespectacled man. "Name another."

"Um... a cormorant."

Hiero fluttered his arms like wings, and he let out a wild screech.

"You!" He singled out Lady Stang-Helion. "Another!"

"A lion."

Hiero hoped his roar impressed her.

"You!" Han targeted Landgrave Vandenberg. "A public figure."

"Gladstone."

Quelle surprise, Hiero thought, having perfected his impression long ago.

"Commodore Goldenplover," Han beckoned.

"Hmm, yes. Well... how about Dickens?"

Thankfully Hiero had had the pleasure.

He cycled through a few more popular figures until he struggled to pitch his voice above the delighted chatter. At Han's nod he sprang over to the fireside, grabbed a poker, and smashed it on the grate. The resounding clang echoed through the room as the dizzy crowd fell silent.

Hiero rose up to his full height, firmed both his jaw and his stance. He stared down each and every member of his audience with the feral eyes of Brutus, and to a one, they cowered. He cocked his arm as if holding a shield, wielding the fire poker like the deadliest of broadswords. He repeated some of the drivel Dahlia Nightingale had cooked up for her character—though he liked to think he improved upon some of her sketchier shadings—until one woman swooned.

With a sizzle and a bang, Han set off one of the medium's fireworks. Someone in the crowd yelped, but few were fooled. When they turned back, Hiero was himself again, waving them back into their seats.

"You see? Mere artifice. A technique any disciplined performer can learn."

Han brought him a glass of water while the debate buzzed, his detractors no doubt currying favor before voicing their objections. Goldie, too, made his way over, a mercurial smile on his lips.

"Two out of three doesn't win the day."

"How now?" Hiero's feigned innocence was by far his worst performance of the evening.

"Her flight. How was it done?"

"Now, Goldie, let's leave the lady some of her secrets, shall we?"

"Given your critique, that's rather sporting of you."

"We charlatans must stick together."

"So it would seem." His smile reached his eyes, but he did not relent. "This mark, alas, will not have his pocket so easily picked. The third stage. Explain."

Just as Hiero made to speak—to lie, it must be said—the door to the drawing room creaked eerily open. The lights in the corridor had gone out. Black and empty as the gaping mouth of a cave, cool air hissed in through the doorway. Silence fell like the slice of an ax. The men, shivering, looked to one another. The women stared into the void, paralyzed by fright.

From the couch Miss Nightingale purred, "Let us in, let us in, let us in..."

A tiny shadow hovered at the threshold, its outline dark against darker. A man cursed; a woman fainted. Miss Nightingale's moans intensified. One specter begat another. A twin pair of Siamese cats slunk into the room, swishing their tails in synchronicity.

No one moved. No one breathed as the felines separated, stalked around a group gathered in the center of the room, their gem eyes glittering in the gaslight. The guests withered away from them like flowers at winter's first chill. Callie rushed forward, grabbed one by the scruff. Both yowled, but only she got clawed. Han shooed the cats away, handkerchief at the ready.

"What the blazes is going on?" Goldie demanded of no one, charging for the door. "Simmons, where are you?"

The lights in the corridor blinked on, and Goldie's head butler crashed into view.

"My lord! They've taken the fang!"

At the bang of the gavel, the uproar began. Reporters swooped down from their perches like eagles after a snake, clamoring for an interview. Bailiffs wrestled their way through the crowds to form a protective wall around the defense table. The accused's mother and sisters spouted fountains of tears while the murdered baby's family looked as if they'd been chained to an anchor and tossed into the ocean. The gallery swirled with infuriated onlookers, a whirlpool ready to sweep under any who dared wade in. Fanny Starling, now a free woman, cowered behind her solicitors, as frail and skittish as her namesake. Only the row of detectives sat stoic as the turrets of the Tower of London, united in their silent condemnation of the verdict.

Detective Inspector Timothy Kipling Stoker had only played a minor part in the case, but its horrors still haunted his dreams. A babe strangled, discarded in an outhouse in the dead of night. Hill Road Manor full of slumbering suspects and enough secrets to suffocate the lot. A neglected window, which might have invited in unforeseen troubles. The rural constabulary had bungled the evidence and delayed calling in the Yard. The facts had been as tangled as a ball of twine, their efforts as useless as a cat's paws at unraveling all the barbed knots.

The primary, DI Kent, had favored the child's nurse for the crime, the same Miss Starling now acquitted. By his present glower, Kent rued his earlier belligerence. Tim had had his own suspicions but, charged with investigating any financial or political motive, was in no position to protest. He doubted any of them would soon forget the photos of little Constance, blue-faced but still angelic, dredged in shit up to her purple neck. Bile flooded his mouth at the thought the murderer today walked free, no matter his suspicions, that another child might be subject to such terror and humiliation. Such was the policeman's burden.

Once the crowd had drained from the gallery, he stood with his colleagues, then followed their funeral procession out. DI Clarke led the charge, followed by DS Palmer, DI Kent, Superintendent Quayle, and DS Littlejohn, with Tim bringing up the rear. The sea of loiterers parted as they moved through the hull of the Old Bailey, but didn't hesitate to spit or froth at the mouth. Vengeance had been denied them; the detectives would do as scapegoat.

The roar of the angry mob awaiting them woke Tim from his somber mood. Hundreds clogged the streets, armed with anything at hand, from skull-crushers like rocks and sticks to squishy projectiles like produce. Local constables did their best to hold back the unruliest elements, acting as human shields, but the crowd was out for blood. Until the defendant dared show her face, the detectives who failed to build a proper case against her would do.

Tim dodged a cabbage as he staggered out into the chaos, chasing his colleagues down the steps toward an awaiting Black Maria van. He hung back as they piled into its long, hearse-like cabin, no different than the criminals they transported. The crowd around them surged, running like dodos into the truncheons of the guardian constables, who sported so many tears and bruises it was hard to distinguish them from the toughs. When Tim reached for his own bat, Littlejohn clamped an iron grip on his wrist.

"Careful, Stoker! A swing of that'll put your eye out."

"I'm quite capable, if you'd like a demonstration."

"Of twiddling your billy? Don't doubt it. But defending your fellow peelers is man's work. Go back to your paper stroking."

"Must have missed you rushing to fend off the mob, *Little John.*"

This earned him a snort. "E division's shout. Get in."

"I will not."

"Stoker." Superintendent Julian Quayle's gunpowder voice boomed over the din. "With me."

Tim threw off Littlejohn, who looked none too pleased, then fought his way up into the front passenger seat. Quayle was already at the whip, lashing out at the horde as well as the horses until finally the back door thumped shut. Two knocks on the ceiling, two snaps of the reigns, and two indignant snorts later, they lurched forward, that section of the crowd smart enough not to risk getting trampled. It was slow going until they turned onto Ludgate Hill Road, the street traffic dense but moving.

The sharp autumn wind stuck tiny pins into the sweaty patches of his skin. Tim flipped up his collar, wishing he had remembered his good leather gloves. He struggled to keep his posture relaxed, his shoulders from huddling lest Quayle think him any more of a lightweight. He had been forced upon Quayle by his superior, Commissioner Winterbourne, after Tim discovered Quayle's predecessor was skimming off an unfair share of the rewards his detectives were gifted for solving crimes. Rather than earn Tim the respect of his fellow Yardsmen and the admiration of his new guv, the move—no more nor less than his sworn duty—had made him something of a pariah.

Though Quayle made use of his talents, he never failed to re-mind Tim of his flaws. Quayle was a man of action, a taskmaster with surprisingly little patience for detail. Tim, on the other hand, was a master of fine print, the elegant script to Quayle's childish block letters. While the other detectives cut a bold swath through the city's criminal element, Tim preferred to excel in anonymity. He did not require a reputation or celebrity to get the job done.

What galled Quayle most was how he needed Tim, precisely because of his discretion. The most lucrative cases were often the ones that involved no screaming headlines or public fascination, but a deft, invisible hand. Rewards were much heftier if the nobility's scandals weren't trumpeted from every newsstand. But instead of seeing Tim as an ally—someone to save him from his shortcom-ings—Quayle instead treated him like a dog that regularly soiled the carpet. An attitude Tim didn't care to encourage.

"Dismal business," Quayle grumbled. "Another target on our back, make no mistake." He shot a glare in Tim's direction. "I suppose you expected this. Should have left you back at the Bailey to celebrate."

"Sir—"

"It was the best evidence we had. The only evidence. You saw how they were, like vultures over a carcass. We had to feed them something."

Tim sighed. "Well, they've made a meal of it."

Quayle hocked up a wad of phlegm, spat it at a passing vendor. Built hammerlike and solid from his boots up, shoulders wide as barbells, there wasn't a delicate thing about him. Not his flat bruiser's nose, not his anvil jaw, not his beef-slab lips, or the plank of his forehead. Not his beady eyes or the grimy blonde curls of his hair. Tim often pictured him as a white gorilla, with all the brute force and gymnastic agility that implied.

"We need a win. Public is fickle. We've still got 'em, even with the dog's dinner we made of this last one, but others..."

"The commissioner?"

"Higher than him. Higher than the likes of you and me could ever climb."

Tim nodded. "They don't like a circus."

"Unless it keeps people spinning their wheels. Distracted. This latest business—"

"Shined too bright a light?"

Quayle snorted. "Got it in one. I've got something that needs your... special touch."

"Is she blonde and poonted?"

Superintendent Quayle let out a grunt of surprise. Tim had caught him off-guard, and he relished the moment.

"We'll make a proper copper of you yet, Stoker." He slowed the horses as they veered onto the Strand. "It's one for them and for us. No clamor, no fuss. No circus on this one. Just quiet, solid work. And a big win, of course."

"Understood. What is it?"

Quayle smirked. "You're always bragging you've got your ear to the ground. You tell me."

Tim crossed his arms over his chest in what he hoped would be mistaken for a gesture of consideration. He secretly tucked his hands into the warmth of his armpits as he chewed the matter over. It would be a case that, on the surface, spoke to his talents: chasing down long-forgotten documents, tracing obscure financial or historical connections, hiding in plain sight. It would involve the noble classes since Tim had learned to elevate his accent. It would involve someone or something their superiors wished to dispose of discreetly. It would also be a trap. Tim was a white whale to them, remarkable but dangerous and capable of drowning them all. He was only a threat to them insofar as they believed him one, but they were true believers.

A thought occurred to him then that fired his blood, such that he no longer felt a lick of the cold.

"Hieronymus Bash."

Quayle's nod confirmed it.

Even as the carriage jostled him about, Tim suddenly felt himself on much more solid ground. He had been following the exploits of the self-affirmed "consulting detective" for months. The gentleman—if indeed a gentleman he was—selected his cases with a care to the most lucrative. Tim was convinced he preyed on the vulnerability of his clients, promising an efficiency and discretion the Met could never match. Little wonder his superiors had taken notice. Something about the man and his methods did not add up. Fortunately Tim excelled at sums.

"At last. What clinched it, sir?"

"What else? A reward." Superintendent Quayle shook his head. "A hundred pounds that could have been ours for the taking."

"A hundred!"

"Aye, and Lord Collins's eternal gratitude. Priceless."

"Bash recovered the moonstone?"

"That he did, and mere days after DI Clarke declared the case unsolvable."

"I see." Tim could not quite suppress a smile. Here, finally, the case that could make his name. If he exposed Hieronymus Bash for a fraud—a man who had bested the Yard's own detectives time and again—then Quayle could no longer deny Tim's worth. "When do I start?"

"Sharpish. The investigation's off book, so keep all your work under lock and key. Everything else goes through me. You'll not breathe a word of it, understand?"

"You think Bash has eyes at the Yard?"

Quayle huffed. "That noggin of yours." He cracked the reins; the horses sped up as they merged onto Trafalgar Square. "What we know about him could fit between my teeth. It's your job to change that. Get me enough to shut him down for good."

"It will be my pleasure, sir."

Hiero was bedazzled. Behind a thin sheet of glass, a world of color exploded, so vibrant that he almost giggled. He envisioned smashing through that frail barrier and feasting his eyes on the buoyant blues, iridescent yellows, ripe purples, and opulent oranges. If only he could shrink to fairy size and bedeck himself in the glamorous butterfly wings, he'd have the perfect frock for every mood, every occasion. Rows and rows of the little jewels stretched out before him, not a one the same. Some were demure, with only a few flecks or spots to distinguish them. Some were flamboyant, one wild but monochromatic color trumpeting their arrival. Some were mysterious, their black, curvaceous wings hiding their true nature.

To a one they'd stolen Hiero's heart. Such as it was.

"Any chance you'd care to contribute to the investigation?" Han asked.

Hiero fluttered round and fixed him with his most ingratiating look. It had no effect.

"How can I when there is such... majesty to behold?"

Now that he had taken a proper look at the room, he found

much to distract him. Though nothing else in Goldie's personal museum matched his collection of rare butterflies for beauty, the treasures of his many African adventures were something to behold. The plush skins of a dozen vicious beasts adorned the walls along with the spears and swords that felled them. Exotic specimens were planted along the sill of the lone window while more robust others stood potted in every corner. Freestanding pillars displayed the most precious items: a marble urn, an ornate headdress, a mummy's skull, a golden scythe, a statue of a fearsome god, a gem-encrusted goblet...

Only one stood empty. A room full of the rarest and most priceless treasures, and the thief had taken a giant tooth. The mind boggled.

"Leave him," Callie instructed. "I'll brief him when we're done." She dragged a tiny brush across the top of the display case, searching for debris.

"Are you hoping the thief left some magic dust?" Hiero queried.

"Residue. *If* it was one of the medium's crew."

"I would have thought them the least likely of the suspects since they were... well, afloat when the robbery occurred."

Callie scoffed. "We've yet to establish a timeline, so I wouldn't go making any grand pronouncements. Go back to your butterflies."

Hiero looked to Han, who betrayed no more expression than before.

"Very well. But if I'm to interrogate Goldie..."

"Mr. Han, will you take him for a walk? I can't concentrate."

"Too suspicious."

"Have him talk to the servants, where he won't do any harm."

"I'm not a child to be dismissed without supper," Hiero protested.

"Then quit your very best impression of one." Callie flicked the last of the debris into a metal tin, then clamped it shut. "The situation is impossible enough without you contributing your usual chaos."

Han frowned. "How so?"

Callie sighed deeply. "Where do I begin? The room was locked with a policeman stood outside the door. The only other exit is the window, and even discounting the hundred-foot drop, none of the plants that line the sill were disturbed. Not an impossible feat, but it was a cold night, and there is not a wrinkled leaf or patch of brown on them. Also, if that had been the point of entry, it's unlikely the thief would have closed the window while he committed his crime since time was of the essence. The plants would have been affected. As there are no secret passages, we return to the door, and to the policeman, *who did not have the key to the lock.*"

"Locks can be picked. Especially, I wager, by policemen," Hiero countered.

"Let us proceed with discounting everyone else in the house before accusing Detective Constable Croke of robbery."

Han nodded. "If we look at them, they will look at us."

"Smart." Hiero gasped. "I mean, oh!"

"Indeed." Callie scanned the room once more with her shrewd gaze. "Not only must we evade detection, but we must disprove the most preposterous theory known to man or mouse."

She gestured toward the pillarlike display case, which betrayed evidence of mauling. A crazed pattern of scratch marks scaled all four of its sides, the feline culprits nowhere to be found after the frenzy that erupted in the wake of the fang's disappearance.

"I daresay the mice will want nothing to do with this affair." Hiero chuckled.

"Don't you dare," Callie hissed. "If *you* hadn't insisted on involving us in this absurd pet project of yours—"

"But it was such pun!"

"Cats, Hiero. I must prove to a group of educated adults that a pair of cats did not steal into this room and abscond with an invaluable prize. Before and after their jaunt to the drawing room to spook us out of our wits."

"We have them by the leash, my dear. Now they must be brought to heel."

She let out a short, exasperated laugh before muttering, "If only I could housebreak you."

"Now that we have discounted all four-legged suspects," Han, always the peacemaker, remarked, "perhaps we might consider some human ones?"

Callie shook her head. "Until we can confirm the how of it, we can't even begin to speculate on the who or the why."

Han nodded. "Be interesting to see what Commodore Gold-enplover has to say."

"Ask and he shall appear." Goldie swept through the door. "How are you progressing?"

"At a bit of a standstill, I fear," Hiero informed him. "We await only your say-so to launch ourselves into the investigation in earnest."

"Yes, well, it has been a trial convincing Blackwood." Already Hiero and his colleagues had been forced to delay till the following morning, due to Lord Blackwood's insistence on calling in Detective Sergeant Abraham Small and his men. Fortunately they had done little more than confirm the lock was undamaged and interview the guests. "He's a bit too straight of an arrow, if you know what I mean."

"It would be the sensible thing to do," Callie remarked. "If you prefer—"

Goldie clicked his tongue. "Nonsense. The fang was mine. If it had belonged to the Society, then. . ."

"So it has no mystical properties?"

"I didn't say that." Goldie's smile turned positively devilish. Hiero always thought there was a dash of the performer in him. "Have I never told you the story of the Fangs of Scavo?"

"No doubt, but we'd do well to hear it afresh."

"Preferably while enjoying some refreshments," Hiero suggested.

"Surely I'm not the only one who's a bit parched?"

"Capital idea. Let's retire to my study, and we'll leave these two to their..." He waved his hand in Callie and Han's direction.

"Oh, I'm certain I've never heard the tale." In a blink Callie was as docile and compliant as a girl half her age. She hooked her arm in Goldie's, curling her dainty fingers around his forearm. "Surely you wouldn't leave me to fend for myself when I could be in your fine company?"

"I fear it is a tale too harrowing for your delicate sensibilities, my girl."

Hiero quickly intervened. "Her sensibilities have the stamina of a thoroughbred, I assure you. Of course you shall join us! And I imagine it would be no bother in an avowed spiritualist's household to conjure up some tea?"

"No bother at all. I'll get my best necromancers on it." Goldie stage-whispered to her, "But don't breathe a word to the cooks!"

The mismatched pair led the procession out of the room. Han, by virtue of his stillness and silence, went unnoticed by Goldie as they settled into the study. Hiero collapsed into one of the two sleighlike leather chairs before the hearth—the kind that invited a late-morning nap. Callie perched on a footstool by Goldie's side in the manner of a favored child or family dog, her gaze adoring.

That girl could charm her way out of a nest of asps, Hiero thought to himself as the tea was poured. Hiero managed to spike his tea without her notice. Goldie, ever his coconspirator in this, stealthily gestured toward his own cup. Hiero caught Han's glint of disapproval from his station beside the door and ignored it, as he always did. A few drams from his flask, and they were ready to begin.

Goldie took a long sip from his own cup, his gaze lost to the flames. "It is a rare occasion when two of the subjects dearest to one's heart intermarry, but such was the case on our trip to the East African Protectorate last spring. Lord Blackwood and I, as you know, go on safari every year. The members of the Spiritualists Society accompanied us on this particular journey, as we had been invited to observe a ritual of special significance to the Mbatha tribe.

"The Mbatha have served and guided us for decades, and we count many as friends. They are vital to the success of our expedition each year. I would not see them harmed. They are a gentle people of joy, of kindness, of faith. They did not deserve what was to come."

"What sort of ritual was it?" Callie asked.

"An exorcism." Goldie let out a slow, fervent breath. "Or that is how we would best understand it. Chiwi, our headman, explained that two of the girls in his village had been acting strange for months: defying their elders, escaping their huts at night, exhibiting inappropriate behavior toward men, and other such mischief. Both had just begun their moon cycles. The village shaman performed the usual purification rituals, but to no avail. They shouted insults, spoke in tongues. These girls had always been adored by the tribe. There could be no other conclusion. Demons had possessed them."

Hiero felt more than saw Han bristle at his words. He hastened to intervene when he saw Callie's cheeks burn a furious red. "Did you yourself witness the girls' behavior before the, er... ritual?"

"We did not. They had been chained to a post in the middle of the tent circle—an odd practice with wild beasts roaming about, but, well..."

"Quite." Hiero himself had difficulty swallowing back his own objections. "Were all the members of the Society present?"

"The founders, yes. Myself, Lord Blackwood, Landgrave Vandenberg, and Baron Stang-Helion."

"Not Lady Stang-Helion?" Callie found her voice.

Goldie chuckled. "The wilds of Africa are no place for a lady of title and refinement. Our lead hunter, Denys Finch, also remained at our camp, though he missed quite the celebration! We were made to feel like kings. We feasted while the tribe danced and sang... You would have admired the spectacle."

"No doubt."

"When it came time for the ritual, we formed a circle. I know you will voice some clever argument, Bash, but it strikes me as significant that it is always a circle. Every culture, every tradition. When calling spirits, you form a circle." Hiero dismissed any protest with a shake of his head. "The girls were brought to the center. The shaman danced and chanted around them. It was, to be honest, rather pedestrian until the wind picked up. Some of the tribesmen stirred at this, but the shaman waved them down. With a black, tarlike substance, he drew symbols on the girls—who were crazed. They bit at him, shrieked at him, their eyes wide and ghostly white. But still he chanted on above their screams, above the howling wind, above the animal cries in the distance.

"When last he stood above them, armed with a cauldron bubbling over with some blood-red brew, one of the tribe's hunters broke the circle with a shout. I only flicked my eyes away for a moment, but it was enough to see the lions prowling around the village. There were two, and they were enormous. The biggest lions we had ever seen! I turned back to the shaman in time to see him anoint the girls, who screeched as if they were being burned at the stake. The lions roared. The tension in the circle was like a live current of energy buzzing through us all. Something cosmic was occurring in that circle, I tell you!

"It was the nearest I've ever come to… to the beyond. The shaman said a final prayer, and the lions retreated, as if at his bidding. The wind quieted. But the night hummed. We carried it with us all the way back to our camp. I retired feeling that something profound had transpired, not only within that circle, but within me. It was three days later we had word of the first attack."

"But what about the girls?" Callie asked breathlessly.

"The girls indeed. They were the first. By all accounts they had recovered themselves. They were as sweet and as merry as before their ordeal. The whole tribe was renewed… until the night the lions came for them."

"You mean they were…" Hiero couldn't bring himself to give voice to the words.

"Eaten, yes. Dragged out of their tents into the night. They recovered their bones the next day. But it didn't end there. The lions came again and again, terrorizing the tribe. Killing one or two each night they invaded. This kind of targeted attack is unheard of. Lions do prey on humans, but not with such relentless determination. But the lead hunter had broken the circle, you see. He'd let the demons out. And the cats' eyes glowed with their unholy light.

"News of the Demon Cats of Scavo quickly reached our camp. Vandenberg is not much of a hunter, but Blackwood, Helion, and I lent our help. For two months we battled them. The Mbatha lost most of their men. They took Finch as well." Goldie stole another sip of tea, then pressed on. "God rest their souls. These cats had the strength and speed of no animal I've ever had in my sights. I can confirm several direct hits—to no avail. We devised more and more complicated traps—nothing fooled them. Then one night Chiwi and Helion hid in two tall trees, hoping to track them to their lair. We… we found part of Helion the next morning, tangled in the branches. Of Chiwi…"

Goldie paused to clear his throat, eyes shrouded with emotion.

"We got them, in the end, with the shaman's help. He performed some blessing… Can't say what it was. By then there was no one left to translate. Vandenberg wanted to retreat to a safer location, but I think we all understood there was no going back until these beasts had been put to ground. The shaman gifted us with the fangs, one for each of the founders. Lady Stang-Helion has been entrusted with her husband's." He sighed. "It was a black business all around."

No one dared break the mournful silence that followed. Hiero looked to Callie for some signal as to how to proceed. Her scrunched nose and furrowed brow betrayed the furious calculations her mind engaged in, all while petting Goldie's hand. The military man himself struggled to appear unhaunted by the ghosts of the past, nibbling at the biscuit he'd dunked in his tea. Han, in his corner, slept on his feet.

Once again Hiero had to fend for himself.

"Surely you don't believe there to be a supernatural element to the theft of the fang?"

"That, chums, is for you to decide. Like any good medium, I am merely a vessel."

"Has anything occurred to suggest such a link?"

"To my knowledge, no. Unless you think it meaningful that it was stolen during a séance, and it was the only item in my vast collection that was taken. The fang of a jungle cat possessed by a demon."

"Logic dictates those points may be coincidence."

"Inferences, rational inferences, might suggest otherwise."

"You think it rational to suggest a tooth carried a demon here from Africa?"

"You think it logical to dismiss a theory out of prejudice?"

"Prejudice! Is it prejudice to look for answers with one's own eyes—"

"Gentlemen!" Callie bellowed. She shot each a pointed look, sighed, then took the floor. "Commodore Goldenplover, thank you for sharing that tragic tale with us. Please accept our deepest condolences, if belated, over the loss of your friends. I'm certain, Mr. Bash, that we can agree on that?"

"Of course. Forgive me, Goldie. It must have been a terrible ordeal."

He shrugged. "It was a battle, but battles I have seen before. Though those lions were, by far, the most vicious enemy I have ever confronted. But thank you, my friends. Many a great man was lost to those beasts. To say nothing of the two precious girls." He pressed his hand over Callie's. "It is more than passing strange, this trouble. The fangs were meant to protect us from further mischief. I was told the shaman cleansed them of whatever fell power they once possessed."

"Oh!" Callie nearly hopped off her seat. "If that is so, then…" She bit her lip as those inner calculations blazed on. "We have three clear motives for the crime. Yes, three. I feel we can dismiss the notion that whomever took the fang was unaware of its history, for the reasons Commodore Goldenplover made clear just now. Therefore the thieves either believe the fang still possesses some demonic or mystical power and aim to harness it—"

"Now, now!"

"Oh, hush, Hiero. What we believe to be true is irrelevant. We did not commit the crime."

"Fair point." Goldie smirked.

"Don't you start as well. It is equally ridiculous to suggest the fang is magic because someone stole it for that reason."

"What's ridiculous is that all this time I have thought you, Bash, to be the brains of the operation," Goldie opined.

"You are easily swayed."

"So it seems."

"Will you let me speak!" Callie glared them both down, eyes a chilly, murderous blue. "If they do not mean to use the fang for ill, perhaps they mean to use it for good. As a protection. Our second possible motive."

"One that would require more intimate knowledge of what befell us in Africa," Goldie proposed.

"Yes! Good. Very good." She wrote herself a mental note. "Though that might apply to the third motive as well. The most ominous. If the fang is meant to protect the founders of the Society…"

Goldie stiffened. "Then I am no longer under its protection."

"And the thieves may strike again," Hiero and Callie said in unison. They locked eyes and shared a look of pure excitement. Complicit as always.

Chapter 2

$\mathcal{T}$im firmed his mask of indifference as he confronted the two tomblike slabs that barred the entrance to Lord Blackwood's townhouse. A gilt green-eyed jungle cat held the knocker in its toothsome maw——a fitting reminder of the predatory world he was about to enter, where "survival of the fittest" wasn't just a rule of nature, but a way of life. Though he had enough experience of the noble class to mimic their mores and manners, he could never give himself entirely to the role. His policeman's instinct, perhaps, or self-preservation. Everyone who belonged in the working class—even at its higher end—understood their place.

In the guise of Mr. Timothy Kipling, importer of antiquities and other frippery from the Dark Continent, this served him surprisingly well. When he first began his undercover investigations for the Yard, Tim feared nothing more than being found out until he realized every single member of the aristocracy played a part. If his accent occasionally warbled, if his waistcoat fit too snugly, if he didn't know the latest gossip from Whitehall or the Palace, it didn't matter. He needed only affect a superior look and stare down his nose at his companion. Imperiousness always won out.

The door swung open before he had a chance to knock. He followed the head butler down an almost Spartan hallway—given the normal excesses of the upper class–dressed in somber hues. No one would mistake the house for anything but a bachelor's residence. They bypassed the drawing room in favor of the library, whose expanse and grandeur astounded.

Tim fought to school his face as he was announced, but he could not help but think how his father would have marveled at this room. Macassar ebony bookshelves lined three of the four walls from ceiling to floor. These interspersed with statues of gods from the various pantheons—the Greeks in flawless ivory, the Egyptians in bejeweled gold, the Celts in gleaming hematite. Thick velvet curtains blacked out the last shimmers of evening. By the far end, a low-hanging chandelier with astrological motifs hovered, like a ring of glowing orbs, over a round table fit for King Arthur himself. A lone candle cast its sallow light on the enormous wardrobe stood behind. In the center of the room, a podium displayed—it could hardly be believed—a giant tooth in a glass box.

Already several of the guests stood transfixed by the incisor with the opal sheen set on a crystal plate, the better to bedazzle onlookers. Various occult symbols were inscribed around the base, wards against the devil-knew-what kind of supernatural mischief. To Tim's mind the only thing that kept the ghouls away was a clear conscience.

"Mr. Kipling." There was an unmistakable note of summons in Lord Blackwood's reedy voice. Tim hurried to heed his temporary master. "How good of you to come."

"It is I who am honored by the invitation, my lord." Tim fought the urge to genuflect.

"What do you think of my latest treasure?"

"Exceptional." Tim tried to convey his gratitude at Lord Blackwood's efforts to establish his identity, all the while praying he need not expound on the tooth's virtues. He had encountered many incomprehensible things in his years at the Yard. This stood among the most confounding. "If only you'd care to part with it…"

"Now, now, Kipling," Blackwood chided as if they were old friends. "We are here to investigate the mysteries of the universe, not to conduct business."

"My lord, as you well know, I am always open to negotiation."

He chuckled. "You old scoundrel. Very well. If you'll follow me, there is a piece..." Lord Blackwood let his voice trail off once they'd ventured out of earshot. He guided Tim to a far corner of the room, where a locked case held several valuable tomes. He made a great show of unlatching the box and extracting a heavy volume, which he eased into Tim's arms with the delicacy of a newborn babe. Tim clamped his mouth shut as he stared down at *The Lesser Key of Solomon*. He did not fake the reverence with which he traced his fingers over the embossed lettering. "You are Mr. Quayle's man, I take it?"

"I am, my lord." He didn't have to fake his interest in the celebrated grimoire. "This is... remarkable!"

"You know this book?" Blackwood's skepticism was plain.

"Derived in part from Weyer's *Pseudomonarchia Daemonum*, though I'm told the ranking is improved, and they've combined it with the *Shemhamphorasch*. Unless this copy is pre-Rudd?"

"It is not."

"Wonderful!" A glance at Lord Blackwood's pinched face, and Tim came back to himself. "And completely irrelevant. Forgive me, my lord. Such rare finds must be commonplace to you."

"Dark be the day that I fail to cherish one of the great works." He plucked the tome from Tim's hands and tucked it close to his chest. "Tell me, Kipling. Are you a believer?"

"I have an interest I would like to cultivate." Which was a version of the truth.

"Mmm." Blackwood nodded, his fish mouth sagging into a frown. "Relieved as I am that Quayle has sent me a man of substance and not one of his gutter louts, I do hope you will concentrate yourself on the task at hand. I'm sure there will be much of interest for you tonight, but do recall your duty."

"It is always central in my mind."

"Good. I have warned your colleagues hereabouts not to acknowledge you, no matter what transpires."

"Colleagues, my lord?"

"DS Small and DC Croke. Hired security, nothing more. There was an incident last week—a minor precaution." Blackwood fixed him with a shrewd glance. "I take it you are not acquainted?"

"Separate divisions."

"Ah, yes. Better still." He slid the *Lesser Key* back into its case, then secured the lock. "We'll confer in my study at evening's end. Until then I think it best we remain apart. I have not your talent for confabulation. I bid you a fruitful hunt."

With that he strode off toward his guests, leaving Tim to wonder what other marvels Lord Blackwood had sealed away in this mausoleum he called a home.

A hush fell over the room. He followed the guests' avid gazes to the doorway. Tim nosed his way through the murmuring crowd until he had a perfect view of... a pair of footmen, who swept back onlookers who had ventured in too close, not unlike a more subdued version of the mob outside the Old Bailey. The head butler cleared his throat with the rigor of an opera tenor. A buzz of anticipation flit from guest to guest until a heady swarm of noise heralded the arrival of... who? The Prince of Wales? The Prime Minister? Her Majesty? Surely only someone of royal blood could command a room before setting foot in it.

A figure loomed in the hallway. Silence fell anew. The head butler gave one last great harrumph... and Hieronymus Bash sauntered in with a little wave for his disciples.

He was the most extraordinary man Tim had ever seen. Tall as an oak but sleek as a panther. Bedecked in opulent mauve velour save for the dragon pattern of his waistcoat, the cape he did not remove billowed with his every gesture. A man in constant motion, posing and gesticulating as if life were a grand comedy, and he its star player. He wore the black waves of his hair overlong and lush, skimming his shoulders as if to frame his face in perpetual portrait. His dense but meticulous moustache ill-concealed his pillowy lips. His skin was of a rich brown hue that pointed to foreign origins or ancestry, but his eyes were the main attraction—black as sin and blazing like a dark star, their mercurial glint could bedazzle the Archbishop of Canterbury. That and the clasplike gold earring that studded his left lobe—a wink at piracy that would have had Tim rolling his eyes if he were not too busy wagging his tongue.

He was, in a word, magnificent. Tim felt suddenly as if all the air had been sucked out of the room. He fought to measure his breaths, to slow the percussion of his heart. He stole a handkerchief out of his pocket—not that anyone was looking at *him*—to blot his hands. If only there was some balm that could dull the tingling constriction in his groin, staunch the flood of shame that suffused him. He hadn't planned to confront his opponent half-hard and sweat palmed and unbalanced. But that, he would learn, was the effect Hieronymus Bash had on people. At least Tim hoped it wasn't just him.

It wasn't. As soon as the footmen retreated, the dam broke. The guests poured over him, by turns flattering and admiring. Those not seeking to seduce him solicited some favor: to find some long-lost bauble, to fetch an absconded relative, to feast as a guest at their table. The star of his celebrity seemingly outshone any reservations they might have about his exoticism.

When at last he tore his eyes away from the dashing Mr. Bash, Tim noticed a bear of a man standing apart from the crowd beside a statue of Osiris. The bushy muttonchops that carpeted his face only added to the menace of his frown. Tim made a mental note to seek the man out later, but for now he had only one appointment. Unfortunately he appeared to be the very last in the queue.

Their host intervened. The guests fell away like heads of wheat as Lord Blackwood sliced through them. This permitted Tim a view of Bash's two companions: an elegant young blonde woman, likely his ward, and a man with such a regal mien he might have been the

Emperor of China, improbably dressed as a manservant. A more mismatched threesome he'd rarely observed.

"Bash," Blackwood hissed, his spine coiled as tight as a preying cobra. "You are not welcome."

"Precisely why I came. You are aware, my lord, that a priceless artifact was stolen right under the noses of—" he scanned the crowd, taking in everyone and everything, until his gaze lighted on a startled Tim "—everyone in this room. Save you, sir. Fascinating. Have no fear; I'll get to you in a bit." He again confronted Blackwood. "I have been charged with investigating that crime, and since you are hosting a virtual recreation of its circumstances—excepting you are fool enough to display the fang *in this very room*—how could I fail to attend? Invitation or no. Besides, Goldie will vouch for me."

"Simply because—"

"—Goldie's fang was pilfered doesn't mean, et cetera, et cetera." Bash yawned theatrically. "My good man, if you're going to put on a show, you cannot fail to invite the main attraction." He addressed the crowd. "Is that not so?"

A chorus of "Hear, hear" and unanimous approval rang out.

"You see?"

"Mr. Bash, this evening's aim is a serious exploration of the—"

A loud snore interrupted him. Bash startled as if being woken from a nap.

"Blackwood, I assure you, no one is trying to prevent you from dissecting the spiritual ramifications of your underclothes. But a real crime has been committed, a crime that may be repeated tonight, in this very room. No matter what you may think of my abilities, I will not sit at home, quaffing port and smoking cigars, while another house is burgled and these fine people are left at risk." If the guests were on Bash's side before, they would now pledge him their firstborn. "May I proceed? Or will you again prove yourself an enemy to common sense?"

Tim could only imagine the expression on Blackwood's face.

Bash confronted it with a cunning smile. In the end no other words were exchanged. Blackwood simply stepped aside to murmurs of approval. Bash and his companions, with an elderly military man in tow, formed a barricade around the giant tooth. Baffled, Tim sought to ingratiate himself with his fellow guests, hoping to ply them for information.

He devoted as much of his full attention as he could spare to them, his eyes lured back to Bash's mesmeric presence again and again. Though Tim was under no illusions as to the Bash's true nature—criminal, if not an outright fraud—there was something undeniably magnetic about him. The way he played to the crowd. The way he flouted authority. The pride with which he carried himself. If that was an act, then it was a convincing one.

Tim would take great pleasure in bringing this wild dog to heel.

A gong sounded, and the room fell silent. The man-bear, his corduroy frock replaced by a cutaway jacket that made him look even more the brute, beckoned them over to the table. Those who had been chosen to participate were invited to take their seats—Tim noted Bash and his crew were not among them. The man-bear ushered everyone else toward an observation area, a gallery of seats a safe distance from the circle itself. He warned the guests not to venture beyond its limits. Bash, of course, commandeered the front row, whereas Tim struggled to find a place from which he could watch the consulting detective and his associates, the spiritual realm being beyond his purview.

A whippet of an officer he didn't recognize, likely the aforementioned Small or Croke, shut and locked the main library doors, then took up guard post. Bash's manservant stationed himself by the windows, apart from the main audience. Both men had their gazes fixed on that godforsaken tooth. Never in the history of the world, Tim thought, had an incisor attracted so much interest.

A whoosh of wind from he knew not where guttered the candle. From inside the wardrobe, a great clamor sounded—a cacophony of bickering voices and jostling movements that eventually resolved into a high-pitched wail. The ursine assistant, armed with a skeletal silver key on a slip of red ribbon, lumbered over. Twice he rapped on the wardrobe door. The wailing ceased. He turned toward his audience.

"Ladies and gentlemen..." His voice, like his bearing, wrestled with refinement. "On behalf of Miss Dahlia Nightingale, I bid you welcome. My mistress regrets that she could not be here to greet you in person, but, whilst you have gathered, she has been communing with the spirit realm. She would like me to remind you that, once she joins you at table, she is not to be touched under any circumstances. She has been in deep reflection within her cabinet, summoning in those spirits you most long to hear from, and only once returned to her cabinet will she exorcise them.

"Please place your hands flat on the table and keep them there at all times. I invite you and the members of the gallery to close your eyes. We will observe a minute of silence, after which Miss Nightingale will emerge. If you please."

Tim lowered his lids to half-mast but could not tell if Bash did the same. The deftest trick of the evening thus far was the man-bear's production of a pocket watch from some invisible fold of his waistcoat. After the requisite minute, just as the guests began to squirm, he took up his key. With a loud clank, the lock retracted. The doors creaked open of their own accord. They revealed a silk curtain inscribed with occult symbols—of no particular significance save decoration, Tim noted. A glance at Bash confirmed he was bored; the tight purse of his lips stifled a second yawn.

The assistant whipped the curtain back, and there she was, undulating in the air like an angel. Miss Nightingale was slight—as birdlike as her namesake—and almost swallowed up by the satiny cascade of her robe. Eyes glowing white with spectral luminescence, she fluttered down from her perch like a tipsy ghost, scuttling over to the table. Her crazed, enlightened look mirrored those Tim had seen on the inmates at Bellevue and would not have been out of place on a

Christian martyr. Her faithful may have kept their eyes shut, but not a member of the gallery—save, of course, Bash—failed to lean forward in their seat, Tim included.

Miracle or horror show, they all had to see what happened next.

Nightingale let out a mad giggle; they jumped. She fell forward, forehead skirting the table top, then launched herself back, nearly toppling arse over teakettle. Lashes flickering, neck twitching, she reached out a spindly, shaking hand. Her assistant jammed a fountain pen between her fingers. With a crow of triumph, she threw herself onto the table. It began to quake. It rose and fell, rose and fell, Miss Nightingale its limp, babbling passenger. Those in the circle fought to temper it, to keep their hands where instructed. It was a close contest, but eventually they managed to subdue both it and their astonishment. They would have clapped, Tim thought, if they had not been so strictly warned against movement.

Fascinated despite himself, he wrenched his gaze back to Bash. Perhaps Bash held some resentment at having been so upstaged because not a twinkle of intrigue or confusion or appreciation lit those black eyes. He perked up when his ward caught his ear, sharing some humorous tidbit that quirked the corners of his lips. Otherwise it was as if he were sleepwalking through a dull dream.

Was Bash so arrogant that he could not even muster amusement? So atheist that he'd discredited Miss Nightingale before she emerged from her cabinet? So petulant that he could not endure another taking center stage? It boded ill of his character, but this flaw might be a boon to Tim. It was easier to wrong-foot an opponent distracted by their own self-involvement. Pleased, if a mite befuddled, Tim turned his attention back to the spectacle. At the moment Bash could not compete.

Miss Nightingale, lips slack, eyes white, rocked in her seat. With her left hand she scribbled out a hasty message.

Spirit writing. Tim had always wanted to witness it for himself. He resented Bash all the more for his having missed which member of the circle the note was for. Or perhaps the spirit world obeyed no such rules. Miss Nightingale's pen tore across page after page as if the hounds of hell gave chase. Her assistant struggled to replenish her stack of paper at similar velocity. The circle members crouched over the table like vultures over a fresh carcass, their clawlike nails almost dug into the varnish. The more furiously Miss Nightingale's hand flew, the farther they leaned in her direction, midwinter flowers craning toward a glimmer of sun.

Bash, the boor, chose that precise moment to go for a stroll. He tapped out a tune with his heels, then sprung to his feet. Bursts of outrage crackled and popped amongst the guests. One woman hissed, another stared daggers. If looks could kill, Bash might have suffered his own Ides of March. With a flourish of his cape, Bash turned tail and disappeared into the stacks. Even his ward looked mortified at his behavior.

Miss Nightingale shrieked, slumped. Everyone gasped. Her pen skittered across the table and struck the base of the candle, which wobbled, snuffing out. Murmurs broke out until the chandelier brightened. Her assistant gathered Miss Nightingale up and carried her to the back of the room, handing her off to the whippet officer stationed at the door. On his way back to the table, he stopped to lock the cabinet doors.

The guests revved into a frenzy of speculation. The assistant silenced them with a curt gesture.

"My lord, if you would care to read out the messages."

Lord Blackwood snatched up the pile of papers and set about sorting them.

"By all means, let's hear what the spirits have to say." Bash startled them all by re-emerging from the library stacks to lean against a statue of Hermes. "They seem to have the gift of the gab."

"Your mockery of Miss Nightingale's efforts," Lord Blackwood pronounced, "is vulgar."

"The only vulgarity here is your appetite for this artifice."

"There are people here, Miss Nightingale among them, who deserve your respect. And compassion, were you capable of it."

"Oh, I have a great deal of compassion. For your late wife more than anyone. Did she send you a *billet-doux* from the beyond, I wonder?"

Blackwood turned the color of cider vinegar, his stare just as acidic.

Bash's ward intervened. "My lord, please ignore this distraction. The rest of us are awaiting news with baited breath." She corralled Bash back to his seat with considerable strength for a young woman. He assayed an indulgent but no less sardonic smirk as she pushed him along.

"Now, then." Blackwood angled the pages toward the light. "I'll ask you all to remain silent until I am done. The first message is for... Valentine." A twinkle-eyed gentleman started, suddenly alert. Blackwood scrutinized the writing for some time. "And appears to be in German!"

A collective intake of breath heralded quite a bit of chatter. Blackwood harrumphed; they quieted.

As he handed the relevant pages over to his friend, he beckoned Miss Nightingale's assistant. "To your knowledge, Mr. Whicher, does Miss Nightingale speak German?"

Tim thought the man-bear's smile might devour them all. "She does not, my lord."

No one missed Blackwood's victorious glint except Bash, who appeared to doze in his seat.

"The next message," Blackwood pursued, "is for Leticia." One of the ladies trilled in delight. "'Darling daughter, do not forget what you promised. Tend to your garden, and you shall reap. Beware of snakes.'" He nodded with satisfaction. "A proper warning, that."

"One I shall heed," the lady confirmed, receiving the scribbled pages as if a precious gift.

"'Tommy, I am here.'" To Tim's surprise, another of the ladies straightened at this announcement. Unlike the others, whose gaunt faces were capped by meringues of hair, her cheeks were round as bubbles and her demeanor of similar buoyancy. "'I miss you, I miss you, I love you. Continue our good work.'"

The lady gathered the page to her chest and sighed. Even Blackwood looked a little wistful.

"Such a noble ability," Bash interjected, spoiling the moment, "preying on the soft feelings of those who have lost."

"What do you know of soft feelings, with a heart like a pitted fruit?" Blackwood scoffed.

"Rotten to the core, you mean?"

"The image speaks for itself." Blackwood surveyed the next page with a frown. "Here's a confounding one. 'Dearest Tim, do not fear. We did not suffer. Remember us as we were. Remember... who you are.' Mysterious, no? Is there a Timothy about I'm not acquainted with?"

Tim felt as leaden and immovable as the statues that surrounded him. He fought for every breath, fought to still his face, fought the sting of tears that pierced the corners of his eyes. Could it be? Could the medium's gift be real? Could... No, he could not allow himself to think of them now. He would have to steal away the page later and... His head throbbed with the pressure of too many memories, conjectures, deductions, like an overtaxed boiler. He thought he might burst. He thought he might be sick. He thought...

"The true mystery, of course, is why you continue with this charade, Blackwood." Tim glared at the back of Bash's preposterous head of hair. "And why the lot of you devote your interest to these pithy messages when yet another treasure is being stolen right under your noses."

Everyone gasped, their gazes shooting to the podium. A strange mist swirled around the crystal base that displayed the giant tooth. An anger-red glow beamed out of the box, bloodying everyone in the room. The rising fog soon swallowed the fang, diffusing the light so that a message in a menacing hand could be read on the glass...

We see all. We know all. We will feed. Signed by a massive, clawing paw print.

Panicked chatter erupted among the guests. Blackwood's guard rushed forward, truncheon at the ready.

"No!" Bash's ward had sprinted between the case and the club. "You can't know what's in there." Before anyone could blink, Bash's manservant swept her out of harm's way and took her place.

"It could be a fell spirit," one man stammered.

"It's the demon cats!" a lady cried. "They've come to curse us!"

"Don't be absurd," her companion growled.

"Calm yourself, Letty dear." The round-faced lady patted one of her hands. To Blackwood she added, "Perhaps we should summon Miss Nightingale?"

"I'm afraid my mistress is too fatigued by her ordeal," Whicher intervened before Blackwood could reply. "But that is like no spirit or demon I have ever seen."

Tim veered his attention back to Bash, who, in his sole intelligent maneuver of the night, had ordered his ward behind him as he examined the opaque glass of the box and its terrible message. Everyone was on their feet, craning forward—some even stood on their chairs. Tim had abandoned his original position to sneak behind and around the gallery, thus providing him with a perfect view of the action.

"It is no demon," Blackwood insisted, striding forward. With the ease of a career hunter, he stalked up behind Bash and yanked him back by the shirt collar. "How have you done this, fiend?"

Blackwood seized him by the throat.

"Stephen! Stand down this instant!" The military man leapt to the defense of his friend.

"You prefer logic?" Blackwood snarled. "Here are my deductions. *You* are the most significant common denominator between the two crimes. You, an uninvited nonbeliever who sneers at the sacred. You have been baiting me and distracting us since you stepped, unbidden, through the door. You disappeared into the stacks just as—"

"Stephen," the military man whispered harshly. "You're making a spectacle of yourself."

Bash's eyes bulged, his face swelling to a beet red that complemented his suit. Grunting, he waggled a finger at the podium. Tim couldn't tear his eyes away to follow it, not when his investigation might be aborted before it had barely come to life. It also wouldn't do to return to Quayle with a murder on their hands. But he could not act without giving his cover away.

Thankfully the same notion had occurred to Blackwood's guard, who dove into the fray. With a succinct "my lord," he commanded the two apart. Blackwood reared on him.

Bash, gasping, husked out: "The fang."

All turned toward the display case. The mist evaporated, and the warning with it.

The fang was gone.

Chapter 3

*B*lackwood immediately did the stupidest thing imaginable. He had the room cleared.

Hiero swallowed hard—it burned as if he had chugged a glass of lye—and hooked Callie by the arm. Han had already fetched him water. Hiero shot him a glance he hoped conveyed *fat lot of good you were when he was choking the life out of me,* and took a sip. Better.

"You." Blackwood pinned him with a glacial glare. He gestured toward the unoccupied far side of the room. "Over there."

Robbed of his most fluent instrument, Hiero had no choice but to obey. Though in truth a moment to regroup would be beneficial. Callie allowed herself to be tugged along, angling her neck for a better view as they passed the podium. Hiero steered them straight for the drinks cart, abandoned next to a statue of Brigid. Han smacked his hand when he reached for the brandy. Hiero expressed his annoyance with a rude gesture and gulped down his water. He had to get his voice back.

He glanced at Callie expectantly. Without wavering her attention from the goings on before her, she nodded.

"I didn't see much. Some sort of residue."

"In?" Hiero rasped.

"The podium? Yes, that's the only explanation. Some sort of piping system. I hope they're not fool enough to open it. The gas..."

"Triggered?"

She frowned. "Possibly. It would have been tricky to time. There might have been delays... There's no telling, really. Han, did anyone approach?"

"No."

Hiero coughed; his throat roared. Perhaps the lion's spirit possessed him? "Why destroy the fang?"

Callie chuckled. "I thought you'd have guessed. They stole it first. Went to a lot of trouble to fashion a replacement. Sense of the dramatic, these rogues."

"Certainly know their audience, with that message," Han said.

She sighed. "Not much help to our investigation. Vaguely worded enough to apply to anyone in the Belgrave Spiritualists' Society, or all of them. Miss Nightingale's scribbling had more detail. If any of it had a purpose beyond spectacle, I wager it was to destroy evidence. The real question is: why trick Blackwood into thinking the fang's disintegrated?"

"Get him off the scent?"

She smiled. "There! You almost sounded normal."

"Still feels like I've swallowed a beehive."

"Ah! Just the thing." She waved at Goldie, who attempted to talk Blackwood down. "Mr. Bash requires a cup of tea, extra honey and lemon."

Blackwood lunged in their direction. "Talk of demons! You blackguard!" Goldie gripped his shoulder, reeled him back. By now Small and Croke both examined the podium, the one tall and angular as a stork, the other as squat and fat as a mole. Behind them in the stacks, Hiero again spotted the unknown guest. The man was not a conspicuous lurker—Hiero had an eye for an easy mark.

Everything about the man rose suspicion, from his too-tight waistcoat to his too-short hair to his scuffed shoes. His demure manner didn't provoke; his plain features attracted no one's special attention. Bookish and quiet, no spark of interest lit his eyes. Not even the copper tone to his hair shone bright enough to draw notice. Hiero might have been convinced the man had lingered in order to peruse the library's trove of books without interruption, if not for the fact that any truly bookish, demure, docile man would have scurried at Blackwood's first bark.

Ergo he was Blackwood's man.

"The stranger. What do you make of him?"

For once Callie looked puzzled. "Who?" Hiero directed her gaze with his own in the shorthand they had long ago adopted. "Oh, I see. Yes. Who is he?"

"That, my dear, is the question." He downed the last of his water, gargled loudly, then spat it back into his glass, which he shoved at Han. He adjusted his cravat, strode back into battle. "You there!" For a shy sort, the man did not startle. "Skulking about. Why do you not abide by his lordship's order?"

Blackwood snorted. "I hardly require you, Bash, to police my guests. Leave him be."

"In case you've failed to notice, you've been burgled. This man is unknown to, I wager, most everyone in attendance, yet he's permitted to observe—"

"Mr. Kipling, show yourself." The gentleman in question stepped out of the shadows, grinning like a simpleton. Most definitely Blackwood's minion. "This man is an antiquities expert of some renown. I see no conflict in permitting him to explore the library while we see to the business at hand."

"You see no harm in giving free reign to someone who deals in antiquities when one of your most valuable trophies has been stolen?!" Goldie demanded. "Good God, Stephen. He may very well be our prime suspect."

"Mr. Kipling is here at my behest."

Hiero scoffed. "Does he not have a tongue, or did you throttle him as well?"

"My lords, I see that I have caused a great deal of bother. Please

42

allow me to introduce myself. My name is Timothy Kipling, and I deal, as explained, in antiquities. That is my principal profession. But I came here not to appraise any item, but to observe."

"And what, precisely, did you mean to observe?" Goldie asked. "An act of thievery?"

"Quite the opposite. His lordship and I had occasion to do business a few weeks ago. I knew he was a longstanding member of the Belgrave Spiritualists' Society since I myself travel in such circles. When I discovered he was holding a séance, I begged an invitation. His lordship was kind enough to agree. But I confess my true purpose in staying"—he glanced around nervously. A feint. Hiero wondered if anyone else had been fooled—"was to observe you, Mr. Bash, in your element. Your exploits have taken on the aura of legend. To be able to watch you conduct an investigation firsthand..."

Pride warred with disbelief within Hiero. On the surface the explanation was sensible. Flattering even. Certainly those green eyes—he could see now they were a dark, leafy green, like the fletches of an arrow—glowed with something like fascination. But being a master of deception himself, he had a sixth sense for fakery. He required no demon spirit to alert him to the fact this man was false. But was that false to Blackwood, or false in his admiration? Or some other gambit as yet uncovered?

There was only one way to find out.

"Dear Mr. Kipling, it is so very kind of you to say so." Hiero laid on the graciousness especially thick. "If only you could convince your patron of my skills, perhaps this investigation could finally get underway."

Kipling stammered unconvincingly. A glance at Blackwood revealed him to be calculating and doing a poor job of reining in his fury. Goldie broke the stalemate.

"A perfectly reasonable request, wouldn't you say, Stephen? That is, after all, why he's here."

Blackwood struggled not to look at Kipling, further cementing their relationship in Hiero's mind.

"Very well. Once the police are done with the room, Bash has leave to examine it. *If* Mr. Kipling agrees to act as my agent. I trust that suits you both?"

Hiero smiled his wickedest smile. "It certainly does. Though I have never before had cause to work in front of an admirer. I may become accustomed. Mr. Kipling, would you care to join us while we wait?"

"It would be an honor."

When Hiero twirled back to face Callie and Han, two disbelieving stares confronted him. He held up a hand to forestall them; accustomed to his improvisations, they did not protest. Yet. The tea with honey and lemon arrived as if on cue. Han preoccupied himself with its distribution while Callie and Kipling acquainted themselves. Hiero took a sip, pretended to savor the cloyingly sweet concoction, then, with everyone distracted, slipped in some brandy. The addition of liquor both seared and soothed his throat. He nursed his drink for a time, pondering his next move, his sore throat the perfect excuse— for once—for silence.

Also for Han to pounce.

"What do you think you're playing at? He will find us out."

Hiero nodded. "Aye, he might."

"And report everything we discover back to Blackwood."

"Quite so."

"To say nothing of alerting the villains—"

"My friend, they are well aware we are on the case. That is our method. That is how we trip them up."

"These are not some petty jewel thieves. There is something sinister to this business."

"Don't tell me that bit of hocus pocus has *you* spooked. What would Erskine say?"

"Erskine never floated in the air like some..." Try as he had to pick up a bit of Mandarin through the long years of their friendship, Hiero, who spoke four languages, still could not decipher a word. "This isn't another one of your larks. These men will have our heads if we fail."

"I hardly see how that's possible since so far the best explanation we have is some occult-obsessed madman is trying to channel the demons that possessed a pair of jungle cats."

"All the more reason why we should leave this to the police."

"Ah, yes, the police." He directed Han's gaze toward the pair of officers at the center of the room, one of whom held a mallet at the ready. "Quite a dependable lot, wouldn't you say?"

"No! Don't!" Callie raced to stop the moronic destruction of the glass case. Han chased after her. "My lords, we cannot know what chemical was used to conjure the mist. It could be toxic."

"Miss Pankhurst, any ectenic force our spirit might have extrud-ed is not harmful to the living," Blackwood said.

Goldie proved more cautious. "We have no evidence of any supernatural tomfoolery. Best tread lightly, eh, Stephen?"

"Unless it was the evidence you were planning to destroy, my lord?" Callie accused.

Hiero fumbled his teacup, hurried to her side. "What my keen-eyed associate means is..." He blinked once, twice. Nothing. "What did you mean?"

"We cannot very well examine the glass case if they've smashed it apart."

"Right." He waved a foppish hand at the officers. "You there, with the mallet. Subtlety not your strong suit, hmm?" The pair glared like rabid dogs straining their leashes. "Off you go. Our turn."

"Mr. Bash, I will decide when they are done with their examina-tion," Blackwood said, seething.

"And I think they would do better to interview the guests," Goldie insisted. "They've been left to stew for nearly an hour. If we've any hope of keeping this quiet, you'd better reassure them and send them on their way."

Blackwood stared Hiero down for a long, dark moment, then relented. He ordered his two lapdogs to heel and quit the room. With a wink in their direction, Goldie followed.

"My goodness, you do have a flair for the dramatic."

Beside him, Callie started. Han inserted himself between her and Kipling, who hovered, eager eyed, by the tea tray. The others may have forgotten him, but Hiero was only too aware Blackwood had left his creature behind. His performance that evening had only just begun.

"All the world's a stage," Hiero proclaimed, reaching out to draw Kipling into his confidence. Taking their cue, Callie and Han set upon the podium.

Kipling had one of the most unremarkable presences Hiero had ever encountered. Everything about him was average: his height, his build, his weight, the pigment of his skin, the shape of his eyes, the size of his hands. A walking illusion. A man who could disappear in a crowded room. Even before he'd taken on his current guise, Hiero had always been a centrifugal force. He admired the ability to hide in plain sight. He would admire it more if he weren't pitted against just such an adversary.

"Mister, er, Kipling, is it?"

"Just so."

Hiero escorted him back toward the circle, where they could do the least amount of harm. In doing so he caught a good whiff of him—you could tell a lot about a man's level of anxiety through scent. Kipling's odor warred with itself. On the surface a strong smell of musk and tobacco. Underneath notes of mint and astringent soap, as well as a hint of sweat. He was nervous—and he had borrowed the jacket. While this fact neither proved his falsehood nor exonerated him, it was more than a little diverting.

"What do you make of tonight's entertainment? You are a believer?"

This gave Kipling a moment's pause. "I am curious. Also a novice."

"Even better. A fresh perspective."

"I suppose. I thought it quite impressive. She was... I hadn't expected... I am, you see, here under somewhat false pretenses. To find myself so engrossed was something of a surprise."

Hiero didn't doubt the truth of that. "That is their métier, of course. To draw you in."

"You didn't seem very engaged."

"I am a cynic."

"And a non-believer?"

"Zealously so."

Kipling quirked his lips up at the side. Interesting. "Do you know how it was done?"

"Better still, I'll show you." Affecting a solemn air, he marched over to the cabinet. He tried the handle—still locked. He searched about for the key, hoping Whicher had been negligent. He didn't want to give away all his tricks...

"Wait." Kipling furrowed his brow. "Did Miss Nightingale leave with the others?"

Hiero shrugged. "I suspect we're about to find out." Seeing no other option, he snatched a lockpick out of the inner pocket of his jacket, then set to work. Kipling's soft gasp only doubled his resolve. He tinkered for longer than he would have liked—but then this entire enterprise was meant as a distraction, so well done, him—when finally that telltale click sounded.

Kipling crowded him when he rose to his feet. That sweaty undertone had intensified such that it put Hiero in mind of other, more pleasurable activities. Excitement, his brain annoyingly supplied, was but another form of arousal. Nothing more exciting than the thrill of the hunt.

The doors swung open with that familiar creak. Miss Nightingale was nowhere to be found, and it looked as though she had taken her magic with her. The cabinet was just that. There were no chains. The angelic sheathes of fabric were part of her costume, able to expand and retract on cue. A few noisemakers, disguised as occult markings, hung on the side walls, hidden by the pinned curtain. A solitary chair tucked into a corner.

Hiero's heart deflated like a balloon.

"Hardly the stuff of dreams," Kipling commented, echoing his own thoughts. "Or mystery. It is somewhat admirable, though, how she makes so much from... this."

"'Admirable' is not the word I'd choose." He launched into a cursory investigation, testing out the noisemakers, examining each element, stepping inside to inhabit her perspective. Not a terribly inspiring view, though his antics amused Kipling. Finding nothing of note, he hopped out again, paced around the perimeter of the cabinet while appearing to give over to deep thought.

On the far side, he spotted it. A foot pedal tucked beneath the cabinet. Hiero slid his sole over the metal slab, then slowly pressed down. A squeal from the center of the room had him grinning in triumph.

A sinuous mist snaked into the glass case.

"It's happening again!" Callie cheered.

"But how?" Han scrutinized the tiny gas jets inside the case before it fogged over.

"Yoo-hoo!" Hiero beckoned them over, so proud he had—at last—contributed something of value that he forgot Kipling entirely.

Until he said, "Most impressive, Mr. Bash," in a tone that might have inspired violence in a lesser soul.

Before he had a chance to gloat, Han dropped to his stomach to trace the paddle's connection to the podium. Callie wiggled her way into Hiero's place. He shooed Kipling to the side so they could both watch them work. For the first time, Hiero felt out of place in the proceedings. He needed a drink but doubted he could pry their admirer away long enough to fetch one.

"Your staff is exceptionally efficient."

Hiero recognized a backhanded compliment when he heard one. "Trained them myself. We receive so many calls for my services that I must delegate or leave some dear friends dissatisfied."

"You traffic in demanding circles."

"Don't I know it."

They shared a rueful chuckle that caught Hiero up short. A glance at Kipling found him similarly startled. He pressed on.

"The real trick in this endeavor will be to secure an interview with Miss Nightingale. Does she receive callers?"

"Not those who have disrupted two of her séances and branded her a fraud." Hiero sighed. "Occupational hazard."

"I don't doubt."

"Fortunately I have more than a few aces up my sleeve."

"Oh?" Kipling smirked. "I didn't take you for a gambler."

Not his first outright lie of the night, but the one that resonated most.

"And how, pray tell, would you take me?" Hiero asked. Kipling's blush spoke louder of his intentions than anything he had said that night. Perhaps Hiero had misjudged him. "Many would brand detection an art, but I've always thought it more of a gamble. Will I find the necessary clues to catch the culprit? Will those clues be enough to lead me to him? Will I be able to prove my case when I find him? It's the ultimate game of chance."

"Not a game, though, to those whose lives are ruined."

"Oh, dear. Don't tell me you're a moralist."

"Isn't anyone who seeks to right an injustice?"

Hiero smirked. "Is there much call for righting injustices in the antiquities trade?"

"Is there much of a gamble in retrieving baubles for blowhards with deep pockets?" Kipling fired back. Anger suited him—the flint in his eyes and the flush to his cheeks enlivened his features. He inched even closer to handsomeness when he realized his mistake and went scarlet. After a long moment of tension, he cleared his throat. "Forgive me. I spoke out of turn."

"Nonsense. It was the most interesting thing you've said yet."

He watched as Kipling bit down on the inside of his cheek, then hissed out, "Is that so?"

A victorious whoop from somewhere beneath the cabinet kept Hiero from delving further. Han had pried a wood panel off of a hidden compartment, revealing a tankard of gas. Dropping down to his level, Callie attempted to shine a candle's light into the space without setting fire to the cabinet.

"Water," she declared. "Our fang was likely made of salt. A generous spray of this would have dissolved it. We'll collect a sample to be sure." Callie traced a length of outgoing tube from the tank's spout down under the carpet, pressing along its edges until its path was revealed. It curved around the table, avoiding the chairs as it wound its way to the base of the podium. Han met her there; together, with the right application of pressure, they removed the glass case. "Not fastened securely. They were that sure no one would disturb it."

"Or touch it and muddle the message," Han added. He daubed a finger across one of the letters. "Grease, if I'm not mistaken."

"The power of misdirection," Hiero murmured to himself.

Kipling raised an eyebrow. "How do you mean?"

"The trick to selling an illusion lies not in making people believe the impossible, but in convincing them that everything is normal beforehand."

"The case appears secure, therefore it is? How philosophical."

Hiero chuckled. "You must go further, Mr. Kipling. The case appears secure, therefore what it contains is of great value. The theft occurs in Lord Blackwood's home, therefore his lordship is not responsible."

"A séance is organized to hide a robbery..."

"Two séances," Callie corrected. "Two similar robberies."

Kipling followed this line of reasoning with eerie prescience. "Quite a lot of bother to conceal something that might have been taken more easily."

"Almost as if someone were trying to draw attention to the crime," Callie concluded with a thoughtful smile. "The question is, what were they drawing it away from?"

"Themselves?"

"No doubt. But what else?"

Fraud or no, he's invested now. Hiero doubted this was the last they would see of the mysterious Mr. Kipling. He couldn't bring himself to regret the fact. Deciphering him would be much more diverting than chasing down some missing teeth. "I think our path is clear."

"We need to speak to Miss Nightingale," Callie agreed. "Alone."

Hiero nodded. "That, I fear, will be easier said than done."

By evening's end Tim had felt like a dog chasing its own tail. Lord Blackwood had done everything possible to incriminate himself beyond twirling the curled ends of his mustache: block their access to the witnesses; dismiss Miss Nightingale and her man-bear, Whicher; and again insist, with maximum bluster, that Bash play no further part in the investigation. Though it was enjoyable to watch round two of Bash vs. Blackwood—a devotee of the squared circle, Tim rarely missed such a prime matchup—he couldn't help but sense the entire affair was much ado about nothing. That Blackwood coveted the fangs for himself.

The stickier issue, the one he had chewed on for most of the evening before Blackwood forced him to swallow, was Bash. His origins were by far the most compelling mystery. But were his activities criminal? Therein lay the rub. Reward and reputation were at stake, and Tim had his orders, but he couldn't help but wonder if he had been sent on a fool's errand. That no matter how he dealt with Bash, he would come out smelling foul, giving Quayle the excuse he needed to be rid of him.

If this was the case—and Tim very much believed it was—only one course of action was available to him: help Bash take down Blackwood and take credit on behalf of the Yard.

Which was how Tim found himself seated on a park bench across from 23 Berkeley Square, Mayfair, a townhouse Bash had inherited from his friend Admiral The Viscount Pankhurst when he agreed to take on his niece Calliope as a ward. Foreign born, as Tim suspected, there was little documentation on Bash prior to that transaction. While he wouldn't be the first noble bachelor dilettante to escape the history books, this spontaneous arrival, as if birthed from the head of Zeus, set off Tim's alarms. Also the gift of a fortune to a man several decades Admiral Pankhurst's junior, although records of Bash's exact age and the extent of his own personal wealth were equally scarce. Though anyone who observed Bash's close affinity with his ward wouldn't doubt Admiral Pankhurst's choice. Perhaps they waited out an appropriate amount of time before announcing their engagement.

Early afternoon, not a creature stirred. Every curtain, save for the bay window on the main floor, closed. No letters had gone in or out—unusual for a house in which resided a young woman of marriageable age. With Corinthian columns flanking the main door and mini-Parthenons framing each window, the white stone edifice had the solemnity of a temple in some sun-baked land. The question was: which god ruled the Bash household?

Tim's money was on Dionysus.

He waited so long after his initial knock that he thought them decamped to a country estate. The door swung open, revealing a giant who would not have looked out of place with the world balanced on his broad shoulders. His long, mangy beard, menacing eyebrows, and wild hair were the antithesis of refinement. Tim's hand trembled as he placed his card in palm of his enormous paw. With a grunt the giant gestured him into the house.

Tim felt as if he had been transported to Catherine Palace. A gaudy Rococo style reigned supreme. Pink, mint, and blue pastels clashed with the wallpaper's intricate floral patterns. Curvaceous cornices and asymmetrical furnishings dizzied the eye. The ivory-white accents that dominated each room hinted at ostentatious luxury, yet as the butler escorted him through the house, the domestic scenes within could not have been more unexpected. A ladies' maid chased a toddler down one of the long hallways, where two older girls played Scotch-hopper. A chauffeur reclined with his feet up on the sill of a large window, smoking and reading the newspaper. A gangly youth fired a pellet-filled shotgun up a chimney to clear the soot.

In the drawing room, Bash's manservant chiseled at an enormous slab of stone. The furniture had been shoved to the side and piled up, leaving him nowhere to sit. The manservant didn't make the slightest acknowledgement of his presence, just focused on his... art? He had carved out an abstract shape that had yet to be refined into something identifiable.

Avoiding the rubble strewn about, Tim retreated to the hearth. The butler still hadn't uttered a word; Tim didn't know if he had gone to fetch Bash or to take his morning constitutional. After thirty interminable minutes of admiring a mural that depicted a Turner-esque naval battle—doubtless a remnant of Admiral The Viscount Pankhurst's residency—and watching the manservant hammer away, Tim was ready to admit defeat.

A commotion stirred in the hall, a clamor of voices in languages unknown. The toddler squealed in delight. Bash breezed in with the child on his shoulder, resplendent in a coral smoking jacket, silk trousers, and velour slippers. Tousled but fresh, as if he had just risen from slumber. He tossed the squealing girl in the air, caught her with his usual panache. A pudgy-faced imp with twin buns of black hair on her head—the manservant's daughter?—she giggled with abandon, demanding a repetition. The maid hovered behind, fretting but unable to scold her master until Bash gave the girl a final swing into her arms.

"Tea! Or... coffee? Mr. Kipling, you look like a coffee man. We have the best. Turkish. Have you eaten? Spot of breakfast, perhaps?"

"Luncheon," the sculptor amended without breaking his concentration.

"Ah, yes, you'll have to forgive us late risers. The business of deduction is best suited to the wee hours. Luncheon, then?"

"Coffee will suffice." Bash had been correct in that assumption.

"Wonderful! You won't be disappointed." He waved the maid away with a vague gesture. "Han, really. Can't you see we have a guest?"

"Yes. You would be more comfortable in your study."

"Oh, quite right." At last he turned his full attention to Tim, who couldn't help but flower under it. Those obsidian eyes mesmerized. The tone of his skin—the rich orange-brown of carnelian stone with gold undertones—allured. Those florid features, though unshaven, welcomed him with the elation of an old friend. Seeing him thus, sleep kissed and relaxed, worked a trick on Tim's defenses. He would have followed that genial smile anywhere. "Have introductions been made? No? Mr. Kipling, this is Han Tak Hai, adventurer, artist-in-residence, and rather useful in a scrap."

"Pleasure," Han muttered without diverting from his work.

"Likewise." Tim struggled not to curl the end of the word into a question. Could he have mistaken Han's somber dress the previous night for that of a servant? Or was his ever-presence at Bash's side just as an accessory to the costume of worldly eccentric the man wore?

Bash clapped his hands together. "There. That's better. Come along, Mr. Kipling."

As they fell into step, Tim straightened his posture and his resolve. He had met charlatans like Bash before. Charm was their first offensive, the shield that concealed the sharp edge of their dagger. Bash indulged him for now. Tim was charged with getting past his defenses, not swooning at his every twinkle.

By Jove, but Bash did twinkle.

"You may have noted a slight"—Bash orchestrated his conversations like a conductor his symphony, his ever-busy hands a guiding metronome—"informality to the household. I'm not one for pomp and circumstance."

"Far be it for me to tell a man how to run his own house."

"I do love a bit of chaos. Keeps things interesting."

"I imagine you like it most when you're the cause of it."

At that Bash beamed. "Very astute, Mr. Kipling. I see I'll have to keep a much closer eye on you."

Tim battled back his blush with every ounce of his will. "It is my hope to give you every opportunity." Bash raised an eyebrow; Tim cursed his clumsy tongue. "I mean—"

"Hold a moment. Do sit."

For all the household's informality, coffee and hot cinnamon buns awaited them. The rich, spicy aroma nearly had Tim on his knees. Bash poured the coffee into little egg-shaped glasses within embossed silver cups, their minaret-like lids set aside. A bowl of whipped butter with muscovado sugar sculpted into a crocus bloom further embellished the tray. Tim barely resisted the urge to abscond with it. The smells and tastes transported him back to the port of Vienna to the out-of-the-way coffeehouses where the merchants and their families gathered before dawn. For a moment the study, decorated in the same bronze and mahogany hues, became this scene of his youth, where his father would smoke cigarillos and his mother would buy him sugar biscuits if he was good.

He masked a pang of anguish by biting into his bun, which mmm-ed away the memory.

"So," Bash resumed, his warm eyes glinting at Tim over the rim of his coffee cup, "you've come to join our investigation."

Caught short, Tim asked, "Am I so transparent?"

"Your eagerness certainly is. And, as I said last night, I am flattered by your attention. But these adventures of ours can be dangerous—"

"I'm no stranger to such hazards, I assure you."

"Be that as it may..." For once he appeared to choose his words with care. "My associates and I work alone."

"Your apprentices, you mean, among them a girl not yet twenty."

"Miss Pankhurst is an exceptional talent."

"So I have myself observed."

"A more rational mind I've yet to encounter."

"Of that I have no doubt." *Given it is she who is the true detective,* he did not add.

"Han provides protection. Helps us out of the trouble we inevitably find ourselves in. We are a small but vital team."

"Of which I would be counted, if only until this matter of the fangs is resolved. Verily, Mr. Bash—"

"Hiero."

"I... Hiero? Capital. Call me Tim."

"Not Kip?"

"Er... If you like."

"I like."

"As you wish." Tim cleared his throat. "I seek to employ your services on a more personal matter. I would consider this an audition of sorts."

"You require an audition when you sought us out on reputation alone?"

"On this matter... yes."

"What does it concern?"

Tim inhaled deeply. In for a penny... "The murder of my parents."

Bash sobered. For all his flounce, he dared not make light of such a declaration. Instead he reached a hand over to cover Tim's own and squeezed. Their eyes met, and in those dark pools, just for a moment, Tim found something like sanctuary. The feeling nearly undid him.

"My deepest condolences."

"It was some time ago."

"But it marked you."

"I... Yes." Tim shook his head to clear it. He would not let the conversation veer further in that direction. "I will say no more until... Sir, to watch you work would be the chance of a lifetime. Last night you dangled a golden carrot in front of my nose—"

"And now you want the brass stick?"

Their laughter broke the tension Tim had been unaware he felt.

"Rather I want to offer you my services."

"*Your* services?" An enigmatic smile played upon his lips. His voice dripping with suggestion, Bash asked, "And just how, dear Kip, do you propose to be of service to me?"

Ignoring the innuendo that melted across his skin like hot butter, Tim responded, "By getting you access to Miss Nightingale."

Bash considered him for a long moment with the sort of avid, terrible scrutiny Tim rarely received. For the most part, Quayle did his best to ignore him. His fellow detectives treated him like a buzzing fly, easy enough to swat away without a second thought. Tim knew what it was to be invisible, to walk the streets like a specter, affecting no one and attracting little notice.

Hieronymus Bash saw him. From the first across a crowded room where everyone was clamoring for his attention, his gaze was drawn to Tim. Again later as he hid in the stacks. And now as he took the biggest risk of his career, revealing some of his personal pain to earn his place on the team. What else did he see? The wolf in sheep's clothing that Tim was? The sleight of hand he was attempting? He had noticed that about Bash—he was not a natural detective, but he didn't miss a trick. Had he clocked Tim the moment he'd walked in the door?

"Five questions." Bash coiled at the edge of his seat, a cat about to pounce. "Answer yes or no. Don't think, just a quick reply. Agreed?"

"Yes."

"Good. That was the first question." He chuckled at his own cleverness. Tim harnessed his concentration, waiting for him to fire. "Are you in league with the Belgrave Spiritualists' Society?"

"No."

"With the medium?"

"No."

"With Lord Blackwood?"

"No."

"Not even a little bit?"

A laugh escaped Tim. "No." He raised a hand to forestall him. "Please, this requires further explanation."

A curt nod. "Proceed."

"Over the years I've had several business transactions with Lord Blackwood, but... he indulged me once because I am of use to him and may be of future use. That is all."

Bash took a moment to digest this. "Will you divulge anything of what goes on during our investigation to Lord Blackwood?"

"No. You have my word of honor."

"Ah, well. That's settled."

"Then I may join you?"

After a final assessment, during which Tim sensed it was not his moral character that was being evaluated, Bash said, "You may. Conditionally. For this one interview. After that we shall see."

Tim couldn't help but grin. He was in. "What are your conditions?"

"Just one." Bash settled back into his chair and took a long draught from his coffee cup. "You must convince my associates."

By the twist in his smile, Tim realized he had scaled but one mount in a long, ever-more-towering range.

Chapter 4

One suit. One solitary, ill-fitting, not particularly flattering suit. How did a man who made his living as an antiquities dealer, hobnobbing with the social elite, survive with a lone, drab, uninspired, and frankly horribly tailored suit? Both the metaphor and the mystery of one Mr. Timothy Kipling, if that was his name.

Hiero watched him jog through the traffic toward them while huddled in his own fur-lined masterpiece of a coat, affronted by the weather. Should he mention the suit to Kipling now that they were on friendly, if guarded, terms, or would that be akin to a declaration of war? Hiero himself did not stand for any criticism of his sartorial skills—not that one received anything other than compliments when blessed with his eye. But no matter his allegiances, Kipling seemed like a man adrift. The price of invisibility, Hiero noted. Kipling didn't want to make an impression, and he succeeded in this. But perhaps success in this area led to constraints in others? Perhaps this very talent was also his deepest flaw?

As these thoughts evaporated back into the great vacuum of his mind, he realized someone shouted at him.

"—threatening everything we've accomplished, and you invite him along because he looked, in your words, 'forlorn,' and he liked your hellish coffee!" Callie let out a blustery breath and shut her eyes. He heard her whisper a count of ten. In a controlled voice, she said, "Hiero."

"Hmm?"

"Were you listening?"

Hiero blinked. "What? Oh, yes. Quite. And I agree."

"You agree you shouldn't have invited Mr. Kipling without consulting us?"

"I do, yes." She shook her head. "Except… Well, how would we have managed an interview with Miss Nightingale otherwise, do you think?"

Callie growled, throwing up her hands in frustration. "We don't know who he is."

"Yet."

"He isn't of any use to us or the investigation."

Hiero looked from them to the hotel behind. "I should think his efforts on our behalf to be obvious."

"It could be a trap. It's certainly a manipulation of some sort. There's no doubt he's in league with Blackwood."

"We have no proof of that."

"Oh, what, because of your infallible rapid-fire quizzing skills?"

"There is a scientific principle—"

"Observation. Evidence. Hypothesis. That is the scientific method. Your instincts are far more biased."

"That remains to be proven."

She snorted. "Does it? Because I recall—"

Kipling hopped onto the sidewalk after a fine display of athleticism. Hiero had certainly enjoyed it. Even though that damned suit revealed nothing of the body beneath, motion hinted at a sturdy frame. Rigorous exercise with no panting suggested considerable stamina. Perhaps not everything about Mr. Kipling was so average after all.

With a hesitant smile, he made his way toward them, surveying their surroundings with those green eyes. "Mr. Bash. Miss Pankhurst."

"Kip."

"'Kip'?!" Callie cursed under her breath. "I was just wondering aloud, Mr. Kipling, why you've chosen to help us with this matter? And spare me the twaddle about hero worship."

"Hiero worship?" Hiero himself marveled, easily distracted by shiny things.

Kipling looked put out. "Has Mr. Bash not explained to you..."

"You must convince her," Hiero reminded him. "That was our deal."

Caught unawares, Kipling stammered out a jumble of words that did not amount to a sentence.

"You see?" Hiero said to Callie. "Harmless."

"Hardly." She crossed her arms under her breasts and frowned. "Explain your connection to Miss Nightingale, Mr. Kipling. How did you come to be in her confidence?"

"I am not, Miss, of that I can assure you." He straightened his posture, taking on the stance of a schoolboy giving his teacher a report. "The bear... er, man Whicher is her booking manager. I wrote to him about a possible engagement, reminding him we had met at Lord Blackwood's the other night. I asked if it would be possible to arrange a private reading. He booked me on the spot."

"So they are not expecting a large party?"

"No. Best to capitalize on the moment of surprise."

"Indeed." Despite her frown, Callie schemed. "Whicher will be there?"

"Of course."

"And how are we to circumvent him?"

"Your man. Isn't he your protector?" Kipling looked to Hiero for confirmation, missing Callie's blush.

Off to the side, Han raised his head for the first time since their arrival.

"You mean we should do him violence?" Callie demanded with more outrage than Hiero knew she felt at the notion.

"Surely there are ways to distract him that do not involve physical harm."

Callie eyed him coolly. "You're awfully thorough for an antiquities dealer."

"You'll find the success of my business, like most, Miss Pankhurst, is in the details." Kipling said the last with humility, though betrayed a spark of bravery when he asked, "Shall we proceed?"

Callie firmed her lips to underline her displeasure, then nodded. She stalked off into the Albion Hotel without waiting for the rest of them. Han chased after her. Hiero, as ever, walked at his own pace until Kipling fell into step with him.

"She has quite a... way about her."

Hiero heard what hadn't been said with some disappointment. "A word of caution, sir. Many in the past have tried, and failed, to snuff out her light. Do not count yourself among them, or our time together will come to an abrupt end."

"I see your servant isn't her lone protector."

"Yet it is what you fail to see, dear Kip, that's far more intriguing."

In the tradition of the grand hotels popping up all over the continent, the Albion was a monument to luxury, from the marble pillars to the gilt cornices to the silk tapestries that adorned the walls. The lobby furniture alone all but begged for someone to commit an act of public indecency on its brocaded fronds. How a humble medium—who made a dishonest living off the sorrows of others, but not wealthy in her own right—could afford a month-long residency told Hiero everything he needed to know about her benefactors. The Belgrave Spiritualists' Society may have been devoted to exploring the spirit realm, but when it came to earthly comfort, it spared no expense.

Callie's expression betrayed a similar observation when they rendezvoused at the lift. The thrill of the hunt had overtaken her earlier anger. Hiero offered his arm, which she accepted. Within minutes they stood before the door of the penthouse suite. Hiero suffered a pang of embarrassment as Kipling, looking for all the world like a street-sweeper dressed for a beloved pet's funeral, clicked the knocker.

They waited. Not a sound stirred from within. Kipling knocked again. They continued to wait.

"Are we certain—"

"Yes."

Finally the door swung open to reveal...

"Thomasina?" Callie exclaimed. It was effortless, the transformation. Hiero might have beamed with pride, but Callie was such a natural, he hadn't really taught her a thing. All at once she embodied the very model of a young coquette. She straightened her spine and lifted her chin. She smiled as if the air itself flattered her complexion. A pair of dimples punctuated the youthful innocence of her face, the sharp glint of her blue eyes softening to a flirtatious sparkle. The picture of demure and ladylike grace.

Lady Stang-Helion lapped her up with a spoon.

"My dearest girl!" She clapped Callie to her bosom like a long-lost daughter. "Have you come to consult with Dahlia? What a treat! If I'd have known, I'd have arranged for us to take luncheon together. Oh, but it's enough that you've come now! And to think we might have missed one another..."

On and on it went until Hiero felt like one of the wax statues in that new museum. Whicher had by this time fully opened the door. By his constipated look, this was not a welcome turn of events, but, fortunately for them, there would be no interrupting one of his benefactors when she was in full mother-hen mode. On the far side, Kipling made a poor show of masking his shock—and his fascination. Not a man who had much experience of women, then. Hiero tucked that little insight away for later contemplation.

Lady Stang-Helion shoved her coat back into Whicher's arms as she drew Callie into the suite. Hiero heaped his own onto the pile, and Kipling followed suit. Thus dispatched, Whicher slunk over to the closet with an extra glower at Han, who smirked and followed them through.

Lady Stang-Helion led the rest of them into a receiving room replete with chinoiserie. A mural of the Great Wall of China played background to wingback sofas in nightingale motifs and chairs like mini pagodas. An abandoned tea service littered the carved mahogany table—the only off note in a sumptuous room.

Hiero caught Han's look of exasperation as he confronted this carnival-mirror distortion of his culture. He gave Han's arm a squeeze as he retreated back to the door to play sentry.

After shooing a returned Whicher off to replenish the tea, Lady Stang-Helion gathered up Callie's hands and proceeded to interrogate her about all manner of tedious social connections. Callie clucked and twittered in all the appropriate places. Hiero sank into a plush armchair and promptly closed his eyes, mentally preparing himself for the next curtain call. Kipling, as lost as a hare at a horse race, perched awkwardly on one of the pagoda chairs.

An eternity later Lady Stang-Helion alighted her owlish eyes upon him. "Do not think I missed you scuttling in behind, Mr. Bash. Nor you, Mr. Kipling. The pair of you are fast friends, I see."

"Birds of a feather," Hiero remarked, enjoying Kipling's scowl.

"Do not tell me your skepticism has prompted you to accuse dear Miss Nightingale of being a thief *and* a fraud."

Hiero took his cue from the chuckle in her tone. "Hardly, my lady. But investigators by their nature must investigate and, thanks to the efforts of your Society brother, Miss Nightingale has eluded us so far."

Lady Stang-Helion nodded. "She is a delicate creature, Mr. Bash. Even one of your cynicism, I am sure, can understand how she is daily assaulted by forces beyond her control. It is an enormous burden to bear."

"No doubt."

"She is a conduit for both the malevolent and the benign."

"A spiritual tuning fork, if you will."

"Quite so." She foisted her most beseeching gaze upon him. "Good sir—"

"Of course, if you were to act the part of chaperone, my lady, it would serve both to alleviate your fears and open a window into our methods, that you might never doubt them again." He ignored the daggers Callie's eyes shot at him from over her shoulder, as well as Kipling's harrumph.

A sigh of relief accompanied Lady Stang-Helion's smile. "You've anticipated my suggestion."

"You see? Miss Nightingale isn't the only one who can read minds."

She trilled with delight. "Oh, Mr. Bash!"

When Whicher dragged in the tea, she urged him to wake Miss Nightingale from her afternoon repose. A hostess down to her bones, Lady Stang-Helion played mum, peppering each pour with anecdotes about her own children. Callie supplied the lion's share of "oohs" and "ahhs" like a giddy falcon circling around for the kill. Shortly after her first sip, she dove in.

"My lady, is it true that you have one of those dreadful fangs in your possession?"

"I do, my dear, but don't fret. Measures are being taken."

"It pains me to think of you alone in your house, some fiend preying upon your every move, looking to strike."

Lady Stang-Helion patted her hand. "Mr. Bash, in her short time with you, she has inherited a flair for the dramatic."

"She is quite right to be concerned, my lady. Whatever measures are underway, I would hurry them along."

"No one has been hurt during the robberies. A house full of guests on both occasions, and the worst anyone suffered was shock."

"Their message doesn't alarm you? 'We see all. We know all. We will feed.'" Callie shuddered. "Hardly the words of a quiet mind."

"Oh, I do agree. Most troubling. But if there is a spiritual cause, then we will have it out at my séance. As you have all observed—some more enthusiastically than others—a medium of Miss Nightingale's talents will not let such threats stand, no matter how idle. Though with the fang removed..."

"Are you so eager to be parted with a piece of such great value?" Kipling queried, perhaps remembering that a man in his profession would.

Her face darkened. "I hold no love for that tooth, nor the means by which it was acquired. I pray someone will steal it. It is no treasure to me."

"I fear there are those conspiring to accommodate you as we speak," Hiero warned.

"Pray cancel the séance you're hosting," Callie insisted. "Why not delay such explorations until the matter is resolved?"

"My dear girl, your concern warms my heart, but I promise you, there is nothing to fear. Lord Blackwood has arranged for his guards to remove the fang from my premises tomorrow to avoid further interruptions. That is the very purpose of my visit this afternoon. Mr. Whicher had voiced similar concerns, and I sought to personally reassure Miss Nightingale."

Hiero wondered if Lady Stang-Helion could sense the mood of the room turn at the mention of Blackwood, a trip wire cranked to maximum tension. Callie did her best to school her expression, but a shoulder muscle spasmed under the strain. Kipling didn't flinch; his stillness told all, and the way he gripped the ends of his armrests. Hiero didn't have to see Han to know his hand hovered over the knife he kept tucked under his belt.

A move needed to be made, and he needed to make it. But which move was the right one? No student of chess, he normally relied on Callie to give some hint of the direction his inquiries might take, but he could read nothing but her eagerness. The silence stretched on, yawning like the orchestra pit at the foot of the stage.

At the climax of his performance, he had forgotten his lines.

A diversion was needed. Something funny. Something frothy. Only one topic that was reliably both: himself.

"Our butler, Lady Stang-Helion—wonderful chap, but rather abysmal at ordering my social calendar. Admiral Pankhurst's man, you know. Beloved to him, can't be rid of him. Must have misplaced my invitation, an oversight I'm certain you'll be only too happy to rectify..."

"Mr. Bash, you are a tyrant," she affectionately teased. "Should you not concentrate your efforts on pursuing these thieves? Leave the spirit world to those with more... open minds?"

"You flatter me, my lady. I had no notion that any one of you took my objections seriously."

A snort from Kipling startled them all. "They don't."

"Is that so, Mr. Kipling? Has Lord Blackwood confided in you?"

"Oh, Stephen is harmless," Lady Stang-Helion chuckled. "Though you do stir him up, and for that, you are most welcome to attend. As are you, Mr. Kipling, if you are considering joining our circle."

"It would be my honor, my lady."

Her gaze flicked back to Callie, who snapped out of her inner conjectures. "And you, my dear? Will you be there?"

"I wouldn't miss it! So long as you swear to me that dreadful fang will be gone."

"Gone and happily forgotten. Stephen has assured me he is taking every precaution. He is the only one who will know of its location, and as soon as the fiends responsible are apprehended, he will return it. The only question is what to do with it then."

Kipling perked up. "I may have some ideas on that score, my lady, if you'd care to hear them."

"I dare say you do."

"Why keep the dreadful thing to begin with?" Callie asked. "Doesn't it remind you of..." Hiero saw Callie's indiscretion was not accidental. Finally a sign! "Please forgive my ward for speaking of things which Commodore Goldenplover told us in confidence within the bounds of this investigation. And which are none of our concern, besides."

Lady Stang-Helion tsked away any whiff of offense. "The tale is his to tell. Only the consequences are mine to bear." Her smile faltered for the first time that afternoon. "As to your question... I did as I was told by my fellows upon their return. I thought it was beastly, but if that creature really did kill my Monty, I wanted my pound of flesh. But I refuse to worship it as Stephen does. What consolation is that? A tooth for a husband."

"You believe their account of the events that led to his lordship's death?"

She sighed but nodded. "'There are more things in heaven and earth, Hieronymus, than are dreamt of in your philosophy.'"

Hiero let out a peal of delight. He charged forward, nearly stumbling over Callie, and fell to one knee at her feet. He snatched her hands in his, which made her giggle, and ardently professed, "'With all my love I do commend me to you, and what so poor a man as Hieronymus is may do, to express his love and friending to you, God willing, shall not lack.'"

"Oh, you are the very devil himself!" Blushing, Lady Stang-Helion shooed him back to his seat.

Kipling's ready gaze caught him the instant he turned, glowing with an intensity that surprised him. His face as closed as a fist and his own fists white-knuckled to the armrests, he could not keep the fire from his eyes—a particular brand of heat Hiero recognized all too well. But what had ignited him? Yet another mystery for him to solve, and he no man's excuse for a detective. Still, Kipling was too flagrant a liar not to figure out.

Whicher, a man no one had missed, waddled back into the room.

"My lady, Miss Nightingale sends her regrets, but she is too drained from your earlier conversation to receive guests at this time."

"The poor dear!" Lady Stang-Helion squawked. "Oh, but you have missed your chance…"

"Perfectly understandable," Callie quickly chimed in. "Perhaps she might spare us a moment before the séance? Or next week? Please inform her that we are at her disposal and eager to experience her talents firsthand."

"I shall, my lady." Whicher's version of politeness looked like he wished he could lift them up, one by one, and toss them bodily out the door. "Miss Nightingale appreciates your patronage."

"As we appreciate her…" Standing, Hiero searched for the appropriate end note. "… decor."

With that, they took their leave.

Tim turned his face into the wind and let his mask slip while Bash and Miss Pankhurst saw Lady Stang-Helion into her carriage. This involved a dance of air kissing and cooing to which he hoped he never learned the steps. Much more familiar to him were the stealth looks and watchful silence of their manservant, who had tracked him from the moment of his arrival. Mr. Han lurked at the edge of their party in that guardian's way, never crowding but never too far.

Sharp with cold and heavy with impending rain, the breeze prickled across his face as if scrubbing it clean of his false identity. In a few minutes, Timothy Kipling, antiquities dealer, would be but a distant memory, along with this ludicrous business. Bash was no better than the mediums he chastised, a flighty windbag chasing butterflies without a net. Or, rather, demonic teeth. Whatever rewards he may have won were down to that girl's intellect, but they were far outmatched here. A ring of thieves this powerful and connected would not bow to their intimidation… such as it was. And if Lord Blackwood had convinced his fellow spiritualists to give him their fangs for "protection," well, he'd already won. Tim would point Small and Croke's superior in the right direction, and Quayle would laugh himself silly when recounted the curious tale of Hieronymus Bash, consulting detective to the noble class.

Except that Quayle was a humorless sot. Still in his crosshairs, failure here would give him enough ammunition to shoot Tim down. He could no more return to him with the ingenious explanation, "They're idiots, guv," than he could allow Small and Croke to take credit for his collar. Bash may be a gorgeous fool, but Blackwood reeked of villainy. And no matter what face he currently wore, Tim was a detective to the core.

Which was why, as soon as they had waved Lady Stang-Helion off, he slipped back into his Hiero-worshipping guise.

"Bad luck, eh, Bash? At least you'll have a chance to interview Miss Nightingale at the séance."

"I daresay, like her namesake, Miss Nightingale will forever hide from us under the cover of darkness."

"Or behind Mr. Whicher's coattails," Callie quipped. "It's a wonder how such ladies ever get anything accomplished, given how often they are indisposed."

"She did sacrifice a generous amount of compensation," Tim noted. "Though I suppose when your benefactors can put you up at The Albion..."

"Ah, but she gained a fair amount of information," Bash pointed out. "As did we."

Miss Pankhurst had the look of a dog with a bone dangling before its snout. "Tomorrow."

"Tomorrow," Bash echoed.

Tim flicked his gaze from one to the other, mouth open, incredulous. Not entirely feigned. They could not possibly mean to... "Tomorrow?"

"Dear Kip." Bash didn't even bother to hide the false sympathy from his smile. "It's been lovely, hasn't it? A smidge of intrigue, a

dash of adventure, a hint of scandal. A tale to tell at your local—
'Hieronymus Bash? Do I have a story for you!' And they will hang,
rabbit eared, on your every word. You'll tell a gentler version to your
children, 'Once upon a time, I was a detective...' And they will
squeal, and your heart will swell—"

"Your point, Bash? And don't embellish."

"This is where we bid you farewell," Miss Pankhurst interjected.
"We've indulged this little fancy of yours long enough."

"This fancy of mine? Need I remind you that I'm auditioning
you for a case—"

"We thank you, of course, for your interest, but murders just
aren't our thing. Too—" Bash performed a whirligig of hand
gestures "—gloomy."

"But incisors possessed by the devil are, what, cheerily eccentric?"

"Of no serious consequence. To anyone."

"Except the toff with the deep pockets, you mean? I told you I
will pay you handsomely."

"Ah, but sometimes a man is more than his looks." Those black
eyes appraised him. "And sometimes he is not."

Tim fought against the embarrassment that flooded his cheeks.
He was no specimen, he knew, but for Bash to insult him thus,
without cause, burned his blood. It took every last ounce of will
within him to continue with his pleas when he wanted to spit in his
face.

"That was unkind. I have ever held your talents in the highest
regard. I seek only to..." He inhaled deeply, pretending some deep
emotion. "You've led me to water. Now let me drink."

Bash raised a quizzical brow. "I don't follow."

"Just what do you mean to do tomorrow? Whatever it is, I
would assist you."

Miss Pankhurst scoffed. "Out of the question."

"Why? I've come this far. I know the players. Whatever you're
plotting, there are benefits to expanding your team."

"We have other allies, Mr. Kipling. Of long standing. Whom we trust."

"Have I done anything to make you doubt my allegiance?"

Bash and Miss Pankhurst both barked out a laugh.

"You've done nothing to prove it," she countered.

Tim shut his eyes. Everything he had worked for, every ambition he had slipped away because he couldn't deceive an overdramatic ponce and a bull-headed girl. He scrambled for a new strategy, scouring the deepest vaults of his mind.

"Very well. Then set me a task."

"A task? To prove your worth to us?"

"Yes. If I succeed, then I shadow you for the remainder of the investigation. If I do not, I will quit you without complaint."

Miss Pankhurst regarded him with open hostility, but Bash could not suppress a smirk of approval. He led her away a few paces, and a heated conversation ensued. At least it was heated on Miss Pankhurst's part. Bash bantered as if he shared gossip at a cocktail party. It wasn't until they returned—Bash visibly triumphant, Miss Pankhurst violently annoyed—that Tim realized he'd been holding his breath.

"One chance," Bash declared with something like relish. Tim wondered if there was an occasion on which he didn't enjoy himself. "One alone. I will pose a question. I demand your most honest answer. If I don't receive it, we are done. Do you understand?"

"I do."

"That was not the question."

"I know."

"Oh, good. Here it is. Ready?"

"Always."

"Mmm. I don't doubt it." A giddy smile. "I mean it now. Prepare yourself."

"Get on with it."

A snort. "I am." His miasmic stare locked on to Tim, possessing him as a spirit might a medium. "What is your real name?"

Tim didn't twitch, didn't breathe. Just stared into the abyss of those eyes, helpless. A million questions of his own floated like bubbles to the surface of his mind, popping against the inside of his skull. Had he already lost? Could his mission be salvaged? Had they always known about him, or was this a recent discovery? Was there any way to continue his deception and still convince them of his honesty?

This last he dismissed. The duke of flounce, the king imp, the handsome dunce he'd thought to fool had instead fooled him. The thief's identity might forever be unknown to him, but Tim he had unraveled with ease. Whereas Hieronymus Bash, whomever he really was, would remain a mystery.

In the end there was only one answer he could give.

"Timothy Kipling."

Bash's smile fell. "Dear Kip. I thought you'd come to play."

He nodded once, then turned to offer Miss Pankhurst his arm. They spared not a backward glace at Tim as they strolled away.

Hiero fiddled with a loose string on his cuff as the carriage jostled through the traffic around Hyde Park. A busy thoroughfare at the best of times, today's stop-start progress and tight quarters were enough to queer his stomach. He had never been one for enclosed spaces, and this cab was particularly snug. Han's bulk spanned the width of the opposing bench, forcing Callie to cram in beside Hiero. After several sharp turns, she was nearly on top of him. For once the comforts of home beckoned, along with the half-empty bottle of single malt he'd hidden in his study. He didn't know when Han had pinched his flask, but as soon as there was air enough to expel such sentiment, they would have words.

"Still licking your wounds?" Han asked.

"Hmm?"

"You're not one to gamble and lose."

Hiero considered that a moment. "Actually I rather think I am." They shared a chuckle, which did little to raise his spirits. "I thought you wanted to be rid of him."

"Not me. I rather liked him."

"Did you?" He twisted his fingers around the string and gave it a hard tug. The meek snap was nowhere near as satisfying as he'd hoped it would be. "I concede that he was an enigma."

"One that you were eager to"—Han's voice dripped with innuendo—"unravel?"

"As it happens, yes. Not in the way you mean, but... Well, I don't see anything untoward about a little professional interest. Seeing as detection is my profession."

"Spiked your curiosity, did he?"

"First time for everything," Callie muttered, not quite under her breath.

"The matter of his true identity, yes. There was something there..." Hiero wiggled his fingers as best he could with his arms clamped to his sides. "In conversing with him, I had the strangest feeling that, most of the time, he was being honest."

"That is unique. To your experience, at least."

"That's what I've been thinking." He met Han's amused gaze with an innocent look. "Do you think I should seek him out?"

Callie interrupted her mental deductions for the first time since they'd sat down. "No."

"After this business is done with, of course."

"We've just got rid of him!"

Han shot a pointed look in her direction. "Wouldn't bother. I have a feeling we've not seen the last of Mr. Whomever He Is."

Mollified, Hiero went back to feeling sick to his stomach. Without a conundrum to contemplate, he rode hard the carriage's every bump and shake. The grimy window only muddled his view of the outside world, though its stench oozed through well enough. He could taste every note of Callie's perfume, trace every wire in her bustle and bone in her corset. With no refuge from his environment and no flask to tipple, he was forced to do something that would forever fill him with awe and dread: ask her about the case.

"So, er... tomorrow."

"Tomorrow." Callie smiled with relish.

"What, uh... what do you think will transpire?"

"How do you mean?"

"I mean..." He steepled his fingers in an attempt to look pensive. "What outcome do you expect from our undertaking?"

She craned her upper body around to glare at him. "You haven't the faintest notion of what we're getting about, do you?"

"I..."

"Hiero, did you hear a word Lady Stang-Helion said?"

"Yes, of course, of course." He drew in a deep breath, if only to buy some time. "But how does that apply to... to us?"

Callie set her mouth in that particular way, seconds away from breathing fire. He watched the color rise in her face and scrabbled for the door handle. Surely being trampled by a horse was preferable to...

Fortunately Han, dragon-tamer extraordinaire, intervened.

"He's right. We need a plan."

"A plan? Simple. We'll drop him at The Grenadier and fetch him when it's done."

"Now see here," Hiero protested, but no one paid him any mind.

"I can deal with this alone," Han insisted.

Callie scoffed. "You will not!"

"If you're seen—"

"I'll go incognito."

Han shook his head. "Too conspicuous. If they catch you, we're done."

"And if they catch you, they'll kill you."

"I can deal with them if I'm alone."

"You don't even know who *they* are."

Han put his hand on her knee; she batted it away. "We might have to split up. You don't know the streets."

"Neither do you."

"I'm fast. I'm quiet. I blend in."

"You're the size of an ox."

"Will someone tell me what the bloody hell the two of you are bickering about!" Hiero demanded. Two pairs of adamantine eyes locked on to him; his stomach lurched. He assayed his most ingratiating smile. "Hmm?"

Callie crossed her arms, her cheeks a traitorous shade of crimson. "Tomorrow Blackwood and his minions are moving Lady Stang-Helion's fang—and likely Landgrave Vandenberg's as well—to a secure location. If we follow them..." She waited for Hiero to make the logical leap. Alas, he could not jump that high. She sighed. "We'll know where he's keeping the fangs. And what he might be doing with them."

"But isn't that rather dangerous?"

"Yes, it is," Han confirmed. "Especially—"

"Don't you dare!"

"My lady..."

"When we set about this business of ours, what did you promise me?"

"That I would never utter those words," Han mumbled.

"Quite right. What else?"

"That unless there was a direct threat to your life—"

"And is there?"

Han grumbled to himself, looked to Hiero, who laughed.

"I believe it's been well established that my opinion is forfeit."

"Right again." Callie straightened, pleased. "I'm going."

Han let out a long sigh, nodded once.

"There! That's settled." Hiero beamed at the two of them. "Now remind me again why we suspect Blackwood is the culprit?"

Callie opened her mouth but seemed to think better of it. "How do you mean?"

"The pedal was behind Miss Nightingale's box."

"True. But anyone could have accessed it. And it's far more likely a wealthy patron has employed a servant or helper as a cover."

"Meaning the person who pressed the pedal isn't necessarily the mastermind behind the thefts?" Han queried.

"Precisely."

"Then why is Blackwood having the fangs removed?" Hiero asked.

"Just as he said. To protect them," Callie explained, "and himself, from being accused."

"And to interfere with our investigation," Han added.

Hiero shrugged. "I provoke him. He retaliates."

"He's a tyrant."

"He's a zealot," Callie corrected. "Doesn't discount him, but his motive is unclear."

"Some mystical balderdash, I wager," Hiero grumbled.

"Could be. But if you ask me, Lady Stang-Helion is the one to watch."

Han considered this. "The loss of her husband."

"Yes. And her close relationship with Miss Nightingale. I don't think it's Blackwood who proposed The Albion, do you? Or who visits with her every day. Or who prevented us from meeting with her." When Callie leaned forward, Hiero almost groaned with relief. He immediately commandeered the extra space. "But she's letting Blackwood confiscate her fang. Or what he thinks is her fang..." Her eyes widened. "Something will happen in transit."

Han nodded. "The thief can't use the séances as a cover any longer."

"Which puts Blackwood back in the spotlight," Hiero concluded, proud to contribute.

"Along with everyone else," Callie countered. "The vandals won't have any obvious connection to the person commanding them. Any one of them could have arranged the theft. Even Vandenberg."

"Or Goldie," Han added.

Silence fell as they each contemplated that possibility. No one rose to the debate, but neither did they argue against it. They all knew Goldie's wiles well enough not to discount him.

Callie eventually broke the silence. "One thing is certain."

Hiero took up her hand. "What's that, my dear?"

"We probably could use another man."

Chapter 5

The pristine columns of a well-kept ledger. Sheaves of letters, their edges blotted red with broken seals. The slashes and curlicues of an elegant hand. The manicured etchings of a well-drawn map. The type of evidence Tim normally gathered during the course of an investigation rarely involved chasing a carriage down Park Lane. Criminals with ink and parchment in their arsenal were meticulous to a fault. One could almost predict their innocence or guilt by the state of their accounts. Tim had to be equally meticulous in his attention to detail; he ignored the minutest sum, the most arcane legend, the meekest punctuation mark at his peril.

His tie garroting his breaths, his every gasp thick with dust and smoke and the foulest stenches imaginable, Tim barreled down the sidewalk like a man possessed. He swerved around prams and vaulted over flower boxes. He dodged carriages as he ran across the side streets. He jogged backward a few steps after a near miss with a street sweeper, then almost collided with a pair of ladies on their afternoon stroll. After a bevy of apologies and a flurry of bows, he doubled his pace. Tim thanked the powers for the traffic; even at a city clip, he was no match for a pair of horses.

He stopped cold when the carriage turned right onto Curzon Street—home for them, then, to strategize the morrow's spate of espionage. After the carriage disappeared behind a row of stately homes, Tim doubled over, hands clamped just above his knees, willing himself not to collapse. Gulping in breath after breath like a man half-drowned, he resolved to add distance running to his exercise regimen and to buy a suit that didn't fit like a straightjacket.

Once he'd regulated his breathing and recovered his wits, he cursed himself. He'd forgotten the first rule of gambling: never try to trump a cheat. He might as well have given Bash the cuffs and keys to shackle him by suggesting he'd perform a task to earn his place among them. What transpired was the very definition of a rigged game, and him the dupe for not seeing it. This momentary folly had hindered him, but he was a detective of Scotland Yard. He may not be accustomed to this sort of legwork, but this was a prime opportunity to hone his skills. To prove to Quayle and the others his instincts were just as sharp as theirs.

Tim took advantage of the walk to Berkeley Square to consider his options. The frigid air helped to clear his mind, though it also crept under his coat and starched his sweat-drenched shirt rigid. His gloves lost, he shoved his hands deep in his pockets, hunching against the intense wind. Not for the first time that day, he wished he'd dressed in his serge and gabardine, with proper boots that covered his ankles. But Tim Stoker's day-to-day wear would not do for Timothy Kipling, and thus he resigned himself to a night of shivering against a lamppost.

Or, rather, a nook across the street from the back entrance to Bash's abode. Once again all the windows were shuttered and the curtains closed. A half hour in the park across the street had given Tim precisely nothing except a crick in the neck. Preparations for the following day's adventures should have been in full swing. There should have been, at the very least, evidence of a light, but the townhouse stood solemn and impenetrable as a tomb. Surely they had not returned home just to go back out minutes later? Had Tim rolled the dice and lost twice in one day?

When he caught a whiff of something buttery, his stomach grumbled so loud he had no choice but to pursue it. His nose—and

tongue, which tried to lick the aroma off the air—led him to the
servants' entrance. The windows glowed with promise, betraying the
hustle and bustle of dinner preparations. Torture though it was to
watch a woman as tall as a willow and as thin as a twig stir, sprinkle,
slice, pound, and pipe ingredients into delectable submission, Tim
bore it, hawkeyed and undaunted. Also fiendishly hungry.

The memory of those hot cross buns tempted him into a rash
action, but he forced himself to keep his distance. Perhaps once Bash
was dealt with, Tim could marry his cook. Surely his enjoyment of
her cooking would make up for his lack in other areas. Or perhaps
Lord Blackwood would be so impressed by his efforts that his
generosity could improve Tim's station, and he'd be able to hire her.
A ramshackle lodging house in Pimlico was no Berkeley Square, but
he didn't doubt such a culinary magician could work wonders.

The boom of that unforgettable voice—which did to his ears
what her cooking did to his other senses—woke Tim from his
daydream of sugarplums and buns. He stole another glance through
the window; Bash, dressed in sober colors and a monkish cape,
chatted with the cook. The arrival of an ornate carriage concealed his
exit, giving Tim a valuable head start. His tie loosed and his
waistcoat unbuttoned, he dashed over to the high street and hailed
himself a hansom. This being London, the driver didn't blink twice
when instructed to follow the next carriage that turned the corner.
The very vehicle they awaited galloped into view as soon as he
climbed into his seat.

The driver made little conversation as they trotted along—the
carriage, perhaps wishing to remain inconspicuous, was in no
hurry—but his curiosity screamed louder than a town crier. A left
turn on Piccadilly surprised Tim since both Lord Blackwood and
Lady Stang-Helion lived in Belgravia. By the time they rounded
Trafalgar Square and veered off onto The Strand, Tim gave up
trying to predict their destination. Nothing could have prepared him
for pulling up beside the stage entrance to one of the more disrepu-

table burlesque theaters. He stared dumbly as the hansom drove forward another block and tucked into a free space. Tim spun around in time to see a hooded figure spring from the carriage and swoop through the stage door. A sturdy-looking older woman with a bird's nest of white hair followed him, teetering awkwardly on what must have been sky-high heels. A patroness? A paramour? Tim's shoulders stiffened with a tension he could not explain.

"Should I continue on, sir?" the driver asked with studied indifference.

"No. I'll stop here." Tim paid him double the usual fare.

He walked around to the front of the building. The row of gas lamps that illuminated the Gaiety Theatre's sign was not yet lit. An honor guard of posters announced that night's burlesque, *Robbing Hood and his Mercenary Men,* starring Henry Irving, Nellie Farren, and the great Horace Beastly, as well as a monologue from *Macbeth* and a pantomime. A few punters milled around the entrance, but the doors were not yet open for that evening's performance. Behind the glass, ushers gave the floors a final sweep, and ticket vendors ordered their desks. Backstage, Tim knew, members of the chorus would be chatting over a smoke while the orchestra tuned their instruments. Crew members would be readying the props for fights and gags, preparing the flies for a quick scene change. Perhaps in this very theater there was a boy like he had been, shy but beloved by this surrogate family, free to explore the wings and the pit, the walkways and the underground passages, to sit in any seat in the house until the audience was let in.

Tim shut his eyes, shuddered. Memories struck at him from all sides. Sitting among the bouquets in a dressing room, trying not to sneeze as his mother stitched the lead actress into the costume she had torn. Shadowing Henri, stage manager at the Théâtre de l'Odéon, as he made his preshow rounds. Clutching his mother's hand all through Charles Kean's performance of Richard II. Laughing until he felt sick at Felicia Thierret in *Tartuffe.* Weeping through *La Traviata* every night for a month after she was gone. The first time he had let a man slide a hand up his thigh and lead him behind one of the columns was during a performance of *The School for Scandal.* Dropped to his knees in a back alley as the theme from *Robert the Devil* rumbled through the wall. Hurried a dissatisfying partner along so he could catch the last act of *The Bride of Lammermoor.* Saved up for a stage-side box so he could admire Horace Beastly's profile, all the while burning to meet the solicitous stare of a hirsute gentleman in the stalls below.

Three years ago Tim had weeded out his unnatural desires by the root, vowing to never step foot in a theater again. Heartbroken that he had to sacrifice his love of drama in order to exorcise himself of his vices, he poured all his passion into his work. Now a temptation far worse than buttery crumpets tested the very fiber of his character. He yearned with every speck of his soul to return to his first love, to sit in his favorite box and dote on the tremendous Mr. Beastly from afar. To feel the faux velvet on the armrests, to admire the gilt angels that decorated the proscenium, to be bedazzled by the glittering chandelier. To be spellbound by the indelible alchemy of music, staging, and spectacle.

There was also the not-insignificant matter of his duty. Bash would be attending that night's performance—an opportunity to observe him in a new habitat, perhaps another chance to persuade him to let Tim join his team. Though the devil only knew why Bash was really here. The Gaiety had something of a reputation, and gentlemen of a certain persuasion were known to rendezvous in its bars and boxes. Not to mention catcall and flirt with each other shamelessly before the performances and at the intervals in full view of the more respectable patrons. Tim also knew more than a few of his colleagues made like wolves among the flock. Arrests at theaters were commonplace, and the Gaiety was one of the best hunting grounds. If he were seen here, even for a legitimate reason, it would give Quayle the ammunition he needed to be rid of him, regardless of the outcome with Bash.

Had he been lured here deliberately? Had Bash, or more likely Miss Pankhurst, used their aristocratic contacts to snuff Tim out? Was he risking everything—case, job, reputation, morality—just by stepping through the theater doors?

There was only one way to find out.

As soon as the doors opened, Tim splurged on a private box. After a sweep of the restaurant and the billiard room, he hastened to it—the perfect perch from which to observe the goings on, but also to avoid catching the notice of any patrolling colleagues. The second he stepped inside, sensory images and remembered pleasures assaulted him. His prick stirred as he slid into his seat, ever conscious of the dark enclave beside him, with room enough to fit two rutting bodies. Tim couldn't help but suffer a tingle of excitement while drinking deep of the heavy air, clogged with smoke, perfume, and the rotten-egg reek of the gas lamps.

With the theater relatively empty, he only had eyes for the stage. Nothing to see with the curtain down, but that didn't stop his mind's eye from reviving scenes from his favorite productions and projecting them against the crimson tiers. He imagined a pantherlike, flamboyantly dressed intruder sneaking in to fill the second chair. While the actors emoted and the audience howled, he would whisper, in a velvety voice, some witticism in Tim's ear. A ruse, of course. He would tease Tim's earlobe with those plush lips, flatter the soft of his neck. He'd slip a deft hand under layers of waistcoat and shirt to worry an already puckered nipple. When the music climaxed, he would pinch with those rough fingers. A bolt of physical and theatrical ecstasy would shoot straight to Tim's cock. He would part his legs, inviting the hand lower so the stranger could knead at the bulge he found there, pluck at Tim's buttons and peel down his placket, seize him as the orchestra raced through another invigorating crescendo.

The chance that, at any moment, one of the other patrons might divert their eyes from the stage and see the swarthy head diving down into his lap was half the thrill.

Intensifying chatter lured Tim back from his half-remembered, half-imagined reverie. He straightened in his seat, praying the tent of his coat concealed the smaller tent in his trousers. He fought to regulate his breathing until the tidal wave of arousal ebbed some.

Outside his box the show-before-the-show was well underway. Undercover nobles with their mary-anns or their mistresses took their places in the dress circle. In the row above and the seats below, those not already spoken for solicited trade by laughing theatrically and flaunting their wares, clicking their tongues in the cooing susurration that signaled their availability. Those men not in flash suits wore gaudy makeup and garish dresses topped with strangling jewelry—a pantomime indeed. Tim had never understood the appeal—if he wanted a woman, he would have bedded one—but neither did he see the harm. Underneath all that frippery waited a manly musk and a ready cock, the thought of which was enough to stir him anew. Three years without had him randy as a stud, his lust nigh impossible to corral.

He wrenched his focus back to the task at hand. A thorough scan of the audience revealed Bash was not in attendance. *Yet,* Tim reminded himself. If he'd gone to the trouble of sneaking through the back entrance, he wouldn't just join the parade of mandrakes and ladybirds along the side aisles. More likely he supped at a private table and would be escorted to his box. Which might very well position Bash directly opposite Tim. It was one of the many gambles Tim had staked his future on that night.

He grew more concerned when the orchestra filed in. As they tuned their instruments, he craned his neck out to spy on the boxes above and beside him. Nothing. He cursed himself for not taking a stroll to the other side of the auditorium for a better view of their inhabitants. Not that he would have been able to resist if he attracted the wrong kind of attention—likely with his prick still sword-ready and his head dizzy with need. Tim would have to chance it at the interval. A mere glimpse of Horace Beastly after all these years should be enough to pop his cork.

The lights flickered; Tim's pulse quickened. Movement on the other side of the auditorium drew his attention. Bash's white-haired companion settled into the stage-side box across the way, but not alone. A petite brunet with a threadbare moustache and lips like ripe plums played escort, though the position of his hands was far more intimate than decorous. Something about the woman struck Tim as familiar, but he couldn't place her. A friend of Lady Stang-Helion's? One of the guests at the séance? If his memory wasn't forthcoming— and who could blame it with the onslaught of distractions?—he would find a moment to discreetly approach her companion. Tim would endeavor to put those scandalous lips to a nobler use than the one his body burned for.

In the pit below, the conductor raised his baton. The house lights dimmed. Still no Bash. Tim resigned himself to having lost the trail and settled in for the show.

The curtains parted to reveal a tranquil woodland road. A placard at the side of the stage revealed it to be "Sure Would" Forest. The audience tittered, primed for the ribaldry to come. A company of green-hooded riders—astride men in horse costumes—gamboled onto the stage, singing of how they were on their "very merry mercenary way." The rollicking ditty soon had Tim humming along. By the time the dashing Robbing Hood brought the chorus to a halt by stealing all of their cloaks and belting out a counterpoint tune, he was hooked.

Few among the cast rivaled Irving, who proved to be a droll and agile Rob, as quick with his wit as with his bow. Nellie Farren equaled him as both Scarlett the Harlot and Maid-No-Longer Marian, at one point bickering with herself over the keys to the famous vandal's heart. Tim had to wait till the second act for Horace Beastly to appear as the bumbling but villainous Sheriff of Not In

Him, but it was worth it for his entrance alone, popping up through one of the traps to deliver a prattling libretto that had everyone in hysterics. Tim had seldom seen him perform comedic roles; a shame, in retrospect, since his impeccable timing and his command of his instrument had the audience hanging on his every whisper.

By the third act, Tim abandoned his seat. Instead he reclined into the corner closest to the stage like a sozzled Romeo, head lolled into a groove of the intricate woodwork, the better to savor every syllable Beastly uttered. In his black tunic and hose, with sleek leather boots and a fur-lined cape as lush as his dark mane, he was magnificent. But it was his voice, deep and sonorous, that most beguiled, purring out threats that would have had Tim dropping, not soiling, his trousers. Under the spell of the dramatists, he could not fathom how he had gone without for so long. As the music swelled and the players sang their last, Tim's heart soared.

And even if, minutes later, he watched Beastly disappear into the wings after the final bow; even if Tim felt more sapped than sated as he staggered back to his seat, he couldn't bring himself to regret the too-brief hour's distraction. Surely he was strong enough to have this without the other? Surely he could reclaim his love of theater without reigniting his lust for its tawdrier patrons? Surely there was some room for leisure and diversion, even in a detective's life?

These thoughts so consumed him that he barely noticed when the curtains inched apart and Beastly, having lost his cape and gained a scabbard, strode to the edge of the stage. He stood poised, as keenly alert as a cobra that had just unfurled its hood, until his audience fell silent. Tim snapped to attention, no better than a child at the circus. His eyes lit with a sulfurous gleam, Beastly scanned across the audience until his avid stare found Tim.

Those trickster eyes, lustrous as black pearls, met and mastered him. Those florid features, greased with paint and contorted with rouge, could not hide what he was.

Who he was.

Shock pounded into Tim like a locomotive. With no air in his lungs to gasp, no flicker in his brain to ignite, he gaped as the lips he had coveted curled into a smirk. Then Beastly launched into the "Is this a dagger I see before me?" monologue from *Macbeth*.

Tim slumped back into his chair, too flabbergasted to absorb the actor's no doubt nuanced and powerful interpretation. Two initials dominated his thoughts: H.B. Two names that equaled one impossible man. Horace Beastly. Hieronymus Bash. But which was real and which the pseudonym? Or were they both false identities, two surface layers shielding someone buried so deep he was nearly invisible? And yet...

Bash/Beastly had just revealed himself to Tim. The recognition was mutual. That smirk... inscrutable. Taunting. As outrageous and infuriating as Bash himself.

Now fuelled by far more than long-repressed desire, Tim's rage burst into full flame. He had been mocked and belittled and humiliated by a common actor. A degenerate and a whore. A charlatan guilty of a far more elaborate deception than posing as an amateur detective. Not only would he have his answers that very night, but Tim would serve Hieronymus Bash, Horace Beastly, or whoever he was to Quayle on a silver platter with a fat red apple in his mouth.

And if he had to spit-roast him first, so be it.

The scene was set. The bountiful bouquets and solicitous notes he received each night after a performance had been tidied away. The green-and-gold pillows on his chartreuse fainting couch had been primped. He'd chosen the blood-red kimono embroidered with emerald dragons for contrast. Hiero had arranged his décolletage to expose a V of chest hair, just enough to intrigue, not disgust, any potential suitors. He'd cleansed himself of all that slap and sweat and powder, though he resisted the urge to perfume. In his experience, not even the Parisian masters could better the potent musk of clean male.

The first hard pound on the door rattled into his bones. Randy and eager, his patrons never gave him long to prepare. Barely had the orchestra played its final note and they flooded the backstage area like the deck of a sinking ship, wave after relentless wave pouring in from the boxes and the stalls. Some sought the easy catch: understudies, minor players, chorus boys and girls. Some had already caught themselves a big fish: Farren had her regular circle of admirers; Irving had wooed and won one of the top investors to secure his place. But those hardier than most, seekers of the Great White Whale—they would storm into his private space and make their demands. Offer him fine wines and delicate bonbons. Gem-encrusted baubles and newfangled trinkets. Access to the most exclusive clubs, the most elegant restaurants, holidays and getaways and every matter of gilded cage. All so he would sing only for them.

Only one such patron had ever claimed victory over his person, his privileges, and so much more. His Apollo, the one who promised him freedom. But it never hurt to cast a wide net in hopes of snaring himself another dolphin.

A quick shake of his head dispelled the memories, and then he answered the door.

"Kip!" Hiero's enthusiasm was genuine, if his surprise was not.

"Mr. Beastly." Gray and swollen as a thundercloud, Kipling's whole body thrummed with suppressed emotion. "Might you spare me a few moments? I'd like to... express my admiration."

"Of course, of course. Come in."

Hiero shivered with excitement as Kipling rumbled past him. He loved nothing more than an unknown quantity, and the man who now hovered in the center of the room as if he didn't know whether to boom or gush had proved wonderfully unpredictable, at least to

Hiero's hornet's nest of a mind. He leaned back against the door, waited for him to take in the intimate splendor of Hiero's leisure palace: the cozy atmosphere, the snug dimensions, the intimate lighting, the availability of several surfaces on which they could recline. Hiero watched Kipling pile shovelful after shovelful of evidence onto the coals of his anger, not realizing that to stoke one fiery emotion was to stoke them all.

Judging by the bulge in his trousers, he was nearing full burn.

"So which is it? Beastly or Bash? Or are you someone else entirely?"

Hiero chuckled. "Ah, philosophy! Never my strong suit."

"I demand an answer."

"Alas, I am under no obligation to give one."

"Who are you?"

Hiero shrugged. "I am as you see me. A man. No more, no less."

"Are you an actor posing as a nobleman, or a nobleman who dabbles in the dramatic arts? A rich man with two ridiculous hobbies, or a confidence man who excels at nothing?"

"Come now." Hiero sniffed. "I'm a ripping conversationalist."

"A professional provocateur, then?"

"I am not the one who appears..." Hiero flicked his gaze downward, pausing a few seconds to admire the one way in which Kipling was not average in the slightest, then dragged it back up the length of him. Ill-fitting suit and all. "... provoked."

Hiero stalked across the floor until Kipling had to look up to meet his eyes, stopping just inches from him, unsure if he was poised to flee or pounce. Kipling's nostrils flared and his chest heaved. He parted his lips in a grimace that seemed to want to both smile and snarl. Hiero was shocked by how much he wanted to kiss them, by the tension that knotted his groin.

"Perhaps I am," Kipling admitted. "I defy anyone not to be in such circumstances. Some five hours ago, you dismiss me for the very same crime of which you are guilty: dissimulation."

"And you've done well in finding me out." Hiero inched closer. "Have you come to claim your reward?"

"I..." Kipling staggered back until he hit the solid wood of Hiero's wardrobe. Hiero resisted the urge to lunge forward. He posed—well, preened—in the manner he knew best displayed his considerable assets. "I don't know what you mean."

"Oh, I doubt that very much."

"I didn't come for..." The hand Kipling flicked to dismiss him instead hung in the air, open but shaking. He nevertheless raked Hiero from foot to forelock with eyes blown wide with apprehension.

"No?" Hiero approached him with caution, giving skittish Kip every chance to fight, to flee. He set a hand in the center of Kipling's chest but kept a respectable space between them. Kipling parted his lips, eager tongue poised to... what? Speak? Wag? Plunder? "Because it seems to me the most scandalous thing about me, the most revealing, the most criminal, is an aspect you are shockingly loath to discuss."

With curious fingers, Hiero smoothed the front of his shirt, plucked open a button. He felt along the taut plain of his pectoral until his fingers brushed over a nipple. When he worried the pert nub, Kipling hissed but did not pull away. Rather he leaned in, his quaking body all but begging to be touched.

"I could feel you there, in your box, even before I saw you. A presence stirring the air. Waiting, watching." Hiero wrenched his arm down, pearlescent buttons popping like confetti. He reached down to cup Kipling's impressive bulge, tracing the length of the even more impressive prick within, hot and stiff as a forge iron. "Wanting."

Kipling mewled, a wild, wounded sound, and bucked into Hiero's palm.

"Is this what you came for, dear Kip? Is this why you sought me out?" Hiero pressed their bodies together, relishing Kip's fitness.

With hungry lips, he caressed the stubbly slope of his neck, his breath a ghost at his ear. "Say it."

Hiero could feel every jitter of acceptance, every twitch of excitement in the body he held. In the end Kipling exhaled in a breathy rush, "Yes."

Too long. Too long without the nip of another man's teeth at his neck, the press of another man's weight into him. Too long without the scent of sweat spiked with desire. Too long without the feel of muscles shifting under skin, the scrape of coarse chest hair, the tickle of mustache, the prod of a ready cock reminding him the person in his arms was wonderfully, unmistakably male.

The list of things Tim should be thinking of at this moment— instead of how his arms might span the vast expanse of Bash's back—was longer than the history of the world, but not a speck of him cared. Not when he could plunge his hand into Bash's satiny swamp of hair. Not when Bash latched those pillow lips to his nipple. Not when he yanked down Tim's trousers with eager hands, wafting a dose of cooling air around his firebrand shaft. For years he had lusted after Horace Beastly from afar, but the reality... Oh, the reality! Trickster or true heart, mercenary or Machiavelli, Bash made his body sing.

Bash flitted out his saucy tongue, laved a circle around Tim's nipple before licking a path down his torso. Tim splayed himself across the front of the wardrobe, widening his stance and canting his hips forward, butting Bash's cheek with the head of his cock.

"So lovely. So eager." Bash's dark eyes glinted with approval. He raked them up the length of Tim's body before locking in.

A raised eyebrow almost brought Tim to his knees.

"Have you been thinking of this? Of us, together?"

"Since that first moment at Blackwood's."

Bash's smile was almost tender. "So have I."

He clamped his fist around Tim's base and set that mischievous tongue to work, swirling it around his shaft and lapping at his slit, tracing under the ridge before slicking back down again, reaching down to fondle his bollocks before sliding him into the hot crevasse of his mouth. Tim cried out, from pleasure, from relief, from the sheer joy of another man's sensual attentions. He burrowed his hands in Bash's velvety mane as he hollowed his cheeks and pulled nearly all the way off before sucking him greedily back in. He fought to keep his hips still, but, with a slap to his left buttock, Bash encouraged him to thrust.

For a time Tim's entire world narrowed down to that elemental connection: his thick cock pushing between Bash's lips, the slender throat that constricted around him, obsidian eyes glittering up at him with a warmth and a wickedness that thrilled him to the core. With the last of his strength, Tim firmed his stance and fucked his mouth, keening each time his cockhead breached the heady threshold.

Even while racing to the finish line, he wanted it to go on forever, the grind and the suck, the breathlessness of it all. The drag across gaudy lips, the plunge into decadent heat. He chased his ecstasy with the endurance of a marathon runner, but in the end, as always, it was a mad dash, a fierce, final pound of flesh on flesh. A gunshot of pleasure and the rapturous recoil as he emptied round after round down Bash's throat.

Tim moaned, pet Bash's forelock back from his brow, the better to see his neck muscles work as he swallowed. He couldn't imagine a more erotic image than Bash's red mouth relinquishing his cock, or the way Bash nuzzled his face into his groin and drank in his scent. His knees as wobbly as a marionette's, Tim sank to the floor.

He suffered a moment's hesitation when he met those enigmatic black eyes anew. Bash looked at him with fondness, but Tim sensed a reticence there. How he wanted to taste himself on his lips, unlace

Bash's robe, and expose every plain and curve of his graceful body. The drape of the cloth concealed whether Bash was still needful. His lust-fuelled courage ebbing along with his afterglow, Tim forced himself to rest a hand on Bash's silk-covered thigh. He leaned in, aiming for a kiss he wasn't sure he'd be granted, giving Bash every opportunity to retreat—but praying he wouldn't.

"Do you want—"

The door flew open. The white-haired woman swaggered in as if she'd ridden to the theater on a particularly unruly horse, her petite brunet companion nowhere to be seen. She took one look at half-naked and disheveled Tim—too stunned to cover himself—and barked out a deep-voiced laugh.

"Is that the antiquities dealer? Good Lord!"

Tim recoiled from the cackling woman, from Bash, from everything that had transpired in the past hour. From the supremely wrongheaded decision to ever step foot in the Gaiety that night or any night. From the vision that now played out before his horrified eyes, of his entire life crumbling to ruin. For the woman who towered above them, despite the peachy hue to her complexion and the gossamer sheen to her wig, bore a strong resemblance to a recent acquaintance.

Namely Commodore Goldenplover. The fact that the commodore, like so many of their persuasion, found both freedom and pleasure in the assumption of a woman's guise, was of no consequence to someone who frequented—and had catted his way around—the theatre like Tim. The fact that one of the main suspects in his investigation now had a front-row seat to Tim's own vices...

"I... I..." Tim hastened to right his clothing, his shaking hands no help at all. He tried to rise to his feet, but the muscles in his legs refused to support him. Instead he huddled against the base of the wardrobe and glued his eyes to the carpet. He swallowed convulsively, the curdled contents of his stomach flooding to his throat as he imagined what Quayle and his fellow officers would make of this, a more glorious downfall than even they could have plotted for him.

"See here, you've spooked him." Before he could protest, Bash made quick work of fastening his breeches and shirt with his nimble fingers. He tossed a glare over his shoulder, but when he turned back to Tim, his look was contrite. "But do permit me the pleasure of reintroduction. Dearest Kip, this is Lady Odile. Odile, Mr. Kipling."

"Good to meet you, er... my lady."

"Dear boy, I wish I could say—"

"Now go on," Bash barked. "Out with you!"

Odile snorted. "I'll be at our usual table, if you have further need of me." She lurched out the door as brashly as she entered but made certain it was closed.

Bash helped Tim to his feet, his arms surprisingly strong for one so naturally tipsy. Though it was Tim who felt drunk on some foul cocktail of loathing and recrimination that made his head heavy and his movements sluggish. Like a hundred-ton boulder on his back, he would lug the shame around for months. If not forever. There was no place at Scotland Yard for sodomites, but there was space enough at Newgate.

It was some time before he realized Bash had not let him go.

"Drink?"

Tim wanted to protest but found himself nodding. Bash eased him over to his ridiculous couch, then busied himself at the drinks tray.

"Don't fret about Lady Odile. She won't breathe a word."

"Until it's convenient." Tim put his head between his knees, felt even queasier when confronted with the mind-bending pattern of the carpet. He shut his eyes, hoping against hope to be magically transported elsewhere.

"I give you my word as a gentleman. In place of hers, of course."

"You'll understand if I'm not entirely convinced of either of your trustworthiness."

"Brain like a roast goose. Stuffed to the tail feathers with secrets, but no one's ever managed to pluck one out of her."

"That's... not the metaphor I would have chosen."

With a firm grip, Bash squeezed his shoulder, then urged him upright. He proffered a tumbler of amber liquid; Tim grabbed it, downed it in one go. A welcome sear down his throat, the hand rubbing his back more so. For all his posturing, Bash seemed a kind man.

"Really." Bash continued as if Tim hadn't spoken. "If you think about it, you've got one up on her and one up on me. You're two ahead."

Tim laughed despite himself. "And yet it feels like I've gained nothing at all." He stared into his glass, the mullioned base far more symbolic of his predicament. "We can't all disappear into a new identity whenever we please."

"No?" He felt Bash's eyes on him and too late realized his mistake. "You've done well enough for yourself on that score."

"I've told you—"

"Nothing of consequence."

"You're hardly in a position to judge, Mr. Beastly."

He let out a wild trill of laughter, gay enough to buoy even Tim's heart. "Isn't that the most delicious name? The theater gods shined upon me that day."

"Mmm. Only slightly more preposterous than Hieronymus Bash."

"Well." His smirk spoke volumes. "That I can't take credit for."

"You don't say."

"My parents, despite their many flaws, had a certain panache."

Tim stole a glance in his direction, smiled. "They did well to pass it on."

"Yes, well, I've improved upon their example considerably." Having the foresight to have brought the bottle with him, he overgenerously refreshed both their drinks. "Now to business."

"Oh, we're talking business, are we?"

"This afternoon." He clicked his tongue. "Most disappointing. But because you have been quite dogged in your pursuit of me and because you have talents that I find..."

"Impressive?"

"... useful, I will grant you one more opportunity to be honest. About your identity, if that wasn't clear."

Tim snorted. "You must be joking."

"I can assure you, dear Kip, that I have never been more serious." Bash considered this. "Possibly. Er, well... this week, at least. Wait... no. Today. I have not been more serious today."

"Are you certain?"

"I am."

"Not even this afternoon, when you first made your demand?"

"Not even then."

Tim swallowed back a chuckle. He should have been mortified. By his own weakness, if nothing else. To come here in pursuit of a suspect and be lured back into a world of vice and depravity. To tangle with the very man he sought to expose. To be exposed himself as a degenerate, putting his career, his future, his entire life in the hands of two men with money and influence enough to ruin him. Yet despite all evidence to the contrary, he found himself charmed.

That did not make him a fool.

"No." Out of the corner of his eye, he saw that eyebrow lift.

"You stand at the gate with the keys to the kingdom, and you refuse?"

Tim firmed his lips as he formulated his reply. "Let me put this in terms you'll best understand: I'll show you mine if you show me yours."

The resulting smile was so wide Tim could have counted his teeth. "Is that a promise?"

After setting his tumbler on the floor, he stood. If he hoped to retain a shred of his dignity as well as resist any of Bash's further advances, he should retreat while he had control of the field. And of himself.

"Make of it what you will."

When he turned for Bash's answer, he matched that mercurial gaze with a challenge of his own, though it took everything he had not to let himself be ensorcelled anew. There may not be magic in the world, but Hieronymus Bash was a wizard of the highest order.

"The Grenadier. Belgravia. One o'clock. Dress... as you normally do. It'll be a day of it, so come prepared. Don't be late."

"Won't Miss Pankhurst object?"

"She won't be joining us."

Tim's curiosity was piqued. "Until tomorrow, then, Mr. Beastly."

Bash raised his glass in salutation. "Until tomorrow, my dear Kip."

Hiero shoved, ducked, and crawled his way through the merry patrons of The Bard and Bullwhip, the bar on the box-level floor of the Gaiety. The density of the crowd was relative to the success of the night's performance, and it had been a roaring one. While one of Hiero's swarthy allure did not go unnoticed by the nancy boys on the hunt for a bit of fun or an easy mark, the sober colors and impeccable tailoring of his suit assured no one dared approach him unless he beckoned first. After all, the best way to hide a renowned eccentric in plain sight was for him to dress like everyone else. Which only underlined the importance of one of his personal mottos: "Clothes maketh the man."

Unbidden, his mind flashed to an image of one Timothy Kipling, professional riddle, drooping over the edge of his couch, suit and life in tatters. Hiero might have predicted someone so sartorially challenged hung on to his equanimity by a thread. What he never could have foreseen was how affecting his unraveling would be. By all appearances Kip had more problems than a few stitches and a bit of hemming would solve. He needed someone to take full measure of his life, cut a new pattern from whole cloth.

Hiero *was* rather deft with a needle and thread...

For an instant the crowd parted, and he spotted Goldie—or rather Lady Odile de Volanges. A flock of twittering mary-anns perched around her window-side booth, black as magpies against the London nightscape. They pecked at one another with catty comments and clawing witticisms, but none had been invited to sit. By the way Lady Odile made eyes at one of the chirpier birds with a slick bill of ebony hair and feathery eyelashes, Hiero had arrived just in time. He swooped in as the dickybird hovered over his seat.

With a communal squawk, they scattered.

"You're a dark horse," Lady Odile opined, as she poured him a full hand of scotch. "Have you been tupping Kipling all this time?"

"If I have, I'm the last to know it." Hiero clicked open his case of thin cigarette papers, counting off two. He poured out a pair of even lines of Turkish tobacco, then stowed the packet. "I had no more warning than a knock at my door before he pounced."

Lady Odile huffed. "Man of violent passions, is he? Naughty things do sometimes come in bland packages."

"He is... unpredictable, to say the least." Hiero wet his fingers on his bottom lip, then set to rolling.

"My word."

"Hmm?"

"Don't tell me you've found another one of your charity cases."

"My..." He twiddled his fingers as if to stoke his thoughts. "What do you mean?"

"I mean you've missed your true vocation. If you've such a yen for public service, you should buy yourself a title and join the House of Lords."

Hiero scoffed. "As if they do anything but fill their own coffers."

"Careful. One of them might overhear."

"I would shout it from the rooftops. I have, come to think of it."

Lady Odile's eyes twinkled. "The soul of a revolutionary. A mind like a bag of cats."

"Cats! Goodness no. Hedgehogs, perhaps."

"Prickly but relatively harmless? Prone to accidental stabbings?"

"Precisely."

The shared a fond laugh.

"My dear friend, I do envy how deeply and truly you know yourself. Some of us..."

Hiero looked up from licking the edge of the paper, frowned. Lady Odile had reapplied her rouge, but there were new smudges under her eyes, not enhanced by the gray-violet circles her powder no longer concealed. Hiero recalled Odile's painful decision to exchange her fiery-red wig for the dove-white confection she currently wore in the wake of his Apollo's passing, a beautiful tribute to their lifelong friendship, to the end of an era. Now he wondered if it was an acknowledgement of Odile's transitioning from the autumn to the winter of her life. Perhaps it was no coincidence she hadn't invited any of those chirruping cherubs for a dip?

"Come now. You're dangerously close to being the next of my charity cases."

"In place of the obsequious Kipling, you mean? I think not."

"You know that word has too many letters. Speak plainly."

"Very well. He's a stranger who, in the space of little more than a day, has brought himself close to you. He's most likely Blackwood's man. Not to mention he now knows secrets enough to ruin us both, and you don't even know his real name."

Hiero smoothed a finger down the length of one of the cigarettes, sighed. He offered it to Odile, who snatched it up. He took up his own, then lit them both. As he sucked in a rush of smoke, he stared out over the river toward the south, the waterway but one of the many invisible barriers between the rich and the poor. Sometimes he longed for the simplicity of life on the other side, even as he vowed to never, ever again fall so low.

"He's hiding a great deal, our Mr. Kipling, but mostly from himself. He won't betray us because we can betray him in turn, and he is terrified of what he is."

"And what is that?"

"Haven't the faintest notion." To see the spark reigniting in Odile's eyes pleased Hiero. "But if tonight was any indication, it's going to be a heap of fun finding out."

She clicked her tongue. "The pair of you deserve one another."

"Was that ever in doubt?" He blew out a plume of smoke, then butted his ashes into Odile's glass. "Speaking of just deserts, or rather just of dessert, where has young Thomas fluttered off to?"

"His father set a curfew after the last incident."

"Oh, my. How deliciously ineffective." At Lady Odile's sniff, he added, "I trust you didn't let him go without indulging in a bit of brown?"

"Of course not. The lad was on me before the curtain dropped."

"Well, you are a devoted chaperone. Lord Henley must see that."

"Quite. Otherwise he wouldn't have been allowed out at all."

Hiero made a moue. "Then I don't see the trouble."

"Don't you? We're in the midst of this garden of earthly delights, but it's merely barrels and barrels of new fruit, freshly plucked from the tree or the vine. If you catch one in season and you treat it well, it may ripen, but nearly all of my indulgences are seedless. Once they rot, there's nothing left to plant. To grow. And they rot so quickly..." Her pale eyes flitted from branch to branch but saw nothing. "You don't know how lucky you are to have found someone like Apollo. Someone steady. Someone loyal."

"Believe me, I do."

Their gazes locked, and Lady Odile shook her head.

"Of course you do. Forgive me. If anything—"

"Perhaps I do need to keep a closer eye on you."

With Goldie's bark of a laugh and sandpaper voice, she replied, "Perhaps you should."

They puffed away in silence for a time, a calm eye amidst the flirtation and revelry around them.

Hiero watched Odile tread water in a storming sea of emotion. He dove in.

"My lady, you must forgive me a moment's curiosity."

It was Odile's turn to be curious. "About?"

"There was a time in your life, was there not, when you were involved with someone... more serious? In your travels?"

She chuckled. "Why do I suspect your curiosity is of a professional nature?"

"Both personal and professional, I'll admit."

"How long have you suspected?"

"Since you censored your version of the events at Scavo." Lady Odile made to protest, but Hiero stopped her. "Oh, it was your right to do so. Not that Miss Pankhurst or Han would have thought any less of you."

"I know they are aware of... the full spectrum of your activities. I simply didn't think it relevant."

"So it's true? The headman, Chiwi. He was your lover."

To Hiero's dismay, her composure crumbled. "He was..." She squeezed her eyes shut against her memories as much as her sorrow. "He was to me as Apollo was to you. But as private as your situation had to remain, ours infinitely more so. He was a tribesman. A husband. A father. He never dreamed..."

"It must have been torture for you when he was killed."

Lady Odile let out a soft cry. "I wanted to feed myself to those beasts! I prayed that they would come for me. I could not grieve. I could not even... To see him that way. Shredded. His face..." With the will of someone who had survived far greater tragedies than this, she collected herself. "I blamed myself. Our sickness. But I see now.

It was a force beyond our control."

Hiero cleared his throat. "Well, that is a matter of opinion."

"Don't start," Lady Odile chided but kept her humor. "If you had borne witness to the things we saw..." She took a long drag on her cigarette, waved the smoke—and sadness—out of her eyes. "Well. It doesn't bear thinking about." She blew away her troubles with a blast of smoke, then shot Hiero a look. "What are you up to, sniffing around my past paramours?"

"My dear, you are the one blubbering into your scotch."

"You led me down the path. Just enough breadcrumbs to lure me along. Why?"

"I haven't the faintest notion what you're on about."

"Hieronymus, don't be coy." She narrowed her eyes. "What, you think I am the mastermind behind these robberies? Because of Chiwi? Are you mad?"

"Certifiable. I have the scars to prove it."

"Answer the question."

"I believe I did."

"Not that question."

Hiero traced circles with his glass, enjoying the clink of the ice until they began to melt under her glare.

"I beg your pardon, but I've forgotten what it was."

If it weren't for her excess of powder, she would have been as red as a beet.

"Why on Earth would I pretend to steal my own fang, hire you to retrieve it, then proceed to steal the remaining three, knowing full well you'll eventually catch me out?"

"Well, when you say it like that..." Their eyes met. He sighed. "One has to chase down all avenues of inquiry, even if they prove as transparent as the spirits you summon."

Lady Odile considered this for a time, then nodded. "I do not have the fangs. I do not want the damnable thing back. If you never retrieve them, I won't be sorry." She raised a gloved hand before

Hiero could object. "Of course the thieves should be brought to justice. And there may be even stranger things afoot. But the fang, if retrieved, will be donated to a museum, threat of demonic possession or no. And perhaps then..."

Lady Odile's eyes took on a glassy cast, reliving scenes of passion and horror Hiero could only dream of. Not that he would sleep well that night. Between Kipling and memory-haunted Odile, he was thoroughly unsettled. Especially since, in disproving one motive, Odile had inadvertently opened the possibility of another...

Chapter 6

Number 4 Whitehall Place, an unremarkable building on an unremarkable side street, suited the most unobtrusive of its detectives just fine. A rectangular two-story stone slab with barred windows, its only flourish the twin gargoyle sentries that flanked the coat of arms over its front entrance, the Yard held some of the city's sharpest minds and a veritable treasure trove of secrets.

Tim skulked through the back door via the nominal Scotland Yard, praying the desk sergeant could not read the culpability writ bold across his face. He wore the same gabardine frock and durable trousers that had defined Tim Stoker since the day he earned his badge, but felt as if bedecked in some Bash-ian riot of color. As if his skin still glistened with a postcoital sheen and his clothes were rank from the rut. As if the only badge he wore was the brand of Bash's lips on his neck or the stripe of his seed on his lapel.

He scurried up the stairs, avoiding the eyes of passing colleagues, which to his mind glowed like the flames under the spit his fellow Yardsmen would roast him on if they ever discovered Tim's predilections. Skimming an extra layer off the reward cream was nothing compared to milking another man. He crept into the squad room, lurching toward his desk. Even as he snuck into his chair, he waited every moment for Bash to leap into the room like a demented town crier and declare to them all—these comrades who treated him with the disdain and incredulity of a bothersome ghost—that he should be in the stocks, not protecting the streets.

In a voice as honeyed as the nightingale's call, Bash would proclaim, "Good sirs, I'm here to report a fox in your henhouse. A wolf, dressed as one of your own, has penetrated your flock. I am something of a penetration expert, having much experience with burrowing, plugging, and inserting of every sort, as well as all kinds of insinuation and infiltration, and I tell you, there is one among you who knows how to pierce to the very core of your hallowed institution. This man!" Here Bash would plunk himself on Tim's lap. "This man, good sirs, is a letch and a catamite. I should know. My body betrays shocking evidence of his depravity." Bash would swing his leg into a straddle as he unbuttoned his shirt. "If any of you would care to peruse…"

Tim could just imagine the manic twinkle in his black eyes. The hirsute majesty of his bared chest. The nudge of his erect cock against Tim's groin as he flirted and frotted to prove his point. Tempting fate as always, but also Tim, the maneuver just another seduction, another irresistible ploy…

Tim shuddered, swallowed hard. He was at once deeply ashamed, yet utterly shameless, to daydream of such things in the law's house. Whispering mantras to himself like a reverse snake charmer, he willed his prick into submission.

"Praying'll not do you much good in the detective trade, Stoker." DS Littlejohn might not have cast as long a shadow as he'd have liked over the desktop, but his diminutive height did permit him to slither up and startle Tim near out of his seat. His lubricious presence also deflated his erection. "The good Lord saves his miracles for those who need 'em."

Tim shook his head to clear it and too late retorted, "Then He must be at your beck and call, considering your solve rate."

"Don't need divine intervention to get the job done." He smashed a fist into his open palm, clicked his tongue. "Just a nose for a lagger and a few tips from the Marquess."

"A Queensberry man, eh? I don't recall ever seeing you at the club."

"Not one for charging at windmills, me. Get my constitutional on the job, don't I?"

Tim swallowed back the bile that rose to his throat and the challenge that seared his tongue. A squirrel of a man with scraggily muttonchops and two flint shards for eyes, Littlejohn looked every inch the East End scrapper. A career criminal in copper's togs, he chose the law because it afforded him carte blanche access to power with no threat of jail time or the noose. His inferior rank also made any fight between them—whether in the boxing ring or the station house—a no-win for Tim. However much he may have wanted to physically and intellectually clobber the DS, he couldn't take the risk.

Wishing he could summon up one of Bash's poetic putdowns, Tim opted to punt.

"Pity, that. I'm sure a man of your wiles would do well on the ticket. A David and Goliath-type match, perhaps."

"Keep dreaming, Stoker," Littlejohn scoffed, then wandered off to flirt with a bench full of female witnesses.

Tim corralled his concentration, refocusing on the long-overdue report to Quayle. He'd barely managed a page when a hush fell over the room. Tim half expected to see Bash's predatory feline form standing in the doorway; instead Quayle planted himself there, impenetrable as a boulder. He fixed a granite stare on Tim, jutted out his jaw, and lumbered off. Every pair of peepers in the room tracked him as Tim gathered his notes and scarpered out. The fleetness of his feet matched the frantic pace of his mind as he scrambled for a way to explain... well, the nothing of his results so far.

Quayle was already seated behind his desk when Tim swept in, clutching his notebook to his chest as if it were the dearest thing he possessed instead of the emptiest. At Quayle's gesture, he kicked the door shut behind him. He considered Quayle's almost-smirk a minor victory. At least he wouldn't be leaving the field without having scored a hit.

"DI Stoker. Report."

"S-Sir." Tim bit his cheek to control his stammer. "I have infiltrated Bash's group and won a tentative trust."

"Tentative?"

"He's an odd duck."

"You don't say."

"Eccentric, brazen, prone to distraction. The true mystery is how he manages to solve any case, let alone so many."

Quayle scoffed. "If he's such a bumbler, why haven't you bagged him yet?"

"His investigative style—if you can call it that—is scattershot."

"The theft of the teeth, is it?"

"Yes, sir. The Fangs of Scavo."

"Ponces." Quayle snorted, a low, bassoonlike sound akin to a fart. "Do you have a lead?"

"We do, sir. We're meeting up this afternoon to pursue it."

"Good." At least it sounded like praise. Might as easily have been a grunt. "Don't let that quack steal your thunder, Stoker. You catch him in some dodgy business so I can put him out of it, *and* you find those missing chompers, tout de bleedin' suite. Lord Blackwood and his gang have deep pockets. It'd be our pleasure to mine 'em."

Staggered, a forceful sneeze could have blown Tim over. If ever he doubted Quayle's intention to see him gone, he couldn't now. The request to solve not one but two cases, bring down someone who had his claws deeply entrenched in the aristocracy, not to mention a thieving noble veiling his crimes under the guise of spiritualism, was as ludicrous as it was impossible. A three, four, or five-man team might manage one of the two feats within a fortnight, if not a month, but a man on his own? Tim would have to conjure up more than a few tricks to escape the box Quayle had locked him in before he drowned.

There was also the not-insignificant matter of giving the very predator he hunted a long whiff of his... secrets.

Tim squared his shoulders, straightened his spine. "Yes, sir."

Quayle's face took on the primitive cast of a statue carved into a cliff face.

"A win, Stoker. Remember. A clean win, or..."

He popped a knuckle with a deafening crack.

Hiero stared into the amber liquid at the bottom of his glass as if it could tell his future. The murky fathoms had far more to say about the sins of his past. Not to mention present tensions, as Han's frowning face reflected there, upside down, which at least made him look like he smiled. Hiero shot back the lot before it could reveal further unpleasantness. The hair of the dog did nothing to relieve the throbbing that pounded at his temples and broke across his crown.

He waved for a refill. Han snatched his hand out of the air and slammed it on the table. Hiero shrieked, the sound muffling his headache for one blissful second before pain shot up his arm. Several patrons turned to glare at them; others went so far as to rise out of their seats. A whistle from the bartender tempered them—for now. A scuffle between foreigners would not be tolerated no matter how generously Hiero tipped the publican.

"What the devil was that for?" Hiero demanded.

"I don't bother to keep track anymore. Just know this: you de-served it."

"I did not!"

"Keep your voice down," Han hissed. His gaze monitored every inch of the pub, all without moving his head, like one of those portraits with the eyes cut out.

The Grenadier was just full enough that the chatter covered their conversation, but not so full they risked being overheard. A high-class watering hole by virtue of its neighborhood, the pub was a favorite with high-ranking officers; no surprise, being named after the Grenadier Guards' triumph at the Battle of Waterloo. Over many a raucous night, he, Goldie, and Apollo had haunted the very booth in which they sat, the military men sharing tales of bloody naval battles. Unlike some of the rougher pubs a few streets away, no one here ever started a brawl or snatched your handbag, which made it the perfect unofficial headquarters for their investigative missions. Or for Hiero to spend a pleasant afternoon while Han and Callie solved their latest case.

But not today.

"I don't see how I'm to blame for supplying us with the very thing we lack. You said yourself we would be better off with another man; I found us one. It was a—dare I say it—logical decision."

"There's no logic in inviting along the man you shooed away only hours before for your own"—Han pointedly dropped his gaze—"reasons."

Callie, who until then was slouched in her seat, hiding under the brim of her cap, absorbed with playing the part of Archie the pageboy, gasped. "Hiero, you didn't!"

"I... It wasn't... You don't..." *Throb, throb, throb.* "Do we need an extra hand or no?"

Callie blew out a sigh, hunched her shoulders. Hiero admired her commitment to her character; even furious as she must be, she deferred to their leader, staring expectantly at Han, who growled under his breath. Hiero feigned his usual level of supreme confidence, regarding them both with a practiced mixture of imperiousness and dismissal, but his performance lacked. For one, concentration proved difficult when a military salute's worth of cannon fire blasting around his head. Secondly a wily, whirligig emotion evaded his every attempt at capture: protectiveness.

No matter what he promised, some inexplicable part of him

wanted to spare Kip the stress of this day. The risk his could-be patron, Lord Blackwood, would find him out. The disdainful looks Hiero's colleagues would cast him. The vain attempts at pretending he and Kip hadn't exposed themselves in ways improper and potentially ruinous. Given how he reacted in the aftermath of their coming together, Hiero didn't imagine Kip terribly well-suited to pretending it never happened. Especially if he, like Hiero, longed for a repeat performance.

They had gotten themselves into quite a pickle.

Han fixed him with one of his indecipherable looks. Sphinxlike and sturdy, he had always played the solid yin to Hiero's slippery yang. "Why do you suddenly trust him?"

"I don't."

"Do you think he will betray us?"

"Haven't the faintest notion."

Han grunted. "I'm trying to understand."

"A fruitless endeavor. How could you when I myself do not?" He winced as a particularly sharp pain stabbed into the corner of his eye socket. "Call it... intuition."

"Not exactly what I would call it."

Hiero couldn't quite commit to his smirk. "No."

"Hardly matters now," Callie remarked. "Here he comes."

The man who strode toward them had the same unremarkable face and average build as Timothy Kipling but was so different Hiero might not have recognized him if Callie hadn't announced his arrival. Not only were the clothes he wore passably tailored, if drab, but they suited him. No more the undercurrent of nervousness and the ramrod stance like an actor who couldn't remember his lines. Instead his brow was set in a newfound determination. Every step he took toward them resonated with authority. Kip's aura and bearing assured his colleagues of his reliability in ways Hiero had not. He even had his blush in check; only a hint of red colored his cheeks when he met Hiero's incredulous gaze. With a proud smile, no less.

"Good day, Mr. Bash."

"Kip." Hiero managed to close his mouth. "You're looking... well-rested." Hiero heaped as much innuendo as he could into the word, but it caused Kip not a creak of upset.

"Can't say the same for you. A bit green about the gills, are you? Rough night?"

"Rather it was quite pleasant. Until the sun rose."

"That is a bother." He nodded a greeting at Han, then directed those keen eyes to a disguised Callie.

Hiero hastened to reintroduce them. "Archie here will be our scout. Won't you, Archie?"

"Right, guv." Callie's accent was as thick as the pomade that slicked back her short black hair.

"This is our associate, Mr. Kipling."

"Sir."

"Excellent." Kip rubbed his hands together as he took a seat. "What's the plan?"

"Mr. Han is our tactician." That did provoke a reaction, much to Hiero's disappointment. Kip perhaps didn't realize how alike he and Han were in their ability to disappear in plain sight. Though Hiero never forgot the common Englishman's jaundiced view of foreigners, he had supposed Kip would have a healthier perspective, if only because of his own secrets. But if there was one thing Hiero had discovered, it was that those who were most cruelly treated could be all the more vicious because of it. "If you would..."

To his credit, Kip's surprise was short-lived. He leaned in as Han explained the particulars of their mission, letting no detail slip by and asking thoughtful questions. Hiero wished he could say the same, but he found the whole thing frightfully boring. His preference, his greatest skill, his raison d'être, was his ability to improvise. To woolgather, as his sister often described it, until he knitted enough scarf to hang himself.

This brought his attention to Kip's neck, stubble already sprouting, though he had no doubt shaved that morning, cords of muscle tightening and flexing as he moved his jaw. Hiero had only had a glimpse of his upper body the previous night. Kip's current well-cut suit kept hidden the fitness of his torso. How did a man who took such care with his physique find himself so lacking in sartorial finesse? Hiero pondered these and other tawdrier mysteries until...

"Good." One by one Han locked eyes with everyone at the table. "Questions?" When none were raised, he concluded, "Very well. Let's be off."

The Black Maria van floated like a funeral barge down the length of the mews, emerging from a bank of fog only to sail into another before weighing anchor behind No. 37 Belgrave Square, Lady Stang-Helion's residence. Peering through the small window of the carriage house loft across the way, Tim could just make out the faces of its four passengers. The driver and the rear guard were unknown to him—no doubt a pair of Lord Blackwood's most trusted men. When the rear doors opened, DS Small and DC Croke emerged, carrying between them a hefty metal lockbox. The effect would have been comical under other circumstances; Small was actually the taller of the two, an upended broom with sticklike limbs and thatched hair. A stout little man with porcine features, Croke had a perpetually glazed look. Lord Blackwood waited for them at the servants' entrance, personally inspecting every moment of the transaction.

Hardly a surprise, thought Tim as he watched them disappear into the house. The remaining guards patrolled the area with militaristic precision, leaving Tim to wonder how, exactly, Han was going to pull this off.

But their precision proved an unexpected boon. After timing out several of their rotations, Tim could predict exactly when their attention would be focused away from the Maria. He slipped a hand mirror out of his pocket and aimed it at the first-floor terrace, where a black-clad figure hid behind one of the columns. Praying there was enough light for a reflection to catch, Tim waited until the guards were almost in position. A few flicks of the wrist and a hard stomp of his boot heel sent the agreed-upon signal.

Mr. Han leapt over the balcony rail, landing on the Maria's roof with a thud masked by the bang of the carriage house doors. Both the guards and the horses reared. Tim lingered at the window while below Bash threw himself into the role of tipsy groom. Tim examined the van's roof, amazed such a large man as Mr. Han could all but vanish atop the Maria. After a curt exchange, the guards ordered Bash back to his duties—Tim's cue to descend. He crept across the creaky floor of the real groom's loft, grateful for whatever combination of exhaustion and drink caused him to snooze through the whole affair. Bash awaited him at the side window, having already traded the groom's coat for his own rather subdued greatcoat.

But then actors must be accustomed to quick changes.

"Has our Icarus landed?" Bash whispered.

"Not quite as disastrously as the boy of myth, thank goodness." Tim pulled out his hand mirror, affixed to the end of a long stick at such an angle as to peer around corners unseen. "He is a marvel, your man. I see why you keep him."

"I think you've got the, er, wrong end of the stick there."

Tim examined his mirrored contraption more closely. "How do you mean?"

"It is Han who keeps me, and has for some time."

"Oh." Tim considered this a moment. "Oh!" A panoply of images of Bash and Han in intimate scenarios played across his mind's eye. "That must be... difficult."

"For him, yes."

"But not for you? Does he permit you to..." Tim found himself fluttering his hand ineffectually. Soon he would be dressing like a peacock and drinking like a gutter rat. "Is that why he objected to my inclusion?"

"*I* object to your inclusion. Yet here you are."

"At your invitation."

"Was it? Well, you were most persuasive, if I recall."

"If you recall," Tim volleyed back, proud of himself for keeping up, "it was you that did most of the persuading."

Bash chuckled softly. "So I did."

They moved toward each other as if by instinct, Bash reaching for his neck just as Tim planted a hand in the center of his chest, though whether to push or to clutch, he did not know. They hovered there awhile, breathing in the other's air, drawn to each other in as many ways as kept them apart. Was it only three hours earlier that he stood outside the Yard, resolved to cast his worries aside and confront his problems head-on? That he renewed his focus on the case, shared secrets and impassioned interludes be damned? Tim struggled to remember anything beyond the cocoon of their near embrace, the warmth of Bash's fingers at his neck, the glint of mischief in his dark eyes.

"Doesn't he mind?" Tim panted.

"Who minds what?"

"Mr. Han. The one who gets to keep you."

Tim wished he dreaded more the smile that curled his pillowy lips.

"What, Han? My..." His laugh nearly spooked the horses. "My dear Kip, there are things between us well beyond your comprehension—"

"Clearly."

"—but *that* is not one of them."

"Oh." For the second time in less than a minute, Tim was rendered speechless. "I..."

A clunk from outside saved him from whatever inanity he would have babbled. Abandoning that gentling touch with reluctance, he

STOKER & BASH: THE FANGS OF SCAVO

raced over to the window and stuck out his mirror. As the events in the mews played out, Bash let out a quiet "Ha!" Pressing against him from behind, the world's most potent distraction joined him in monitoring Small and Croke's progress as they heaved the lockbox out the door.

"Blast!" Tim secured the stick to the window frame so they could continue to watch as they exited. "We've tarried too long."

Using a carriage wheel as leverage, he hoisted himself up and out the window. He turned back to help Bash, who only stared at him, incredulous.

"That was quite a feat."

Tim urged him forward. "Hurry, or we'll miss them."

"You go. I'll rendezvous with Miss—er, Archie, and meet you back at the pub."

It was Tim's turn to be incredulous. "Don't you care to see where the fang ends up?"

"Han will make a full report."

"What if he's caught?"

"Then you'll speak for him."

"If I can keep up."

"I have every faith in you." Bash paused. "Excepting the part where I don't trust you. And you might still be in league with the enemy. Drat!"

With a good deal of grumbling and very little grace, Bash managed to haul himself out the window. With no time to consider all he just said, Tim instead led him around the back of the carriage house, where there was enough of an alleyway for them to bolt for the street. Bash's huffing and puffing blighted out any sound of the approaching Maria. Fortunately when they reached Halkin Street, the van was still parked by Lady Stang-Helion's rear door.

A relief, except for the posse of horse-bound constables waiting to play escort but steps away. Bash once again proved his singular way with words when he rounded the corner and exclaimed: "Oh, bugger!"

Five pairs of eyes, bright as bloodhounds, fixed on them. Only the sixth widened in surprise.

"Sir!" a young officer gasped.

For an endless minute, Tim struggled to place him. "Constable Hobbs, isn't it?"

That *was* it; Hobbs nodded proudly, pink to the tips of his ears.

"Are you one of Lord Blackwood's men, sir?"

"Hang on a minute," the constable at the head of the posse protested. A scrappy lad with a hard mouth and a pugilist's nose, he cast an assessing look down at Tim. "You know him?"

Tim well knew how unsteady the ground beneath him had become. He felt rather than saw Bash's avid interest in the constables' conversation. Bash might be a fool, but he was a clever fool. One false move and all Tim's careful preparation, all his gamesmanship and bargaining, would be for naught. Though his stomach rumbled and his nerve quaked, he affected an air of adamant superiority.

"Worked the Artherton trouble with him, didn't I?" Hobbs supplied for him.

"A dull business," Tim seconded. "The constable here was the only bright light."

"What you doing here?" the puglike officer demanded.

"Consulting. Along with my associate, Mr. Horace, an expert in African artifacts." Tim darted a glance at Bash, who had produced a monocle seemingly out of thin air. "As the van is full of the, er, cargo, Lord Blackwood thought it best if we hail a cab. We're to follow you."

Tim stared expectantly at the lead constable as the seconds lurched by. With every interminable tick, he became more aware of the dangers of the situation. He had no idea how close the Maria was to joining them. Whether Blackwood sat at the front or in the cabin, or if he had arranged his own transportation. He waited, heart in his throat, for the constable to ask the obvious: his name, his rank, his identification. Revealing any of these might win him this battle, but would he lose the war? He could feel Bash beside him, spine curled and claws at the ready, a cat about to pounce. Though he felt as meek as a mouse, he had to project a leonine strength.

He met the constable's scrutiny head-on. Eventually the young man nodded.

"Bates, hail a cab for the gentlemen!" he called to one of the rear officers. "We'll be quite a procession, sirs, so mind you don't get cut off. If you're having trouble, tell your driver to whistle at one of us. We'll escort you directly."

"Thank you, Constable…"

"Drake, sir."

"You have our gratitude, Drake. I'll be sure to commend you to Superintendent Reid at E Division."

This earned him a lopsided smile out of place on such a rough face. "Much obliged, sir."

Tim tipped his hat to them both before dragging Bash over to the waiting hansom, parked behind the back riders. He jogged over to have a quick word with the driver after glimpsing the Maria's approach. Tim swung into the cab an instant before she lurched forward. Wherever it might lead, the black procession had begun.

Any moment he might have spared admiring this stroke of luck, or pride felt at having turned a bad situation to his advantage, evaporated the second Bash opened his mouth.

"So you're a policeman?"

Tim hoped his laugh sounded more genuine to Bash's ears.

"Heavens no. I'm consulted, as the lad said, when there are thefts of this nature."

"Which is how you came to be in Blackwood's employ."

Startled, Tim shifted around to face him. "The day I take a penny from a man like Blackwood for such a foul purpose is the day I truly am possessed by a demonic spirit."

"But you would take money from him for a righteous cause?"

"If he had a mind to sell one of the rare occult texts in his collection, I would impose a fee, yes. A man has to make a living."

"And a gentleman in your profession can't afford to be too discerning."

"Brave words from a man with two public faces."

"I assure you I have many more than that."

"Oh, I don't doubt." Unsettled by Bash's accusations—both direct and implied—he struck back. "I wonder which came first, Mr. Beastly or Mr. Bash? Did the gentleman of leisure take to the stage, or is the actor giving the performance of his life?"

Their eyes locked, Bash's more wounded than defiant. A flicker of some soft, unidentifiable emotion lit his face, fleet as the bat of a hummingbird's wing. His usual expression of indulgent amusement settled in its wake.

"You ask an awful lot of questions for an antiquities expert."

"For an amateur detective, *you* are frightfully indifferent to the matter at hand."

Bash snorted. "On the contrary, dear Kip. I have at this very moment caught the scent of the only mystery that truly matters."

"Is that so? And which is this?"

With sensual deliberation, Bash raised his left hand, undid the button at his wrist, then slowly pulled each finger out of his glove. He peeled back the leather until his elegant maestro's fingers were exposed, fanned them out with flourish. He raked them across the back of Tim's hand where it rested on the seat between them, gently turned it around. They stroked over his palm and cuff before stretching out to twine with his own. No matter how calculated the gesture, that indelible connection had every nerve in Tim's body singing.

"I think you know."

A hard jostle broke the spell. Tim recoiled as the cab began to list to one side. A spindly figure leapt onto the scrap of space before the cabin. A spate of arguing outside heralded a pound on the front window. The door wrenched open and, before they could stop him, the boy Archie swung inside.

It was, alas, a two-person cab; he took up an unenviable position on Bash's lap and slammed the door shut.

"Well," Bash drolly remarked, "that was unexpected."

"I should say so!" Archie twisted his torso that he might glare at Bash directly. "Did you mean to leave me behind?"

"Consider this: is there a way I might answer that won't incur your wrath?"

Archie's response was a low growl, which Tim suspected was a "No."

"Did *he* put you up to this?" Archie demanded.

Tim did a double take. "What? Me?"

"Not you." Something in the boy's look of annoyance struck Tim as familiar, but, accustomed as he was to people's indifference, he couldn't place it. "Mr. Han. If this is his way of keeping me out of things—"

"Don't fret. You could not be more in. Things, as you say, happened quickly—as they do—and there wasn't time to alert you, stationed at the front as you were."

"And who was architect of that plan, I wonder."

Bash waved his hands about but seemed unsure where to rest them to avoid Archie's person. Instead he clasped them together.

"Not I, I should like to point out. For the second time, I might add."

"And I'd have you repeat it until you're blue in the face, if only—"

"See here," Tim sharply interjected. "Do you normally address your employer in such a tone? I should wonder he gives you any work at all."

Whatever protest he might have made died in his throat. Stunned silent, Archie gawked from Tim to Bash and back again, then promptly shut his mouth, turned away, and stared dead ahead.

"Sorry, guv," he muttered.

Tim narrowed his eyes, the sudden lowering of the lad's accent further drawing his suspicion.

Bash dismissed any concern with a click of his tongue. "No need. It's your fire we admire, Archie." He gave his back an awkward pat. "We'll certainly have need of it once we get... er, wherever we're going, I suppose."

Far from being soothed, the boy hunched his shoulders and tugged down the brim of his cap. Though still suspicious, Tim regretted his strong words. It was no business of his how Bash conducted his affairs, and certainly he had his eccentricities. Tim refocused himself on the mission at hand: their pursuit of the Maria. All other matters, including, thankfully, Bash's bold flirtations, were a distraction he couldn't afford.

Much sooner than expected, the Maria came to a halt in front of the middle door of a block-long stretch of red-bricked houses.

"Vandenberg," Archie announced.

They stared at one another, waiting for someone to take action, neither Tim nor Archie willing to overstep the tenuous bonds of their individual agreements with Bash.

Who looked as if he were settling in for a long nap.

"Off you go, lad," Bash urged.

"I will not! You'll leave me again."

"Don't be ridiculous. It would be foolish to leave you here when we could have left you before."

"You did leave me before!"

Bash let out a dramatic sigh. "I've explained that. If you want to play detective, then off with you! Go detect!" He shooed young Archie away with a fluttery gesture. Scowling, he scrambled over the barrier and scooted off down the lane.

Once no longer in sight, Bash extracted a flask from his inner pocket and took a generous draught. He then dangled it in Tim's direction but was refused. He stole another sip before stowing it away, then settled into himself like an owl on a branch and shut his eyes.

Tim permitted the silence to stretch on for several minutes, enjoying the chance to observe Bash in repose, unfettered by his own concerns and Bash's flamboyant personality. He did not look innocent as he dozed, as some do, only less himself. His attractiveness was somehow muted by tranquility. Awake and animated, he bedazzled. But relaxation humbled him, helped one peek behind the curtain to see the mechanics of his performance. Tim wondered if he ever allowed himself a day off from being Hieronymus Bash, or Horace Beastly, or if the performance had become his life.

Perhaps Tim would never unravel the enigma of his identity because the man he once was no longer existed.

After a brief delay, Archie leapt back onto the cab, startling them both. He paused on the slip of platform behind the horses to catch his breath, where Tim noted his pink cheeks and delicate features gave him an almost feminine aspect. He cocked a hand on his hip as he leaned on the barrier between them, in a manner almost resembling...

"Come quick," Archie managed between gasps. "Vandenberg's refusing to cooperate. Blackwood's in a state."

They sprang to action as inconspicuously as possible, taking advantage of the constables' distraction to sneak around the back of the cab, over the small white fence that penned in the front gardens, and behind a fortuitously placed hedge. They crawled along on all fours—never let it be said investigations weren't work—until within earshot of the building's entrance, where Blackwood played the part of battering ram and Vandenberg of fortified battlement doors. Which was to say their quarrel heated up.

"... only way of keeping us safe."

"By removing the very things meant to safeguard us?" Vandenberg demanded. "For the last time, I will not participate in this ludicrous plan of yours."

His voice like a discordant flute, Blackwood protested, "Valentine, I've consulted four different mediums and two card readers. The signs are clear."

"The only sign that is clear to me is that this time you have gone too far. No one has been hurt."

"Yet."

"In that you are correct. But it is you, my friend, who are playing with fire. I can only pray it isn't Tommy who will be burned."

"Now see here!" Tim imagined Blackwood gathering his energy during the pause that ensued until his rage glowed white hot. "Everything I have done from the moment this awful business began has been to protect her. And you, if you weren't such an ox."

"Better to have a bull's head than a rabbit's heart. You speak boldly, but I hear the pitter-patter, pitter-patter under every word." At that Bash poorly stifled a snort. "I saw the horrors of that place same as you, Stephen. I have not forgotten them. But if we act rashly here, we'll suffer the same fate. That is my final word on the matter."

"Valentine, see reason—" Blackwood blurted before the door slammed in his face.

Bash poked his head up an instant, likely unable to resist a glimpse of Blackwood in defeat, but Archie shoved him in the direction of the cab. They tucked snugly into their seats with no one the wiser by the time Blackwood made his way to his carriage. They waited until the procession continued on to indulge in speculation, their voices masked by the clamor of the busy London streets once more.

"Reckons he's something of a white knight, that Blackwood," young Archie remarked after squeezing himself in between them. Despite the grime on his clothes, a disturbingly floral scent wafted off him. "And Lady Stang-Helion's his lady fair."

"You think there's something between them beyond friendship?" Tim asked.

"Got a nose for it, don't I."

"That certainly casts his actions in a different light. Perhaps he's been trying to protect her all this time."

Bash barked a laugh. "You think him blameless?"

"Perhaps," Tim replied. "Perhaps not. He's not beyond suspicion, certainly. But if he's courting Lady Stang-Helion, I'd be curious as to when his suit began. Before or after her husband's death?"

"And if she's having it or giving him the cold shoulder," Archie contributed.

Tim chuckled. "Precisely. Though it's possible Vandenberg has the same ambition, and what we witnessed was two rams bashing heads rather than a bull and a bunny."

Bash, easily amused, giggled. "Aesthetically I prefer the latter image."

"So what's Blackwood's game?" Archie pondered, much to Tim's surprise. He hadn't been aware Archie was so well-informed on the particulars of the case. "Why's he risking taking away the fangs when they're meant to protect them? Why don't Vandenberg trust his friend? I thought they all believed in that hocus-pocus."

"Perhaps Vandenberg thinks it all a lark," Bash said.

"What of the events at Scavo?" Tim asked. "I imagine that many bodies would make a believer of the hardest skeptic."

Bash scoffed. "They were *attacked* by lions; they didn't turn into them. Perhaps the cats were rabid. Perhaps the villagers had done something to anger them. Perhaps an enemy or a rival set the beasts upon them every night. Superstition has only one function: to obfuscate the truth."

To say this stream of logic took Tim aback was an understatement. "I think that's the most solid line of reasoning you've ever followed."

"Don't fret. I won't make a habit of it."

"Sorry, guv, but that don't track," Archie said. "If Vandenberg don't think the fangs work, then why is he keeping his?"

Tim stepped in, as this appeared to baffle Bash. "To keep it from Blackwood? To keep Blackwood from having the entire set, if Vandenberg suspects he's behind the thefts? Because he himself is the culprit? For some indiscernible motive as yet unrevealed? Choose your poison."

"That's rather elegantly put, Kip. Well done," Bash complimented.

Archie sniffed, unimpressed. "I'll hold my wager until we know where we're going."

"And what manner of mischief awaits us there," Tim seconded.

A sharp elbow to the side shocked Hiero awake; a hand clamped over his mouth muffled his cry. His head rolled around like a cannonball loose on the deck of a gunship, his vision rocking in counterpoint to the motion of the cab until both came to an abrupt stop. He took a deep breath, pinched the bridge of his nose. Sleep hadn't been plentiful enough, but at least his headache was gone. After a series of slow blinks, he got his bearings.

Hiero discovered he had no idea where in London they were, if they were indeed still within the city's limits. The incline of the street and the openness of their surroundings pointed north, as well as the chessboard of chimneys across the rooftops. Closer to the cab loomed a fortresslike building, a hulking stone monolith with slit windows and a caged entrance. When Blackwood wanted something hidden away, he spared no expense.

Their cab, no doubt at Kip's instruction, had hung back a block to break from the procession, hopefully unnoticed by the constables at its rear. Kip settled their tab as Callie—in her Archie guise—craned forward to watch as the first riders clopped into the gated courtyard. The Black Maria, which, for all Hiero knew, now contained little more than a fresh litter of puppies and their exhausted mum, diverted from the horse-bound guards once behind the gate. The possibility of there being a back entrance was good news, though Han's prospects for escape were looking grim.

Callie read his mind on the matter. "How will we get him out of there?"

"No idea."

"Was that supposed to reassure?"

"I'll remind you he wanted to do this alone. With good reason."

She huffed. "Being that you would be well away from here, swaddled in your robe and slippers, nursing from a bottle of 1856 Romanée-Conti and coddling one of your 'gentlemen's pamphlets'?"

"Among other lesser alternatives."

She shook her head but seemed to have cast off her concern in favor of annoyance. Hiero would harbor enough for the pair of them. Callie gritted her jaw and hunched her shoulders before Kip slipped back into the cab. Once home they would have to review the personage of the young ruffian Archie. She'd let it slip once too often, in circumstances he now believed were far more dire than he first suspected. Though it was hard to hold to such an impossible conclusion whenever Kip shot those fern-green eyes in his direction. In fact, it was proving extremely difficult to hold to any conclusion at all in his presence. But then Hiero had never been renowned for his mental prowess.

"Area's a bit rougher than expected. There's a chop house across the way where we might set up watch, at least for now. I expect they'll grow suspicious if we linger too long, and I'm not sure how to explain about the boy."

He looked expectantly at Hiero for reasons beyond his comprehension.

"Give 'em enough coin, they'll forget everything they ever knew," Callie as Archie insisted.

Kip scoffed. "What happens when Blackwood's men come pound on their heads?"

"Excellent point," Hiero acknowledged with added oomph when the cab driver banged on the roof. "For later contemplation. Let's be off!"

With its heavy burgundy curtains and squat medieval chairs, Jock's aimed for elegance but settled for oppressiveness. The restaurant equivalent of a dungeon, its patrons had the look of inmates rather than diners, with the lifers sequestered in the darkest corners and a chain gang of regulars ringing the bar. A trowel-faced woman grunted when they requested the large table by the window. Hiero chose to be optimistic and escorted his party over himself. The menu was scrawled on a chalkboard beside the bar in an illegible hand. Fortunately it consisted of standard fare: roast meats, bangers and mash, pasties, puddings, and tea. Hiero ordered a large pot and scones for the table. Neither of his companions looked peckish enough to be more adventurous, at least for the moment.

Kip had been right in that the window seat afforded them a perfect view of the goings on across the street. Or rather the nothing that stretched on for well over an hour. With both the Maria and Blackwood's carriage gone from view, half of the posse of constables loitered around the front entrance, chatting like girls at a garden party. The other half, including Hobbs, Bates, and Drake, had accompanied the Maria.

The glamorous life of the consulting detective, indeed. With his twin terriers, Kip and Callie, on the scent, and after consuming two of the leaden scones, enough tea to stain his teeth, and half his pack of tobacco, Hiero turned his mind to hunting bigger game. The other patrons were a maudlin bunch: an elderly couple, fallen from a higher stratus but not far enough to be counted among the poor, on their weekly excursion; a roughshod group of men skiving off their normal duties; a nervous young man struggling to make conversation with his sweetheart; an artistic type scribbling intently into his journal. The men, he thought, were the most propitious of the bunch, if they didn't break his kneecaps just for glancing in their direction.

With Kip and Callie engrossed, he strolled over to the bar and ordered a whiskey. He rolled another smoke, careful to lean against the brass rail without letting himself recline. The trick was to make yourself appear vulnerable enough that they might play with you, but solid enough to avoid any real danger. Like most tightropes, he'd learned to walk it long ago.

The men ignored him for so long that he resorted to tapping a coin on the worn wood surface, its varnish melted by many a pint.

"Keep that up and you'll lose it." One of them finally bit. With a mess of hair more ash than blond and knuckles that had cracked more than a few skulls, he had the air of a ruffian choir boy.

Hiero's favorite kind.

"What, this?" He displayed the coin in the center of his palm with his best flourish, then, with a flick of his hand, vanished it.

"What the bleedin' hell?" Blondie demanded.

"No need to get religious. You've only made yourself a shilling."

"A what?"

"Check your pocket."

The man gave Hiero his best dubious squint, but, by this time, his friends had gathered. He dug a grubby hand into his pocket. His eyes popped wide. A cheer rang out when he proffered the shilling, and the clamor started. Hiero only hoped he had enough tricks up his sleeve to hold their interest until he'd earned enough goodwill that they wouldn't try to rob him. There was a bad apple in every bunch, and he'd met his fair share when his quick hands were the only thing saving him from the gutter. But he also knew men like this had more bad nights than good and deserved to forget their troubles for a while.

To that end, after doling out all the shillings in his pockets, he asked, "Do any of you fine gentlemen have a deck of cards?"

Three hours and every trick in his arsenal later, he'd finally earned his supper—on the house, for his whole table. The group of workers dispersed, well-lubricated and without trouble. Hiero continued on to entertain the patrons at several other tables, all of which dined longer and ordered more. The owners, Ruta and Jock, were so pleased with the results that they begged him to come back the next day. Instead Hiero convinced them to lend him their table until closing, which he returned to with a sense of satisfaction. Till he remembered there were five more hours to while away before they could even contemplate venturing out of doors.

Fortunately Callie had ordered him a heaping plate of roast pork and applesauce, along with some vegetables and a savory bun. Kip had fortified himself with the bangers and mash—not a surprise given he was such a sausage lover—while Callie had stayed in character and indulged in a huge slice of roast beef. They ate in peaceable silence, the day's adventures enough to make anyone ravenous, with more to come. Ruta's buns could have been used as door stops, but Jock knew his way around a roast, seasoning the meat with unusual spices that were echoed in the sauce. A glass of port would have proved a fine conclusion to the meal, but Hiero settled for the house whiskey and the last of his tobacco. He puffed out rings of smoke as he reclined back as best he could in such a hard, boxy little chair, his mind and gaze drifting until they landed on one Timothy Kipling.

Kip's green eyes scrutinized him like a specimen under a microscope. Neither Kip nor Callie had left their table, or its perfect view, since they arrived, but those eyes observed him with the detail of a Darwin tracing the origin of some new species as he plied the locals with spectacle. Once or twice, when Hiero accomplished one of his more complex sleights of hand, Tim lifted thin, red-flecked eyebrows. Otherwise Kip examined him with all the flair of an undertaker's assistant.

The delicious frisson that shivered beneath their every interaction now returned as Kip's scrutiny grew more intense. No challenge in his expression, only the skein of tension that always stretched over him, which cracked here and there, but hadn't broken. Yet.

The night was, after all, still young.

"Something you're curious about, dear Kip?"

An almost-smile curled the corner of his lips. "The world is full of curiosities."

"Any one of particular interest at the moment?"

"A great many. Was there something that you cared to inquire about, Bash?"

Hiero let out a soft chuckle. He was almost comically easy to provoke.

"Nothing comes to mind."

"Well, then. I hope you've kept those cards."

But not without a few surprises of his own. "Shall I play a trick or tell your fortune?"

"And here I thought you put no stock in the spirit world."

"Only where there's a chance to turn a profit." A hearty laugh had Hiero staring at the undulating muscles under the skin of his throat. What he wouldn't give for a private room and a chance to reacquaint himself with that meaty neck. Among other substantial parts of Kip's anatomy. "What's your game?"

"Ecarté. Loo. Dummy."

"Goodness. I didn't take you for a gambling man."

"Depends on what's at stake."

When their eyes met again, Hiero watched him calculate what to say and when to say it, what to hold back and what to slowly reveal, how much he could risk emotionally without losing his... what? Soul? Face? Job? Self?

He's not accustomed to anyone seeing him, let alone taking notice, Hiero reminded himself. *When someone does, he's like a moth to a flame. I just have to singe his wings a little. He's too wary of being burnt to let me in.*

Hiero dug the pack out of his pocket, sat up, and began to shuffle. As restless as he was sedate, Callie announced someone had to keep watch for Han's signal, whatever it would be, and left to walk the building's perimeter. Hiero waved her off. Well into their second hand, he asked, "What brought you to the antiquities trade, dear Kip? Family business?"

"Of a kind. My father worked as foreman for a small shipping company that specialized in the international transport of luxury goods—precious metals, jewels, works of art, ancient artifacts, and the like. They worked closely with the acquisitions departments of the British Museum and the National Gallery. So I've been around treasures my entire life. Some of the world's greatest came through our doors."

His features took on the gilded cast of memory. "I remember sitting atop a crate that housed the tablets excavated from the Library of Ashurbanipal as A.H. Layard argued rates with a clerk. Mama worked nights and slept during the day, so the warehouse was my playground. They called me 'The Inquisition' because... well, because I harassed all the archeologists and museum staff about their newest acquisitions. Eventually I knew the provenance of certain pieces better than the junior staff sent to fetch them. By exploiting the right connections, I..."

"Became the man you are today."

"Something like that, yes." Kip absently plunked another card on the table, still mired by the fog of reminiscence. Or perhaps his keen mind had caught back up with him since he grimaced. "I've just incriminated myself, haven't I?"

Hiero chuckled. "The thought had occurred."

"Do you think I mean to pinch the fang from Blackwood while you're distracted elsewhere, if we do indeed manage to infiltrate the fortress across the way?"

"I'm rather terrible at predictions. I prefer to wait for a leopard to show his spots."

"Yet you tell fortunes."

"Ah, but that has nothing to do with seeing into the future and everything to do with being in the moment. Knowing how to read the subtle expressions of the inquirer. Hearing what they don't say as much as what they do. Filling in the blanks they give you with exactly what they want to know. Satisfying the need they cannot express."

"Rather like an act of emotional thievery."

"True. But in this case, they beg to be robbed."

Kip let out a sharp laugh. "So in the end, you are no better than Miss Nightingale."

His feathers ruffled by this, Hiero chose his next words with a care he rarely showed. "My audience knows they are being fooled. They delight in it. They come to be distracted, to be entertained."

"But surely most of those attending the séances seek the same sort of distraction and entertainment."

"Some, I'm sure, but not all. Look at Lady Stang-Helion, seeking word from her husband beyond the grave. Blackwood's increased power and fortune from pseudoscientific discoveries. Even Goldie's lost his pocketbook, if not his soul, to that lot. It all comes back to... what did you call it? Emotional thievery." He saw that during his speech, Kip had trounced him. He surrendered the remains of his cards with a pout.

"Says the man who permitted me to accompany him only after our little interlude."

"That was not—"

"Wasn't it?"

Kip had nearly won on both fields and looked entirely too smug. Hiero paused to regroup as he considered his latest hand of cards. Rational thinking had never been his strong suit. His normal strategy in such situations was to admit to everything and nothing at all.

"My dear Kip, how can I possibly respond to such an accusation? If I defend my actions, you will continue to think me suspect. If I confess to ulterior motives, you'll never consent to an encore. And an actor of my caliber loves *nothing* more than an encore."

When Kip pursed his mouth with that familiar, constipated look of horror mixed with arousal, Hiero considered it a personal triumph.

Kip cleared his throat not once, but twice. He leaned forward over the table's edge, his gaze fixed somewhere in the vicinity of Hiero's chin, and whispered the words through sheer force of will, "Well, if you play your cards right..."

Too shocked to laugh, Hiero simply gaped. "Does this mean you are considering a return engagement?"

His face crimson and his hands quaking, Kip murmured, "You know of my great passion for... the theater."

Hiero did laugh this time, for a touch too long, until Kip let out a low hiss and buried his face in his cards.

Chapter 7

$\mathscr{T}$hick as a chimneysweep's sooty porridge, the fog descended at midnight. The clouds had hung low all evening, like rows of snuffed paper lanterns. But the witching hour put the finishing touches on the dismal atmosphere, garlanding the streets in gray tulle. Even from Tim's vantage across the street, Blackwood's fortress looked like little more than an amorphous lump; a hill impossible to map, let alone scale. Whatever signal Bash and his man agreed upon, they would not see it from their current vantage. To say nothing of the increased challenges of infiltrating the building without clear lines of sight.

After three hours inside, Blackwood and all his men had decamped, leaving not a single guard in place. A mystifying strategy—or a galling amount of hubris. Not a soul had scuttled across the lawn or slipped past a window since. Either Blackwood's faith in fallible safeguards like gates and padlocks was absolute—and, having met him, it was a distinct possibility—or some warrior caretaker awaited them inside.

Either way, Bash appeared in no hurry to find out. After nine tricks of ecarté, he had smoked and imbibed his way into a near stupor. Archie popped in on occasion to make his report, which would rouse him for a short while, but then he'd signal for another whiskey, insist they play another round, and doze off midsentence. All in all, it was an evening for the ages. Now the barkeep, having shooed out the last of the customers, gave them the eye. Tim did his best to ignore him. Hopefully Bash's little card tricks had earned them another half-hour's goodwill, at least until Archie returned, that they might together decide how to proceed. That a lad of fourteen had more sense than the so-called consulting detective who presided over this case said everything one could about Bash's methods. Such as they were.

Sooner than anticipated and to Tim's great relief, the door flew open and young Archie shouted out, "A light! A red light in one of the windows! Hurry, sirs! The hunt is on!"

Bash's eyes flew open. He leapt to his feet with the nimbleness of a far more sober man, waving a hand at the barkeep to fetch his greatcoat. "You're certain?"

"I climbed the gate. Nothing else to be done in this fog, guv. Even if they had seen me, I'd have been gone in a flash."

"Unless they'd had dogs," Tim reminded him. "Still, you've done well."

"The message, lad. What was it?" Bash demanded.

"'Back door open. Proceed with caution. Left, right, stairs, right, left, left. Wait in the office.'"

"You've taught them some sort of code?" Tim asked, incredulous.

"Obviously," Archie snipped. "You coming or what?"

Bash tossed a few coins on the table, then urged them out into the brume with a whisk of his hands. Tim reeled from the fact he was steady enough to follow them.

Archie shoved a slight, girlish hand into Tim's that they not get separated, waiting for him to link up with Bash before venturing into the dense fog. Taking advantage of the obscurity, Bash hooked on to Tim's arm, that mischievous twinkle the brightest thing for miles. Though no carriage or rider would dare navigate such sightless streets, they walked slowly.

The tall spikes of the fence thrust into view as if aimed directly at them. Archie guided them along its perimeter until they reached the opposing side. One of the neighboring buildings encroached upon a rear corner. Its bricks could be scaled, as Archie ably demonstrated. After this a small, careful jump to the top of the fence.

As Tim tested his weight on the bricks, Bash whispered, "Hold a moment."

"What?"

"Run around to the front and open the gate for us." This to Archie, who looked closer than ever to outright rebellion. "There's a lad."

"It will be locked," Tim explained for him. "They're careless, but they're not imbeciles."

Bash absorbed this for a moment, weighing his options. "Give me a boost."

Tim was halfway up the wall. "It's far too high. If you've not strength enough to propel yourself across, you won't be able to pull yourself up and over."

"Or up that wall, I should think."

Tim sighed. "True enough." He hopped off easily but noted Bash's flinch as he shot toward the ground. Interesting. After shaking off the jolt to his legs, he positioned himself near Bash, cupping his hands to receive his foot. As he shifted his weight onto Tim, he closed the distance between them to kissing close. He patted Tim on a ruddy cheek, then proceeded to use him as a human staircase, stomping on his shoulder and grazing his jaw as he wiggled and wobbled his way up the fence.

Tim didn't wait for the thump of Bash's landing to launch himself up the brick wall once more. The leap across was even more intimidating than Bash worried, the fence spikes in view but nothing visible below them. With a silent prayer, Tim overleaped the whole fence. He sailed over the spikes and dropped into the soup. Landing at Bash's side, he fell into a roll. It was the first time he has used his police training for anything remotely physical.

Despite the omnipresence of the fog, they crossed the compound with caution. The bank of clouds diffused the blink of the red light into a rosy aura that emanated from one of the rear windows of Blackwood's fortress. As they inched toward the cage that surrounded the back door, Tim rested a hand on the hilt of his truncheon, sheathed in a secret compartment in his coat. He wondered if Bash was armed with anything besides his overdramatic tendencies, then berated himself. Of course not.

Bash kneeled to pick the cage's lock, repeating the feat on the inner door. Tim couldn't pass judgment on his long pause before easing it open. On the one hand, every second they lingered risked discovery; on the other, the devil only knew what awaited them on the other side. Archie took the lead, easing the door open and creeping into the black.

Just enough murky light inked through the windows to sketch the basic blueprint of the entranceway. Bash anchored a grip on Tim's wrist in a far less flirtatious manner, steering him through the shadowy fathoms as if his arm were the rudder of a slow-moving boat. Tim ticked off the coded instructions as they went: left, right, stairs, right, left, left. How Archie found the various turns in the almost lightless corridors, he could not say, but it wasn't the first thing Tim had ever left to faith.

After a harrowing journey inching up the stairs through total blackness, the blazing rectangle of the second-story door promised light in abundance. On the top landing, Bash took the lead, peering through a crack before yanking it wide and waving them in. As below, so above: not a mouse stirred. The office would have been easily found were it not for the astounding view from the upper hallway, lined with windows that overlooked a cavernous space at the building's center.

A labyrinth of interconnecting cages dominated the space like some ancient glyph writ large. To Tim's astonishment a pride of lions prowled through this metal-bound terrain, looking as sweet as kittens as they played and napped or picked over the bones of some unfortunate creature. Agog, the three of them glued themselves to the glass. Several larger sections had been outfitted with every possible comfort for the lions beyond an actual veldt: an in-ground watering hole; a grassy, palm-shaded oasis; several rock outcroppings; and a few artificial caves. One large, blood-streaked section appeared to be gated off—a hunting ground. Several piles of bones littered the area near the outermost wall, some still webbed with viscera.

Fresh kill.

Tim shivered, both appalled and awestruck at seeing such magnificent beasts so caged. Unless Blackwood had a regular supply of antelope—not the most ridiculous assumption given their recent discovery—the bones were likely human.

"The ultimate security measure."

Bash snorted. "That, my dear Kip, is somewhat understating the situation."

"There's the lockbox." Archie pointed to a curious-looking boulder in one of the rock mountains. "Protecting their own. Reckon they know it too."

"Certainly explains the absence of guards," Tim remarked. "I wonder what other treasures he's got hidden in there."

"Ah-ah!" Bash tisked. "You know what they say about mixing curiosity and cats."

Tim couldn't pry his eyes away from the pile of boxes long enough to laugh.

"Come on," Archie urged. "Mr. Han's waiting."

They navigated their way to the office with little trouble, each still in a daze of disbelief and conjecture. Dominating Tim's thoughts were two major questions: who had been fed to the lions, and how would Blackwood retrieve the fang? As safe as it was in the lions' den, surely it could not remain there indefinitely.

He expressed as much as soon as they were reunited with Mr. Han, who had his ear plastered to Blackwood's safe as he carefully turned the lock. At least not all of his lordship's secrets would have to be pried out of a lion's jaws. Mr. Han held up a silencing hand, then clicked the lock into its final position. A tug at the handle resulted in nothing more than a loud clank.

"Come now, man, what news?" This from Archie, who perched on the edge of the desk.

Bash strayed to the window, which offered an even more elaborate view of the labyrinth, but also, fittingly, of the machinations around it. Tim stationed himself near enough to observe without turning his back on Mr. Han and awaited his testimony.

"For my money, the man is innocent," Mr. Han declared to a chorus of protests. "Maybe only of the thefts, but he's no swindler."

"Tell us everything," Archie insisted. "From the moment of your departure."

"I doubt you're interested in tales of dodging pigeon droppings and holding fast to white-knuckle turns." Mr. Han chuckled. "I didn't hear much. Had to sneak in after they'd unpacked the Maria. But I saw how they got the box in there. Poor things, they must keep them half-starved. Dropped a couple buckets of raw meat into the feeding area, then cut them off from the rest while they stashed the box. They're smart—took all the ropes and pulleys with them, so there's no way for some thief to do the same. Weld the locks shut and saw them open every time. We're not getting in there."

"Someone did," Tim pointed out.

Mr. Han nodded. "One of his own team. Tossed him in with the cats as a warning to the others not to cross him. I've seen some things in my time, but..." His face said everything he could not.

"That poor, dear lad." Bash beckoned them over. "Look."

Sure enough, a scrap of red-headed scalp was flung over the crushed remains of a police helmet. The gravity of the situation weighed on Tim's chest like one of the lions' boulders. "Hobbs."

"But this is madness!" Archie cried as if for all of them. "A copper's life, all to protect an enchanted tooth! He can't get away with this!"

"He won't," Bash vowed.

"He must." Tim's raised hands were poor defense against their communal ire. "If he's innocent of the thefts, which I admit is looking more and more likely, then calling in the Yard will only scare the culprits away."

"You mean if the fortress full of lions hasn't already."

"The police know," Mr. Han reminded them. "DS Small and DC Croke were here when the boy went in. I'm the only reliable witness to the crime, and I'm..." He gestured to his face.

Archie spoke for them all when he let out a huff of frustration and kicked one of the legs of the desk.

Tim felt adrift. Unbeknownst to his companions, a detective of Scotland Yard *had* been alerted to the murder—of a fellow officer, no less—but was as powerless as they to do something about it. His word would hold more water than that of a foreigner, but he hadn't witnessed the crime. Quayle would welcome the news of Blackwood's innocence where the thefts were concerned, but charging him with the murder of a policeman without reliable evidence was career suicide, and Tim already had a gun to his head. Especially since it was Bash he was meant to deliver, stripped of his false identity and pretensions, not the man who would be donating their reward.

If he wanted to save his career, Tim had no choice but to deliver both Bash and the thief to his superiors. The question of whether such a career was worth having would wait for another day.

"We'd best make a thorough search," Tim announced, only to discover Archie doing just that while Mr. Han had returned to safe-cracking. Bash remained at the window, fixated on the goings-on below.

Tim walked over to the filing cabinet and set to his task, rifling through the various contracts and ledgers found there. Finding nothing but the minutiae of lion-keeping—food deliveries, health and welfare details, cage maintenance, and something he would charitably call "waste removal"—he soon joined Archie at the desk. For a boy from the streets, young Archie's reading skills astonished. He zipped through employee records and reference books as if he could memorize each page wholesale at nearly three times the rate Tim progressed. But here again they discovered nothing of note unless the particulars of tranquilizing large beasts fascinated.

With a definitive click, Mr. Han announced his conquest of the safe. Tim and Archie crowded around him for the big reveal. They were not disappointed. An indecent amount of money packed the bottom shelf, making Tim wonder how much more, if any, the lions protected. Mr. Han smacked Archie's hand back when he reached for it.

"Come on!" Archie protested. "He won't miss it."

Mr. Han chuckled. "Probably spiritually connected to every penny. He'll feel a disturbance in the auras."

"I rather think this is his petty cash." Tim shook his head, marveling that such an amount could be but a drop in the bucket for a man like Blackwood. "Payoffs, salaries, the like. He can't very well fund his more questionable enterprises through a bank."

The second shelf contained documents of a more private nature, as well as a red notebook that immediately caught the eye. Tim nabbed it before Archie could, unhooked the small latch, and stepped aside to peruse the interior. Rows upon rows of coded entries spanned every single page until late in the book, teasing Tim with their hidden revelations. He wished he had more time to pour over Blackwood's records, to correlate and cross-reference to his heart's content. This he excelled at: an intricate cipher, a money trail, dubious accounting. With space to work and evidence like this, he could find the necessary loophole, the one his superiors at the Yard couldn't ignore.

But that, of course, was not his lone assignment.

"What's up there?" Tim asked his companions, sliding the journal in beside his truncheon in what he hoped was an inconspicuous manner.

"Rifle cartridges," Mr. Han replied.

Archie scoffed. "Looks like only Lord Zealot is allowed to kill one of the cats."

"Not surprising," Tim remarked, "considering the expense involved in bringing them here." He considered the open safe for a moment. "Of more pressing interest: if this is what he leaves for thieves to find..."

"Then what's in those boxes?" Archie finished for him.

Tim turned to inquire after Bash's opinion, but he was gone. Then the roaring started.

With a slam and a spin, Mr. Han shut the safe, sped out the door. Tim and Archie chased after him, cursing the fact he had the lantern. The race tested all of Tim's skill and some of his endurance—exhilarating. He'd missed this part of police work, running through the street at breakneck speed after a pickpocket or a shoplifter, all senses on high alert. But he stopped short when they broke into the labyrinth chamber, the enormity of the space and the rankness of the smell hitting him like a wall.

He'd done his tour of the coroner's tombs, but nothing had prepared him for the stench of carnage, the primitive, bestial reek of the lions and the remains of their prey. The killing floor was closest to the entrance, so it was impossible not to stare at the last of Hobbs and those pitiful others of whom Blackwood had made an example. A few growls echoed off the walls, but the roaring had ceased. Bash stood just beyond the iron bars that enclosed the lounging area; either he had tamed the lions, or they no longer perceived him to be a threat. One female prowled the edge of the cage, but the others lazed about in small groups.

Digesting, Tim thought with a shudder.

"Were none of you even curious?" Bash asked as they approached. "What a rare chance."

"We're a sight more interested in solving the crime, guv," Archie reprimanded.

"That'll keep. But this…"

One glance through the bars, and Tim understood what he meant, even if—in typical Bashian fashion—he hadn't alerted them to his absence. To be only steps away from such vicious, almost mythical creatures stirred something in Tim that had him measuring his breaths and clearing his throat. Laying about or pawing at each other, they looked as innocent as overgrown cats. There was a sensual element to their savage grace; the way their tawny hides undulated over muscle and bone made Tim want to reach out. But the hard, feral look the lioness shot his way as she passed chilled any tactile impulses. These experienced hunters knew exactly how to lure you in. Much like the one who currently stood mesmerized little more than a paw's length beyond the cage.

Bash's decadent lips stretched into a smile so open and adoring that Tim suffered a small—and completely unwarranted—pang of jealousy. Bash looked as if he would dive into the pride and embrace every last one if given the chance. Tim didn't doubt they could have left him there for days. But given they had already lingered far too long, they'd best be off. He was about to say as much when he saw them.

They streamed in from both ends of the labyrinth, their black garments and masks doing nothing to conceal that they were a gang of brutes. Archie grabbed Bash by the arm and shoved him into a dark corner. Tim extricated his truncheon. A glance at Mr. Han confirmed he would take the right stream while Tim handled the left. Archie armed himself with a stray plank of wood and took up a central position to finish off any stragglers—how, Tim hadn't the faintest notion, but Archie had proved his usefulness in other areas, so why not hand-to-hand combat? Tim, thankfully, had the experience of both the boxing ring and riot control, though he had never taken on five thuggish assailants in one go.

First time for everything.

He steeled himself for the fight. Behind the bars, the lions stirred, snarling at the new invaders. Tim fought to banish all thoughts of ripping flesh and cracking bone from his mind. With enough ingenuity, a man could be fed through those bars.

A quick scan of the players told him no ringleaders were present, which implied added men and resources outside. One thing he was sure of: these were not Blackwood's men. But given the many boxes of treasures and secrets the pride currently used as lounge chairs, they might not be after the fang. Neither did they look to be in a bargaining mood.

Tim stood his ground, tried to look as menacing as the beasts. He double-fisted his truncheon, ready to strike with either end. Behind him the sounds of chaos had already erupted. He prayed Mr. Han wouldn't send more goons his way as the first pair sidled up, hands at their sides and eyeing him coldly. The air between them vibrated with unreleased tension. Tim recognized the sensation from the ring, relished it. His primal instincts revved and his adrenaline spiked in the seconds before they charged.

The first gave himself away by going high with his left. Tim leapt over his attacker—gone low—and, with a thwack, broke his hand. A bit of footwork evaded the second, but not for long. The man dodged; Tim's kicks swung wild. One finally clipped the thug in the jaw. Tim recovered while number three—a giant—lurched forward. Those massive fists pounded Tim like a mallet. He dove for the giant's stomach, hammering punches in. A fist to Tim's kidney, and he was screaming. Desperate, he slammed the butt of his truncheon into the man's bollocks.

That bought him a few seconds of head spinning and lion snarling. He shoved his boot into number two's chest, sent him flying into a nest of claws. The last two spread out, circling him from opposite sides. Tim glanced over at Mr. Han instead of following them. To Tim's relief, his five thugs kissed the floor. Mr. Han urged Bash out of the corner, toward the door where Archie hid, ready to brain any further invaders. Tim signaled—subtly, he hoped—for them to run, wishing he could give a proper warning as to what might be waiting for them in the courtyard. Hopefully the fog would still be a help, and they could escape undetected.

Number four, short and stocky, flinched. Tim spun around to meet number five—a wrecking ball launched from behind. A jab of the truncheon under the jaw had him reeling, then stocky was on him. His arms pinned, Tim wrestled his attacker to the ground but could only bat at him like an insect on a window pane. Assaulted by a vise of pure muscle, Tim's shoulder popped its socket. His truncheon clattered as he kicked back, aiming to heel the stocky man in the groin. Tim writhed and wriggled, making him fight for every grip. He pried his good arm out by strength alone, elbowed him in the ear.

The stocky man howled. The lions roared. The wrecking ball recovered and knocked him out.

"Unhand him!" Hiero bellowed, overlooking the fact that pounding your fist into someone's face was not, by definition, a form of restraint. Kipling hung in the air a moment, a leaf caught on the breeze, but a second blow toppled him. Something shifted inside Hiero at the sight of him so brave and bruised, a tightness in his chest more constrictive than fear. This wasn't his fight, and yet there Kipling was, leading the charge. Or rather being trampled by it.

The scene before him resurrected the Roman Colosseum. A chorus of roars underscored the painful percussion the gladiatorial thug played on Kipling's face. A stout, injured fellow cheered him on with bloodthirsty glee, not intimidated by the close proximity of jungle predators. This amidst a nest of masked baddies in various states of injury or unconsciousness. Who would reign supreme? The answer seemed obvious until Han's timely intervention.

With a flurry of lightning-fast chops, Han dispatched both the gladiator and his cheering section. Kipling slumped onto his side, his face as raw and red as a slab of beef. Hiero raced into the nest of vipers—wounded, but vipers no less—before Callie could stop him. Plucking his handkerchief out of an inner pocket, Hiero dabbed at Kipling's cuts as he surveyed the damage. First he'd proved more clever than Hiero originally thought, then more dedicated, then more daring… Was there no end of indecipherable clues to Kip's mysteries? Kipling could have turned and run at the first sign of trouble, but instead he felled nearly as many brutes as Han before one got the better of him. And such an unexpected display of athletic prowess was only the tenth most confounding thing about him. Though it did explain the muscles.

"Stop mooning," Han snapped, "start lifting." He hoisted Kipling to his feet, then hefted him over his shoulder, Hiero fretting all the while.

"The very definition of nondescript," Callie muttered to herself as she examined one of the least-conscious thugs. "Criminal class, but that's to be expected. Of greater value would be to know who they are working for."

"But shouldn't we…" Even Hiero didn't know what he was suggesting.

A nearby groan answered him readily.

"Hurry," Han urged. "They're rallying."

Callie scoffed. "Then see that they don't."

"Kipling needs a doctor."

"He'll wait. *We* need to figure out who's behind this. Especially since they've turned murderous."

"Blackwood is the murderer. These thieves are just thieves."

"Certainly. But what are they here to steal? Who pulls their strings? How did they know to come here—ahh!" One of them grabbed Callie by the ankle. With her free leg, she stomped on his face. "We should take one home. Which looks the smartest, do you think?"

Hiero snorted. "I believe the term is 'least moronic.'"

"I've only got the two arms," Han griped.

"Oh, I expect Hiero and I can manage him." She skipped over to the nearest wall, which displayed a veritable rogues' gallery of chains and manacles. Devilish didn't begin to describe the gleam in her eyes. "With these."

"And just what are we going to do with him once we're done?"

But she'd already selected one of the smaller sets. Hiero could think of no objection but was reluctant to leave Kipling's side. Especially when doing so involved something deeply unpleasant.

"We'll deliver him to the Yard."

"So that he can report us for kidnapping?"

"Goldie will know what to do."

"Now we're involving Commodore Goldenplover?"

"Why must you always…" Callie marched over to a likely victim and dropped the manacles with a great clatter. The noise roused the lions, who'd returned to their roughhousing, the chance to observe human behavior a poor substitute. Several stalked the length of the nearest bars. This did little to deter Callie. "This case is a menace. There's not a lick of concrete evidence, our best lead's been discounted, we've been stymied at every turn, and now we're to trundle back home to play nurse to a liar." Hiero grunted an objection, which she dismissed. "That man is no more an antiquarian that I'm—"

"Ah, yes," DS Small queried as he rounded the nearest corner of the labyrinth's perimeter. "Just who might you be, lad? And do introduce us to the rest of your mates."

"It's Bash, sir," DC Croke declared, forever at his heels.

"Yes, I can see that." Small sighed, shook his head. "A little breaking and entering all in a night's work, hmm?"

Hiero strode toward the officers as if walking to center stage for his soliloquy.

"You seem to have the advantage of me. I don't recall us being introduced, Officer…"

"Oh, I'll be happy to make the formal introductions, sir. Detective Sergeant Abraham Small, here to arrest you on his lordship's behalf."

"Now, now, my dear DS…" Hiero found himself looking up at the storklike man as he approached. "Something of a misnomer, your surname."

"A whatsits?"

"You're very tall. For a Small, I mean."

The smirk that had started to twist the DS's lips firmed when DC Croke guffawed. "That's what I'm always saying."

Hiero flicked a knowing gaze from Croke to Small. "My condolences on your choice of partner."

"Forget him." Small peeled back his coat to reveal a row of handcuffs dangling from his belt. "You lot are coming with us. You're nibbed."

"I assure you we're nothing of the sort."

That hint of a smirk returned. "Care to put a wager on it?"

"I'm not in the habit of taking easy money."

"Could have fooled me."

"You wound me, very tall DS Small." Hiero unbuttoned his own coat, revealing… a silver pocket watch chain. "Tell me, do you intend to take us to the station house, or to Blackwood?" Small opened his mouth, then shut it again. "Ah, so you are enacting the part of security guard, not officer of the law."

"And you're on the wrong side, no matter how you slice it."

"Am I? What have I done?"

"Are you joking?"

"Do I look amused?" Hiero couldn't help but smile at that, his eyes meeting Small's slate grays in challenge. "Our investigation into the theft of the fangs led us to this place. When we arrived we saw this gang of ruffians stealing into the building. We gave chase, following them in through unlocked doors. As you can see, my man handled them tidily. Mr. Kipling was less fortunate. Once the dust settled, we saw that we were in some sort of secret zoo. Which belongs to Lord Blackwood, you say? Curious." Hiero stroked his chin as he considered this "new" information. "Fortunately the pair of you turned up just as we were deciding whether to cart them to the Yard or send my boy for a constable. Though why Lord Blackwood would have two dedicated policemen watching over such a fortress in the dead of night... Well, it's his prerogative. Surely there's nothing of value here. Nothing of interest to, say, the Home Secretary..."

"And what if there is?" Croke sneered before Small waved him into silence.

"Well, then I'm certain he'd love to hear all about it," Hiero affably countered. "As would the judge at our arraignment. And the headlines, of course. Can you imagine? 'Celebrated Detective Saves Lord of the Jungle's Lair.' 'Attempted Theft a Cat-astrophe.'" Oh, and my personal favorite, 'Local Coppers Get Bashed.'"

Expression stony, Small crossed the distance between them until they stood nearly toe to toe, one of the rare men to force Hiero to look up. His height, along with the fierceness of his stare, akin to that of an avenging god. To his credit, Hiero wasn't cowed. His time as a card sharp had taught him when to call a bluff.

"I'll spare no detail with his lordship."

"As it should be," Hiero insisted. "You'll deal with this... riff-raff?"

"I will," Small confirmed. "If you breathe a word..."

"I cannot speak of what I never saw."

"And them?" He nodded toward Callie and Han.

"A boy and a foreigner." Hiero shrugged. "Who would believe them?"

Small pushed so far into Hiero's space that he almost wondered about his intentions, then—after glaring at him for a short eternity—blew out a long, foul breath.

"Go."

Hiero hung there a moment, teeth bared in his widest smile until a flint of hesitation sparked in Small's eyes. He performed his most theatrical bow and waved his people out.

Chapter 8

A piercing squeal shot Tim awake. He vaulted upright. His head throbbed. His vision listed like the needle of a drunken compass. He blinked, found a reference point: a round little face with pouty plum lips, punctuated eyebrows, and two tight buns of hair. Her face hung in the middle groove of the baseboard like pagan tree carving—the sort of wild-eyed imp that would steal into children's bedrooms to lure them on nighttime adventures.

Seeing him awake, she squealed again, a sound that sliced like an arrow into one ear and out the other, followed by a trill of laughter more akin to rifle fire. Yet when she popped back down behind the baseboard, Tim found he missed her. Until her mother burst through the door, hurling invectives in her sharp-toned native tongue like daggers to his temples. They locked eyes; she gasped, scooped up her daughter, and raced from the room, shouting, "Mistress!"

Tim collapsed back onto the rather abundant nest of pillows and tugged the sheets over his head. A head currently under repair, if all the pounding, aching, and swirling were anything to go by. The muscles of his face felt as if they'd been flattened by a mallet. It hurt to form an expression. His hands were no better, swollen to gorilla size as if he'd gone two hundred bare-knuckle rounds. The rest of him, however, was as snug as a pearl in an oyster's shell. Tim had never imagined awaking in Hieronymus Bash's bed—his fantasies hadn't involved an actual bed—but this one was even more luxurious than anything his unconscious mind might have conjured.

The room far improved upon the cold, cramped lodgings he rented from crabby old Mrs. Lester—not a surprise given it was three times the size. The theme—and it was the type to have a theme—was chess. An ornate set crowned a small table by the window, each of its adversarial chairs in the appropriate color. The wrought-iron furnishings, with insets of mother-of-pearl, reminded one of a knight's armor. A rooklike motif dominated the wallpaper. The quilted coverlet depicted tessellated pawns; the tops of the bedposts alternated the shape of the king and the queen. Disorienting for someone who had been bashed on the head—and wasn't that a telling turn of phrase—but otherwise rather like a grownup's playroom. Though given Bash's affinity for cards, Tim guessed this was Admiral The Viscount Pankhurst's doing.

But there was no doubt who was responsible for the satiny teal shift they'd swaddled him in, which wouldn't look out of place on a South Seas concubine.

The clamor of the household blew in through the crack in the door. Tim stole a few peaceful, if pained, moments trying to piece together the events of the previous day. His initial fear that he had given in to some half-baked seduction of Bash's had evaporated with the fog of sleep. Yet Tim found he longed for that delusion compared to the reality: Blackwood guilty of murder but so far innocent of the thefts, a half-dozen suspects with none showing promise, a few scattered clues but none leading to the location of the stolen fangs, an attack upon them by unarmed assailants with no clear motive. All of which left Tim feeling like one of the pawns on the nearby board, facing an unpredictable opponent who planned twenty moves ahead. And he didn't even know what sort of mischief had transpired after he was knocked out.

He burrowed farther under the covers, doing his best impression of a turtle.

The door creaked open sometime later. The smell of broth lured him back into the light. Miss Calliope Pankhurst started at the sight of him—giving some indication as to the extent of his bruises—but held the tray she bore steady. The sight of the steaming bowl, along with savory buns that looked just as cloudlike as their sweet forbears, a pot of tea, and a slice of pâté drew the entirety of his attention as she made her way toward him.

"Don't tell me I scared the serving girl away. You shouldn't have to wait upon me, Miss Pankhurst," Tim rasped, his throat tacky with disuse.

"I wanted to see to you myself." Her face betrayed not the hint of a smile. "Given that you were almost beheaded."

"Rather my neck is the only part…" Just then a tight stitch knit into the top of his spine. In truth he was a shambles from the shoulders up. "Has the doctor been?"

She nodded. "This morning. And will return at teatime. He said to fill your stomach and test your wits before he prescribes anything, so eat up." By this time he had propped himself up on the pillows. Calliope set the tray astride him; he caught the scent of jasmine as she leaned toward him, with an odd undercurrent of pomade.

But soon the homey smell of chicken broth overtook Tim's senses, stirring memories in him that threatened to wet his eyes and heavy his heart. He restrained these as he waited for her to exit, but, to his dismay, she seated herself on the edge of the bed. Tim shoved away memories of his mother's kitchen—useless to dwell on such things now, even battered as he was—and concentrated on meeting her incisive stare. In another world, one where his desires weren't demented by cruel fate, she would have been the perfect muse for his artful affections. The Rapunzelesque trellis of golden hair. The frosty blue eyes. The cupid's-bow lips she always firmed to look more serious. The aristocratic cheekbones and angular jaw. A switchblade Aphrodite. Intelligent, savvy, discerning—she would make someone an excellent wife.

Instead he craved everything she was not: dark and sensual, flibbertigibbet and flamboyant, cunning and mysterious. The only trait Calliope and Bash shared was an unhealthy dose of curiosity, which had served them well... until it hadn't. Which brought to mind...

"Where is Mr. Bash, may I ask? Was he injured?"

"Ha!" She chuckled mirthlessly. "His Majesty doesn't grace us with his presence until midafternoon at the earliest. Though to be fair..." She caught herself before she could finish.

"Hmm? What?"

"Let us speak plain, Mr. Kipling. A fitting test for your wits, I'm sure."

Tim nodded, sneaking a bit of soup to fortify himself. It was even more heavenly than he could have imagined. He cursed her for lingering.

"What are your intentions toward my guardian?" she demanded.

Tim's spoon hung in the air halfway to his mouth. "My intentions? I should think they were clear by now, dear lady. I intend to help him solve this case."

"I am no more dear to you, Mr. Kipling, than a scorpion is to a frog, so I'll ask you to stow such embellishments." With a clank and a splash, Tim's spoon fell back into his bowl. "I understand you act with deliberation. What confounds me is your purpose. And don't spout that drivel about admiring our work. An admirer who counted among his clients our chief suspect would have fled the moment Blackwood's name was mentioned. Instead you doubled your efforts to be one of us and show no loyalty to Blackwood whatsoever. A man of character and morals would have reported my guardian to the police a hundred times over by now, or at the very least set about ruining his reputation. You have done neither." Her accusatory tone softened as she warmed to her subject. "I'll admit a part of me still believes you mean to betray us... But you've also given us ample evidence to use against you. And we have wealth and status on our side. So enlighten me, Mr. Kipling. Why are you here?"

Tim drew in a deep breath. He reached for one of the fluffy

buns as a stall tactic, all too aware of the chill of her stare as it prickled the less-damaged side of his face. The builders who had taken up residence in his skull still hammered away at his gray matter. His hands had swelled the size of anvils, and his spine felt as if it had been spackled together like shoddy brickwork. But as he chewed buttery morsel after buttery morsel, he knew that to answer her would be to admit defeat. There was no going back from outing himself. He may not have much of a career left after these cases, but he would abide by his duty and do his best to solve them. A Sisyphean task, perhaps, but being a policeman was all he wanted from the moment he returned to his parents' shop and found their mangled, blood-soaked bodies.

He finished the bun, then sipped down two more spoonfuls. "I'm afraid, Miss Pankhurst, that my actions must speak for themselves."

"That is your final answer?"

"That is my only answer."

She bunched her lips, no longer able to contain her irritation.

"Would you permit me to tell you a story while you eat, Mr. Kipling? To pass the time until Hiero awakens."

Tim saw the opportunity to wrong-foot her and kicked. "Curious, that."

"What?"

"Your familiarity."

"He is my guardian."

"True. But surely you must be aware of the rumors."

A genuine laugh, if only of disbelief.

"The rumors, yes. I assure you I've heard them all."

"No doubt."

"Your point?"

"I've made it. You are familiar."

If her stare was chilly before, it turned glacial. But she permitted a smirk to twist her lips.

"That is, in a roundabout way, the crux of my tale." She snatched a bun from his basket—icicle eyes glinting at his horror-stricken reaction—then settled in for the telling. "Once upon a time, there was a dashing second son to a man of means and title, born some fifteen years after his older brother. Both became navy men and had illustrious careers, if in different wars. The second son married late and out of convenience. He was a scoundrel of the highest order, you see, but his career had stalled a bit because he was too long out of society, so he bought himself a wife. And proceeded to ignore her for the next decade, drinking, whoring, and gambling when he wasn't away fighting. Any prizes he won didn't last him long. When he was at home, he beat and berated her, paraded her around the drawing rooms but never spoke a word to her otherwise. Gave her a pittance of an allowance. As Hiero often says, the show was spectacular, but the backstage was mayhem. When he finally left her—ruined in every way but socially—he didn't even have the grace to die. Instead he left on a mission and never returned. Without the Royal Navy's official confirmation, he could not be declared dead for seven years. Therefore she was not permitted to remarry and salvage her life. Instead the poor woman, as so many do, went quite mad.

"But there were two good things left in her life, though she was by then too exhausted to see them as such. The first was her daughter. She had shielded the girl from her father as much as possible—which was quite enough, as it turned out. It helped that the child's uncle, the second good thing, doted on her. A much older bachelor, he swept in when his brother abandoned them. He brought them to his home and treated them like his own. The girl went from a life of near destitution to complete freedom: to learn what she wanted, to go wherever she fancied, to do things no other little girls were allowed. He taught her the rules of society, but also how to flout them and not get caught. He gave her back her life and gave her mother the best of care. For the first time, this girl was loved.

"So when she learned some people considered his way of loving unnatural and wrong—a crime, even—she knew she had to protect him at all costs. When he invited a particular friend of his to reside with them, a rich foreigner hoping for an entree into British society, she embraced him. And she came to love this eccentric man as much as her uncle—because he was wild and fun and beautiful—and the love he had for her uncle was fierce and true.

"For five blessed years, they led enchanted lives. But, as in every fairy story, the enchantment can't last forever. When her uncle announced he was sick... She had never known such despair. She had been young when her father left. This was different. This was gutting. But her uncle, true as ever, found a way to protect her from what might have been. His friend, though perhaps not as well-equipped, took on his mantle. And, yes, his fortune grew, and he had new responsibilities in the household and the girl's reputation to safeguard, but he has adapted. If anything he has invited more people under his parasol to be shielded from the rain. In fact, he is now known as a collector of sorts, and people in our larger acquaintance sometimes bring him others to help. He is no saint, I assure you, but he does know his way about the world.

"And so he has collected you, Mr. Kipling. And here we are. And I must ask you again... Why are you here?"

Tim watched as she dug her thumbs into the crust of the bun and ripped it apart, reeling from her tale. Calliope scooped out the spongiest part and popped it in her mouth, her face registering a flicker of enjoyment.

That was, he thought, the difference between them. Her story compelled, but pluck at one of the connective threads and it started to unravel. Over and over again, she had been protected from the tragedies in her life. This might have been due to her age or her sex, but Tim pinpointed her caste as the culprit. Unlike so many women of lower class he had known through the years, and a great deal many men, there had been an alternative to the worst-case scenario for her. Money to fund it. Social options—disagreeable ones, but options just the same. Miss Calliope Pankhurst would never have found herself in a workhouse, or trolling the streets, or scrubbing her fingers to the bone. Something better invariably colored the horizon.

Not so for him. Tim could fall—or someone might push. The result would be the same. Cast out of his profession. Disgraced, unemployable. Perhaps prison. Perhaps even execution. And then who would avenge his parents, good people struck down in their prime? Was his failure to be their only legacy? Were the compassionate whims of a confidence man his only recourse? Was she offering him the same shield that protected her through the onslaught of her girlhood? Because he saw no other way to vanquish Blackwood or the true thieves or Quayle's machinations. Tim had little money and no power or social options. All he had was the goodwill of Hieronymus Bash and his merry band of amateur investigators.

Tim was not by nature a gambling man. Still, he had no other choice but to roll the dice.

"My full name is Timothy Kipling Stoker. I am a detective inspector with the Metropolitan Police."

Hiero's scowl threatened to devolve into an outright pout. His mind, ever ready to leap before it looked, had imagined far more outlandish scenarios where the true identity of this unremarkable man—even his secret was mundane!—propped up by a bouquet of pillows in Hiero's favorite armchair was concerned. The bastard son of a duke attempting to solve his savage murder in order to be granted a hefty reward. An agent of the Department of Imports looking for proof of Blackwood's illegal immigration of a pride of lions. The envoy of a mystical cabal tracking the rise of spiritualism in London. Hiero had wanted to believe he was anything more than a policeman. The obviousness of this conclusion was in itself dispiriting.

For a moment Hiero wondered whether Kip—at least his pet name remained intact, though this, like everything about him, disappointed—had attempted to entrap him through their backstage interlude, but no. The crisis he had suffered was quite genuine and made much more sense in light of his true mission. As for that, Hiero didn't need to guess.

"I have been tasked by my superiors with learning all I could about the consulting detective Hieronymus Bash, with the aim of ending his interference in matters that should be investigated and resolved by the police."

Hiero surveyed the detritus of Kip's face, acknowledging—if only to himself—the beating might give it more character. He looked exhausted but alert. How could he fail to be whilst giving them the rope with which to hang him? Hiero mentally set aside the reasons for such a bold move and considered him. The tightness of his jaw— those neck muscles strung taut as a violin's bow—as he spoke, forcing the words out. The crinkles of skin at the corners of his eyes and across his brow, evidence of the pain he'd been enduring before this whole ordeal even started. The way his hands trembled even while gripped the armrests. The way his rigid spine fought the urge to slump in shame. The way he had not changed out of one of Hiero's gaudiest robes, fastened like a straightjacket around his solid frame. Those green eyes shifted to confront everyone in the room, save Hiero.

Kip perhaps thought—mistakenly—that he would perceive anger there, or affront, or, worse, indifference. Hiero felt none of those things, only bored. All this drama, and he played only a minor part in it.

"If you think I'm about to start calling you 'Stoker' or... or, gracious, 'Timothy,' you are gravely mistaken."

"I..." Leaf-green eyes met his at last, bewildered. "Do you understand what this means?"

"I really must insist that you call me 'Hiero.' This 'Bash' business is so... middle-class." He waved a hand as if to clear the air, then launched himself to his feet. "Now as you all know, I'm not one for formality, but we've recently suffered a rather galling defeat, and I believe we must reassess the situation."

"As *I* said to you just an hour ago." Callie sighed. "Word for word."

"What can I say? I'm an excellent mimic."

"Just... just... Bash," Kip stammered.

"Hiero," he corrected.

"I don't care!" He'd surprised himself with that exclamation, but not for long. "Do you not hear what I'm saying? Scotland Yard is investigating you. I may be the first, but——"

"You're not the first."

"I... What?"

"They've sent others. Just constables at first, then a sergeant, and another detective. Credit to you, we sniffed them out before the first introduction. Han has a particular talent in that regard, so well done, you." A grunt from Han didn't slow him in the least. "My dear Kip, our methods may be a bit unconventional, but we are far from innocents. When you act as a Robin Hood, you must expect a few Sheriffs of Nottingham along the way."

"If you but allude to my role as that of Maid Marian, I'll slit your throat," Callie warned.

"Little John?" Hiero suggested. "No! Little Archie."

"Hold on." Kip raised his hands to avoid further confusion. "That was you? I... uh... No, of course it was." He shook his head, refocused on Hiero. "You give your winnings to the poor?"

Hiero twiddled his fingers. "Mmm... after a fashion."

"More evasion!"

"Says the police inspector in the antiquities dealer's clothing."

"Better than a scoundrel tarted up like a richer scoundrel."

Hiero gasped, secretly pleased. "Take that back!"

Kip sighed, pressed ache-blunting fingertips into his temple. "I do. I'm so very sorry. A thing has been set in motion that I'm powerless to stop, and I've endangered you all."

"Nonsense." Hiero crossed the room, laid a gentling hand on the nape of his neck. Kip's face as he gaped up at him was a portrait of shock Hiero found most evocative for the hope that limned his features. There was nothing more compelling, to his mind, than a person given his last best chance to change his life. He rubbed the base of Kip's head, attempting to soothe away some of that ache.

"You're not casting me out?"

"Don't be silly. You're one of us now."

"But I deceived you."

"Whilst doing your duty. Did you ask for this assignment?"

"No. But I was happy to receive it."

"Why?"

Kip struggled, but eventually the truth won out. "Before this I dealt mostly with financial crimes. Ledgers, accounts, government documents. Such work is not well-regarded by my superiors. Or peers."

"The headline chasers."

"Quite. This was my one chance to prove them wrong."

Hiero smiled down into that stricken face, something like the flutter of wings in his breast. "Then let's do so."

"You mean to help me prove to them you are a fraud?"

"Stranger things have happened." Hiero laughed. "My dear Kip, you must know by now that there is always a way."

"Mr. Stoker." Callie's ice-queen guise had melted slightly. "*This* is what we do."

"I don't understand."

"You will." She gestured Hiero back to his seat. He plunked himself on the arm of Kip's chair and refused to budge. "We'd best get on with it."

At her signal, Han threw that morning's newspaper onto Kip's lap. The headline shouted: "Cat-Tastrophe at London Zoo: Copper Mauled by Lion."

"Of course." Kip scanned the article, shaking his head more vigorously at every line. Hiero redoubled his massaging efforts. "An unimpeachable cover-up on Blackwood's part."

"Hobbs?" Hiero queried.

"Undoubtedly."

"Curious. I do wonder if there was enough of him to, er, move."

"Either that or Blackwood owns a few scribblers."

"More interesting are the aspersions this casts on Small and Croke's motives last night," Callie noted. "Not monitoring the place, as they claimed, but fetching the remains to erase Blackwood's crime."

"A pretty penny that must have cost him," Han commented.

"If that's where it ends." Kip meticulously refolded the paper. "If they cover for this crime, why not for the others?"

"Which means their investigation into the thefts, such as it is, may be corrupt."

"Just so."

"Blackwood's still lacking any motive for the robberies," Callie countered. "If he can take possession of them by claiming to protect them, why resort to theft? Our focus is too unilateral. We can't discount the other suspects just because Blackwood's involved in known criminal activities."

"I agree." Hiero felt Kip straighten his shoulders as he grew into his natural role as lead investigator. "Our objective now should be to try to disprove Blackwood's guilt and consider the other suspects more closely."

"Disprove?" Han queried.

"It's a technique we use in financial cases. There are a host of ways in which Blackwood could have perpetrated this crime, due to the fact that he has unlimited resources, and therefore anyone or everyone could be his agent: Miss Nightingale, Mr. Whicher, Small,

Croke, others... The possibilities are endless and impossible to prove conclusively, especially since much of the information involves private transactions. We must search for the outlier. The thing that proves his innocence without a doubt."

Han grunted. "What if there's nothing to be found?"

"That in itself is revealing. At best another suspect will come to the fore. At worst we will have a better understanding of how he did do it since certain scenarios will have been eliminated. And of course our investigation into the others might bear fruit."

Callie's normally implacable face betrayed the hint of a smile. "That's rather ingenious. I can't think why those growlers at the Met mean to force you out."

"A poor appreciation of the finer things." Hiero gave Kip's shoulder a squeeze.

Kip gave another shake of his head, perhaps still wondering why he hadn't been chucked out. "Flattery, alas, is of no use to us. We need a plan of action."

"The logical course is to attend the séance at Lady Stang-Helion's in three days' time," Callie said.

"But she doesn't have her fang," Han said.

"No," Kip elaborated. "But all the players will be there, and it will be a prime opportunity to observe their interactions."

Hiero chuckled. "And provoke them into certain... revelations."

"We know what you'll get up to, but what about the rest of us?" Callie batted her eyelashes in mock innocence. "I suppose I'm relegated to interviewing Lady Stang-Helion."

"I don't know of anyone else who has her wrapped around their little finger."

This earned him a smirk. "True."

"Seen in a certain light, she does have the strongest motive," Kip reminded. "Try to excavate her feelings on the subject of the fangs. Mr. Han, your silent stalking skills will be a boon where Whicher and Nightingale are concerned."

"As you wish."

"And I'll have a chat with Lord Blackwood," Hiero declared.

"Actually... no." Kip had retreated back behind his reserve like a rabbit to its warren, his hands clasped on his lap, fingernails cutting into his palm. "I... Blackwood is funding my investigation. It was he who provided my entree into the Belgrave Spiritualists' Society."

A tedious hush fell over the room. Tedious to Hiero since he had gathered as much from the night of their first meeting, but Han glared at Kip, and Callie fought for composure.

"How much have you known, all this time?" she grit out.

"No more than you. I was originally assigned to investigate B— Hiero, if you'll recall. I wasn't told what case you were working. I'm not sure my superiors were aware of the theft of the first fang. The introduction, and a stern warning to keep him informed, was all Blackwood gave me."

Both of Hiero's dogs stopped growling, but neither of them would forget that niggling detail anytime soon. Nothing to be done about it. Kip would either rise to the occasion or deserve their ire.

"And you mean to mine this connection, tenuous though it may be, for gold?" Hiero queried, nudging them all toward the obvious conclusion.

Kip nodded. "Blackwood doesn't know I've been discovered or where my allegiances lie now. It's possible that, in a private moment, he might confide in me. If I can gain his trust."

"Which will mean giving him something of use," Callie said, her lips in a moue, "about Hiero."

"Or by appearing to," Hiero hastened to reassure her. "A nugget of lead we can paint into fool's gold. With three days to prepare..."

"And only his word Blackwood's been sold the lie, not the truth."

To Hiero's surprise, Kip himself responded with "Is this what you do, then? Pretend to trust until the first obstacle? Wait until I stumble to exact your pound of flesh? Say the word, Miss Pankhurst, and I am gone."

Callie shut her eyes, drew in a deep breath. Hiero recognized one of Han's patience exercises. Han had performed them often enough throughout the long years of their friendship. No doubt Kip would soon be a convert.

"I'll banish no man to his ruin while he might still be of use." She regained something of her composure. "And you will be ruined, won't you? If you fail to provide evidence against Hiero?"

Kip blinked in acknowledgement of the truth of her words, his face ashen.

"You must be already in revealing yourself to us." Her balloon of righteousness popped. Everyone deflated, sagging into their chairs as if the very air leeched their energy. "Why do it?"

"It was my duty."

"No. Why tell us the truth?"

Kip shrugged. "It was the right thing to do."

Silence fell anew, more resonant than the first. Hiero let it reverberate through them for a time until he could stand it no more. What was the point of such silences, if no applause followed?

"Vandenberg. We've not considered him."

"Quite right," Kip encouraged. "He refused to have his fang protected. There must be something there."

"But should we wait so long to interview him?" Callie asked. "The séance will not be an ideal time, especially to air any bad blood between him and the members of the Spiritualists Society."

"Perhaps you should call upon him in your official guise, Stoker," Han suggested. "Police business."

Hiero clicked his tongue. "Of course not. Better to maintain the dissimulation. No, Kip and I will arrange a private interview under far more relaxing circumstances since our dear Landgrave is a great amateur"—he swooped his arm through the air with flourish—"of the theater."

Kip coughed out, "Will you... Will you be performing?"

"Heavens no. Vandenberg traffics in more rarified circles than the Gaiety. We shall attend tomorrow evening's premiere performance of *The Merchant of Venice* at the Lyceum. Vandenberg is a sponsor, so he is certain to be there." He clapped his hands with relish. "We must plan meticulously. Han, summon Monsieur Henri."

"Who's that now?" Kip asked.

"Why, my tailor." Hiero planted both hands on his shoulders and squeezed with all his might. "Dearest Kip, you're to finally be fitted for a proper suit!"

This news was, needless to say, not received with acceptable enthusiasm or gratitude, but Hiero wasn't bothered. If he could not have the mystery of Kip's identity, then by Jove, he would have his fun.

After doing his best impression of a pincushion all evening, Tim escaped back to the chess room to collect his things. Such as they were. Though laundered, pressed, and sewn, they were a ruin. Having just paged through book after book of the finest fabrics, he noted the wear on the elbows and knees, the fraying at the cuffs, the sweat discoloration around the inner collar. While he still considered it a minor victory to have left Hiero's study with his sanity intact, with his livelihood in jeopardy, now was not the time to invest in a new wardrobe. But Tim began to see himself how others—one clothes-horse in particular—saw him. The reflection did not flatter.

But then no one in this upside-down house was who they seemed. Over an informal dinner in the basement kitchen—with the servants, the chatter so lively and the host so boisterous Tim nearly wept for joy—he had occasion to observe them all, these so-called charity cases. How did Minnie, a taciturn former slave from the

West Indies, end up as cook/matron in a tony Mayfair townhouse? How did Angus—Scot, carriage driver, and former addict—go from the opium dens, where he met Jie, the ladies' maid, to the refuge of Hiero's household? Their daughter Ting held place of pride on Hiero's knee the entire meal, such that Tim almost began to envy their playful familiarity. The butler's story, Tim discovered, was tragic. Aldridge, an American actor acquaintance of Hiero's, had spoken up too many times to the wrong theatre manager and had his tongue cut out. But where did Mr. Han hail from, and why was he treated as Hiero's equal by the other staff? Why was Miss Pankhurst permitted to work with him unchaperoned and sit kitty corner to him at dinner? Why, every so often, did Tim think he heard a distant shriek? The house itself was peculiar.

Yet for all he was by nature a quiet and dutiful sort, a part of him delighted in the chaos. Certainly he could not help but be intrigued. What detective would fail to be by such an unusual group? And to give up such power so freely, as if to do so made them lighter, not heavier. All through the meal, he expected to feel the weight of their secrets as boulder after boulder was heaved onto his shoulders with every revelation. Instead they acted as balloons, buoying him up out of his pain and anxiety into the giddy air of those who truly respected one another. He was the ultimate stranger in a strange land, but, for a time, he could pretend he was one of them.

The real heaviness was in the weight of his tattered clothes, which challenged his waning strength as he dragged them on. The thought of the haranguing Mrs. Lester would give him for not returning the previous night, oblivious to his bruises, made his feet feel leaden. His body's aches intensified when reminded of his creaky, sharp-springed cot, his gloomy wallpaper, the rust-rimmed basin that would match the bloody water as he cleaned his wounds. He struggled to fasten his buttons with his ham-hock hands, wishing for his mother's brisk but loving touch, for the jokey rivalry of talking sport with his father, for the family of which Hiero's collection of urchins and troubled souls had so agonizingly reminded him.

But temporary alliance or no, Tim did not belong here.

Another shriek sliced through the pleasant din that echoed up the stairs, unnerving Tim such that he almost missed the odd sag to the left side of his frock coat. Leaving the mystery of the caterwauler for another day, he patted his outer pocket, then remembered the notebook he had stashed in the inner seam. Throwing off his coat as if it were on fire, he dove back into its folds, fumbling with the small inner pocket button awhile before tearing it clean off. Muttering curses, he extricated the notebook as if removing a thorn from a lion's paw. He need not have worried. Hiero's staff was eccentric but thorough. They had removed the book prior to washing. Tim flipped through its delicate pages with renewed awe and an overabundance of excitement.

This world he knew. Arcane scribbles and obfuscating etches. Neat rows of cryptic annotations. Reams and reams of data with no clear source or subject. The notebook might contain something as mundane and vulgar as a timetable of the cats' defecation or as precious as a list of the treasures in all those lockboxes. There was only one way to find out. The long night that stretched ahead suddenly looked a lot less lonely. Tim hastened back into his coat, cradling the notebook to his chest as if it contained the secrets of the known universe.

Hiero swaggered in bearing a bottle of Scotch and two tumblers along with a predatory air. He had imbibed generously all through supper and the tailor's visit and likely hadn't stopped when Tim slipped away—it was something of a miracle he still stood. And so beguilingly at that, his smoking jacket loosened to expose a tempting sliver of that luxurious pelt and his black mane tousled as if he'd already been abed.

Tim caught his breath, bit down the side of his tongue. He

clutched the notebook with both hands, his virtue (and sanity's) only shield.

"Fancy a nightcap?" The glasses tinkled like a fairy's charm. "Oh, don't make that face! I swear by all the Muses, my intentions are purely platonic. Well, perhaps not entirely, but I gave Callie my solemn oath that I would let you rest tonight. But I am, of course, willing to break it if you are so inclined. Only we must be quiet, otherwise she'll be accompanying us to the theater tomorrow night, and that simply will not do. How else am I to lure you into the dark corners of our box?"

He'd closed the distance between them during his little speech and gazed down at Tim now with firecracker eyes. Tim shut his own, breathing in the spicy, virile scent of him, not daring to speak. The lust was so thick in his mouth it was as if he'd grown a second tongue. The potency of the spell Hiero cast over him with but a gleam and a smile terrified. If not for the very real, very sore state of his body, he'd have already been on his knees.

When Tim pried his eyes open, he saw Hiero had taken a welcome step back. And his eyes had lost some of their luster.

"Going somewhere?"

"To my flat." Tim couldn't bring himself to say the H-word in relation to that dismal place.

"Whatever for?" Hiero's look was not merely of shock, but of hurt. "Have we not made you comfortable here? Is the bed too coarse or unfamiliar? The room too draughty? If there's something particular you require, Han can fetch it. I know we're an... unconventional household, and certainly it takes some time to grow accustomed, especially for someone as..." He waved his hand so furiously Tim feared he'd drop the glasses. "As you..."

Tim caught his hand, plucked the tumblers out, and set them on the nightstand, snatching the Scotch away for good measure. He still had no idea what to say to Hiero once this was done, surprised by his vehemence and somewhat moved by his concern. The truth won out.

"It is my place of residence. It was exceptionally kind of you to care for me whilst I was indisposed, but I'm on the mend and..." Another shriek interrupted him, further muddling his already muddled thoughts. "Who is that? Do you hear it too, or did that blow to the head affect me more than I thought?"

Hiero assayed a sheepish look. "Madwoman in the attic."

"Ha-ha." But Tim couldn't repress a smile. "Who is she? Your paramour? Wife? A servant your eccentricities drove around the bend? Miss Pankhurst's disgraced mother?"

He would have continued, but Hiero went white as a ghost.

"Never again doubt your skills as a detective, dear Kip."

"What? You mean Lady..."

"Mrs. Pankhurst. Lillian. Yes. She's... Well, as you can hear, she has... transcended this earthly realm, as they say. Well, her mind has. Except on Sundays, when she dresses in her finest, pops down for tea, drinks an entire bottle of Bordeaux, and falls asleep on the divan. She's quiet most nights but has a keen sense for when there's someone new in the house. But please, don't let her chase you off. She'll calm down once you're introduced."

Tim stared at him, jaw agape, unable to think of a single thing to say.

"She's not alone, so don't fret on that account. She has a nurse-maid, Agnes. Sweet girl. We don't see much of her since old Lil's quite the patient, but you'll like her. Wears a long braid that she loops... Never mind." Not for the first time, Tim couldn't decipher the mire of emotions that twisted Hiero's face, though he noted concern, defiance, and, to his shock, nervousness. "Kip. Please stay. Blackwood... well, there's no telling. Other unknown dangers, that sort of thing. I won't lay a finger on you. Solemn vow. Just... this room. Another. Whatever you want. But please... stay."

He took a moment to savor something rare and momentous when it came to the wily ways of Hieronymus Bash: the upper hand. Then he smiled.

"Well, if you insist."

"I do." Hiero sighed. "Wonderful. That's settled. Now drink?"

"One," Tim underlined, poorly schooling his face. "And I mean it. Just one. I have some work to attend to."

With his fingers he played a swift tattoo on the cover of the notebook. He formally presented it to Hiero. As his magician's hands fluttered through the pages, Tim was hard-pressed to say which he desired to know more thoroughly, Hiero or the secrets within.

Chapter 9

The man who made his entrance at the top of the grand staircase astonished no one but Hiero. Cut to perfection by Monsieur Henri, his single-breasted tailcoat elongated his torso and emphasized his trim waist. His kerseymere trousers with silk-braided outseams hugged his powerful thighs and calves in ways even Hiero judged to be too licentious. Hiero had insisted upon his U-shaped waistcoat in ebony satin embellished with tourmaline buttons, and his string tie. He could not be seen with someone in anything less than the latest fashions.

Though he twisted his gloves like a dishrag and his silk top hat was under his arm, not on his head, Timothy Kipling Stoker looked every inch the British nobleman. Hiero could not deny the irony of making someone who went unnoticed look commonplace in a different social setting. It tickled him too much. But he would not have his Kip attract any untoward attention, especially of the predatory variety. Even the Lyceum, that bastion of civility and culture, housed its share of sexual deviants. Having to ward off rivals as well as spies would douse Hiero's desire before it had a chance to burn.

The first licks of flame kindled low in his groin as he met Kip at the bottom of the stairs. His look must have conveyed much of his thoughts since the object of his perusal turned the color of the carpet—a bold vermillion. On impulse Hiero invaded his space, snatching the hat out from under his arm and setting it ever so gently atop his head. When met, those verdant eyes shimmered with something like amusement, something like gratitude despite the healthy amount of reserve Hiero always perceived there.

For this he didn't blame Kip in the slightest. *Hiero* would have doubted the honesty of his own regard in Kip's position. Once upon a time, Hiero's affections were as flighty as his manners, flitting like a hummingbird from flower to flower to flower. But his dearest Apollo showed him a different way, made him a constant lover, if not a better man. If ever there was a heart in need of patience, persistence, and fidelity—attributes Apollo had in spades—it was Kip's. If only as tribute to the man who saved him, Hiero owed Kip an initiation into the ways and means of a worthy lover.

Once the night's business concluded.

"'How far that little candle throws its beams!'" Hiero stepped back for a better look at him. "'Sir, you have bereft me of all words. Only my blood speaks to you in my veins.'"

Kip snorted. "'You speak an infinite deal of nothing.'"

"So shall read my epitaph." It took a surprising amount of self-control to avoid taking Kip's arm as they made their way toward the carriage. "And how goes your love affair with Blackwood's little book? Do I need to fetch the scissors?"

"How do you mean?"

"Scissors, enemy of all paper. You tinkered away the better part of last night and most of the afternoon. I was beginning to think you'd absconded back to that... room of yours."

"You've never seen my rooms."

"Precisely."

Kip tipped his hat to Angus at the carriage door. The driver smiled. Former reprobates tended to be excellent judges of character, Angus included. If the staff had taken to Kip, then... Well, the future would reveal itself in time.

"The code Blackwood uses is a Vigenère cipher, a variation on the classic Caesar cipher that is thought impossible to crack. Basic alphabet replacement, though without the keyword... I consulted some of the books in your library. Admiral Pankhurst has quite a few tomes on the very subject, one of which has a theory on how it might be deciphered, but I've yet to hit on a satisfactory result. It might help to consult a proper mathematician..."

"Egads." Hiero shuddered. "I shan't ask again."

Kip chuckled. "Code-breaking not your cup of tea?"

"Certainly not. I prefer mine dark and robust and..."

"Turkish?"

"Quite."

"Like your coffee."

"And my baths." Hiero caught his eye. The red flush returned. "Have you ever been? They're most rejuvenating. A long hot soak and a bit of pampering can provide a tremendous release."

"I don't doubt." Kip cleared his throat, forced his eyes away. "And no, I've... But Landgrave Vandenberg. What's our plan of attack?"

Not an artful change of subject, but Hiero didn't fault him. After all, this was only stage one of his evening-long seduction. It wouldn't do to culminate too soon.

"We'll walk the salons and bars, let ourselves be seen. I'll send him an invitation to dine with us during the first interval. He won't be able to abandon whomever's accompanying him, but will likely stop by during the second. If he does not..."

"He's avoiding us."

"Mmm. We'll have to be a bit underhanded."

"Bribe a steward?"

Hiero cackled. "Kip! You *have* done this before."

"I'm a detective inspector, not the Archbishop of Canterbury."

"No." Hiero still chuckled. "Despite your piousness, I can't envision you as a man of the cloth."

"My... You've entirely the wrong impression of me."

"Do I?"

"Yes."

"All this time, it's you who's been playing a part?"

Kip grunted. "Your whole life is a performance. Do not think I haven't had cause to wonder whether we've shared one genuine moment together."

"Oh, we have." Hiero did his best impression of the cat who had gotten the cream. "One in fond particular comes to mind."

He had anticipated another gorgeous blush; instead Kip's features hardened.

"But is this not just another starring role in another thrilling production? *The Foppish Gentleman and the Foolish Detective.* Another ruse to... to 'scape the serpent's tongue." He gripped his gloves so tightly Hiero thought he heard them tear. "I'm nothing but another mark that needs deceiving, another player in the great drama you've made of your life. You've not only discovered my weaknesses—the things that call to me by night—but you've mastered them! How I could ever have resisted you..."

Hiero shrank from his outpouring of emotion like a violet from the sun. He had no answer that would suffice him, no proof of his good character or honest intent, for he had intended to manipulate him. At first. Perhaps, in a way, even now. And he would make him no promises. But neither was he indifferent to the reality of Kip's circumstances. Nor did he wish to cause him pain. Was it so wrong to show him a little attention, a little affection? Nurture him as he had been nurtured by Apollo? Even if it was fleeting?

"Then do."

Kip raised his gaze. "What do you mean?"

"Refuse my advances. Reject my insinuations. If I affront you, deny me."

"I..."

"It was never my intention to act against your wishes. If you believe anything of me, believe this. Say the word, and it stops now."

Kip could not have looked more startled—or disappointed. It buoyed Hiero's spirits.

"Everything? The flirtation, the innuendo, the seductions? All of it, at my word?"

"You've only to give it." He scrutinized Hiero's face with tragic eyes, recording every curve and arch, scanning for any hint of deceit. On Kip's own troubled mien, a battle raged, one Hiero recognized all too well. When one had been beaten down every time he'd inched out of the hole, another climb seemed not only unfathomable, but impossible. He could only reach a hand down and pray Kip grasped it.

Kip swallowed hard, lowered his eyes anew. Hiero wanted to shake him out of submission, but he could only wait for him to sever their tentative alliance.

"'What would be the fun in that?'" A trace of a smile lit those dour features. "I gather that's what you'd say."

Hiero couldn't help himself. He beamed. "Something of the sort."

"I've misjudged you. Forgive me." Kip shuddered, balled up his gloves. "I'm just so bloody nervous."

"Ah. Well, I've the perfect remedy for that." He hopped over to the opposing seat, cupped Kip's cheek, turned his face toward him. At his soft gasp, Hiero paused, hovering near enough that his intentions were plain.

And savoring the moment. The jaw against his palm tensed, but Kip's mouth fell slightly open. Their breaths mingled, misting over their lips. Hiero stroked his fingertips through his sideburn bristles, the glints of red catching his eye. He marveled at Kip's lovely, freckled pallor at this vantage, his eagerness to take charge of his own desires clashing with his poorly concealed vulnerability. Hiero waited him out, offering but giving him every chance to refuse. The pretense Kip had been forced into temptation ended there and then. If he wanted—and Hiero could feel the intensity of his want in the grip on his side, the intimate cant of Kip's body toward him—then he had to take what he wanted.

A low, bawdy laugh heralded what Hiero thought was Kip's retreat, reclining back to notch his neck on the top edge of the seat cushion before drawing Hiero down atop him. With a purring sound that rumbled down straight to Hiero's groin, Kip pawed a thumb across his bottom lip, then delved deep. It was the maneuver of a man accustomed to quick, clandestine bouts of sex, not lovemaking—a lesson for another time. For now the sensuous tangle of tongues, the hot press of his taut body, and the slow thrust of hips sufficed. Hiero moaned into his clever mouth, forgetting their mission, the location, everything but how Kip's tang reminded him of the taste of his luscious cock.

As if in answer to an unspoken command, Kip's most impressive attribute prodded into his navel, urging Hiero's still-thickening shaft to come out and play. Kip parted his legs, inviting Hiero between them. His rather delicious submissiveness forced Hiero to revise his earlier opinion as he moved them into alignment, then set a sultry, grinding rhythm. He surrendered Kip's mouth to breathless panting in favor of gorging on his sinuous neck. It took everything in him not to leave a mark—such a decadent slope of skin all but demanded goring.

Lest he assume Kip had entirely given over to him, he kneaded his way down the length of his back and over his buttocks, demanding he quicken his pace. Hiero knew they should flick open a few buttons, shed a few layers, but they were too far gone. Besides, a sticky mess would mean a dash home. Once home it would be no trouble at all to lure Kip to bed for a proper rut. The theater and Vandenberg could wait on the morrow, but this, the strange alchemy that burnished them gold—this required some serious, ardent, and oft-repeated experimentation.

The carriage lurched to an abrupt stop.

Kip groaned, which pleased him enormously. Hiero leapt up,

caught the door before Angus swung it open.

"Once more around, I think. Wouldn't do to be too early."

"Of course, sir."

When Hiero turned back, Kip had righted his posture and shut his eyes but said, "Smart. Thank you."

With his clothes mussed and his hair winged, he looked delectably wanton. Hiero hard-swallowed a surge of regret. "Not my first time."

His red-roughed lips curled in an unmistakable smirk. "Nor mine." Never before had a sentence piqued Hiero's interest more. "Still, it wouldn't do for the Lyceum."

"No." He basked in the view a moment longer. "Let's get you righted."

"In a minute." To Hiero's shock, Kip's gaze, when foist upon him, simmered with lust. He visibly struggled to control his breathing, to calm what was raging only seconds before. Kip shifted in his seat, slicked his hair back into some semblance of style, but still didn't tear his eyes away. "Must you always look so..." He gave his head a violent shake. "Afterward. We'll continue?"

"As many times and in as many ways as you care to."

"Good." Kip exhaled a long, cleansing breath. "If you would help me..."

Hiero kept his touches light, his fingers desperate to linger, to delve. He anticipated their afterward more than anything in a long while. By the time the carriage came to a second, less sudden halt, they had both resumed the guise of distinguished gentlemen, betraying nothing but poise, gallantry, and, in Hiero's case, a certain unhinged quality. But Hiero didn't think he was alone in feeling a gentle if constant tug in Kip's direction, as if their earlier unquenched passions had bonded them in ways deeper than carnality.

As they walked the bars and salons searching for Vandenberg, they chatted politely, their conversation as fluffy as a valmouse. But every so often he would catch himself reaching for Kip, or Kip reaching for him, only to halt inches from the other, eyes penitent but yearning, posture rigid with self-restraint. Normally Hiero would use such anticipation as fuel for his slow-burning desire, little sparks of temptation that would fire into an inferno by night's end. With Kip he had to snuff out each one lest his insides be reduced to embers before long.

A welcome distraction to the interminable chore of locating Vandenberg.

When the trumpets sounded, they had no choice but to find their box. Hiero again had to restrain himself from taking Kip's arm as they followed the madding crowd through the corridors. He spared a polite greeting for the few acquaintances they passed, but thoughts of Kip consumed his mind. Specifically the hows, whens, and wheres of their later encounter. Would Kip agree to a second night at the house, or would they couple savagely in his dingy little flat? If they managed to secure Vandenberg by the second interval, could they be off soon after? This added new urgency to their mission. Was Kip really as submissive as he seemed, or was that simply a result of his past indiscretions? How many and of what variety were those encounters? And would he be amenable to sharing a few of these tales with Hiero once they were well and truly sated?

He became so distracted that he barely noticed the usher escorting them into their box. Indeed he missed Kip's request that their curtain not be opened yet, the generous tip he paid the young man, and the click of the lock after the door shut. When Kip shoved him against the far wall and dove in for a kiss, he yelped, surprised.

For a moment—a blissful, delirious moment—he gave over to the onslaught of his sweet mouth. Kip pinned his arms back, that finely wrought body thrumming with need, but kept a sliver of space between them. He pulled away with far more delicacy than he'd pounced, finishing with a soft peck that did nothing to stop Hiero craving more. Kip capped this brash but welcome action with a fervent look, then retreated as if nothing had happened.

"I did mention this isn't the Gaiety?" Hiero said.

"So you did." A hint of his earlier smirk returned. "Are you sorry?"

"That word isn't in my vocabulary."

"Don't I know it."

Hiero chuckled, then stole a moment of his own to take in the sight of Kip thoroughly enjoying himself. "How is it that you become more of a mystery the more you're revealed to me?"

Kip shrugged. "I've made you a promise. Now to work."

Hiero couldn't suppress his groan. "If we must." He took his seat as Kip saw to the curtain. The crowd at the Lyceum twittered politely, branches upon branches of these magnificently plumed birds soaring up to the rafters. No catcalling or ruckus here. Gentlemen stood faithfully beside their companions as they chatted with friends, ceding their chairs to visitors. Ladies leaned toward each other while maintaining statuesque postures, fans raised every so often for a private word. The few mistresses in the audience stuck out like foxes in a henhouse, their décolletage a touch too fulsome, their jewels a smidge too garish. The men who squired them too powerful for anyone to make a fuss.

Spying a renowned critic in the box across from theirs, Hiero growled under his breath.

"Is it Vandenberg?" Kip committed the faux pas of edging too far into Hiero's personal space. Eyes turned in their direction—*they* had now been scoped by the lady hawks in attendance, who would swoop in during the first interval. Normally Hiero thrived on such attention, but they were there to hunt, not be caught in their talons.

"Worse. Andrew England."

This earned him a grating chuckle. "Oh, dear. He hasn't been kind to our Mr. Beastly."

"He is a pustule on the ass of this great city."

Kip guffawed. "Are you quoting one of his reviews?"

"He would go in for this kind of"—Hiero dismissed the entire audience and production with a curt gesture—"soulless pageantry."

That sobered Kip. "You don't care for Shakespeare?"

"I most certainly do. He is one of the only gods in my pantheon, along with Sophocles, Moliere, Congreve, Pushkin, and Goethe."

Kip appeared to give the matter some thought. "I can't quarrel with that. Is it the theater itself that displeases?"

"How could it? Look at the detail on the proscenium, the lustrous glow of the floodlights, the marble, the gold, the velvet, the pristine acoustics. It's a cathedral of the arts, the likes of which would convert the most savage of brutes. Rather the managers and their esteemed patrons have kitted the place out with every luxury, every innovation, save the one that matters most."

"Dare I ask?"

"Proper actors."

Kip pressed his knuckle to his lips for a time before remarking, "But Mr. Lance is the toast of London."

Hiero let out a bovine sound by way of a reply.

"Mr. Gordon?"

He scoffed.

"Surely you cannot find fault in the mesmerizing Miss Lamb?"

Hiero sighed. "An improvement on the hysterics of Miss Dahlia Nightingale, but only that."

"I suppose your Shylock was a sight to behold."

"Rather my Antonio is considered by those in the know to be the definitive interpretation. Irving, of course, nabbed Shylock—that peacock. Still, I'm hardly of age to tackle such senior roles. In time I shall prove the command performer."

Kip just then regarded him in a way that might have been mistaken for fondness. How desperately Hiero wanted to reach out and pet his freckled cheek.

"How good of you to abase yourself in the name of our investigation."

"It rather is, now I think on it."

"And in your distraction, you'll have every opportunity to locate Vandenberg while I... Well, I confess I was looking forward to the performance."

Hiero waved away his contrition. "Leave it to me. If you find it in yourself to enjoy this..." He twiddled his fingers in the direction of the stage. "Have at it."

The applause as the lights dimmed drowned out his response. When they rose again on an Antonio so foppish one might consider him the owner of a brothel, not the titular merchant of Venice, and a Salanio so rotund the hilt of his sword kept poking him in the belly, Hiero scanned the opposing boxes for their prey. Like the paintings in a portrait gallery, the reams of dour-faced nobles took on a sameness that had Hiero flicking his eyes and ears back to the stage. A mispronounced word, a dropped cue, an ungainly cut to the text—every misstep tugged at his attention like a neglected child. To say nothing of the beatific look that overtook Kip's face as he beheld the massacre of a sacred script happening on the stage. (The thought of Kip enjoying such a travesty did give Hiero pause.) In his fern-green eyes a bedazzling spectacle played out, his plain features transformed by utter emphatic delight. Timothy Kipling Stoker loved the theater. And Hieronymus Bash might very well adore him for it.

The spell broke during the scene before the first interval, when Hiero realized he hadn't located Vandenberg. After a thorough scan, he spotted him in the balcony audience, his glittering eyes and that white-blonde hair like a beacon in the night. Better still, he sat with a group of men—likely his fellow patrons of the arts—from whom he might easily absent himself for a few minutes. Hiero scrawled off a hasty note and snuck it out to the usher. With luck this might all be over after the first interval. Then he could spirit Kip away to a more private location.

The minutes dragged by with no telltale tap at the door. Hiero attempted to refocus his attention on Kip or the dreadful actors, but to no avail. The lights blinked out, the curtain swept closed, and applause thundered through the hall. He had missed his window.

As soon as the house lights rose, Kip spun around. "You can't possibly—"

"Pedestrian."

"But Gordon—"

"Too overwrought."

"Surely Portia—"

"Frosty. Misjudged."

Kip snorted. "Is there nothing here to please you?"

"Most assuredly." Hiero shifted his leg until their thighs pressed together. He felt the muscles flexing under Kip's skin as he fought to stifle his reaction. They had been ignoring the fact of their proximity, but now the knowledge flared back to life, bright and searing as the tip of a forge iron.

A tap on the door snapped them apart.

"A note, sir. And a bottle of Glenlivet with three tumblers."

"Thank you." To Hiero's surprise, Kip intercepted the tray, tipped the usher, and poured himself a dram, which he downed in a single gulp. He included Hiero in the second round, reclining back against the wall of the box instead of retaking his seat. Hiero felt more than saw the force of his gaze, lust reflected in its recesses. Not a wisp of wariness clouded them, much to Hiero's relief. "The note."

"Hmm?"

"What does it say?"

"Ah, the note." As he perused the contents, Hiero fought to conceal his dismay. Which was to say, by the end it was writ bold across his face. "He's invited us for a drink at his club after the performance. Hmm. A trap, do you think?"

"If it were, he'd invite us to his home. Most likely the sort of public privacy that keeps secrets safe but sends a message."

"You think him false?"

Kip shrugged. "Everyone involved in this affair has something to hide. Present company included."

"Ha! Do you include yourself in that estimation?"

"Most certainly." That guarded little half smile made a reappearance. "Of which you are well aware."

That recessive lust floated to the fore, as gaudily green as an algae bloom.

"Come here."

"No."

"Why not?"

"Because I want to." Kip's hand shook as he refilled his glass. "This place... one like it... is where I learned to..." He swallowed hard. "They are forever linked in my mind. I should never have let you lure me here."

"Don't be absurd." Hiero stood, moved toward him, but stopped at a respectable distance. He waited until Kip's breathing slowed, another dram of amber liquid caressing his tongue and throat as Hiero, at present, could not. "Tell me."

For a moment he thought Kip might bite at him or bluntly refuse. But stories, especially tragic ones, ached to be told. Hiero knew this only too well.

"After my parents..."

"No. Earlier. How did you come to love the theater?"

"Mother." Kip sighed. "A seamstress. She repaired costumes. Easy work to find in a new city, especially since all theater people know of each other. A letter from Monsieur Étienne at the Opéra de Paris got her in the door; her talent kept her there. I went with her when I was small. Even when I wasn't, I would join her when I could. It was... Well, I don't need to explain."

"A home away from home."

Kip nodded, seeming to stare out at the distant stage, but really at the shadow play of memory he projected onto the closed curtain. "When they were gone, it was the only way to feel close to her. We used to watch the plays together, you see. *Hamlet. Tartuffe. Faust.* Commedia dell'arte. Burlesques. Pantomimes. Anything and everything. A youth seated on his own night after night, even one as unremarkable as I, draws notice. The wrong kind... and the right. By day I clerked for one of my father's associates. By night I found relief. In the shadows of a private box. In a nook backstage. In the alley behind the stage door. Until the police came sniffing around my employer's business, and I impressed an inspector with my fastidiousness. I grabbed at the chance to turn my life around with both hands and never looked back."

Hiero stood aghast. "You *abandoned* the theater?"

"I forsook the ways that would see me hanged, if ever I was caught. The theater included." He raised his lids, smacked Hiero with the full force of his stare. That emerald cast gleamed, lustier than ever. "Until I was forced back whilst chasing down the man who would reacquaint me with my old ways most... persuasively."

"And now?"

"It's all I can think about." He fumbled for another dram, but Hiero stopped his hand. The heat of that single touch nearly unmanned him, but he held fast to the fact they would expose themselves publicly, if nothing else.

Instead he stole the bottle away, cradling it to his chest like a colicky babe.

"Don't be greedy." After measuring out a final draught for himself, Hiero corked the bottle. "There will be time enough for such indulgences." He took a step back, gestured toward their seats. "Come now. The final act will soon begin."

With a grateful nod, Kip shuffled back to his chair, keeping an honorable distance. Hiero drained his glass, wishing he could free-pour the bottle down his throat. Only a few more hours, he reminded himself, until they were blissfully alone.

As the carriage horses neighed their annoyance at the post-theatre traffic, Tim grabbed the reins of their discussion and held on with all his might. He was an officer of the law, not the heroine of a Gothic romance made vulnerable by the charms of a seductive rogue until he lost everything. His virtue may be long gone, through no fault of Hiero's, but while a glimmer of hope that they might solve this case remained, he must redouble his determination. Which did not preclude a later relaxing of the rules, but for now, a suspect's interrogation loomed, and Tim needed to keep himself well informed.

If only to avoid any further slips of the tongue in the form of kisses or confessions.

"Vandenberg," he said to Hiero. "What do you know of him?"

Hiero steepled his hands under his chin as if in mockery of a thinking pose.

"He's an amiable sort. Something of a bon vivant, from what I'm told. Never had much cause to speak to him before this sorry business."

"You've not conversed with him?"

"Only briefly at Goldie's séance."

"Nor encountered him socially?"

"We don't traffic in the same circles."

"Have you made inquiries into his business holdings? His family scandals? Extracurricular activities?"

"Whatever for?"

"Have you done any investigating at all beyond asking Commodore Goldenplover if he would be at the theater this evening?"

"Didn't want to alert him to anything, did I?"

"Then how did you know he would be here?"

"Like anything else. I *presumed.*"

Tim couldn't help but laugh. "Miss Pankhurst truly does carry all the weight in this little enterprise of yours."

"I take exception to that remark."

"Is it your vanity or your pride that's insulted?"

"My sense of honor, if you must know."

"Ha! So those are your parameters. Petty larceny in the name of fun, acceptable. Disrupting séances with heckling asides, acceptable. Fraudulent representation of self, acceptable. But don't for a second suggest he's outmatched by a girl."

Hiero shot him a jaundiced look. "Nonsense. Our partnership is predicated on two inviolable tenets. The first that we both play to our strengths. She is, as you say, the coal-burning engine, and I am the screaming burst of smoke."

"And the second?"

"That I never, under any circumstances, presume her to be less than capable because she is a woman."

Tim opened his mouth to reply but found he had nothing of substance to add. He had embarked upon this investigation with so many presumptions and, like a row of tin soldiers, a flick of Hiero's ever-busy hands had toppled each one.

"But you're right to criticize. I should have consulted her before…"

"Launching headfirst into an interrogation with an unknown quantity?"

"You detectives and your righteousness."

"The job does require it on occasion." Tim scoffed, reminded of some of his colleagues' antics. "Less than one might expect."

At that Hiero raised an eyebrow. "A conversation for a quieter day. For now, what have you, dear Kip, learned about our landgrave during the course of your research?"

"Capital of you to ask," Tim teased, pleased by the resurgence of his smile. "Like many nowadays, by the time Vandenberg inherited his title, there was little fortune left to speak of. The money had gone long before the Prussians annexed the landgraviate of Hesse-Kassel in 1866, leaving his father powerless as well as almost penniless. But he and his firstborn son retained the title of landgrave, which I suppose became their calling card. Even in youth Vandenberg was, as you say, a bon vivant. A standard education with no skills, but many charms. Loved the outdoors—hunting, fishing, sport. He was a favorite at balls, renowned for his wit and his warmth. Thus it was easy for him to marry into money, an English girl of Dutch heritage with a sizeable dowry and a father with a nose for shrewd investments. So his life of luxury continued on apace."

"Ah! I can report that she fell ill soon after they wed, and that they are, by all accounts, devoted to one another."

"So he's not of our persuasion?"

"Not at all. I don't believe I've ever heard him linked to anyone other than his wife."

Tim nodded. "My research bears that out. He has his interests—it's no wonder he fell in with Goldenplover, Helion, and Blackwood given his passion for hunting—and his philanthropic work, but otherwise, he remains at her side. His holdings are the same that his father-in-law set up for him over two decades ago, overseen by the same firm. He signs where they tell him to and cashes the checks."

Hiero shrugged. "Mine is a similar arrangement."

"Save for the amateur detection and playhouse moonlighting, you mean?"

"Quite so." He wiggled his still-steepled fingers. "He's something of a blank canvas, wouldn't you say? Few of his sociability and humor are painted in such bland colors. There must be something untoward about the man."

Tim grinned, tickled by these basic deductions. They would make a true detective of him yet.

"If there is, my dear Hiero, we will discover it."

Despite his declaration of resolve, Tim felt far less confident as he descended from the carriage and stared up at the handsome house on St. James Street that was Vandenberg's club, Brooks'. He permitted Hiero to lead them into its elegant, if somber, confines, the military reds and Oxford blues that dominated the decor the only brash political statement made within its walls. Brooks' reputation was one of quietude and conviviality: a good meal, a meticulously stocked cellar, a comfortable atmosphere, a jolly bit of conversation. A Brooks man's temper never ran high; he enjoyed the spoils of his station in life and kept his more controversial opinions private.

Or confined to a well-appointed corner of a room too vast for eavesdropping, to which the porter escorted them. Tim again considered Vandenberg's strategy, arranging for them to meet in a place where Hiero would be forced to mute some of the loudness of his personality, and any overzealous arguments would get them thrown out. A defensive maneuver Tim did not mistake for caution.

Vandenberg looked every inch Prince Albert's twin in his spoon-backed blue velvet armchair—indeed Tim wondered why he hadn't set his sights on the Queen herself when wife shopping. He casually perused one of the evening papers, a pipe crooked in the corner of his lip and an amber-colored wine resting in a crystal decanter on the table before him. The Teutonic chill of his face in repose underwent a spring thaw when he spotted them, melting with warmth and welcome as he bid them sit down.

"I must confess I was thrilled to receive your note, Bash," Vandenberg gushed. "Please forgive the change of location, but I couldn't miss the chance to show you off."

If any of the other members had taken an interest in their arrival, they had yet to show it.

"I am, as ever, more than willing to provide an evening's entertainment." Hiero winked. Tim actively fought against the rolling of his eyes. "As you may have heard, my investigatory team has taken on a new member. May I present Mr. Timothy Kipling."

"A pleasure, sir. A great pleasure." Vandenberg's grip, like everything about him, was effusive. "Would either of you care for a cigar? Tobacco? I've ordered a truly exceptional Riesling for us, but if you would prefer port, whiskey... Our cellar can make real your wildest imaginings."

Tim accepted a cigarette out of Hiero's stash—an image of that feline tongue swabbing the paper invading his mind—and ordered a scotch. Hiero sampled the Riesling as one might sup from a lover's sacrum, to Tim's discomfort and Vandenberg's delight. A tray of fruit, nuts, and cheese fit for the Olympian gods had been laid across the table. Tim's stomach gave an appreciative rumble, but there would be time for feasting at a later hour. For now he forced himself to relax, to believe himself among peers, to look with the eyes of a faithful hound but to listen with the ears of a fox.

"How did you enjoy the play?" Vandenberg twinkled at them. "Come now, your honest opinions."

Tim interrupted as soon as Hiero opened his mouth. "Riveting! I have never been so moved by Shylock's plight as in Mr. Lance's interpretation. His Richard III impressed, but this was by far his finest performance."

Barely concealing his glare, Hiero remarked, "Though Gordon—"

"—was by turns fearsome and tender, troubled and beguiled. A triumph!"

"The staging—"

"Magnificent!"

"The costumes—"

"Decadent!"

"Miss Lamb—"

"—like an angel of justice brandishing her fiery sword. My only quibble..."

"Yes," Hiero hissed. "Do tell."

"... is that the orchestra was, at times, a touch too bombastic. The actors, after all, must be heard."

Vandenberg nodded vigorously. "I felt very much the same. Indeed I already sent word to the conductor."

"Then you are, as Commodore Goldenplover has said, a shrewd patron of the arts."

Vandenberg chuckled with false modesty. "If I'd have known

you were such an amateur of the theater, Mr. Kipling, I would have stood you an invitation long ago."

"It's Kip among friends," Tim amiably corrected whilst dodging the daggers Hiero shot in his direction.

"And you must call me Val." His smile never dimming, he considered them both. "In truth I was wondering when you'd come knocking, Bash. Millie and I even have a wager going."

"I do concede that it was an inevitability. If you've any light to shed on this dark business…"

Vandenberg's eyes made a quick sweep of their surroundings. "Don't know that I'd color it in such hues, sir. A few trinkets taken. No one killed or injured. An inconvenience, surely, but nothing more."

"Then you don't care to see the thieves brought to justice?" Tim asked.

"Certainly they must be. But I hardly think extraordinary precautions are required."

"Is that why you refused to let Lord Blackwood protect your fang?"

A hint of menace enlivened Vandenberg's glittering gaze. "One of the reasons, yes."

Tim nodded. "And you've no fear, as some of the other Society members do, of… spiritual retribution? The message at the last séance was quite explicit."

Vandenberg laughed outright. "The greatest danger to my fellow otherworld explorers and I is the risk of taking the entire enterprise too seriously. Some of them, how shall I say it… expect too much of the outcome."

"I wonder," Hiero queried as delicately as possible, "if the villagers of Scavo would agree?"

Vandenberg took a long, thoughtful sip of his Riesling. "That was, as you say, a dark business. But the real crime was in allowing themselves to get swept up in the myths and folktales of savages. To them, of course, the lions were cursed by their gods. They have to believe that to live in such a place. To survive with such predators all around them. And certainly this pair of beasts did not behave in the expected fashion. Does that mean it is the work of the devil? They were animals. They were hunting, not playing the violin."

"And yet you stayed?"

"Of course I stayed! Their spears and arrows would never have saved them. And..." He dropped his voice to lure them in. "It was the most glorious hunt I will ever know. How could I not try to bring down such prizes?"

Tim took a long drag on his cigarette, hoping the smoke would char away some of the foul taste in his mouth. He had encountered men far more ruthless and uncaring than Vandenberg before; when one did the work of financiers and governments, one became accustomed to sangfroid. He could only pray Hiero didn't give the game away. He looked as if he'd been punched in the gut.

"Sensible," Tim eventually replied. "What are your thoughts on who might be committing these crimes? Surely you have a theory."

Vandenberg quirked a smile, glanced at Hiero. "You are the glove and he is the brick. Is that it?"

"Rather Mr. Kipling is the newest addition to my team of hobbyists. I am currently testing how he does in the field. What's your estimation?"

"He's impressed me so far. His methods are a bit obvious to those who are used to playing predator, but they are effective nonetheless. He's slowly and methodically backing me into a corner I won't be able to escape without answering a critical question."

"And that would be?"

"What do I know of the activities of one Stephen Tiquin, Earl Blackwood?" He turned back to Tim, his smile as wide and glinting as a great white's. "Is that not so?"

It was Tim's turn to chuckle. "You've found me out."

"And yet you would have your answer."

"I would."

For the first time that evening, Vandenberg's face took on a severe cast. "There are many who fear Stephen, but I do not. I have no secrets, you see, and he is something of a collector. In times of strife, the weak flock to the powerful. And he is not without compassion, at least at first. But it comes at a price. Few are powerful enough in their own right not to pay it, even among our peers. As to this affair of the fangs..." He shrugged. "It isn't like him. Too loud. Too public. Stephen is a man of precision. If you cross him, he will use quiet and cunning to have his pound of flesh."

Tim was preoccupied with absorbing all that had been said, when Hiero asked, "Has he any weaknesses?"

Vandenberg's smile turned wicked. "Only one. Lady Stang-Helion."

Chapter 10

"To Berkeley Square, Angus, and quick about it."

Hiero felt something akin to the leonine hunger with which the Scavo cats must have hunted the villagers as he watched Kip mount the carriage steps. The anemic glow of the streetlamps provided just enough shadow to contour his taut buttocks, an effect further enhanced by the tight cut of his trousers. For hours he had waited—as they attended the play, as they interviewed their witness, as they bantered about art and sport until Hiero wanted to slam Kip down on the nearest settee and fellate him in full view of Brooks' membership.

He had not, but only just. For one whose modus operandi was causing a scene, Hiero was surprisingly out of his element when it came to the delicate push-pull of gaining information from a source. Part of that—Kip had that very night taught him—was lingering after the formal interview. The subject, having divulged at least some of his secrets, might drop a few more once the topic turned to less weighty matters. No doubt Kip had gleaned some from Vandenberg. Hiero had been too preoccupied with imagining the ways in which he would unravel him. How he would strip him of that magnificent suit piece by piece until Kip quaked with—

"The more the evidence disproves Blackwood's involvement, the more reluctant I become to trust it. What do you think?"

"Hmm?" Hiero had been thinking how remarkable it was that he could desire someone so unremarkable with such ferocity, but even he knew that didn't fit the question. "Oh, whatever you think, dear Kip."

"You have no opinion? Suspicions? Interest?"

"I believe I've made my interest plain." Hiero leapt over to Kip's side of the carriage and insinuated himself between the door and his person. He traced a finger down the row of buttons on Kip's shirt, flicking open the two that bound his waistcoat. He rested his hand on that ridged abdomen, roused by how it undulated with Kip's every breath, which had quickened deliciously.

"H-had you heard any rumors about B-Blackwood and Lady S-Stang-Helion?" Kip shut his eyes as if steeling himself against a blow but also reclined his head back, exposing the cords of his neck. Hiero's tongue grew heavy in his mouth.

"That is more Calliope's domain. You must ask her. Tomorrow."

Hiero watched him swallow hard, the bob of his Adam's apple testing his patience.

"Where shall we go?"

"Wherever you'll feel the most at ease."

Kip barked a laugh between gasps of breath. "I doubt there's a place in all the world where I'd feel safe doing..." A nudge against his little finger alerted Hiero to the rapid advancement of Kip's arousal. He leaned in, plucked at his tie with his teeth, anything to liberate that sleek slope of neck. "Part of the fun, I suppose."

"Mmm."

Hiero rose, Kip's tie between his teeth, to meet eyes the dark green of northern pines. He dropped it to claim his lips, slender but ardent, which Kip opened to him in ways he wouldn't have but scant hours ago. Kip canted his legs to invite his body in until they were chest to chest, thigh to thigh, tongue to questing tongue. They kissed as if they needed to conserve air, with an urgency and aggression that startled Hiero. Too well he now pictured Kip's early years fumbling in the shadowed corners of theater boxes or the rain-slicked alleys of Soho. How his older patrons overwhelmed him with sensation, made him a feral, desperate thing, ready to submit to any indignity in satisfaction's name. They had taught him to coil himself tight as his desire mounted, waiting for his partner to snip free his orgasm. It would take a lover of means to make him crave a slow winding up, a patient and thorough unraveling.

In time Hiero could be that lover. For now he would begin with a quick anatomy lesson.

"What do you want?" Hiero growled into his ear before darting down to maul his neck. "My hand, my mouth, or my prick?"

Kip's grind and moan answered, lacking somewhat in specifics.

"What's that, hmm?" Hiero laved the little dip at his collar, held Kip's torso as he arched toward him.

"I owe you…"

"Oh, I'll exact a fitting payment, never fear."

Kip twined his fingers in Hiero's hair, pulled his head up for another breathless embrace.

"Your prick," he panted upon release, falling to his knees and extending himself out along the seat. The member in question swelled to an aching hardness at Kip's beckoning. Hiero loosened the placket of his trousers lest he burst through it. He had played possum to many a suitor before the night Apollo begged him to "part my arse like a ship's prow," but seeing Kip so trusting, so graceful, so alluring in his passive pose, was proof Hiero hadn't been made for it like him.

Kip spooked when they sensed the carriage slow. Hiero stilled him with a touch, then rapped on the roof.

"The scenic route, if you would, Angus!"

Grateful the dense wood muffled the driver's response, Hiero pet Kip as he would a nervy stallion, from his unruly mane to his meaty buttocks. With stroke after stroke, he soothed him, sneaking in an extra squeeze or grope on each turn until Kip attempted to maneuver a hand between his legs. His thoroughbred properly stoked and his own desire chomping at the bit, Hiero knew it was time to start the race.

He grappled with Kip's jacket as he tugged it down and off his arms, the better to dig out his shirttails to expose that lust-flushed back. Kip's hands joined with his as they disposed of his trousers, commanding his wrists until Hiero palmed that massive, ready cock. A few tempering jerks were all Kip sought, his grunt of relief swallowed by the seat cushions. Hiero lingered there awhile, marveling anew at his length and girth until a trickle of seed warned him to make haste.

"How long?" he asked, shedding his jacket.

"An eternity."

They chuckled together. Kip reached back to seize his hand. Hiero did him one better, pressing his shaft into that sweat-slick crease. His heated breaths tickled Kip's nape as he stretched his body over his sculpted back. Rocking his hips gently, almost languidly, a hiss from Kip had Hiero scrabbling for the oil he kept in a secret compartment under the seat. Kip vibrated with laughter at the sight of it. Hiero took advantage of this mirthful interlude to work him open, a daub of oil, a finger, two, until they were both gasping, growling, ravenous things. Until his dogged, dependable Kip cursed a blue streak and demanded to be fucked.

Hiero obliged. As he pushed into Kip's scorching-tight channel, as that beautiful, sensual grip enclosed him, as he attuned himself to his every twitch of resistance and droop of relaxation, the last sweet and terrible bind Apollo held around his heart snapped. For it had been years since *he* had done this. While part of him listened attentively to Kip's every grunt and moan, echoes invaded his mind of Apollo's whimpers as his disease-ravaged body bore Hiero's tender ministrations one last time. He measured his thrusts as he had then, his grip loose on hips far more solid than Apollo's skeletal form. The flesh beneath his fingers now pink and freckled, then parchment white and spotted with bed sores. If only Hiero could have given him a send-off akin to the welcome to which he was now treating Kip. Near the end Apollo was too frail, a wraith of the man who once dropped trou in the middle of The Gaiety's backstage to prove his aged body still had its allures.

Hiero grimaced against the emotion pricking at the back of his eyes and throat, bowed his head as he penetrated to Kip's molten core. Perhaps he should have invited Miss Nightingale to this little erotic séance. Apparently he had his share of ghosts to exorcise.

"All right?" Kip panted, craning around as best he could despite the primal need that must still be burning through him. The pricking turned to stabbing when Kip cupped his face.

"Mmm. Quite." Hiero still couldn't open his eyes, couldn't bear the sympathy that paled the rut-red from his cheeks.

"Old wounds?"

"Something like."

"Should we stop?"

Hiero took a deep, cleansing breath, nuzzled into his consoling palm. After a final thought for the past, he dared a look at his present: a troubled but giving man, an adventure unlike any he'd ever known, a tryst that—before it turned maudlin—blazed like an effigy on Guy Fawkes night.

He stole a quick kiss, then shoved him back down. "Never."

Kip chuckled, nudging Hiero back into action with interior muscles that gave his flagging erection a stiffening jolt. In answer he took hold of those firm buttocks and improved his angle, hammering at Kip's gland with such acuity he nearly saw stars. Double-fisting the seat cushion, Kip bit down to stifle his ecstatic cries.

Hiero never had a lover devote himself so completely to their mutual pleasure. Kip submitted in name only; with every pinch and flex of his channel, every writhe of his sinuous back, every parry to his thrusts, Kip empowered their connection until Hiero blissfully and utterly gave himself over to him. When finally their raw, keening dance reached its crescendo, Kip stammered a half-meant endearment and came with a shout. Hiero rammed himself into that climactic clench and found his own end, laughing as a heady, golden feeling suffused him. Heavy and giddy and altogether too adoring, he stayed within Kip as long as he could, wrapping his arms around his torso and burying his face in his neck until only the scent of their sex fed his still-grieving brain.

Hiero knew he did not have to let his memories of Apollo go to have Kip, but the possibility comforted him all the same. Kip twined their hands over his chest, conveying more in that simple gesture than any words could.

"You're a prince," Hiero whispered, pressing a solemn kiss between his shoulder blades. Kip made a drowsy sound of contentment.

The door wrenched open, and a dark figure swooped inside. Good thing it was only Han.

"You have my word this will not happen every time," Hiero assured Kip, who did his best impression of a turtle recoiling into its own shell. He shot Han a murderous look. "Have decency, man! Avert your eyes!"

But Han had already set to counting the fibers in the curtain tassel. "Is that what you call tupping in a carriage? Decent?"

"I do. If we cared to be indecent, we would have done it on the steps of Buckingham Palace and given Her Majesty a better show than the one we attended."

"I should have known what delayed you."

"Why?" Kip had found his voice but struggled with his shirt. Hiero batted away his trembling hands and set about righting him. He received a small but grateful smile for his trouble and almost lost himself anew in the desire to kiss it wide again. It was a relief to know they weren't done with each other, that these interruptions hadn't yet scared Kip off. One of the advantages of seducing a man with little left to lose. "Has something happened?"

"I'd say. There's a man parked outside the house. Long black coat, silver buttons. Hat shaped like a... *liúlián.*"

"A durian," Hiero translated.

"A what?"

"A fruit with a shell. Round. Delicious."

Kip snorted. "Are we having it for tea or trying to identify this mystery man? Do you think it's one of Blackwood's thugs, Mr. Han?"

"Perhaps." Han's face betrayed exactly what he thought of Kip's prickly attitude.

Hiero hastened to translate yet again. "What he means is it's a policeman. Whether one in league with Blackwood or..."

Kip nodded, grim-faced. "He hasn't moved? Hasn't tried to enter the house?"

"No. Miss Pankhurst thinks it's nothing, that if they had wanted to attack us, they would have done so. I disagree."

Hiero sniggered, got a pair of hard looks for his trouble. "Waiting for me, no doubt, before they invade. If they mean to invade. In your experience, dear Kip, do villains and other dubious sorts usually advertise their nefarious schemes before they commit them?"

His palpable relief at the realization lifted a weight off Hiero's shoulders, one he hadn't even known was there.

"No, they don't. It's a message, but from whom? Is there anyone who hasn't warned us off who might feel the need to? Or who has and might care to emphasize the point?"

"Perhaps your bosses are simply checking up on their investment," Han remarked, sharp as a knifepoint. "You've produced few results so far."

"Han!" Hiero objected, but Kip waved him off.

"I take your meaning. It's past due I make my report, at any rate, and a visit to the station would not go amiss given the activities of Blackwood's police associates."

"You mean henchmen," Han insisted. "Bought and sold as easily as your superiors."

"I mean men who are not of the rank and quality found at Scotland Yard. There's a conspiracy here, I grant you. But until I have proof it goes as high as we suspect, I'll not blacken the reputation of a fellow officer."

Han huffed. "If only to save your own skin."

"I'm well beyond saving. You've just seen proof of that." His gaze, full of more than either of them could express in present company, fell on Hero. "I'll catch the omnibus."

"You will not!"

"I must. We can't chance my being seen returning home with you, no matter what general has set a sentry outside your door. My injuries are no longer reason enough to delay."

"I'll have your doctor claim you're still recovering."

"And they'll believe the evidence of their own eyes. Not to mention the hundreds who saw me at the theater."

"You'll not sleep in that hovel." *Instead of my bed,* Hiero did not add.

"It's a room like any other."

"What if there is an attack?" Hiero blustered, not convincing even himself, but not willing to concede. "Who will protect you? We should stay together. Strength in numbers and all that."

"I'm not an invalid, no matter what your doctor is prepared to claim. I'll consider decamping for the night if someone awaits, but to my club."

"The policemen's sporting club? Hardly reassuring."

"You may accuse the Met of various and sundry crimes, but they tend not to murder their own in one of their private establishments."

"You've yet to convince me I should let you leave that seat, let alone the carriage."

"It's rather good, then, that you have no choice in the matter." Kip glared in Han's direction to ward him off, then gathered Hiero into intimate proximity. "I've had the most unforgettable evening, my dear Mr. Bash. I do hope we might... take in a bit of theater again once this black business is behind us."

"You have my word as a gentleman."

Kip chuckled. "That promise would bear more weight if you were a gentleman."

Hiero's lips twisted into a reluctant smile. "You know me too well."

"Not yet. But I will. That's a promise."

With that he slipped out into a night full of lurking shadows and a long, sleepless wait till morn.

Hiero searched after him for a time, then turned his gaze inward. The workings of his mind were, at their best, akin to the cogs of a watch that had been soaked in syrup, smashed by a toddler, and shot into the sea. He now wrestled to enforce some form of order and found himself being repeatedly slammed down on the mat. With Kip around, everything had become so much clearer: what he lived for, what he strived for. Without him his brain took back its place on the merry-go-round of spectacle and sensation.

"Why him?" Han appeared genuinely curious in that older-brother way of his.

Hiero wanted to perform an elaborate series of gestures designed to bedazzle and distract, but his longtime friend knew all of his tricks. Besides, it didn't pay to evade the one person he could be honest with. If only the truth of the matter wasn't eluding *him*.

"I can't say for certain."

"He's no Apollo."

"Of course not! Why would you say such a thing?"

"It bears saying. As it bears repeating: he may be at this very moment betraying us to our enemies."

"Don't be absurd."

"What is it Erskine always said? 'The best magicians never think themselves—'"

"'—above being tricked.' I'm aware." Hiero pinched the bridge of his nose. He and Kip should have been sneaking into the townhouse through the back entrance, tiptoeing up the servants' staircase with hands linked before bursting into Hiero's room and collapsing on the bed. Or Hiero atop Kip atop his bed, both raring for a second tangle. Curse his enemies for stealing away his first night of leisure in two long years. "How do you know I'm not the one doing the deceiving, luring him in to learn the last of his secrets?"

"Have you learned any?"

"Some. Personal anecdotes and the like. I believe I've earned his trust."

"And has he earned yours?"

Hiero regarded him for some time before he spoke. "We both know that I don't trust anyone."

Han nodded, mollified if not pleased. "At least you have not forgotten Erskine's most important lesson."

Tim dodged overcurious looks and too-long glances at his finery as he ambled through the far-from-deserted streets of Pimlico. Unsteady on his feet and moony eyed after his intoxicating interlude with Hiero, he couldn't quite bring himself to worry about the stranger darkening his lover's doorstep. Han, after all, was a formidable fighter, and he doubted their enemy would attack the household. If the maneuver was meant to inspire fear, he would not succumb to it. Not when his head bobbed along like a child's balloon tethered to a string, his muscles ached from vigorous use, and in the deep recesses of his heart shimmered a rosy-fingered dawn.

Yet the closer he got to his rooming house, the more the reality of the situation threatened to cloud his sunny view. Tim may have been dressed like a lord, but there was no elderly lover waiting to gift him a fortune before he shuffled off this mortal coil, which was how—he suspected—Hiero had come up in the world so swiftly.

Theirs could never be more than a forbidden affair, not the privately fervent, publicly amicable companionship Tim now realized was necessary to the harmony of his very soul. To say nothing of that fact he was still required to deliver the truth of Hiero's identity to his superiors, a fatted calf to be butchered on the altar of their greed. And he the human sacrifice to appease the gods of high government.

No matter how many times Tim erased these dark thoughts, their inky tendrils would bleed through the parchment of his mind, staining him with doubt, with despair. Their task was so great and their resources so paltry. Did he take Hiero at his word, or were his intimate attentions just another form of confidence scheme? Could the man who rode his body into the heavens truly fall so low as to report him to his superiors? Would he be, in the end, a lone voice shouting in the wilderness?

Whilst zipping around the final corner, Tim startled out of this bleak reverie. There on his doorstep lounged DS Abraham Small, a pile of ash by his boots and a toothy glint to his smirk. He smoked with his fist coiled around his cigar, chomping at the end as he sucked in gray fumes. He leapt to his feet and blew into the air, a train's stack come to life.

"Well, if it ain't Mr. Timothy Kipling in his Sunday best." Small had nearly a foot on him and used it to his advantage. Even several paces away, Tim still had to look up at him. "What business might you have with DI Stoker, I wonder? He lives here, don't you know? Though come to think of it, he ain't been seen for a few days."

Tim had always thought the best defense against such teasing was stillness and silence. He straightened his stance, crossed his arms, and waited Small out, his face the picture of patience save for one quirked eyebrow. If Small had been planning to attack him, he wouldn't have made himself known. Inwardly Tim struggled to cool his curiosity, which, fuelled by drink and the dregs of afterglow, fired hot. No doubt the officer monitoring Hiero's house was none other than DC Silas Croke, which quieted the last of his worries. No one that pudgy and priggish would get the better of Mr. Han.

"Funny we're investigating the same crimes, but yours leads you to the opera house. Though I bet under all that finery, those toffs are no better than the crooks we collar."

"I couldn't say. Though I dare say Lord Blackwood has an opinion or two on the matter. Why don't you be a good lad, peek out of his pocket, and ask him?"

"Don't you thumb your nose at me. Last I checked, we're on the same side."

While every nerve in his body screeched in outrage, Tim smirked. "Officially."

Small scoffed. "Thanks I get for coming to check if you're still with us."

"With whom, exactly, would that be?"

"The living." Small swaggered toward him, hips loose but silver eyes menacing as he scrutinized Tim's face. "Must have tarted you up with enough powder to choke a whore to cover all them bruises."

Tim held firm under his examination, the "stillness" half of his mantra playing on a background loop in his mind. At the forefront a knotty tangle of intuitions and impressions regarding DS Small. His sinister birdlike looks and his obedience to Blackwood had seen him cast as a villain in the various pantomimes of the crime Tim regularly played out for himself. But the possibility remained Small had been lured into his current position whilst visions of promotions and headlines danced through his ambitious head. Much like Tim before him, he wouldn't have been able to refuse a direct order, even if he somehow predicted the outcome of his assignment to Blackwood. Such powers of divination were the bread and butter of mediums like Miss Nightingale, but not milquetoast talents like Small. Throw in a ramshackle background, a street-smart education, perhaps even a wife and a few nippers to support... Small hardly needed a tragic flaw to explain his motivation.

Which didn't mean Tim had to like him.

"Why are you here, DS Small? And which of your masters are you serving at present?"

"Only one man who rules this roost, and you'd do well to remember it." Small craned his head to glare at Tim from on high. It was like being stared down by the crow atop a weathervane. "In the—what's it called?—melee the other night, someone broke into the boss' safe. Left the cash, left the cartridges. Didn't even blink at the big-ticket items. Know what that boodler nabbed?"

"I'm ninety percent certain you're going to tell me."

"A red book, totally worthless. No value to anyone save the boss." Tim feigned disinterest, met his eagle-eyed look with one of indulgence. Channeled a bit of Hieronymus Bash for good measure. "You wouldn't happen to know where it scarpered off to, eh? Not seen it on the desk of London's first consulting detective, have you?"

Tim didn't have to force out his laugh. "Bash isn't exactly the book-reading type."

"Take your word for it. But you are, ain't you, Stoker? That's how you got your nose so far up Quayle's ass, innit?"

The accusation relieved Tim. Small didn't exactly have his ear to the ground when it came to Yard politics. He saw their encounter for what it was: a roustabout.

"And what do I stand to gain from stealing from Lord Blackwood?"

"Depends on what's in the book, don't it?"

Tim bit his lip to keep himself from smiling. "I hardly see how that matters. My orders are to discredit Bash and find the thieves. Last I checked, Lord Blackwood had hidden the third fang in a very secure location. That hardly points to his guilt. Not to mention that he's one of the victims of the crimes."

"That's the thing, though, ain't it, Stoker? You never know who's telling the truth. Only one thing you can trust as a detective, ain't there?"

"Instinct?"

Small's grin revealed thin, incisive teeth. "Exactly. And mine tells me you've got something to hide."

"Don't we all, DS Small? Isn't that why we do what we do? Investigate other people's lives so that no one looks too closely at our own?"

Tim saw at once he'd rattled him. Small's stare intensified, boring into Tim's eyes, a pickaxe mining for a shard of rare diamond.

"Answer the question. Do you have the book?"

"I don't." Not a lie, exactly, as he had turned it over to Miss Pankhurst for safekeeping.

"Do you know who does?"

Trickier, this. He summoned the Bashian Muse. "No."

Whatever wild gods he'd called down in that instant must have favored him because Small finally backed away a step with the air of a man burdened by far more earthly forces. Tim empathized only too well with his position, stuck between the pillars of law and the bedrock of their society: the wills and whims of the aristocracy. But neither would Tim take on any extra burdens. Small's problems may not have been entirely of his own making, but they were his and his alone.

"If you happen across it," Small all but snarled, "send word. If you know what's good for you."

"I will."

"The boss has his eye on you, DI Stoker. Keeps saying he could use a man with your... talents. Think about that while you're out there working for Queen and country."

"I can promise you, DS Small, that the thought will never be far from mind," Tim replied, clear and calm over the hammering of his heart, the terror-shriek ringing in his ears.

"See that it's not." With that Small turned on his heel and strolled down the street, casual as you like.

Once he was out of sight, Tim hobbled over to the door to his lodging house and collapsed inside. In a blind panic, he raced up the stairs, knifed the key into his lock, then broke into his rooms with the stealth of a prowler. When satisfied no further threat lurked, he bolted the door and sagged back against it. The weight of his theories, connections, conjectures nearly crushed him; he felt like a boulder teetering on the edge of a cliff, where the slightest whiff of conviction might send it crashing down.

The most imminent threat: Small might at this very moment be rallying Blackwood's henchmen against Hiero. He believed Tim when he said *he* hadn't seen the notebook, but that didn't mean it wasn't in Bash's possession, the why of it notwithstanding. A search of the townhouse would be the only way to know for certain, and it might serve the dual effect of dismantling their investigation. But would Blackwood sanction such a maneuver against a fellow nobleman, even one he disliked? How much of the Met did Blackwood have in his pocket? How intimidated was he by Bash's influence? They simply didn't know enough. The intangibles of the thing drove Tim mad.

More maddening still was the realization he could not warn Hiero or run off to help them. If Tim revealed his suspicion of Small's intentions in any way, it would alert a tyrannical enemy to the fact of his betrayal as well as risk the revelation of his identity. To say nothing of the ruination of his career, his chance of solving the case, every goal he had ever set for himself... His only choice was to trust Hiero could protect himself. At least that option, unlike everything else, was supported by tangible evidence.

Over and over Tim replayed the final moments of the night of Hobbs's murder, searching for the tiniest scrap of insight into Small's intentions. Could Small and Croke have been watching them the whole time? Surely the dense fog precluded that. They also would have intervened before Hiero's party reached the lions in order to shield Blackwood from an accusation of murder. But if they hadn't seen him, Hiero, and Callie enter, then how did they later see the gang of thugs? What brought them to the warehouse? Happy coincidence?

Another notion niggled at Tim's brain. When had Blackwood discovered his notebook was stolen? And was it Blackwood himself who made the discovery, or did others have access to the safe? How did Small's suspicions fall on them when the gang of thugs was also in play and a far more likely culprit? The warehouse stood unguarded most of the time. Surely the notebook could have gone missing at any time. Undoubtedly Small was exploring all his options, but perhaps there was another agenda at work here, one Tim couldn't yet see.

Riled and restless, Tim worked through the problem, as well as all the options available to him, for several minutes. All galled, none satisfied. And none blighted out the memory of that pantherlike body pinning him to the seat, of mustache-prickled lips that nipped and licked at his neck, of hands that clutched and cradled him. Of a house and a life that had been open to him from the start; him, the wolf in sheep's clothing. Of a little girl with almond eyes giggling as her Uncle Hiero tossed her, over and again, into the air.

Resolved, Tim found his legs again. He would go to Hiero, alert him to the threat of Small and his makeshift army, make good the kindness that had been lavished upon him. He scoured his rooms, focusing the cyclone of his mind into one singular, devastating force. He reminded himself it was nothing more than another puzzle to solve: how to stage the room so no one knew he'd left, how to escape the building without detection, how to reach Berkeley Square as quickly as possible, how to sneak into Hiero's townhouse without being spotted by Small's network of spies.

If they did invade, they would discover him there. It was a risk he would have to take, if only in service to his conscience.

Chapter 11

*H*iero curled into his favorite armchair as if into the arms of a long-absent lover, seeking a form of comfort it could not give. Already their tussle in the carriage felt not like the summit of togetherness toward which they'd been climbing, but the high that preceded a precipitous fall. He'd been flailing ever since to recover after Kip's sudden departure, to silence Han's unspoken but obvious misgivings as they sped back home, to catch up with Callie's efforts to pack the servants off to their Devonshire hunting lodge. To find a way to confront the turnip of a man still planted in front of their home, rifle sprouting from his left shoulder.

He shut his eyes, counted in time with every pulse of pain chipping at his skull. The old fear, the one he hadn't suffered in years, paralyzed him now, clamping around his wrists and constricting his back. A cinching belt around his neck; the crush of arms across his chest; the bite of the metal on his cock and balls. The insect buzz of all those eyes watching, evaluating, shaming. Swarming around him, suffocating him.

The clink of the glass Callie deposited on the side table broke the spell. He grabbed the tumbler, drank greedily, liquid courage searing down his throat and pouring heat into his roiling gut. She perched herself on the edge of the accompanying seat, still in her evening dress but having discarded her wig in the midst of the tumult. Her short, matted black hair licked at the lobes of her ears, stealing years, if not the worry lines, from her young face.

He'd only that day discovered she and Han had purchased the adjoining house last fall, in whose cellar hid a secret door to the underground river. A second carriage house a few blocks over, with another convenient underground passage, had also been secured in the event they required a means of discreet escape. While Hiero was grateful someone had prepared for this eventuality and the servants had absconded without threat to their safety, he felt a goodly dose of unwarranted outrage.

If Callie and Han had been able to predict there would eventually be danger to their household, why had they not included him in their plans to protect against it? Had he become so superfluous to their concerns—or worse, such an anvil around their necks—that they didn't feel the need to warn him of the consequences of their actions? Hiero acknowledged he at times behaved in a reckless, if not downright foolhardy manner as regarded his personal well-being. Perhaps he had never considered the consequences to those around him before now? And if that was the case... Why?

The door clanged open, and Kip raced in, Han but a few strides behind him. Hiero's concerns, if not his persistent headache, evaporated like a mist.

"You're here! Excellent. Callie has done us the great service of dismissing the servants, and she and Han are sure to keep a weather eye whilst we—"

"They're coming." Kip bypassed Hiero to stand before the hearth and address the room. "That is someone, or a gang of someones, may be on their way at this very moment. I've no idea what sort of arsenal they might bring with them, but we must away."

"How can you be sure?" Callie asked as Han moved to the street-facing window and peered around the edge of the curtain.

"I encountered DS Small on my front stoop when I arrived at my lodgings, on the hunt for Blackwood's notebook."

Callie nodded. "It was only a matter of time before they discovered it missing. But surely you gave him reassurances?"

"I did."

"Did he believe them?" This from Han, who had rejoined them. "It's Croke. I should have known him before, but he's so... forgettable."

"I cannot say. My powers of evasion are not the equal of some." His verdant eyes sought Hiero out, half-bashful, half-imploring.

Callie sighed. "You shouldn't have come. If they discover you here, you'll have broken faith with them."

"I know."

"He thought it worth the risk." Hiero thrilled at the sprigs of color that bloomed on Kip's cheeks. "The question is... do we?"

"How do you mean?"

"If we flee," Han explained, "we all but confirm to them that we have the notebook. The question becomes if we are investigating the thefts and not Blackwood, why did we take it?"

Callie turned to Kip. "Why did you take it?" She held a hand up to Hiero when he made to protest. "I don't mean to accuse you; I would have done the same."

"It's written in code. We hadn't discounted Blackwood at the time."

"We still haven't," Han reminded them.

"Precisely."

"But you must see the problem from their perspective," Callie pursued. "If you, Mr. Kipling, are looking out for Blackwood's interests, and you come across a notebook in cipher—you, a detective renowned for dealing with such crimes... Why do you take it?"

Hiero grunted. "One of us might have recognized it for what it was."

"I would not have. It looks to my eyes like a normal ledger," Callie said.

"All the more reason we must crack its code," Kip insisted. "But first I must assure your safety. Is there no place to where you might decamp for the duration?"

"The duration of what?" Callie demanded. "Today? Tomorrow? The night of the séance? Another week? Until the case is resolved?" She exhaled a long, tortured breath. "I'm afraid I agree with Han. If we leave, it all but confirms our guilt."

"To say nothing of the other valuables here that cannot be so easily moved," Han put in.

"But if they come…" Kip insisted.

"Let them come." Even Hiero felt the stab of her icicle eyes as Callie stared them down each in turn. "They will find no notebook here."

Hiero considered, then reconsidered, then considered her words again. After several beats, he remained confused. "What do you mean?"

"Mr. Stoker, you say DS Small was satisfied that you did not have the notebook in your possession? Very well. It shall return to your lodgings with you."

To Hiero's astonishment, Kip appeared impressed by this plan. "Of course. But not to my lodgings, to the Yard. My Superintendant reserved one of the evidence safes for my investigation. I learned how to change the lock code, just in case."

Hiero should have been impressed by this bit of devilry but felt despondent.

"Lord Blackwood isn't the only one who can hide things in plain sight," Callie complimented.

"I'll continue my work there," Kip added. "I'm more certain than ever that the key to all of this is in that book."

Visions of enclosing them in his boudoir while his friends stood vigil faded before Hiero's unwitting eyes. "But you mustn't—" He appealed to Kip, but to no avail. He turned to Callie. "He won't be—" In desperation now he reached pleading hands out to Han. "You can't allow—"

"You'll brief us tomorrow, Kipling, after checking in with your guv," Han instructed.

"I will."

"Good."

"Do send word if anyone invades. I'll do my best for you, if it comes to that."

"Yours will be the first name off our lips," Callie confirmed. "Your real name, that is."

"I'll consider myself warned."

After a final peek through the curtain, Han gestured toward the door. All this was enacted before Hiero like a shadow play on a cave wall, in another reality he could not comprehend.

"You've only just come," he insisted, launching out of his chair. On cue Callie escaped to fetch the notebook, and Han slipped into the hall. "You're a terrible tease, you know."

"It's one of my better qualities."

"I've half a mind to toss you out myself."

"A pity, then, that I'm leaving of my own accord. I do enjoy the occasional vigorous show of force."

Hiero permitted himself a smirk. "You're hardly a shrinking violet. It does flatter a man when someone comes running to his rescue."

"I suppose I shouldn't spoil the effect by admitting it was the servants I hoped to save…"

Hiero paused, pinned him in place with his eyes. "Only the servants?"

Once upon a time, his Kip would have flushed crimson. Now he took a few measured steps toward Hiero. "I suppose not. There's Miss Pankhurst to consider, of course, and Mr. Han."

"Both innately capable of caring for themselves."

"So I've observed." He stopped, leaving an indecent amount of space between them, and seemed to watch Hiero's chest rise and fall for a time before glancing upward. His face—so undistinctive, so regular—opened as he turned toward him, pale as a moon flower. The budding emotion Hiero perceived there thrilled and terrified him. "And what of you? Who cares for you when there aren't wolves at the door?"

A pounding fist on the front door shocked them both apart. Kip raced to the window, peeked out, cursed. Han's black silhouette filled the door, a scrap of red under his arm, ordering Kip out with a curt gesture. Before Hiero knew what he was about, a hand gripped his own, squeezed, then slipped away. Han ushered Kip into the bowels of the house—his house, his fortress, his hideaway, its walls veritably papered with secrets—whilst Hiero stood, paralyzed anew before the fire.

Every strike to the metal door resounded in his head like a knell. He heard again the wails and shrieks of those around him, smelt again the reek of blood and piss and human filth. Felt the belt buckle dig under his chin, the straps chafe his wrists, the vise prick into the center of his brow. All the sterling and gold in the world wouldn't keep them from sending him back if they found him. He had been what they had accused him of being—too bold, too frivolous—his fame and fortune no sturdier than a house of cards.

The wolves had come to blow the house down.

The cock of a rifle brought him back to himself. Hiero took quiet inventory, unsure what strange alchemy of events had twice now ensorcelled him with the bleakest moment of his past, but unwilling to delve further. He upended his glass into his mouth, joggling free the last few drops of scotch, then inhaled a deep, revivifying breath. As he turned toward the exit, Hiero realized the throb in his head no longer echoed the bangs on the front door.

Silence emanated from the hall. On tiptoes, he inched toward the frame and cautiously peered around its edge.

Poised like Artemis before a wild boar, Callie pointed her rifle at DC Croke's porcine snout. His sneer slowly disintegrated as the gun's barrel drew nearer until she had backed him out onto the stoop. Hiero hurried to her side, but she had no need of him, carefully shifting her aim to target any one of the five thugs collected around Croke, a sounder no match for his goddess of the hunt. He felt more than saw Han fall in behind them, the whisper of his twin blades as they bisected the air tickling Hiero's ears. Since his own stare lacked menace, he crossed his arms to keep from waffling and affected a smug grin.

"State your business," a re-bewigged Callie demanded, aiming for Croke's cavernous nostrils.

"Now, Mistress, we have no quarrel with you—"

"You have no quarrel with any member of this house. We have broken no laws, committed no crime. You have no cause to enter without permission, a privilege I will not grant you."

"Now see here—"

"What I see, Detective Constable, is a group of men attempting to enter my home without warrant. As a subject of this great kingdom, I am permitted to defend myself in such circumstances."

"Not against the police," one of the thugs chipped in.

"Can you produce evidence that you are acting on orders from your superiors at the division house? If so, show it, or fetch them here to explain themselves. You will not step a foot in otherwise." Before Croke could squeal out a retort, she added, "Are these men all officers of the law? If so, let me see your badges."

Croke huffed out a breath, pushed his way over the threshold, calling her bluff as she had called his. Callie punted to the right and blasted off a round, exploding the head of a sculpture at the end of the walkway behind them. Croke stepped back out again.

"Give us what we want, and we'll leave you be," Croke rallied after another lengthy standoff. He nodded at Hiero. "He knows what we're after."

"A right bollocking and a stay in the clink?" Hiero guessed in his best south-of-the-river accent. "Mr. Han, would you be so good as to send our boy out with notes to Mr. Charles at the *Times*, Mr.

Hawk at the *Sun,* and Mr. Chambers at the *Standard.* Tell them we've solved the mystery of the home invaders. The police themselves are involved. *Quelle scandale!"*

Croke went so white he might as well have blabbed it all himself.

Hiero continued, "We've told your little friend, and now we're telling you—"

"And we don't care to repeat ourselves," Callie warned.

"Precisely, my dear girl." Hiero narrowed his eyes and firmed his mouth, summoning up the Muses for another climactic speech. "We are investigating the theft of the fangs. Your esteemed employer, as one of the victims, is not considered a suspect unless he, through you, continues to provoke us. We have turned our attention elsewhere. Do not goad us into taking a closer look at your—and thus your lordship's—enterprises. If you bother us, or any of our associates, again, you'll force our hand."

"And mine is on the trigger." To underline her point, Callie poked him between the eyes with her muzzle.

Croke and his gang stood their ground, snorting and snuffling like a herd of ornery cattle. Finally he spat on her slipper, then trundled off down the walk. She kept them in her sights until they'd piled into a too-familiar Black Maria and bustled off into the darkness. Hiero slammed the door shut before she'd lowered her gun, grappling with the locks as he fought to steady his shaking hands. With everything secured, at least for a time, he pressed his pulsing forehead into the night-chilled door. Only a scant few hours ago, he'd known bliss for the first time in years. Now he suffered its opposite—true terror—which had been equally elusive since Apollo welcomed him into his home.

A home he was, all things considered, ill-equipped to defend.

"We've caught them out!" Callie whooped with a girlish glee that would have served her poorly minutes earlier. "By the look on his face alone, they must be responsible for the home invasions."

"Which does nothing to further our case," Han objected.

"Perhaps, perhaps not. I do think we can rule Blackwood out as a suspect, even though his list of crimes grows by the day. I wonder what our Mr. Kipling will make of it?"

"I can't imagine he will match your excitement."

She chuckled. "I daresay not." He heard the safety click on her rifle, the familiar sound of her tucking it under the arm. "Though I believe that's enough excitement for one night, even for me. I'm off to bed, Han, unless you care for some company while keeping watch?"

Hiero wished he could scream as loud as the silence that accompanied Han's internal deliberations.

"Take your rest while you can, my lady."

Hiero knew she smiled and stole a kiss from his cheek and mouthed some stern instruction regarding his well-being. He knew he should turn away from the door behind which a million dangers schemed and plotted their downfall, but he could not. They had bluffed their way out of danger twice now; Blackwood and his cronies would not be dissuaded a third time. This little game of theirs had become deadly serious, and he was a jester with a slapstick.

The same two hands that forever lifted him out of harm's way now gripped his shoulders. Hiero let Han steer him back to the warmth and comfort of his study, back to the bottle of spirits that would, as ever, banish the worries that weighted him.

Jab-jab, jab-jab, jab-jab...
Unh-unh, unh-unh, unh-unh...
A = E, B = S, C = Z...

Tim pounded his fists into the leathery hide of the heavy bag. Every slam of his knuckles compounded his injuries from the other night, but he didn't care. The pain helped him order his inner chaos, set his discordant thoughts to an overriding rhythm.

Jab-jab, jab-jab, jab-jab...
Unh-unh, unh-unh, unh-unh...
$A = E, B = S, C = Z...$

With his flesh consumed by his boxing routine and his brain distracted by the previous night's carriage tryst, his higher faculties could make connections without the white noise of his urges and aches. Tim had hit a wall—metaphorically speaking—with the Vigenère cipher. Forced to accept he would not have the notebook decoded in time for the séance at Lady Stang-Helion's that evening, he had escaped to his club awhile to silence the alarm blaring at the back of his mind by running laps until he could barely stagger off the track. The exertion hadn't proved distraction enough, thus his masochistic matchup with the heavy bag.

Jab-jab, jab-jab, jab-jab...
Unh-unh, unh-unh, unh-unh...
$A = E, B = S, C = Z...$

As he fought to maintain his pace, his stance, the minute adjustments various trainers had suggested over the years, Tim loosed his thoughts. They chased down his every theory like hounds on a rabbit hunt, nosing into burrows and darting through brush until they caught a whiff of their prey. He knew he was close, so close to snaring the keyword. If only he could leave his body awhile, let his mind race.

He nearly managed it whilst under Hiero's sensual command, but he was too overwhelmed by his first bedding in years to concentrate. Tim wasn't convinced a second interlude would yield the desired results. He was too raw, too needful, too owned by a plentiful kiss, a generous touch. Even now the bite of each impact, the gnaw at his biceps and upper back, wasn't enough to turn off the echoes of their sex.

Until DS Palmer all but tore him away from the bag, marching him over to the water bucket and shoving the ladle between his lips.

"Easy there, mate. You were swooning. Got some bonny lass keeping you up nights?"

Tim gaped at him, reeling from the fact someone at the Yard had shown concern for his well-being. A junior member of Littlejohn's posse, Palmer routinely snubbed him.

"Something like that."

Palmer gave a knowing nod. "Should have guessed. You've been more skittish than a church mouse lately. The lads thought you'd been given the boot."

"Hoped, more like," Tim muttered to himself.

"What's that?"

"Heavy assignment. Fifty boxes of legal documents to read through in five different languages. I go to them; they don't come to me."

Palmer chuckled. "Say no more! It's a good deal we've got you on the squad, and make no mistake." Tim smirked, wondering if absence truly did make the heart grow fonder, or his fellow officers were just relieved someone else took on the financial cases. "Noticed you've got a kink in your shoulder there. Stooping over a desk all day'll hunchback you right quick. Want me to give it a crack?"

"Maybe next time. Hurts enough as it is."

"I don't doubt." Palmer plucked the ladle out of his grasp, dunked it, then forced another scoop of water on him. "Drink three more of these, then hit the bricks. The guv's sent for you." Tim had sent Superintendent Quayle a predawn note requesting a meeting, but hadn't expected to hear back so soon. "Give the hippos my regards."

"What?"

"You're off to the zoo."

The ladle fell back into the bucket with a loud clank. Little wonder the DS had been kind—he might soon be rid of him. Tim had yet to unravel where in Blackwood's web of influence Quayle was snared. Was he part arachnid like Small and Croke? Cocooned and paralyzed like Lady Stang-Helion? Or did he hover on the outskirts, avoiding those sticky, silken filaments by sending a fine selection of flies his way? Was he simply following the orders of those on high, or had he been recruited? Was this summons a chief calling an errant officer to heel, or that of an eight-legged fiend luring a buzzy newcomer to his death? Would Tim be the latest officer to meet a tragic end at the lion house?

After washing up and dressing, he scrawled off a hasty note to Hiero and set off for the train. The short journey north gave him little time to plan, but the mile-long walk from St. John's Wood Station through the Regent's Park Gardens gave him ample time to prepare. If only he'd had time to consult with his favorite master manipulator. Hiero, no doubt, could wheedle out clues as to Quayle's true allegiance whilst convincing him he hadn't a brain in his skull. His cunning tongue and clever hands worked in ways near mystical—and if Tim wanted to keep what few wits he had about him, he needed to stop thinking about Hiero's more appealing attributes.

Better to question his intent, as any good investigator should. Tim held no illusions as regarded their affair. They burned with the intensity of twin suns, especially when embroiled, but past suitors had whispered many pretty promises to him that, in ecstasy's wake, they had no intention of keeping. Tim had murmured a few of his own, in his greener days. His chemistry with Bash was no more predictable or durable than a streak of luck at the track. Something to be enjoyed when it happened, but not something to bet your savings on.

Hiero was not what he seemed, but not in the way Tim had expected. He championed Bash because, in his own roundabout way, he did good. Their goals, if not their life philosophies, aligned. The only unfortunate consequence was that said goals made enemies of some terrifically powerful people. Time would tell whether Tim's career would be swept away with the tide. But the shelter of Bash's affections certainly made it easier to weather the current storm.

A constable at the zoo gates waved him through while a representative of the Zoological Society made excuses to a group that had travelled up from Greenwich. As Tim strolled along the empty tree-lined road, he conjured his mother's ghost to his side and extended her an arm. Phantom susurrations swirled around him, memories of her encouragements and cajolements as she spirited him toward the squat, gaol-like building around the bend. They had gone to visit the new hippopotamus—Palmer's warning was somewhat prescient in that regard. As he approached the menagerie, the brays, squawks, and roars of the creatures housed there replaced the wisps of her lilting voice.

A live-wire tension coiled within Tim when he entered the vacuous main hall. Colorful signs and decorations hung limp in the static air. Three shadowy tunnels, the yawning mouths of mountain gods, blew their foul, bestial breath at him. The judgment of a thousand invisible eyes fell upon him. Tim consulted the map and chose the left corridor, reverberant with growls. Quayle would be at the lion cages.

Too late he realized he had no proof of Quayle's summons beyond Palmer's word. Small and Croke and their crew might be at that very moment poised to strike, the hare and the tortoise hunting... What was he? A mole? An otter? A beaver, perhaps? Hiero would have known. Tim passed the thylacine hutch, thinking of his lover. Sleek, predatory, with flamboyant stripes—oh, yes. Pity the zoo didn't house any panthers.

But it had acquired one white gorilla. Quayle came into view, hunched in his usual Neanderthal stance as he stared into the lion cage. An area that was missing, if Tim was not mistaken, any actual lions. Had Blackwood added to his pride?

"Stoker." Quayle wasted no time on niceties. "Report."

"I was told you wanted to see me, sir."

"You were told correct. I'll have my say once you have yours. Report."

Wrong-footed from the start, Tim fought to regain his mental balance. He'd wanted to wait Quayle out, get a sense of where he stood from his initial comments. A bit of banter, even. Quayle hadn't given him any tea leaves to read. For the second time in less than a day, the investigation called upon Tim to channel the stalling tactics of one Hieronymus Bash, master of illusion.

"A grim business, this." Tim indicated the cage where PC Hobbs's remains had been left for the police to find—not that Quayle had any clue as to the actual circumstances of the constable's death. "The station must be fired up."

Quayle grunted. "I've had nothing but thunder and brimstone from them for days. Top brass wants it closed sharpish."

"Any leads?"

"Not a one." Quayle moved toward the cage, gripped the bars. "Truth be told, we still can't figure out how he got in there. He was a slight lad, but he wouldn't have fit through. Zoo Society don't exactly leave the key out for any old sod to pinch. Caretakers don't even go in there unless one of the cats is sick. They toss the meat in though the bars."

Tim paused just long enough to allow him to come to the logical conclusion. Even distraught—and make no mistake, the burden of solving the murder had only quieted, not stolen, Quayle's bark—he had a mind like a steel trap. Tim wondered if he simply didn't see it, or didn't want to see it for whatever reason, nefarious or otherwise. Regardless, on this he was duty bound.

"But that's your answer, isn't it?"

Quayle dropped his arms. "Explain."

"They throw the meat in through the bars. There's no evidence of a struggle, no blood on site."

"So they do him, chop him, and pitch him in, piece by piece."

"Like bits of bread at a duck pond. Charnel house version."

Tim suspected Quayle's curt laugh covered a more visceral response.

He absorbed this new information for a moment, then backed away from the cage. "Opens up motive. Could have been anyone, anywhere."

"They'd still have had to break in here at night, take the time to do it. These creatures are precious... but not quiet. I imagine the zoo is well guarded. The clamor alone would have drawn them."

"You got it in one."

"I suppose the men on duty report no unusual disturbances that night?"

"That's what they say. Which is whatever those Society mucks want to hear."

"The same mucks leaning on you to tidy things up?"

"The very same." Quayle let out a sigh that snarled at the end, turned on his heel. "Any more of my cases you wanna solve? Maybe one of the two you've been assigned?"

"Sir..." Tim struggled to interpret Quayle's earlier comment about the powers that controlled them both. He made his resentment plain, but how deep did his allegiance run? Tim didn't stand a chance of knocking out a man like Blackwood if he couldn't shake enough trees to get justice for Hobbs.

"Stop wrinkling your brow and speak plain, Stoker. Bash. Leads. Anything?"

"Yes. Maybe... It's too soon. I've only just gained his trust."

"Tick-tock, Inspector."

"Yes, sir. I know, sir. It's only... we're so close to nabbing whoever stole the fangs. I just need more time to sniff them out."

"Caught the scent, have you?"

"Closing in, I'd say." Tim crossed his fingers. It wasn't a lie if you believed it could be true, was it? "I may have a name for you as soon as tomorrow."

"That so?"

"Lady Stang-Helion is holding a séance this evening. We will be there and better prepared than on prior occasions. We've vetted the participants, gathered the relevant evidence, and we'll see what transpires."

"You think they'll try again?"

"Not for a fang. Lord Blackwood's taken hers to a secure location. I predict they'll cause some sort of ruckus out of protest."

"Go for one of the nobles, that sort of thing?"

Tim met Quayle's penetrating stare with a stiff-backed confidence he did not feel. For the first time in his life, he wished he could twist and twirl words like a baton, distracting his audience with a flourish whilst secretly maneuvering toward the next spectacular revelation. Alas, Tim dealt in facts and truths, not convenient truisms. If only he could learn to wield those as deftly...

Inspired, Tim answered Quayle's scrutinizing eyes with a keen look of his own. He reminded himself he only treaded water before an inevitable sink into the abyss. His career had ended the second he revealed himself to Bash and his cohorts. Perhaps sooner. Perhaps the moment the curtain parted and Horace Beastly strode onstage in all his villainous glory. Perhaps later when he found heaven on a fainting couch. Perhaps he'd never stood a chance from the second Quayle assigned him the case.

There would be no recovery from failing to give Hiero up to his peers. Quayle had asked, but they had demanded. Men like Blackwood, who thought nothing of watching lions make a mash of an innocent constable. So oblivious they made a game of stealing from one another with hundreds of humble lives in the balance. The sport of vengeful gods, and both he and Quayle were theirs to kick around. Against such an epic canvass, how severe could the punishment for an honest question be? What could Quayle do to him now that he wouldn't in a few days, or weeks, or months? Tim would never ascend to the heights of the aristocracy. He would be broken and shamed and made to beg.

Better to have his fun before the fall.

"Yes and no. The identity of the potential victim is anyone's guess." Tim approached Quayle cautiously, aiming to emphasize his diminutive stature compared to the bestial chief. The thought occurred that Quayle would not look out of place in one of the cages. "The identity of the thief..."

Quayle snorted, the huff of a waking dragon. "Spill it, Stoker."

"Our betters, sir. Will they allow it to be known? Am I jousting at windmills? Or will I be encouraged to find a more... practical solution to the case? Like a promising young constable who imbibed too much one night and accidentally flung himself to the lions."

Quayle chewed this over like a piece of rotten cud. He sighed, then nodded back toward the empty cage. "Ask yourself this, Stoker. What did they do with those cats?"

Tim shook his head, uncomprehending.

"Shot 'em, didn't they?" A second heavier sigh. "Lions are lions; they do what they do. No man can help that. But they still killed 'em." Tim recoiled—from Quayle or from his answer, he didn't know. "I expect word from you by end of day tomorrow. Dismissed."

Chapter 12

Sefton House, at 37 Belgrave Square, stood as squat and bland as its mistress was round and jolly. The front steps, at a mere two, lacked the grandeur of some of the most regal homes. The white stucco face swallowed rather than reflected the moonlight. But the octagonal entrance hall more than made up for the exterior. On four of the eight walls hung portraits of the Barons Stang-Helion, each posing with the main motif on the family's coat of arms: a lion. While the latest, Montague IV, was dressed in mundane hunting gear, his predecessors had been more bold, each wearing the skin and headdress of their latest kill in the manner of Heracles.

"I daresay the hunt of wildcats is something of a family tradition." Hiero meandered over to the most garish of the four, that of Montague II. "Perhaps one that extends to courtship rituals?"

Callie hissed, lifting her skirt to kick him in the shin. In her light-blue satin gown and lustrous blonde wig, she looked an Alice in search of Wonderland, the effect marred by her scowl and tendency toward physical violence.

"Do try, my dear, dear guardian"—she leaned in as she pretended to straighten his tie—"not to give the game away before our turn on the pitch."

Hiero sighed. "If I must."

"You must."

"If you say so."

"I do."

He raised a theatrical brow. "Have you been sneaking off with Han to watch that *danse brute* they call a sport?"

"I have. You should join us sometime. It's quite your sort of thing. A gang of burley men jam themselves into something called a scrum—"

Too near for comfort but not for discretion, the butler cleared his throat. Callie took Hiero's arm as they followed him down a long, ornate corridor. Instinct caused Hiero to shiver when a diminutive figure fell in at his left. He glanced over to see Kip match them stride for stride—with a wink in Hiero's direction—and stifled a sigh of relief. It was the first he'd seen of their do-right detective all day; a brief exchange of notes at some ungodly hour of the morning informing him Kip would not, as expected, rejoin them before the séance. Hiero had absolutely *not* fretted for the better part of the afternoon over his well-being, the potential hazards at the sporting club, his interview with Superintendent Quayle, what sartorial travesty he would bedeck himself in that evening, and whether he would agree to a private interlude after their clue-collecting concluded.

An aesthete and a detective in his own right, he hadn't lost so much as a second's worry to such trivialities. Nor a wink of sleep. If anything he'd been focused on his own toilette. The grooming of his mustache. The primping of his hair. The tailoring of his mustard-colored velour waistcoat. The selection of the appropriate dress coat, in a dark teal, and gloves. With the addition of his finest cape, militaristic gold embroidery lining the collar and the edges, Hiero and his party arrived at the ballroom door ready to wow.

Double doors in the French style parted to reveal Lady Stang-Helion's very own crystal palace. Great gilt trellises embossed with glittering stones framed the mirror-paneled walls. Cupids danced and flirted among the clouds on the frescoed ceiling, capped by a crown-shaped skylight. Six chandeliers dripped with more diamondlike shards than the necks of her most distinguished guests, their constellation of lights bringing out the stars in everyone's eyes.

After the bullfrog-throated butler announced them, Hiero measured out seven regal steps, paused for effect at the expected gasps and cries of the guests...

For two endless minutes, no one so much as glanced in their direction. With a surreptitious squeeze to his elbow, Kip whispered his excuses and hurried off in search of Blackwood. Lady Stang-Helion bustled over, arms outstretched... and swept Callie away with little more than a cursory nod in his direction. Hiero counted out seven more steps, stopping near several circles of guests, but not a one parted to invite him in. He spotted Goldie in deep conversation with Vandenberg by the window and set off in their direction, only to be waved away with a discreet gesture. He scanned the rest of the ballroom for potential marks, but to no avail.

He had been blacklisted by a society skilled at closing its ranks.

Undaunted, Hiero grabbed a waiter, stole two flutes of champagne off his tray, and sauntered over to the staging area. There more hocus-pocus paraphernalia awaited the gullible like a scaffold dressed as a carousel. Arcs of empty seats encircled a small rectangular table with two opposing chairs. Plain and brown, their legs barely a cut above the woodpile—the better to underline the transparency of the medium. Nothing to see here: no tricks, no feints, no fraud. Just a gargantuan crystal ball with a gem-encrusted silver base through which the secrets of the otherworld could be divined.

Glinting with the insight of an all-seeing eye, only the heartiest among them would resist that bauble's lure. One of the purest tricks in a magician's arsenal: the power of suggestion. Nothing Miss Nightingale—or any medium, mesmerist, or would-be sorcerer—could conjure held sway over her victims like the visions they projected into the ball. Hiero wondered where they had concealed the smoke valve. Hidden in the base, perhaps? The table looked too thin for a false bottom, but then that, too, might be an optical illusion. Well-funded, that Miss Nightingale. No penny-ante fireworks and hand-painted mirrors for Lady Stang-Helion's pet. But then few mediums bunkered down at the Albion. Hiero crept closer, dragged a finger under the table's edge...

A shout had him twirling about, searching for the offended party. A second shrieking cry pointed true north. The background chatter was loud enough, and the argument distant enough, not to attract the notice of the guests. Or perhaps they watched without looking, in the aristocratic way, monitoring his every move despite their air of disdain. Someone—three guesses as to whom—had branded his ear with a "danger" mark, no better than any other cow in the herd. He'd see what they made of him slipping past the sheepdogs. He wandered in the direction of the stage door: a servant's entrance that, when closed, melded into the wall. Fortunately whomever now bellowed like a bear in heat had left it open a crack, through which Hiero disappeared.

As soon as he crossed into a tight, dim corridor, waiters swarmed him. Babbling his apologies, he exchanged his two empty flutes for full ones before shooing them off. Hiero inched down the passage-way, the hubbub from the now-open door behind him blighting out the argument until his first major obstacle presented itself: turn the corner or descend the stairs? He glanced down the staircase in time to catch a familiar wiry-framed detective sergeant slip into the shadows. Were Blackwood's hounds sniffing about? And if so, why? The clatter of plates from below scared him off the scent, and he veered further down the corridor... then leapt back again. Pressing himself against the wall and peering around the edge of an open door, Hiero wasted no time in congratulating himself on this piece of real detective work as he spied on Mr. Whicher and Miss Nightingale yowling like two cats in a bag.

In German. Curious, that. Fortunately he was fluent.

"For the last time, you will go out there, and you will give these people what they want!" Whicher smacked at the arms that wrapped around his leg, careful to avoid Miss Nightingale's head despite his anger. Her face couldn't have gotten any redder in Hiero's estimation, swollen with tears and buried in the knee of Whicher's trousers. She clung to him like a child to its mother's skirts, collapsed on the ground so he dragged her with every lurching step.

"I can't! Please! I've seen it! The demon eyes! The walls drenched with blood!"

"Oh, you've seen it, have you? Who told you—the spirits? Who was it—the ghost of Hamlet's father, or did Mephistopheles himself ask you to sign his book?" Hiero couldn't help but be impressed by the ease with which he quoted the classics. But then it came as no surprise to learn such a trickster once tread the boards.

"Please! This is serious! Something isn't right."

"What's not right is you pitching a fit like the grubs we play to." He dug into her shoulders and tried to push her off, to no avail. "Pull yourself up, by the fates! Have some dignity! They'll ask for you any minute."

"I won't go! I won't do it!"

He finally managed to pry a hand loose. With a kick and a twist, Whicher freed himself, yanked her off the ground, and threw her into a chair. "You'll do it, or I'm done!" He slammed his fists on the arms of her seat, prodded his face toward her until they practically kissed. "Eight years, Dahlie, we've been at this—clawing our way out of the gutter into the bars and music halls, onto the stage to the top of the billing, then finally, finally into a few drawing rooms. Finally we've been noticed. They've been pouring money into our pockets, and I, for one, am not going back to porridge for dinner and seven shows a week! And neither are you!"

"Chris…"

Whicher pushed his body in so close Hiero began to calculate how he might intervene if things took a darker turn. Whicher caught her by the chin, bore his wolfish eyes into hers until he overtook everything else. "I won't say it again. Ready yourself for the performance, or I'm done with you. We'll see how willing that fine lady is to help you when you haven't got a penny to your name. You might want to remember that you've always been too good for washing dishes, or polishing the silver, or nursing their little whelps. You might want to think on how we got ourselves into this mess to begin with and just who got you out of it."

He stared at her for another minute, her concession an almost imperceptible nod. He straightened, grunted his approval, and marched out of view. Hiero heard the click of a lock. She crumpled into sobs, not hearing Hiero's careful footsteps until he was nearly upon her. Only after he thrust a half-empty flute in her face did she glance up, her eyes blown wide with shock.

"Champagne?"

She looked from the glass to his face and back again, wailed in anguish.

Hiero shrugged. "If I must..." He downed the remnants in one gulp.

"If you're here to unmask me, then do as you must."

"Ah-ah-ah! Not quite as simple as that, I'm afraid, but I do see how you would think me the solution to all your problems." He offered her his handkerchief, a monogrammed affair in buttercup yellow. Perhaps if she held it under her chin, he might glean some insight into her character. He still pegged her for a charlatan—a leopard recognized its own spots, after all—but if *she* believed herself in danger, there was something afoot Kip and Callie should know about. "That is, of course, why you lured me here. Insurance."

She sniffled quite prettily, then honked her nose like a goose giving birth and folded the handkerchief over to dab at her eyes. These stall tactics worked insofar as Hiero kept his distance. He fetched a chair, installed himself across from her so there would be no means of escape. At least no honorable means.

"I don't know what you're on about. I didn't even know you

were here."

"You knew I would be here. You just put your plan into motion earlier than expected. Quick thinking is a trademark of the profession, and you're nothing if not skilled."

She sighed. "I don't know why I bothered. I knew you wouldn't believe me."

"I don't." Hiero twiddled his fingers. "And yet I do. What do you fear will happen if you take the stage?"

"A horror."

"I assume we are not speaking of the quality of your performance, or any theatrics you and your partner might get up to?"

She huffed in affront. "No. This is..."

"Intuition?"

"More than that." She wiped a shaking hand across her cheeks, straightened her back. "I know what you think of me, Mr. Bash, but you're wrong. I have the sight. I've felt the tremors ever since I can remember."

"Tremors?"

"In the air. In the ground. On my skin, on my scalp. In my teeth. I know when something's coming. I don't know what. I don't know how. I can't bark on cue like a trained dog. That part... Most of it, you're right, is an act. If you ever press me outside of this room, I'll deny it, but... but the tremors are real. They've never been wrong. We need to get away from this place right now." The performer in her, perhaps, couldn't help leaning forward, lowering her voice, reeling him in. But was it really all for show? And if so, why go to such pains to convince him? "Something is coming, Mr. Bash, and it won't be stopped."

Hiero regarded her for a long time, even after she reclined back and crossed her arms under her breasts. A stalemate of sorts, and one he was powerless to break. Even if he believed her—and still now he noticed every facial cue, every miniscule gesture, all meant to put him at ease. A master class in persuasion.

But no one would believe *him*. To them he was the boy who cried fraud. They didn't care when he accused her. They wouldn't listen if he came round to their point of view. They wanted their spectacle, and they would have it, no matter the cost.

They were, if anything, more than eager to pay.

Tragically he did believe her. Or more specifically, he believed that she believed. To Hiero, "tremors" was just another word for "intuition" or "fear" or "the trouble that I've stupidly gotten myself into." Her tremors warned of the disintegration of her and Whicher's black enterprise, of Lady Stang-Helion's doubts, of Lord Blackwood's threats, of the thieves' dissatisfaction with the part they played in the proceedings. *"We see all. We know all. We will feed."* The reality of these threats may be questionable, but her belief was not. Dahlia Nightingale was terrified of retribution for her crimes, but that did not mean anyone other than Dahlia Nightingale need suffer for them.

"Your premonitions, as always, bear the ring of authenticity, my dear Miss Nightingale. But I, too, hear a tremor beneath. Of remorse. Dare I say... of guilt?"

Violence erupted in her face. "You poncey, prissy, spiteful peacock!" She hurled the handkerchief at his chest. "You... you ignoramus! You're no better than they are! You deserve each other!" She flew to her feet, kicked back her chair. "When the blood starts flowing, I hope you're the first to drown!"

With his eyes Hiero followed her to the window of her cell, then dropped them to his lap. There the infected handkerchief lay like a gob of honey candy some stroppy infant had spat out. On the only clean corner, poking out, were his initials, H.B., a signal flag to Whicher if he should return. Hiero shrunk back from the handkerchief as Miss Nightingale gave over to her sorrow, contemplating a host of disagreeable options.

A solitary figure smoked by the first-floor balcony rail, watching the procession of jewel-box carriages below as they opened to reveal their glittering wares. From a drawing room done in confectionary colors—icy meringue green with shortcake-pink accents and *croque-en-bouche* amber glaze—Tim observed Stephen Tiquin, Earl Blackwood, with as much professional sangfroid as he could muster.

Even at his advanced age, Blackwood cut a dashing figure, with his silver mane of hair just a touch too long to be in fashion and his lithe frame all but vibrating with suppressed energy. From behind he appeared as lean and cruel as one of his jungle cats. A pity too-bushy brows and a guppy mouth mired the effect, to say nothing of his almost comically thin voice. Little wonder he had to pay others to intimidate for him—not that Tim's pulse wasn't pounding through his veins like the footfalls of a long-distance runner. Blackwood may not look the part, but he could play it.

Crossing onto the balcony proper, Tim forced himself to forget everything at stake—his career, his reputation, the safety and sanctity of those he'd lately come to hold dear—as he took the first step.

"Kipling." Blackwood welcomed him without turning. "I'd hoped you'd seek me out."

"Forgive me for not doing so sooner, my lord. I've been entrenched—"

"Yes." His airy voice clipped the end of the word like a broken flute. "You've done well, by all accounts."

"I dare say Superintendent Quayle's reports have been far from sterling." Tim inched to the right, angling for a view of his face. Not that his unreadable expression revealed anything, but part of Blackwood's power came in denying. "I've come to explain—"

"Superintendent Quayle serves a purpose and serves it well. If not for men like him, grunting and sweating under a weary life, we princes would not be free to capitalize on certain... opportunities. Opportunities you, Mr. Kipling, have enabled through your continuing efforts. It is a long and perilous endeavor, digging to the heart of a man. So far I am quite satisfied."

"That makes one of us, my lord."

Blackwood took a long draught on his cigar, blew out a stream of perfect Os. "A skilled hunter, Mr. Kipling, does not make haste. He chooses his position and lies in wait, for hours, for days, for as long as it takes to lure the beast into his sights. Those who beat the bushes and listen for the dogs make a mockery of the sport. Any predator of merit exhibits two traits: patience and cunning. You have set your trap. Let no one pressure you into springing it."

"I will abide by your wisdom, my lord."

"See that you do." Blackwood chuckled, a hoarse, hiccupy sound. When he finally turned, Tim wished he hadn't. Exposed beneath his assessing stare, Tim's shoulders constricted and his throat pinched as if the noose were already tightening. If they did manage to expose this man and his crimes, how would he survive it? "As to the matter of the fangs, I would appreciate any insight you might have."

"How do you mean?"

"Lady Stang-Helion's incisor is secure, but the first two have not yet been recovered due to Bash's interference, and Landgrave Vandenberg is being... unhelpful. I would see this matter resolved before the final séance next week, which offers the thieves yet another opportunity—"

"Say no more, my lord."

"So you have, as Superintendent Quayle explained, been running an investigation concurrent to Bash's? You are quite the ball-juggler, Mr. Kipling."

"I..." Tim swallowed back the swarm of retorts and ribald comments that buzzed into his mind. If Blackwood meant it as an insinuation, Tim could not rise to the challenge. "I have come across some promising new evidence that may bring us close to a solution."

"You and Bash?" Behind the thicket that topped his eyes, Tim thought he saw Blackwood wrinkle his brow.

"Myself and the Yard, my lord."

"Ah. The pennyroyal 'we.'" Blackwood whinnied with laughter, startling some of the horses below. But his features settled into a brood as dark and menacing as any storm cloud. "This evidence you have, Mr. Kipling, should it bear fruit, you will present it directly to me. When you have a name, you will come pour it in my ear, and my ear alone. Do you understand?"

Tim didn't have to feign his astonishment. "But... my lord..."

"Mine alone." He inhaled deep of his cigar, expelling fumes thick as hellfire. "I have need of clever, loyal men in my various enterprises, Mr. Kipling. Men of discretion. Men of guile. Fear no further reprisals from your superiors. I've got my eye on you."

After following another fleet of servants back into the ballroom—and pocketing an entire tray of canapés for later—Hiero dusted the crumbs off his lapel and struck out in search of his team. To no one's surprise save his own, they awaited him by the drinks trolley, standing to the side with the stiff formality of a couple suppressing the urge to quarrel. Kip had kindly fetched him two fingers of scotch, though he snatched the glass away when Hiero reached for it. Callie anchored him to her side, and together the three of them strolled the perimeter of the room in a manner not in the least conspicuous. At all.

"Where have you been?" Callie demanded in a harsh whisper. "Lady Stang-Helion insisted I fetch you after your blatant perusal of the scrying space. I had to pretend to fancy Lord Rathbone—Lord Rathbone!—in order to cover the fact that you'd all but vanished from the room. Please tell me you did not steal down to the liquor stores."

Hiero scoffed. "That was only once, and you must admit old Boney was being stingy with the wine."

"You don't particularly care for wine."

"Not of that vintage! 1870 Vinaigre du Lac Boue, if you ask me."

"You're evading the question," Kip interjected.

"By defending against accusations of incivility."

"Of which you are guilty." Kip followed at a close step behind them, hovering by Hiero's left ear like one of his better angels. "Now where were you?"

"With Miss Nightingale."

Hiero felt more than saw Kip's smirk. "Need I be concerned?"

"For my virtue? Never. She behaved in every way the lady."

Callie snorted. "If by 'lady' you mean…"

"A blubbering mess who raved about doomsday visions and telltale tremors and things that go bump in the night."

"Come now," Kip insisted. "You must have learned something of use."

Hiero indulged in a theatrical shrug. "Only that she speaks German. And she may—may—have warned me against some dark menace that threatens us all."

"Imminent?"

"Mmm. She does not wish to perform tonight. She covered her objections in spiritualist claptrap, but she is genuinely frightened. Of Whicher, primarily. The man is more bully than guardian. I'd go so far as to call him her keeper."

"Hardly evidence of guilt *or* insight," Callie remarked, "given what transpired during her last two séances. Did you sense anyone other than Whicher pulling her strings?"

Hiero laughed. "Poor girl has enough with one master to wind her up." He glanced back at Kip, whose frown grew contagious. He'd already infected Callie and now worked his dark influence on Hiero himself. "And what of your interview with the unofficial Chief Justice of London Town? I take it you escaped the noose?"

"By a hair." Lawn-green eyes met his, limned with worry. "He seeks to recruit me."

"But you're already his man," Callie objected. "Or is there another wrinkle you've yet to straighten for us?"

"This would be a permanent position as one of his henchmen. He thinks himself my very own Pygmalion, ready to breathe life into my career if this case or Superintendent Quayle should stall it."

"'Twas Aphrodite who did the breathing, I'll have you know. Mine was the definitive interpretation of the love goddess as seen in *Pig Male Lion, a Story of O,* a three-month sellout at the Strand Theater."

"A performance you may reenact when at your leisure." Callie reared on Kip. "What of the notebook? The thefts? The murder? Did he make any mention—"

"None. Of any of it. I don't..." Kip sighed, shook his head. "I don't think he's aware that the notebook is missing. Or of our invasion of his vault that night."

"Unexpected. But not illogical."

"No."

Hiero didn't much care for the keen look that passed between them, but then, his objections, if noted, would have been ignored. "What do you mean?"

Kip opened his mouth to explain, but Lady Stang-Helion, accompanied by Lord Blackwood, had taken center stage and called them to attention.

"Welcome, welcome, dear friends and fellow spiritualists, to another evening of otherworldly investigation. Tonight is the third event in the Belgrave Spiritualists Society's month-long showcase of Miss Dahlia Nightingale, who has been invited to predict the futures of those among us brave enough to sit across from her through her crystal ball. Her findings are certain to amaze and delight!"

Enthusiastic applause thundered through the ballroom as Lord Blackwood stepped to the fore.

"But first we must tend to a graver business. Most of you here tonight bore witness to the shocking thefts of two of the Fangs of Scavo, those totems which protected us from a great demonic evil. The shaman who spelled the fangs did so to keep the spirits of two bedeviled lions from exacting their revenge. That protection is now gone. But Miss Dahlia Nightingale—seer of sights more wondrous and terrible than those we suffered on the Dark Continent—has agreed to perform a cleansing ritual to shield us if the fangs are never recovered. While I have every expectation they will be"—Hiero noted Blackwood did not even flinch in his direction—"as any medium of worth will tell you, one can never be too cautious. And you will play audience to this awesome display of her powers."

An anxious murmur travelled through the guests, but no one dared contradict Lord Blackwood—not even Goldie and Vandenberg, though their clenched jaws and flinted eyes revealed much of their opinion.

"Do take your seats now, everyone, and we'll begin," Lady Stang-Helion invited.

"What do you make of this?" Callie asked them as they hurried to grab seats in the front row.

"Nothing good," Kip sighed. His nervousness surprised Hiero. He reasoned it must be due to his mistrust of Blackwood and not any spirit-related nonsense. Or so he hoped.

The chandeliers dimmed to settle the guests, with only the smallest, above the table, at full gas. With a thunderous boom, the vaultlike doors of the ballroom closed and locked, charging the atmosphere with tension. Footmen drew blue velvet curtains across the windows, blighting out the moonlight. The guests were caught in a bulb of light in the middle of the cavernous ballroom, as if trapped in the crystal ball at its center.

Whicher emerged out of the blackness at the far side of the

scrying area—dressed in trousers and tails!—balancing a silver tray on one hand that bore a rune-inscribed wooden box. With great ceremony, he unhooked the latch, flipped the lid, and plucked out small white... stone? Rubber? Pastille? The choler-red tint of his neck fat as it bulged over his collar, evidence of recent anger, intrigued Hiero far more. Who wrangled Dahlia while Whicher performed the first vital steps of the ritual? And how would they explain away the medium's absence? Showmanship, after all, only accounted for so much. Mr. Maskelyne, the famed illusionist, hardly quaked in his boots.

Whicher raised the little bar of gleaming something into the light and presented it to the spectators. With an awkward flourish— truly no one could find such a boorish man mysterious, could they?—he walked to the head of the table, counted five paces outward, and bent to the floor. With a speed belied by his bulky frame, he traced an imperfect circle around the table—chalk! It was chalk—then marked out four equidistant points with an X. He gestured for the four hunters to gather near, placing each of them on one of the marks.

"The four points of the compass," Kip whispered, to which Callie nodded. "Blackwood north, Vandenberg east, Goldenplover south, and Lady Stang-Helion west."

Before he could say more, the lights went out. A few ladies gasped, the buzz of their conversation silenced by the arrival of Miss Nightingale's procession. Four veiled and robed servants holding candles escorted her into the scrying space. As the chandelier above dimmed to an eerie glow, the medium laid hands on the crystal ball, closing her eyes and falling into deep contemplation. The servants handed off their candles to the four hunters. Miss Nightingale's dress, of celestial blue, evoked the stormy watercolor whorls of a Turner; a trident crown stirred the black waves of her hair. A wisp of lavender smoke snaked into the glass orb, twisting toward her outstretched fingers before plunging back inward.

A vent, Hiero thought, impressed despite himself. *How novel.* A sudden burnt-syrup smell permeated the air. *Still needs a bit of refinement.* Miss Nightingale trembled and twitched with the effort of summoning Beelzebub-knew-what down to her. Hiero felt the different tiers of the audience slowly succumb to her spell: first the zealots, then the believers, then at last the skeptics. Even Kip and Callie appeared transfixed, their moon eyes lustrous with intrigue and excitement.

It was, Hiero had to admit, quite a show.

"Ye two fiends, with souls as black as raven's wings and a blood-lust that knows no bounds!" Miss Nightingale bellowed with arms outstretched and a murderous mien. "Ye two heathens who prey on the meek and the pious! Who gorged on the hearts of two innocents and devoured their people! Ye two demons who stalk the four noble hunters who sent you back to hell! And ripped this kind woman's husband from her untimely soon! Ye who hiss and scratch and roar, I call ye! I beckon ye! I challenge ye! Come! Come to me, devils, and meet your doom!"

She glared into the blackness beyond the circle, legs rooted but arms quaking, grunting from the strain. A low rumble, like a saber-tooth's purr, reverberated through the hollows of the room. A few titters escaped the nervous nellies in the audience, quickly shushed. The anticipation was so thick Hiero felt he could take a bite, though perhaps that was the purview of the ghostly beasts. When finally the purring and the tittering and the tension had reached its zenith, Miss Nightingale's eyes rolled back into her skull. In a voice as deep and loud as an entire pride, she roared...

"We see all! We know all! We will feed!"

She fell to the ground, snarling and convulsing. A gentleman doctor leapt to her aid. Whicher shoved him back. Goldie and Vandenberg betrayed a hint of confusion as to what, if any, part they were meant to play in this overwrought theatrical. Lady Stang-Helion looked stricken. Only Blackwood stood still, beatific as a monk at evensong, his face bathed in candlelight. Hiero couldn't quite stifle a sneer, interrupted by Miss Nightingale rolling onto her front, then stretching out on all fours like a lion waking from a catnap. Panting and grunting as if she suffered a particularly violent bout of constipation, she curled into a ball. Hiero assumed this was the "containment" part of the ritual. After wrestling with herself for a time, she treated her audience to a final hiss, which became a whimper, then a meow.

Finally Miss Nightingale lay still to rhapsodic—and unwarranted, in Hiero's estimation—applause. Then, stunning everyone, she lurched to the side and vomited up a foamy green substance.

"My word," Callie gasped, sotto voce.

"Commitment," Hiero noted. "Always the key."

Several audience members rose to their feet. Whicher ordered them back with a click of his tongue. Miss Nightingale slowly recovered herself, rising to her knees and murmuring an enchantment over the green puss. In one graceful movement, she swooped up to her full height—exceptional gymnastic abilities, Hiero had to admit—and full majesty. One by one she moved to each hunter, gripping a hand into their chests and staring deep into their eyes. Most accepted this with piety, but Goldie poorly stifled a chuckle. She returned to her crystal ball, cupping the orb like a lover's face and, gazing provocatively into the otherworld—

A sudden jolt shuddered the doors. A collective gasp, then a few giggles.

Another blow, stronger now. Stillness reigned.

Then it began, a steady, constant battering, invaders at the castle gate. At first no one dared move. Anxious murmurs. Creaking doors. Whicher and Nightingale broke character, exchanged a look. Goldie, Vandenberg, and Blackwood fidgeted, concerned. The pounding continued. The sound of splintering wood joined the cacophony. A lady screamed; another fainted away. Even Callie grabbed his arm. On his periphery Kip bent to his boot, then stood, truncheon in hand. Hiero fought to maintain his superior air above it all. Certainly this was part of the spectacle.

Until the pounding ceased, and the lock clanked, and the doors flew open.

Until two very real, very liberated lionesses stalked into the room.

"No one move!" Goldie barked, walking cautiously over to protect Miss Nightingale, who appeared more spooked than anyone.

Blackwood, shaking off a stupor at seeing his prize beasts let loose, moved to shield Lady Stang-Helion. Several ladies made to flee, but their gentlemen friends held them firm. Hiero wanted to race off with them, wanted to be anywhere but here. The fluffy creatures that so fascinated him whilst behind bars terrified him when only fifty paces away, even if, by their blinking eyes and groggy movements, they hadn't quite woken from a dose of tranquilizer.

Callie sunk her nails into his arm. "Han. Where is Han?"

Hiero couldn't find the words to reassure her. There was no telling what foul mischief had transpired beyond the confines of the room.

"They've been drugged," Vandenberg observed, somewhat late to the party. "We haven't much time."

"Open the servants' passage," Lady Stang-Helion instructed the poor footmen caught in the room. "Get everyone out."

"No!" Goldie warned. "Outside. There might be others." He'd been joined by Whicher, who helped him turn the table into a barricade, crystal ball and all. Vandenberg grabbed a chair while the brave head butler upended the candelabra.

"Others?!" Miss Nightingale's breaths came sharp and short, her earlier performance no match for the horror that afflicted her now.

Fully recovered, Blackwood took charge. "I'll lead them. Get the guns. Tommy, who has the keys to the cabinet?" Lady Stang-Helion gestured at the head butler. "Open that door now! File out in an orderly fashion. I don't want to hear a sound." They moved to the head of the crowd at judicious speed, and then they were gone.

To Hiero's shock, Kip called after them. "Spears, long knives, anything that could be of use." Then he was at Hiero's side, shoving a chair into his hands as he pushed him toward the servants' passage. "Clear the block if you can, as loud as you can. And by Juno's crown, be careful. They're still out there, those who did this."

"You're not staying!"

"I must."

Callie fished a whip out from under her skirts. "And so shall I."

"You'll do no such thing!" Hiero shrieked, near hysteria. "You are my ward, and I order you to come with me this instant. And you..."

"Miss Pankhurst, you must go." Kip drew her in to whisper. "Save your talents, if not your hide. And get us those guns! Blackwood's likely absconded with Lady Stang-Helion, leaving us to be slaughtered."

"Kip," Hiero bleated.

"Take Miss Nightingale with you, and don't let her out of your sight."

"*Kip*," Hiero demanded with the gravitas of a Lear. "Your promise."

He gripped Hiero by the neck, as close as seemly to cupping his face. "And I intend to keep it. But duty calls. Do your part, see these people safe, and *fetch us some weapons* so we don't all die here." A bloodcurdling scream erupted from the back, echoed in a terrible roar. "Go now!"

The guests at the servants' passage rioted, surging toward the exit as the lionesses stalked toward the barricade. Callie dragged him away from Kip's haunted green eyes and the maddened crowd, toward the furthest window. Dumb with terror, he watched as Vandenberg retreated back behind the table while Kip broke off legs to use as spears. Goldie and Whicher had done a fair job of creating a chair-and-candelabra bramble against the cats, which might hold.

For a minute.

Only once Callie had conquered the latch did he notice Miss Nightingale bundled into herself against the wall behind the crowd, sobbing and shaking as if she had for the first time seen a ghost. Then Callie threw him out into the cool evening air and slammed the window shut on the chaotic scene.

She turned to him, her face a misery, and fell into his arms.

"You're a dark horse, Kipling." Tim noted the gleam in Goldenplover's eye and wondered if he was enjoying himself. Neither he nor Vandenberg betrayed a hint of fear despite having lived through a nightmare that would have sent some men raving.

Tim, by contrast, was wretched with sweat. His fingernails had cut grooves into the wooden pike he gripped. He kept his stare locked on the two snarling cats out of fear that if he blinked, he died. Only the occasional roar drowned out the inner voice that cursed him five kinds of fool for not following Hiero and Callie out the window. The situation and their disorientation had so far kept the beasts at bay, but who knew what other tricks those who had unleashed them had up their sleeves?

"I rather think I'm the main course."

A gruff laugh sounded to his right. "I mean to say you've got a lot of bottle for an antiquities dealer."

"My travels have been quite extensive."

"Oh? Spend time on the veldt, did you?"

"No. But there isn't a creature on this great earth my father didn't import from some far-flung locale. We had our share of incidents."

"So one might say wrangling is something of a family business?"

Tim heard the smirk in his voice when he said, "Of course, I've heard tell you're quite adept with a stick."

"A rifle would do me better." The only thing more perilous than the lionesses were Commodore Goldenplover's innuendos. "Do you think Blackwood will return?"

"I'd take odds against it." On his far side, Vandenberg scoffed. "If we live through this, I'll ask you to tell me just how deep in it he's sunk."

"If we live through it, I'll shout it to the moon." The lie lay heavily on Tim's tongue and his heart. What if those were his last words? What if his promise to Hiero came to naught? What good was he—as a detective, as a policeman, as a man—if his provocations led to this? Was he indirectly responsible for this wild gambit? And how many men's lives could be laid at his feet?

Tim snapped back to attention when one of the cats pawed at the fence they'd made of the chairs. The other roared, a war cry sharp as a knife to the gut. Tim's chest heaved with locomotive strength, pumping blood to every tensed muscle, every poised limb, to the mind that scoped the slightest tremor in the air.

A flicker of movement on the far wall drew his attention in time to see Mr. Han slip out from behind a curtain, rifle in hand. The angle was bad; he would hit one of their hind legs, startle them into lunging. He seemed to know it, melding into the black to continue his painstaking course around to the safe side of the room. Tim searched for a distraction that wouldn't end in slaughter. If only someone could bring a chandelier down on the cats without blowing the whole house. For the first time in nearly a quarter of an hour, he took his eyes off the lions to do what he did best, scrutinize the details for the one niggling little—

The first lioness crashed through the fence. The chairs smashed to kindling in her wake. She pounced on Whicher, sinking her fangs into his neck and stealing the scream from his throat. Vandenberg launched his table-leg spear, missed. Goldie leapt the barricade and ran up behind her. He stopped cold when she ripped out Whicher's throat. A geiser of blood showered over them, exposing bone and viscera.

A woman wailed. The second lioness sped toward Goldie. A shot rang out. The cat reared, veered, and raced toward its attacker. Two more shots and it hit the floor, claws shrieking across the expensive tile. Mr. Han looked as if he'd gone for a Sunday-afternoon stroll by the river.

"Out, out, out!" Goldie commanded. "Val, check the windows. Kipling, grab Miss Nightingale and secure the servants' exit. You, Han, is there any shot left?"

They scrambled for the doors, the lioness gorging on Whicher just feet away. Tim's instinct urged him to flee, but his detective's savvy insisted he remain and observe. Goldie, with preternatural calm, inspected the gate, then reloaded the rifle. Vandenberg concluded his inspection of the windows and enlisted Han in closing the main doors. Tim gathered the sobbing heap that was Miss Nightingale into his arms, fighting her into the corridor before handing her off to Lady Stang-Helion who, along with Blackwood, had returned in time for the final confrontation. Sharing a grim look, Tim and Blackwood strode back onto the scene in time to see Goldie drop the second cat.

He lowered his rifle and let out a long sigh.

"Well." Blackwood kicked the lioness off Whicher's remains. "What's done is done."

One of Hiero's most winning characteristics—at least to his own mind—was his intimate knowledge of his limitations. He was an able mimic and a good listener. He excelled at creating a diversion. He was a loyal companion, a skilled lover, a sartorial devotee, and a gentleman of manners. What he was not, however, was a man of action. Or as it happened, a lion-tamer.

Slumped onto a bench beside—irony of ironies—a statue of Sekhmet, he cowered before the barrage of aristocratic ire that assaulted him. Ladies in gowns more garish than a French whore's paste jewels and gentlemen windbags with more bluster than the evening breeze crowded him, demanding, in tones ranging from imperious to despotic, that he *do something.* What that something was, beyond fetching the police—one of the footmen had already set off for the local division house—and preventing anyone from leaving—which the servants had well in hand—baffled him. Even he was sentient enough to guess who the culprits were. Whether they could be apprehended was a matter beyond his purview. But the same ninnies who ignored him when they suspected he'd finger one of their own now raged at his inability to control a primal force of nature.

Ungrateful louts.

Hiero tore a leaf from one of the nearby shrubs, twirled it by the stem. It was the color of Kip's eyes when darkened by desire. Would he ever see their like again? How was Kip faring? Was he already dead? Had Hiero condemned him to this fate from the moment he lured him into the confines of his dressing room at the Gaiety? Were they both mad to target Blackwood, a man with more secrets than sense? He glanced up at the chorus of angry yobs screaming for his head and wondered, not for the first time, how this little adventure of theirs had gone so wrong.

Then he remembered who he was and that he didn't care. He hopped to his feet, angling toward one of the more operatic women, her jewel-plated bosom thrust forth like a scorned Brunhilde. Hiero dangled the leaf before her grimacing face, then with a flick of his wrist, made it disappear. Caught midmelisma, she gaped. Hiero swerved his empty hand back and forth three times, feinted left, and reached for her right ear. She slapped his hand away. He smirked. She bared her teeth. He let out a belly laugh, repeated the gambit.

With a skeptical grunt, she allowed it. Hiero plucked the leaf out from behind her lobe and presented it to her with a graceful bow. Her reaction couldn't be described as charmed, but at least she had stopped screaming. He was about to repeat the trick for the next Valkyrie when Callie—speaking of bearers of bad news—shoved her way through the crowd.

Which immediately turned on her, barking like a pack of rabid dogs. Callie raised her fan above her head, held it for all to see. The crowd's clamor quieted. With a clack, she shucked the fan open and waived them all away like the gadflies they were. A few tried to protest, only to confront her glare. None dared defy a lady of such sterling reputation, second only to Lady Stang-Helion herself.

"One day you must teach me how to do that."

"Couldn't be bothered." Callie clapped the fan closed but couldn't hide the tension at the corners of her eyes and the edges of her mouth. "I've sent a boy to the Yard. Any word from inside?"

"None."

They'd returned through the front door after making their escape, Callie committed to assuring there were no other cats in the house. An open cage had been left abandoned in the corridor that led to the ballroom, its provenance unknown and its purveyors vanished. They found Han defiling the weapons cabinet and defended him from the matron, only to be shooed into the back garden with the rest of the guests. Callie muttered about some conspiracy among the house staff, but nothing could be proved without a more thorough investigation.

"Oh, what are they doing in there!" With no one else to accuse, she turned on Sekhmet, stabbing her fingers into the goddess's stone heart. "I suppose you're pleased! Your minions wreaking havoc, innocent lives..." She blinked rapidly, staving off a fury of tears. "But you've got it wrong again, you see. Chaos doesn't expose villains; it hides them. You've given them shelter—and a cause!" She spun back toward Hiero, jaw set and eyes brimming. "Blackwood will emerge from this victorious. Mark me."

"What you fail to recall, my dear, is that he cannot lose. The best we could have hoped for was to put a chink in his armor."

She scoffed. "I cannot embrace such a jaundiced view of the world."

"You'd best, if you care to live in it."

She opened her mouth to counter him when shots exploded from the ballroom. Everyone stilled. A desperate, terrific cry pierced the air. Callie gripped his arm fit to break it. Nothing for more heartbeats than Hiero dared to count, then a final booming shot.

No one moved. No one breathed. The patio door cracked open, and Lady Stang-Helion emerged, a wailing Miss Nightingale in her arms. Callie made to meet them, but Hiero held her back, locking her to his side. Some magpies hovered around the two ladies, but most chirped and chattered amongst themselves. Various servants scampered in and out of the house to consult with Lady Stang-Helion; Hiero heard mention of calling a doctor for Miss Nightingale, who appeared otherwise unharmed. Some time later, Lord Blackwood, wearing a mask as brittle as an eggshell, came out to address them.

"Ladies and gentlemen, fear no more. The danger has passed. The two"—did Hiero imagine a quaver in his voice here?—"beasts some foul person set on us have been dealt with. The house is presently being searched. Please accept our sincerest apologies for the inconvenience. Further refreshments are being dispatched, and there is ample seating for those who require it. Detective Inspector Enwright is on the scene and is at this very moment dispatching constables to help with the evacuation. After a short interview, you will be permitted to return home. Again—"

They charged him like a ravening herd of cattle, snorting and bellowing, incensed. Callie nodded toward the gate, and they slipped away, around the front and up the stairs for the third time in as many hours. A gaggle of constables concentrated on receiving their orders took no notice as they darted around them, down the corridor, and past the empty cage. They found Han as he exited the ballroom. Callie yelped despite herself, running to him, stopping short of throwing herself in his arms. The look they exchanged was pregnant enough—Hiero didn't care to chance the real thing. He left her in Han's capable hands and set off in search of his own green-eyed knight.

He froze at the entrance to the ballroom, eyes only for the mangle of flesh that once was a man. Hiero knew he should look to the others, tally hair color and facial features, but he couldn't bear the thought of what they might add up to. Had it come to this? Had his posturing led Small and Croke to defend themselves in the most fiendish way possible? Or was this monstrosity the product of Blackwood's maniacal mind, trusting in his creatures to do his bidding when unleashed upon the masses? Was this how their story, barely begun—Stoker and Bash, detectives at large—would end?

"There you are!" a familiar voice called out. Footsteps—shoes, he never wore the proper shoes—clopped toward him, and a gentle hand covered his forearm. "Whicher, poor sod. Nightingale's inconsolable. I still don't know what to make of it all."

Hiero smiled into the plain, humble face of which he had grown so fond. He felt the aftershocks quiver through Kip's grip on him and discreetly covered his hand with his own. Dahlia Nightingale's predictions—tremors, escape, "Something is coming, and it can't be stopped"—echoed through his mind. Where before he might have locked every door and erected even higher walls against the possibility of supernatural phenomena's existence, he now permitted a small crack, barely a fissure, to open.

"A rather drastic way to be upstaged, if I may say." Hiero chuckled. "Not even Henry Irving would have been so bold."

"You've hit on it precisely. None of the crimes we've seen so far—with the exception of Hobbs's murder, but those were quite different circumstances—have been so severe. The thefts of the fangs may have put the members of the Scavo Four in danger, depending on your beliefs, but an attack of this scale..."

Hiero shrugged. "Macbeth began by killing a king, which led to all-out warfare. Hamlet meant only to shame his uncle, and we all know how that turned out. The tragedies tell us that certain events, once set in motion..."

"But where to next? An attempt on Vandenberg's home? Setting a match to his gas pipes? A new gunpowder plot? The mind reels." Kip shook his head. "I must decipher that notebook. I'm more convinced than ever it can impose some order on all this chaos."

"An impromptu escape? Capital notion." The more Hiero reconsidered Miss Nightingale's advice, the more he embraced its fundamental rightness. "Let's rejoin the rest of our party posthaste and run from here as fast as our legs can carry us!"

Kip laughed, a jarring sound that disrupted the solemn atmosphere. "Hold a moment. You must speak to DI Enwright if you want to escape suspicion."

"Suspicion? Have I or have I not been engaged by persons"—he glanced up to see Goldie striding toward them—"swiftly approaching to solve this very case!"

"Nay, *I* have been engaged to solve it. By Scotland Yard, if you recall. A fact that cannot be known by DI Enwright if I mean to maintain my cover. Which is in your interest as well. So you'll permit yourself to be interviewed, and you'll flounce and flop around, as you do, evading every question asked, and in so doing, you'll send Enwright down the path of our choosing, well out of our way."

Hiero sighed theatrically. "Well. If you insist."

"I do."

"I suppose that is the superior plan."

"Rather. A superior intellect devised it."

Hiero raised a pointed brow. "It is fortunate that you possess other attributes much admired by me, else I might be prompted to take offense at such a comment."

"Note that I said 'intellect,' not 'intelligence.'"

"Your flattery skills require some work, my dear."

"Much like your detecting skills, Mr. Bash."

The pair shared a conspiratorial smile, released their hold on one another, and turned their attention to Goldie.

"Hiero," he proclaimed as if to his assembled sailors, "a word."

"But of course."

Kip dutifully ceded the field. "I'll hold off Enwright until you're... available."

They strolled toward a far corner, well away from Whicher's grisly remains and Enwright's nosy questions. When they stopped, Goldie angled his body so his back was to the room. He was not of a height to conceal Hiero, but then, he well knew the extent of his poker face. On occasion they'd found themselves in stickier situations than even this.

"I'm afraid, dear chap," Goldie loudly expounded, "that your services are no longer required." Hiero did not have to feign his shock, even when Goldie gave a subtle shake of his head. "You must see that, under the circumstances"—Goldie mimed the continuation of their conversation as he lowered his voice to a whisper—"it is vital that you persist. After what transpired here today, I fear that you are the only one who might bring some truth to light." In a more authoritative tone, he declared, "The local division, as you can see, have the matter well in hand. Of course you'll be compensated for your efforts thus far..." Quiet again, he added, "Our only hope in surviving this menace lies in you. Are you confident you can operate without notice?"

Hiero considered this. With an officer of the Yard embedded among his team, a tyrannical noble with henchmen and man-eating lions on the hunt for his head, and only the skill of a brilliant but untested young girl to rely on, true confidence just wasn't in the cards. Good deal Hiero didn't believe in that clairvoyance poppy-cock, recent events with Miss Nightingale notwithstanding.

"Goldie, you know I live for the glow of the footlights."

He looked confused. "You're declining to continue?"

"Meaning I know," Hiero emphasized, "how to put on a show."

"Ah! Yes, well..." Goldie met his eyes with a pointed stare, confirming their agreement. At top volume he concluded, "It's good of you to understand. If you'll share everything you have dug up with DI Enwright, we'll all soon be able to put this infernal business behind us."

He clapped Hiero on the back, then escorted him into a different sort of lion's den.

Chapter 13

Silence blanketed them the entire carriage ride home. Wedged in beside Han's bulk, Tim looked to the moon—the only celestial body that had a hope of distracting him from Hiero. On many a troubled night, he had sought out her radiant grace. The grand dame of the sky, her pale face hung over him like that of an indulgent mother. Her remoteness a reminder of the vastness of the world and how inconsequential his place in it. Just a flicker among millions basking in her light. One could not cling to loneliness whilst contemplating the moon.

Tim stole a glance at the family that meant to adopt him, marveling at their resolve, their openness, their eccentricities. A travelling circus in finer clothes. But would he run away with them? Even now he harbored doubts as to Hiero's forthrightness, Miss Pankhurst's acceptance, Mr. Han's motivations. What happened once they solved the case? Would they embrace him, an unemployable man of limited means and lesser showmanship? Each of them lived to perform, but he preferred to beaver away backstage. Tim had imagined this his one great adventure. Leading to promotion, of course, and better assignments, but not necessarily the public's notice. He'd been confident he could operate as London's first uncelebrated detective. Had he been a fool? Naive? Worst of all, self-deceiving? Was there an actor in him after all?

No. Nothing had changed for him. He would live through the

looking glass for a time in this world of gorgeous mad hatters, girls who grew ten sizes too tall when on a case, and sculptors who masqueraded as menservants. He would revel in the sense of homecoming that already suffused him when he spotted the house at 23 Berkeley Square from afar. He would topple Blackwood's tower of secrets and soothe his savage beasts. He would give in to every sensual thrill, crow at every conquest. Then he would retire disgraced unless, by some feat of prestidigitation taught him by the man who'd branded himself Hieronymus Bash, he managed to save his job.

And every night Tim would look to the moon and remember the lunacy that had bewitched him for a spell.

Heavy with the night's horrors, they crawled into the house. With no servants to greet them, they dropped their coats onto doorknobs and gesturing statues. They drooped against the backs of armchairs and the fronts of end tables as Mr. Han made a sweep of the upstairs rooms—no predators to be found, fanged or otherwise, thank the stars. With a promise to meet in the morning, Hiero led the charge up the stairs with Miss Pankhurst and Mr. Han close on his heels. Tim saluted them wordlessly, then searched for a means of lighting his way to the kitchen. After turning on every fixture save those that illuminated the back stairs, he fumbled through a cupboard for a candle when a shuffling step startled him.

Hiero, in slippers and a crimson robe, eyes glittering like shards of obsidian, reclined against the cupboard door in a pose that recalled one of Delacroix's nudes. He had exchanged his trousers for a pair of silk pajamas, the dark pelt on his chest peeking out of the V at his collar. His face, Tim realized, was similarly exposed, bare of the powder he must meticulously apply on a daily basis to lighten the tone of his skin. Tim couldn't help but undress him with his eyes.

"Who are you?" He could not help but speak aloud the thought that had haunted his mind since before they met.

"I'd do better to ask what you're about at such an ungodly hour?" Hiero let the question hang in the air, preening. "Come to bed."

Tim shut his eyes, resisting the urge to rake Hiero's pantherlike frame anew. Also to fall to his knees and uncover for himself what lay under all those satiny layers. "Coffee. Surely you've got coffee. Strong. Turkish, no doubt." Something clicked for him then, but he recognized it as another distraction.

"Somewhere, I suppose, but I've something better to help you sleep."

"I can't. Sleep, I mean." Tim wrenched the cupboard door from under his arm, shutting it. When Hiero swerved in his direction, he took off down the hall. "Where, by the powers, is the switch to the kitchen lights?"

"If you've need of refreshment, I'm sure Han—"

"The notebook, Hiero. I must decipher it. Lives are at stake. It cannot wait another night."

Tim heard him sigh. "With a clear mind—"

"Is that what my mind will be after you've had your way with me?"

"And some goodly hours of rest..."

Tim spun around, confronted him head-on. Hiero slid to a halt mere inches from his face. They hung there, panting, yearning, sizing each other up like fighters before a bout. *So easy,* Tim thought, to relax his stance and lean inward, to invite his plump, whiskered lips to ply his own, give himself over to the force of Hiero's intoxicating embrace. To lose himself in the black wells of his eyes, gift himself to a lover of skill. Already his blood quickened, already his skin tingled in delicious anticipation of that first heady touch. Prickles of exhaustion at his extremities only intensified his desire to be taken hard and fast, to be used with vigor, then dropped into dreamless slumber. In Hiero's bed, his powerful body within reach should Tim require any further... release.

And what mischief would Small and Croke wreak whilst he slaked his lust? At what cost his satisfaction?

No. Tim would bring this to an end, then he would fulfill his promise to Hiero.

"Do you think they are at rest, those fiends who sought to feed us to the lions? When they hear that not a single one of their enemies has been gored, do you think they will fetch their pipe and book and cozy in by the fire?"

Hiero scoffed. "They would be the better for it." Hiero raised a hand to his cheek; Tim stepped out of his reach. A touch, he knew, and he would be lost.

"Take care. You're coming dangerously close to expressing concern for my well-being."

"I'll do more than express it, if given the chance."

"After the case is resolved, I'll be happy to entertain all fervent gestures, formal writs, and impromptu declarations."

"So noted." Hiero swooped into his space anew, parted lips hovering over Tim's tense brow, ghosting his palms against his chest.

Every cell in Tim's body surged toward him. But he had only to imagine the consequences of such a choice and sobered.

"But if, in the meantime, you require some persuasion..."

Tim caught him by the wrists, pushed him gently away. "You are tempting beyond words and generous beyond measure to take such an interest in me. But if one more person is harmed due to my inability—"

"Say no more." With a flick of his arms, Hiero pulled out of his hold and caught up his hands. Tim had barely had time to react when he said, "Coffee. Black, I presume?"

"Milk and sugar."

"Ah, the English." Hiero shook his head. "Go to your little room and take up your book. I'll bring it up. And stoke the fire."

"It's hardly a little room."

"It is if you're alone. You'll see."

Tim laughed, suddenly reluctant to let him go. "You... you know how to make coffee? The mystery deepens." Hiero opened his mouth to speak, then, by his look, thought better of it. In a flurry he kissed the knuckles of both of Tim's hands, and, with a final squeeze and a swat on the arse, urged him toward the study. Tim got as far as the door before he glanced back in time to see the glow of the gaslights illuminate the back stairs.

The pot of rich, potent coffee and glazed almond biscuits Hiero had left him were but a distant memory by the time Miss Pankhurst joined him sometime after dawn, pert as a schoolgirl on her first day. Her lack of makeup somehow enhanced her angular face. She had clipped up her short black hair at the sides. Tim ripped his eyes away when he realized she wasn't wearing a corset under her utilitarian dress. After little more than a nod in his direction, she set to work helping him decipher the notebook—which in all the tribulations had never made it out of Tim's pocket—quickly spotting the path he had not yet taken and scribbling out a few variances.

Tim refocused on the numbers until his hands shook. The chime of the clock alerted him to the fact three more hours had passed. He staggered over to the window and threw open the curtains, hoping a breath of fresh air might revive him. He'd not quite conquered the latch when he felt a looming presence behind him. He turned to find Mr. Han in his normal state of hulking repose, his look flirting with amusement. Upon spotting a full breakfast buffet laid out on a side table, Tim ceded both the latch and his dignity, racing to grab a plate. A pile of kippers, eggs, bacon, and jam-slathered bread later, as well as a tangy relish so good he almost licked the jar clean, Tim nursed his third cup of tea by the open window whilst Miss Pankhurst detailed her findings on a newly acquired chalkboard.

Hiero had wandered in sometime between Tim's second and third cups and currently snoozed in a wingbacked chair under a bundle of multicolored blankets. As he had yet to reapply the skin-lightening powder he wore in public, Tim allowed himself to admire his unvarnished face, gilded by the sunlight. A sudden violent desire to drop the powder box into the Thames consumed him. How dare anyone judge Hiero's natural looks as aught but beautiful. Tim stifled the urge to set eyes upon every inch of his skin.

Miss Pankhurst grunted behind him. With a piercing screech, her piece of chalk ricocheted off the board and plopped into his tea. Tim set aside the murky substance to rejoin her at the desk. She stared at her latest results with a mulish expression as if she could will them into some sort of rational order.

Tim was only too aware of the growing hopelessness of the situation. A Vigenère cipher used a *tabula recta*—a square table of alphabets, each row made by shifting the previous letter to the left— to encrypt a message. A keyword of variable length was matched to the text, then the message filtered through the table to determine the code. This way, a letter like E, which in a Caesar cipher would always be replaced by the same letter, say S, would be exchanged for a different letter at each reoccurrence. This made it impossible to trace without the keyword as a guide to which letters replaced the Es and others. A few years earlier, a German cryptographer named Kasiski discovered a method of deciphering a Vigenère by recognizing other types of patterns made by the keyword, but this only worked if it was of a reasonable length, somewhere between four to ten characters. A longer keyword—a sentence, for instance—would be virtually impossible to decipher.

As Tim feared was the case here. His current method involved attempting to guess what keywords Blackwood might choose. He had started with the obvious: "lion," "Belgrave," "Scavo," "Thomasina." He'd graduated to rudimentary sentences, hoping the more common words within them might reveal a pattern. He'd felt keenly the constraints of his knowledge about Lord Blackwood, so he'd delved into his history, applying any relevant anecdote or fact to the code, to no avail.

As he reviewed Miss Pankhurst's work, Tim struggled to keep the frustrations that roiled in his very full stomach from bubbling up. An overflow of anger would serve no one but the villains who'd lit the fire under them. He gratefully accepted the fresh cup of tea Mr. Han poured him, took a generous sip. Though a queasiness lingered in his gut, Tim found the fortitude to return to his list of common sentences and assign one to Miss Pankhurst.

To no one's surprise, she glared at him. "No. No more, Mr. Stoker, until you convince me that this Sisyphean task is more worthy of our time than the real detective work to be done."

"'Real detective work,' I'll have you know, Miss Pankhurst, is not the stuff of screaming headlines and penny dreadfuls. More cases are solved by examining the facts and figures than chasing some hooded rapscallion down a dark alley. The public may be captivated by feats of derring-do, but a judge demands evidence. This case is long on suspicion but too little on proof."

"But surely after last night, a case can be made against Small and Croke."

"Perhaps." Tim regarded her a moment, this clever girl who hid so much but wanted the world. She had been playacting detective for too long, using Hiero's talent for embellishment as a shield as much as a mask. It was time she be put through her paces like any officer of the law. Tim parked himself in the desk's chair and crossed his arms, giving her his undivided attention. "Explain."

She hesitated. "Mr. Stoker—"

"You claim there is enough evidence against DS Small and DC Croke to convict, Miss Pankhurst. Well, then, convince me. Make your case."

Miss Pankhurst met his challenge with a set jaw and a determined look. "Very well."

She glanced around the room for any props she might use to make her argument, but found only avid gazes. At the sound of shouting, Hiero had roused. He currently nursed a large cup of reheated coffee whilst still swaddled in his coat of many colors. Mr. Han, having taken up Tim's vacated spot, smiled in encouragement, the first such expression Tim had ever seen brighten his face.

"Let's begin with recent events. Only three parties are aware of Lord Blackwood's fortress of secrets: his lordship, his henchmen, and us."

"But what of the gang of thugs that attacked us?" Mr. Han asked.

"Ah! I will come to that." She shined a grateful grin in his direction.

"It should also be said that, when interviewed, Lord Blackwood betrayed no sign of being aware that we know of the fortress' existence or of the fight there," Tim added.

"Which also points to Small and Croke being the architects of last night's adventures." She ignored Hiero's harrumph of displeasure. "They alone were in possession of all the facts, they have firsthand knowledge of how to transport Lord Blackwood's cats, they have a history of intimidation—as we have seen for ourselves—and they have reason to want the people in that ballroom harmed."

Tim clicked his tongue. "And what is the reason?"

"Greed, of course." She warmed to her narrative. "For years they have served Lord Blackwood. Bullied for him. Stolen for him. Helped him amass the great pile of boxes the lions guard containing riches and secrets that would make them exceptionally wealthy men."

"Theoretical riches and secrets until we decipher the notebook."

"Verily, Mr. Stoker. What do you imagine he keeps in there, his collection of medieval goblets?"

"Proof, Miss Pankhurst."

"Coming to that." She pursued her narrative. "Small and Croke learned well from their master's conniving ways—perhaps too well, for they sought to emulate him. They stole the fangs from the first two noble houses. As policemen and security guards, they alone had unfettered access to the fangs and could have replaced them at any time. Blackwood even helped them do so by hiring them to transport the third fang. It would have been child's play to switch out the tooth in the lockbox for one of their fakes when they were enclosed in the back of the Maria for the journey to the fortress. We threw the only wrench in their works, by being there later that night, when they came back with their very own gang of thugs, likely to liberate the cats and steal the caged boxes."

Tim held up a hand to pause her. "You've hit upon something there. But if the thugs were in cahoots with Small and Croke, why did they not enter with them?"

"Perhaps they went to retrieve the notebook," Mr. Han contributed.

Miss Pankhurst shook her head. "But they would have found it missing and suspected us immediately."

"Not if our fight interrupted them. Or they had to be certain it wasn't in Lord Blackwood's possession," Tim said.

"We spoiled their plans." Hiero shrugged. "As we've seen, they don't have a knack for improvisation."

"We can't all be John Hare."

"Speak for yourself."

Miss Pankhurst cleared her throat. "If I may. Their intention last night was to do away with Blackwood before he discovered them and keep all his treasures for themselves. Why else would they try to derail our efforts to solve the case? Why else seek out the notebook, if not to understand the value of what Blackwood has gone to such measures to protect? They are, unquestionably, the villains we seek."

"Bravo, my dear!" Hiero applauded her conclusion. In his corner, Mr. Han nodded in fervent agreement. Miss Pankhurst evidenced a trace of a blush, her hands clasped tightly together in anticipation of Tim's verdict.

He sighed, steepled his fingers. "A likely scenario, I agree. But where is your proof?"

She carefully considered the matter, undaunted. "The fangs will be found in their possession. As will other paraphernalia used in the robberies."

Tim frowned. "These are policemen, Miss Pankhurst. More

well-versed than the average criminal in ways of covering up their crimes. More importantly you have failed to support your conjectures with concrete evidence. A theory, however reasonable, is not enough for an arrest. And if, as I suspect, all three of the fangs are in Lord Blackwood's boxes, that will imply his involvement. And the contents of those boxes may prove revelatory in a number of ways. As we have already seen, he is in deep with the police. Who's to say what he may have over the commissioner or the Home Secretary?"

"But why would he set the cats on himself?"

"He was the first to flee," Hiero pointed out. "Quicker with an excuse than even I."

"And in no rush to return," Tim added. "We'd not have had guns if not for Mr. Han."

Miss Pankhurst let out a blustery breath. "I hadn't thought of that."

"Motive." Tim rose to his feet and erased the board, then searched around for the missing bit of chalk. Callie proffered the box. "The most difficult aspect of any crime to prove, especially where theft is concerned. Valuable items are valuable to everyone, therefore everyone has a reason to steal them. In this case, all of the suspects have one clear motive: power. Blackwood wants to maintain his power. The other members of the Scavo Four may want to secure it for themselves or wrench it away from him." He wrote out the word *power* in large block letters. "I would amend an earlier point, if I may—we have no proof that only three parties know about the fortress of secrets. Others may. That is a weak link in the evidentiary chain." He turned to address them. "Other possible motives?"

"Revenge for the events at Scavo," Mr. Han said.

"That's merely a cover for the crimes," Miss Pankhurst objected.

"Or the motive behind them," Tim said. "Commodore Goldenplover and Lady Stang-Helion may both have good reason to doubt the official version of events. Perhaps that led them to Blackwood."

"Last night Lady Stang-Helion and Lord Blackwood appeared rather more intimate than before." Hiero lathered on a great deal more innuendo than necessary to that statement. "She wouldn't be the first, of course."

Miss Pankhurst scoffed. "Speculation."

"Every bit of it." Tim shot a hard stare at each one in turn. "We have theories and suspicions—at the risk of sounding a bore, what we need now is *proof.*" He picked up the notebook and slapped it on the edge of the desk. "The contents of those boxes, once revealed, will point the way forward."

"If," Mr. Han sighed, "we can decipher the notebook in time."

"Precisely."

"And what are we less—" Hiero waved his hands. "—practically minded folk to do in the meantime?"

"Chase after this." Tim underlined the word *power* on the blackboard. "Find out who really has it, who wants it, and why, and how close they are to getting it. Get me times, dates, appointments. Evidence we can marry to a clear motive. In a word… snoop."

Hiero let out a gleeful whoop. Tim had to applaud his enthusiasm. Even Mr. Han appeared less stoic than usual.

Only Miss Pankhurst made a moue. "You mean reinterview all the principal suspects?"

"As a pretense, yes. But what you're really searching for is—"

"Don't say it." She exhaled deeply. "I understand."

Before Tim could offer further encouragement, someone rapped on the front door.

Everyone froze.

Hiero pressed a knuckle to his brow. "Does no one send a card before making a social call anymore?"

"There's been no one to receive them," Callie whispered. He could see her mentally tallying the time required to ready themselves. Foolish, really, to flounce about unprepared when under siege.

"And their intention may not be social," Tim warned, ever the spoilsport.

Hiero considered a mad dash up to his dressing room, then realized that would require movement. "I daresay Small or Croke wouldn't have bothered with niceties."

"They didn't last time." Callie tapped out the seconds of silence on her arm as if taking the moment's pulse.

A minute passed and the rapping continued.

Hiero and Han exchanged a knowing look. "If you would."

"No. Let it be me." Kip fussed with his clothing, not straightening so much as rumpling in a different way. Hiero waved him over, set to work. "If it is Small and Croke, they won't override a fellow policeman."

"And how will you explain your presence here?" Callie asked.

"I rather think we're beyond that," Hiero remarked.

Kip nodded. "If they've come, it's not to discredit me." He turned his attention to Hiero's busy hands, the corner of his lips quirked in an almost-smirk. "If it isn't them, how long do you need?"

"An hour, two at the most."

"Prima donna."

The bid at humor surprised Hiero, given the morning's tensions. A glance at Kip's face betrayed not a hint of fear, only amusement and something... softer. A feeling Hiero couldn't help but reflect back at him despite his every instinct on high alert. "Roper."

"Stump."

"Skupter."

Kip lifted a hand to Hiero's face, fingertips hovering over the arch of his cheek. "Don't powder yourself." Hiero flinched, stunned by the reverence in his tone. "Let them see you as I do."

Before he could formulate a reply, Han returned. Which was

something of a shock given they hadn't noticed him leave.

"Vandenberg," he announced, "and he's not alone. Hurry."

"I'll help stall," Kip said.

Hiero and Callie raced off to dress.

A half hour later, having tamed his hair, trimmed back the bramble of his mustache, and wrangled Callie into a corset, they strolled into the parlor as if onto the promenade deck of an ocean liner. One glance at Vandenberg, and Hiero wondered why they bothered. He looked like something out of a folktale, pale and bedraggled, with tufts of white-blonde hair poking up like a straw crown. Kip appeared more rested, though the only complimentary word Hiero could summon up about him was the maroon circles beneath his eyes contrasted with their muted green.

But the true revelation was the elegant if skeletal woman tucked against Vandenberg's side. Swaddled in more layers of linen and lace than a Corsican nun, Landgravine Millicent Vandenberg's spirit flickered like a guttering candle. Her fading English rose complexion worked against the serenity of her features, her dark eyes and translucent skin giving her a sinister air despite her smile. She trembled such that the only thing she could hold was her husband's hand. Fortunately he doted upon her, flouting propriety by anchoring an arm around her waist. He even lifted her teacup to her lips whenever she gestured in its direction.

"My lady!" Callie rushed to her side. "What an honor it is to meet you." The two women fell into deep conversation, such that Vandenberg ceded his hold to Callie.

"I suppose that dispenses with the formalities." Vandenberg bowed his head to Hiero without rising. "Please forgive the intrusion, Bash, but after..."

Hiero shooed his concerns away with a whisk of his fingers. "No need. It is I who should extend my apologies. I'm afraid you've caught us a bit understaffed."

"Kipling here says you've sent them away."

"A precaution."

"So the events of last night were not unprecedented?"

"I cannot speak for others, but I certainly found it to be a novel experience."

"What I mean—"

"Your meaning is clear," Kip interjected. "What remains less so is the reason for your visit."

Hiero sighed inwardly. "What my rather overzealous associate is trying to say is... how can we be of service?"

Vandenberg laughed, a brittle, broken sound. His blue eyes, normally twinkling with mischief, grew as bleak and fathomless as an arctic sea. His gaze drifted, sinking to the floor. Heavied by an unknown burden, his sharp features sagged. Only his connection to his wife kept him tethered to the conversation, a nudge of her shoulder compelling him to speak.

"What you must understand is... I was the one who survived. Thrived, even. I have a worthless title—not a penny left by the spendthrifts who preceded me. Rather a mountain of debt I could never hope to scale. I'd been raised by a profligate who thought an honest day's work consisted of hours at the whorehouse, drinking and gambling and the rest."

Kip grunted. "Sir, I'll remind you there are ladies present."

"This lady," Landgravine Vandenberg said, in voice so rich and sonorous they were all momentarily astounded, "is far more scandalized by my law-father's neglect than his actions."

Callie huffed in agreement.

"My one stroke of luck was I looked like a storybook prince," Vandenberg continued as if none of them had spoken.

"With the heart of one," Landgravine Vandenberg added.

He lifted his gaze from the carpet to lock eyes with her.

"You are my judge and jury in this, as in all things, Millie." Vandenberg turned back to the room, having regained much of his noble poise. "I had many, many cousins who were not so fortunate as

I. Where my mother gifted me with blues and golds, my father's siblings chose homelier mates."

"Poverty can be much improved by comeliness," Callie concurred.

"Well said. And so as I soared, others..." Vandenberg sighed. "I tried to help as best I could, but my allowance could only be stretched so far."

"Especially when your generosity was not used to improve their circumstances," Landgravine Vandenberg said.

"Quite. My cousins had learned at their fathers' tables. They proved much quicker studies than I. So I sought to help in other ways. A letter of reference to secure an apprenticeship. A kind word to the parents of a son or daughter with a healthy dowry. A sponsorship for travel abroad."

"An introduction to wealthy patrons whose belief in the spirit realm meant promotion of their séances to all their equally wealthy friends." All eyes turned to Kip, who shrugged. "My condolences."

Hiero lost control of his face, unsure of whether to beam with pride or frown with sobriety. His features fixed into a muddle of both. "Whicher, you mean?"

"My cousin's eldest, Christofer," Vandenberg confirmed. "And thank you, Mr. Kipling."

"So Miss Nightingale..."

"His sister, Astrid. My cousin's daughter."

Landgravine Vandenberg cleared her throat. "We thought it best to preserve the illusion until we had consulted with you, Mr. Bash. The girl might escape this with her reputation intact."

"Of course." Hiero glanced at Kip, who nodded. "She is, after all, a victim of this terrible tragedy."

"We'll treat the matter delicately," Callie added, "but we will have to investigate."

"I pray you will do more, and soon," Vandenberg said. "These fiends are out for blood, and I fear the police have made little progress, with most of them in Blackwood's pocket."

He'd opened the door, and Callie leapt through. "The guests last night did seem rather cross with him. But you cannot think—"

"I know not what to think. How anyone who lived through those dark days in Scavo could..." Vandenberg shook his head. "If he didn't order it done, surely he was the intended victim."

"You've hinted at less legitimate associations of his before, but we've found no proof," Kip said. A half truth, Hiero judged. "We've our suspicions but no hope of convincing a higher authority unless someone like yourself will testify."

Vandenberg groaned. "Have you heard a word I've said?"

"Every one."

"Insinuations, my dear Val, do not a case make," Hiero commented. "If you truly wish to protect young Astrid—"

Unmoved, Vandenberg inquired, "Do you remember, Bash, during our last interview, when I told you Blackwood was something of a collector?"

"Mmm."

"Well..." He shut his eyes, made a releasing gesture with his hands.

"Ah." For once his befuddled associates looked to Hiero for clarification. "He's been collected."

A chorus of sighs further depressed the room's atmosphere.

"During the unpleasantness at Thomasina's, thieves invaded our home. I believe you can guess their intent."

"The fang." A quaver of alarm reverberated through Kip's tone, one Hiero didn't care for. "Is it gone?"

"No. But other more personal items were not spared. And the state of the place... Claw marks, Bash, slashing the doors, striping the wallpaper. Bloody paw prints staining the carpets. My portrait a ruin, the message ripped into its canvass—"

"'We see all. We know all. We will feed.'" Kip sighed heavily. "Was anyone...?"

"No. But it does give one pause." They hardly needed follow Vandenberg's glance to his wife to retrace the line of his thoughts.

Callie threw her arms around Landgravine Vandenberg. "Oh, thank goodness you're all right! Did you see them? Did they threaten you?"

"Don't fret, dear. I'm perfectly well." Landgravine Vandenberg gave her a few weak pats on the back. "Slept through the whole ordeal. My maid woke me once they'd gone. Val's study suffered the worst of it, and the trophy room."

"Would that they had taken the infernal thing. Then this black business would be done, and I..." Vandenberg continued to gaze at his wife—her withered face, her adoring eyes. "I hid it, you see, in the one place no one would dare to look. Not even demons such as they."

Landgravine Vandenberg coughed a laugh into her handkerchief. "Under my pillow."

"Have you communicated with the police?" Callie asked.

"To what end?" He leaned forward as he beseeched Hiero, as if to get down on his knees. "Bash, you must put an end to this. I'll double whatever Goldie's paying you."

"My dear Val, you know as well as I that it's adventure, not money, we're after. And this has been a merry chase, but you're right. A most unnatural murder has been committed, and many more attempted, and I cry foul." Hiero imbued his last statement with just the right level of gravitas.

Kip picked up the baton. "Your continued cooperation will be key. No matter their penchant for stealing secrets, the thieves have shown they want one thing above all: a complete set of fangs. With your help, we would set a trap for them."

"My help? Whatever do you mean?"

"The final séance. You must convince Miss Nightingale to perform."

"Her brother is not a day in the ground, and you want her to...

to put on a show!"

Hiero pressed the back of his hand to his mouth to hide his smirk. Yes, Kip had the right of it. He contemplated several delectable possibilities until hitting on: "Not *a* show. *The* show." He stood as all eyes shot toward him. "Anyone with sense will be terrified of returning, so we must devise a scenario that will prove irresistible. Given what transpired last night, a return engagement is already rife with danger. We need only add a soupçon of intrigue, a dash of novelty, and slather the whole thing in high emotion… Yes! I have it." He paused to savor their undivided attention, almost licked his lips. "The widow Nightingale—her husband mauled before her very eyes—knows his soul is not at peace. How can it be when the person who set the lions upon him still walks free! On the night when the veil between the living and the dead is at its thinnest—better known as All Hallows Eve—she will channel all her powers through the last remaining fang to summon Whicher for a final moment together—and to discover the name of his murderer!"

He hung there, finger pointing to the sky like a statue of some ancient Roman politician, waiting for his applause. The response was somewhat underwhelming.

"Oh, bravo," Landgravine Vandenberg croaked out, to which Vandenberg hissed, "Millie!"

"Brilliant." Kip's smile was subdued by the limitations this imposed upon him. One week to make sense of the notebook and devise some manner of entrapment for the séance.

"It's a bold sort of madness, I'll say that." Vandenberg blew out a breath. "How do you suppose I'm to convince her?"

Callie reached out, linked hands with the couple. "By explaining it's the only way to avenge her brother's death."

"Val," Landgravine Vandenberg urged, "we must."

"And how can we be certain others will attend?"

Hiero laughed. "And miss the spectacle of the year? I think not."

Chapter 14

As the lonely toll of the grandfather clock reverberated through the house, Tim slumped back in his chair and yawned. After hours upon hours of staring at the chalkboard and pages upon pages of nonsensical scribbles, even the glow of the fire stung his eyes. He canted his chair further away from the hearth and stared into the shadows, not daring to lie down lest he be lured into sleep. He mulled another trip down to the kitchens, but even the promise of Hiero's coffee and sugary biscuits wasn't enough for him to brave the cavernous hollow beyond the door.

Tim had sequestered himself in the study for so long that a place without figures and grids, letters and ciphers felt strange to him. An upside-down world where fine ladies cropped their hair and wore trousers, servants looked to their masters to watch their children, and the valet was more lethal than any decorated soldier. In the wee hours when the nonsense words of the code started to form their own black language, he sometimes imagined he could still hear the terrible shrieks of the madwoman in the attic, as if she haunted him from afar. Or perhaps the cries emanated from his own subconscious, warning him of what horrors would rack the city's noble houses if he failed in his task. Though for all he knew, he could have been risking his sanity and livelihood for the secret to Blackwood's family cider recipe.

Three nights of industry had yielded not a single pattern of note.

Tim chased each hint of repetition down, searching for a nugget of insight. More often he found crumbs, two-letter recurrences that were meaningless without a larger context. If there was one. Tim suspected Blackwood had used a key longer than twenty-six letters for the very same reason as the root of his frustration: it couldn't be deciphered unless someone guessed right.

At the quarter-hour chime, he stared into the shadows on the far side of the room, unable to shut his eyes against the bleaker and bleaker scenarios playing out there. His career was sunk however the case concluded, an inevitability from the second he laid eyes on the man who called himself Hieronymus Bash. But how many lives would be chained to the anchor with him, waiting to be pitched overboard, if he failed here? The answer was as unknowable as the notebook's secrets. But watching the world above the waves fade away as the deep fathoms of ocean claimed him was not a fate he would resign them to without a fight. As long as he was badge and duty bound, he would swim, he would struggle, he would hurl himself against the tide.

Several sheathes of paper and the remainder of the inkpot later, Tim pitched his pen at the wall. The tip entrenched itself in a portrait of one of Callie's long-faced, long-dead ancestors. Too exhausted to laugh, Tim collapsed his head into his arms. With his ears muffled, he didn't hear the footsteps on the stairs, the hiss of the hallway lights, the light tap on the doorframe. Tim let out a soft groan, his self-disgust doing battle with the incipient droop of his lids until a familiar voice startled him out of his chair and almost atop the desk.

"You've improved it. I didn't think it possible." Hiero—or rather Horace Beastly, just returned from another triumphant performance as the Sheriff of Not In Him, as evidenced by the ring of greasepaint across his neck—gestured toward the painting. "What inspired you to..." He fluttered a hand in the portrait's direction. "Pique or exasperation?"

"A bit of both, I fear."

"Mmm." Hiero surveyed his working area as if it emitted a foul odor. Which, given that he hadn't bathed since the night of the attack, was entirely possible. "So I thought."

The firelight glinted in his black pearl eyes, focused on Tim's haggard face. Tim felt no more substantial than one of Miss Nightingale's spirits, drifting in and out of existence. Hiero was like a creature of myth summoned to vibrant life, an elf or a satyr or a sprite, crackling with suppressed power. His recent board-treading was only partly to blame. He burned as if lit by a thousand inner fires. How Tim longed to be warmed by them. There was a coziness to his slinky frame, like a calico curled in your lap. Tim could get lost in him. Perhaps he already was.

"How did you fare tonight? Another standing ovation?"

Hiero scoffed. "Irving's proving something of a flattery whore. Twice now he's joined me onstage when I'm meant to bow alone. He claims it's better to present us as rivals, but I know his game."

"Played it yourself?"

"Indeed. And I always come up trumps." He chuckled to himself. "He forgets who has the director's ear. And favor."

"Oh? What sort of favors?"

Hiero clicked his tongue as he made his way around the desk. "For a man of the theater, Bob's one of the least adventurous chaps in the trade. Married for ages, with more children than sense."

"I see why he permits you such... liberties."

"Like many of our ilk, he never lets morality get in the way of good business."

Tim sighed. "The sort of code I myself should embrace."

"Not till you embrace me first."

He permitted himself to be drawn into Hiero's arms, pressed against his solid, sensual frame. Tim lifted his head to seek out his plush lips, but Hiero cinched him in. Tim drank deep of his scent, as rich and spiced as the coffee he served his guests. His head found a comfortable perch in the crook of his neck. Hiero held him with a strength and security Tim hadn't known since boyhood; he gave over to it with the zeal of a cranky child. Failure and exhaustion had somehow regressed him, with Hiero forced to play parent as well as lover.

But just as his fatigue threatened to overwhelm him, Hiero pecked a path from his brow to his temple with his whiskered lips. He paused, as if awaiting permission, and Tim remembered both his promise and his refusals—one for every night since the attack. But the confidence man at the core of Hiero read his mark rightly. Tim required him; more, he *wanted* him. Wanted to forget, wanted to delay, wanted to feel something other than useless. Wanted to be, if only for a stolen hour, the man he saw reflected in his glittering black eyes.

He snuck a hand up to Hiero's collar and unlaced his tie. Plucked open a button, two, and spread the halves wide. Imagined his legs being parted in a similar fashion as he suckled the notch at the base of his throat. Rubbed his cheek into the downy pelt that cut off at Hiero's collarbone, so silken Tim could be forgiven for judging him half-man, half-mink. Rose to his tiptoes to nudge his stiffening cock against Hiero's answering bulge. Attuned all five of his senses to this mystery of a man who, from that first night in the dressing room, had given Tim his all.

Hiero backed him against the desk. Tim needed no help in hitching himself up and parting his legs so they were face to face, chest to chest, groin to groin. Hiero palmed his jaw, pawed a thumb across his bottom lip to prepare his mouth for plunder. Tim tongued the tip, lured the forceful digit in knuckle deep, an action mirrored below by the canting of his hips. Their gazes locked in intimate challenge, Tim fellated the thumb with all the talent of a youth who'd spent three nights a week at the mercy of some lusty theater patron.

But unlike those rakes, with their leering looks and their sweaty hands, Hiero slowly withdrew. He took a moment to brush his cheek, pinch his chin, stare into his eyes before claiming Tim's mouth. His kiss was everything, tying Tim up into an impossible knot before unraveling him, hitch by hitch, loop by loop until, giddy and pliant, he gave himself over to Hiero's tender care. Hiero stood him up, stripped him bare, disappearing buttons and clasps and hooks with his magicians' fingers as well as waistcoat and shirt and trousers and unmentionables. Not an inch of him escaped his roving hands. Hiero escorted him over to the divan before mapping every groove and curve of his skin, making him croon and writhe and beg.

Beg to be used. Beg to be sucked. Beg to be thrown over and fucked. But the man he barely knew at all could somehow divine what Tim hadn't even realized about himself until that moment—that he longed, more than anything, to feel safe. So Hiero tucked him tight against the cushions and pressed his still-clothed body over him. Kissed him long and deep until Tim felt he couldn't breathe without those lips on his. Kept an arm anchored around him even as his teeth scraped the soft of his neck. The satin of his shirt roughed Tim's nipples. His sin-hard cock clamped between their bodies, he worked an oil-slicked finger to his core. If Hiero's hold was the weight dragging him down to the bottom of the ocean, he would happily drown.

"So wanton," Hiero murmured into his hair. "So magnificently wanton. You deny and deny yourself… Is that part of the pleasure, I wonder?" He drew Tim's leg around his waist, bucked his hips once, twice—their swollen pricks jousting until Tim's leaked just enough to salve Hiero's second finger.

Tim felt its glorious stretch, relaxed into its careful, expert penetration. With eyes only for Hiero, he ran his fingers through that velvety mane of hair, caressed his smooth cheek.

"Why do you hide?"

All the more handsome for his surprise, Tim watched his avid eyes consider a number of replies before punting.

"How do you mean?"

Tim traced the line of greasepaint that still bisected his neck. "Your color. Your beautiful color." He didn't think he imagined the tinge of pink that lit Hiero's cheeks. "Damn them for forcing you to be less than you are."

"Ah. How unlike you, my dear, to have it all wrong. I am the one who denies them."

"They don't deserve the truth."

"How well I know it."

Tim shuddered through the first fierce burst of sensation as Hiero kneaded his gland, purring out a low moan as he bore down on his deliciously invasive hand.

"And me?" he huffed between jolts of pleasure. "Will... will I ever know you? Truly know you?"

"This is hardly the time for philosophy."

"I want to, Hiero. I want... all of you."

All at once he withdrew his heady fingers. Tim heard more than felt him tear at the placket of his trousers, but the hot length of Hiero's cock sliding against his own registered brilliantly well. Tim lifted his head in time to watch Hiero anoint them both with an amber stream of oil, batting his hand away so that he could do the honors of coating them. A thorough grope and a hiss from Hiero later, Tim indulged in a long, hungry kiss before flipping him on his back and straddling his hips.

"All of you," Tim declared before impaling himself on his ready cock.

He shut his eyes once he pushed down to the root, reveling in the fullness, the sense of completion, his every fear and flaw exposed to his molten black gaze. He held until his thighs trembled and his back clenched, until the need cleaved him nearly in twain, until Hiero gripped into his buttocks and let out a strangled grunt. Like a carriage horse under its master's lash, Tim flew, riding Hiero with rare abandonment. He forced out of his mind all thoughts of codes and ciphers, enigmatic men and mysterious circumstances—the solution was in this: the pounding of turgid flesh, the parry and thrust of newfound lovers, the slow implosion within.

As Hiero's adoring eyes bore witness to his ecstasy, Tim grew bold, prying one of Hiero's hands up and curling it around his cock, craning over to take bristly lips and textured tongue, gorging himself. Hiero nurtured this voraciousness, twisting them together until it was difficult to tell where one began and the other ended, reaping Tim's passion that he might sow it back into the fertile ground of his body.

Tim held fast to Hiero as he keened, trembling, cursing, erupting in their commingled hands, relishing the answering gush of heat that filled him so perfectly. They hung there awhile, swaying, snickering, the pleasure so bone deep Tim feared his own had turned to jelly. Eventually Hiero collapsed back onto the cushions. Tim sank down into his arms, still thrumming, already yearning for a second tangle. He chased those bawdy daydreams into sleep, his mind finally blissfully at peace.

But not for long. He bolted awake some hours later, though not quite upright—there was the not-insignificant matter of Hiero spooned against his back. To say nothing of the leg curled possessively around his own, the arm clamped to his chest, the snortles of breath steaming his nape, and the sword-ready prick sheathed between his buttocks. Tim burrowed farther into his tender hold and gripped into the hand over his heart, deciding his nighttime revelations could wait upon the dawn. He hadn't shared a bed since those lonely, sorrowful nights in the orphanage after the loss of his parents, and the kicks and shoves of those wiry boys simply did not compare to this splendor.

If Tim could have this, only this, a sacred memory to conjure up on sleepless nights after his disgrace, all the shame and rejection and recrimination would have been worth it. To know that for one shining moment he was cherished, however ephemeral Hiero's affections proved... He might very well survive the trials to come.

Tim set aside thoughts of how he had been transplanted to Hiero's room—for, despite the chiaroscuro play of moonlight and shadow across the walls, there was no mistaking who inhabited this particular space. Hiero embraced the color palette, if not the artistic refinement, of his namesake: bloodletting reds warred with hellfire yellows, bronze grotesques jeered at puce tapestries, jet-black busts outdid garnet-encrusted vases. The satin sheets that enveloped them were the scarlet of an overripe peach, the swarthy coverlet like a panther's hide. A fresco of Botticelli's *Primavera* dominated the ceiling, the nymphs replaced by comely youths. Every countertop and night table was clogged with baubles and keepsakes, to say nothing of the array of colognes, tonics, and paints suffocating the base of the mirror.

Yet somehow Tim felt right at home. Though he had no love for self-decoration, as a boy he would take refuge in the costume racks while his mother sewed. The flouncy dresses, the shiny fabrics, the ruffles and lace made wonderful tents or turrets or cocoons—any shelter he could imagine. But in none of these childhood cloud castles was he cozied up to a slumbering beauty.

Ever since he met Hiero, Tim had collected a treasure trove of memories to rival those of his boyhood. It hadn't gone unnoticed he had not felt so vital, so cherished since the singular comfort of his mother's arms. Whatever game they played—and Tim was not such a fool as to believe Hiero's motives to be pure—he would ache when it ended. But he had survived more gutting sorrows, and he would survive this, in time.

"My dear, if you think any louder, you'll draw a crowd."

Tim chuckled. "It's your fault for giving me so much to think about."

"I fear you've rather missed the point of our little interlude."

Ignoring him, Tim gestured toward a statue of a Grecian woman dressed like a Parisian whore, complete with feather headdress and full makeup. "That, for instance. How could one look at that, and not think—"

"Thalia, Muse of Comedy? You'll find them all over the house—the Muses, I mean. One of Apollo's obsessions, as interpreted by Han. Though I do feel my additions have improved her. Don't you agree?"

"She's certainly memorable."

"You see? A conversation piece."

To his dismay, Tim suffered a pang of jealousy. "I'm sure many have sung her praises. Or simply sung to her. Isn't that's what's done?"

"Quite so." A silence, then a squeeze. "She had a great many admirers in Apollo's time. That is to say before I came along. She's been rather lonely since he passed, the poor dear. She doesn't much care for my frivolities, so you must do well by her."

"Can't carry a tune, I'm afraid."

"Oh? I am surprised. You were quite vocal earlier. Perhaps if you were in the proper mood..."

The hand that covered his heart stroked down to his navel, hovering just a tease above his lengthening prick. Hiero caught the edge of his earlobe between his teeth, worried the delicate ridge with his tongue. The slow rotation of his hips stirred Tim's desire, evaporating all thoughts of lovers past and future out of his mind. No matter who Hiero had been then, or who he would be once Tim was gone, the man with him now made no secret of his need of him. Tim turned in that giving embrace and took his mouth, sliding atop that powerful—and needlessly clothed—body.

He broke off the kiss when he realized just how clothed Hiero was—clad in a dense night shirt that extended past his wrists, with silk trousers beneath, only the same dark V of hair exposed at his collar. A glance at Hiero's face betrayed something Tim had never perceived there—apprehension. Not quite fear—not yet—but Tim sensed if he pressed the matter, he might fracture the understanding between them. So he returned to his ready lips, considering all the while how he might undertake to pleasure a man who would not reveal himself.

Hiero sighed. "You're wondering."

Tim lifted his head, but only so that Hiero could read the emotion writ bold there.

"Readjusting, if you must know."

"But you're curious."

"I'm a detective. Perils of the trade."

Hiero laughed, but there was no humor in it. He stroked his hands down the slope of Tim's back, cupping his taught buttocks and marrying their cocks, Hiero's trapped between two layers of fabric. Somehow this only intensified the sensation. "Allow me."

"Oh, yes..."

With a discreet movement, Hiero freed himself, then recoupled their pricks in his large hand. Tim let his lids droop to half-mast, his brow pressed to Hiero's own, their heated breaths mingling as they pumped and bucked. They found their rhythm with ease, Hiero the maestro and Tim the instrument, the fevered pound of his hips reverberating across their skin, into their flesh, deep within their bones. Tim moaned out an aria to Hiero's Muse, testifying to her in that carnal language only gods could comprehend, every whispered half word misted across Hiero's cheek. Too soon Tim felt that pinch in his balls, that singular pressure in his core. The tide of ecstasy swelled deep within, surging such that he cried out as he spilled, to Thalia and Hiero both.

Hiero released himself to wring out every last drop from Tim, who twined his fingers into his hair and bit hard into his neck as he rode out his passion. He found those lips anew, drank as though starved of them, then darted downward before Hiero could protest. He dared a glance up once positioned over his wilting prick, stalled the fear in his eyes with a clasp of his hand.

"Allow me. Please. The privilege." When Tim sensed resistance, he dipped his head down to lick up the length of Hiero's foreskin.

"Let me give you this."

Hiero examined him for a time, perhaps considering, perhaps admiring. Hiero nodded. He anchored his fingers in Tim's short locks, Hiero's erection resurrected by the mere graze of his lips. But the time to pamper and tease had passed. Tim laved his tongue tip into Hiero's slit, then worked his way down the shaft in elongated swirls until he swallowed him down to the root. A sharp intake of breath from above, and he set a daunting pace, retracting his foreskin and sucking him in deep, worshipping the one part of him that was hard and real and true.

He'd pulled almost entirely off and returned for a second helping when he felt the first tremor. Their earlier play had driven Hiero almost to the brink; he needed only a nudge from Tim to tumble over. Hiero dug his hands into Tim's scalp, arching his feline hips to meet, to delve, to fuck his mouth, emitting a soft growl with every penetration. His rhythm stuttered, he spit out a half-cursed "Kip!" and the headiest of libations poured down Tim's throat. Punch-drunk on pleasure and pride, he milked Hiero until his quakes subsided. Crawled up to plant a triumphant kiss on his slack mouth. Hiero lolled his head on Tim's shoulder, permitted him to tuck his sensitive prick away, too woozy in the aftermath of their loving to do anything but offer his embrace, which Tim curled into, supremely content.

"Zeus be praised for hidden talents," Hiero declared as he locked his arms around Tim. "As a man of a certain persuasion, I've always felt a considerable debt to the Greeks. That was beyond divine."

"Is there a god of carnality? If so, we'd be better served honoring him."

"Or her. Aphrodite, perhaps?"

"I dare say the types of things we get up to are somewhat beyond her remit." Eros came to mind, but Tim thought their relationship complicated enough. "Perhaps we'd best raise a glass to Dionysus and have done with it."

"Men lying with men as one of the Mysteries? I approve." Hiero grunted. "But as usual there's no one to fetch the wine."

Rather than move, Tim relaxed further against him until he could feel the coarse thatch of Hiero's chest hair against his cheek. "One might argue the act itself is a sort of dying and rebirth."

"*Le petit mort.*"

"Precisely."

"Does Miss Nightingale practice mesmerism? She could initiate us."

"I fear I find you far more entrancing." Tim felt Hiero smile at the compliment.

"Then I look forward to our next bacchanalia."

Quietude embraced them for a time, but neither slept. His mind alert, Tim marveled at his own ease. Something about Hiero invited such calm, his whirlwind personality forcing one to center and still. "Curiously Blackwood is something of an adherent."

Hiero scoffed. "Of mysticism? That's been well-established, my dear."

"No, of Dionysus. There's a whole shelf in his library dedicated to—" Tim froze. "The key... the key!"

He leapt off the bed. His head swam, eyes scrambling to make sense of the strange moonlit room around him. Hiero shot out an arm to steady him. Remembering himself, Tim turned back, smashed a kiss to Hiero's gaping mouth. "Thank you," he whispered into his mustache.

With a gleeful yawp, he stole one of his lover's discarded robes and dashed off to the study, muttering calculations as he raced down the stairs.

With the gas lamp lit and a fresh sheet of paper before him, Tim wrote out *Lesser Key Solomon* in large block letters. By the time Hiero joined him—with a steaming pot of coffee and a mercurial smile—Tim had already drawn out the full *tabula recta*. He flipped open the notebook and applied the keyword to the first line of code.

After delivering his cup of heavily creamed coffee, Hiero settled into his favorite armchair to watch him work.

Ten breathless minutes later, Tim found him there, beaming. "We have him."

Chapter 15

OCTOBER 31ST, 1873

*H*iero regarded himself in the hallway mirror, evaluating every aspect of his dress from every possible angle. He'd chosen his most dramatic ensemble: his coat and trousers the red of a young cabernet, a black velvet waistcoat embroidered with a panther motif, a wing-collared shirt with string necktie, a cape with gold underlay, and buff kid leather gloves. While the others milled about his study, busy with last-minute preparations for the final séance at the Vandenberg manse, he practiced each of the seven emotive poses of drama as well as several gestures he knew would be required that evening. With the eagle eye of a longtime actor, he made minute corrections and adjustments, ever striving for perfection of form. He might not be playing to his usual audience, but that did not mean they deserved any less of a show.

"I pray you've devoted as much time to learning our conclusions as you have to grooming your mustache." Callie, looking no less the part in a striking royal-blue gown and cascading blonde wig, observed him from the study door. "As there's the very real chance we could be lion fodder before the night's through."

"Have you ever known me to drop a line?"

"No. But normally we have a solid notion of whom we're there to accuse."

"It is with the greatest professional pride that I remind you I am a master at improvisation."

"Though not nearly as adept at self-defense." Han emerged from the study bearing a pillow, upon which rested an opal-hilted revolver. He presented it to Callie. "Your weapon, miss."

"Surely there's no need for such measures," Hiero protested.

"Of course there is. Don't be a fool."

Hiero shrugged. "Guilty."

"But as he so often reminds us, he's our fool." After slipping the pistol into a hidden pocket in her voluminous skirt, she linked arms with Hiero, steering him back into the room. "Keep your wits about you tonight. If there are any sudden revelations you fear might turn the tide, defer to Mr. Stoker or myself."

"With pleasure."

Though the room more closely resembled a war bunker than a place for private consultation, with its elaborate maps, secret dossiers, and lists of potential targets, Hiero had eyes only for Kip. Hiero had coerced him into a sea-green waistcoat that made the blue flecks in his irises phosphoresce. Kip folded one of the many notes on which the evening's events hinged with origamic precision. After sealing its envelope, he wrote out the address in a tidy script, set it down beside the others, and pushed back his chair to reasses the totality of their plans. Kip looked every inch the cautious, humble, milquetoast public servant, and Hiero wanted to devour him.

Only one lion would roar that night—the one sitting at his desk, preparing to pounce.

"Ready?" Hiero asked.

Kip let out a blustery breath, shook his head. "I have no idea."

He laid a hand on the deciphered copy of Blackwood's note-book, stroking the cover so tenderly Hiero was almost jealous. Then he remembered how Kip had woken him that morn, with kittenish pulls at his neck and lascivious tugs at his cock, and pitied the notebook its lack of tactility. He watched as Kip resisted the urge to flip through the first few pages, to recheck the findings one more time, remembered the pride with which he'd presented the completed decoding to the group only the day before. Hiero did not mistake his hesitation now for anything other than what it was: the knowledge their final gambit signaled the end of his career.

"A wager before we go. What do you think?"

"You mean to take odds on whom among our acquaintances is a thieving, murderous fiend?" Han asked with his own special form of amusement.

"We've bet on worse."

A grunt. "That we have."

"Well, I for one think it's a capital notion," Callie said. "But what spoils go to the winner? Surely not a financial reward."

"No, I dare say there will be enough of that to go around." Hiero considered the matter, twitching his fingers as if operating some magical calculation device.

"The satisfaction of being right?" Kip suggested, which earned a collective groan.

Even from Han, who contributed, "The offending party's fang?"

"Alas, I fear such an item would not be ours to take."

"Never stopped us before."

"True." A glance around the room proved to be no help at all.

In his corner Kip assayed a playful smile. "How about a night at the theater in the company of Horace Beastly, revered thespian and genial raconteur?"

Han scoffed. "Hardly a prize, that. I've lived through too many to count."

"And I don't see how I'm to profit," Hiero seconded. "Unless... other arrangements could be made, should I prevail?"

"If you prevail, I'll eat my fan." Callie's nod concluded the debate. "That's settled, then. Time to risk it all. Who is the chess master who has been moving our pieces across the board, gentlemen?"

"Blackwood," Han said. "Once a deceiver, forever a deceiver."

"Lady Stang-Helion," Hiero declared. "It's always the quiet ones."

"Ooh, that was my guess!" Callie smacked him on the arm. "Never count a woman out. Although..." She pursed her mouth in that familiar moue. "It does seem somewhat unfair to assume a puppet master. I'll wager Small and Croke acted alone."

"A brave choice," Kip complimented. "Bonne chance."

"Et tu, Kip?" Hiero didn't like the frown that marred those pale features. "Come now, pick a horse."

"You won't like it."

"I don't particularly care for anything about this foul business. Now whom do you peg as puppet master?"

Kip sighed, rapped twice on the notebook's cover. "Commodore Goldenplover."

"Interesting," Han said, his tone conveying an approval that disturbed Hiero.

"Let me explain—"

"No need." Hiero forced himself to smile.

"Blackwood does have four entire boxes collected on him," Callie said, "but to do this..."

"We must be prepared for every outcome," Kip warned.

Han nodded. "Agreed."

"Then let's away," Hiero urged. "Only look up clear. To alter favor ever is to fear. Leave all the rest to me."

A funereal atmosphere enshrouded the Vandenbergs's drawing room. The guests marched in like the condemned to the scaffold. They sat in solemn, disparate pairs, their whispered conversations never rising above the eerie drone of a lone violin. The Teutonic color scheme and shabby, faded grandeur of the furnishings—evidence of the lady of the house's long illness—lent themselves to further sobriety. A mummified butler waited by the empty yaw of the door for guests that would never come.

Despite the alluring promise of scandal and vengeful spirits on the wildest night of the year, only the founding members of the Belgrave Spiritualists' Society had bothered to attend. Though she and Blackwood had arrived arm in arm, Lady Stang-Helion perched herself by Landgravine Vandenberg's chair, chirping polite nothings in her ear to keep her awake. Vandenberg vibrated such that he was nearly a blur, torn between receiving his guests and seeing to his beloved's comfort. Commodore Goldenplover had taken charge of the drinks tray, assuring that everyone—himself most of all—was well-liquored.

With the gravitas of an ancient king, Blackwood, seated in the host's chair, watched the evening play out, an enigmatic smile curling the edges of his lips. He fixed his eyes on Miss Pankhurst and Hiero by the window, who chatted as if they attended a far livelier gathering, clinking their champagne flutes and snickering behind their hands.

After securing all possible escape routes from both the room and the house, Tim performed his only trick, that of the invisible man. His stage: the puddle of shadow beside the curtained box from which Miss Nightingale made her entrance. His able assistants: a faulty gas lamp and the snobbery of his fellow guests. His magic: a visage so plain, so utterly forgettable that it slipped out of one's mind even while Tim stood before them.

Only one man's glinting eyes shone in his direction every so often like a lighthouse beacon searching for the lone survivor of a capsized ship. Fortified by that black, if sparkling, light, Tim attuned his senses to the tensions in the room, seeking out the false notes, the hesitations, any scent or sign of danger. He heard only Miss Nightingale's muffled weeping from within her cell as she came to terms with the role she would play in the night's proceedings. Tim prayed her conscience was the night's only casualty.

The shrill cry of a cuckoo clock startled them all. While a footman raced to silence it, Vandenberg chuckled. "Relic from another time."

"Aren't we all?" Commodore Goldenplover quipped, but no one save Hiero bothered to laugh. Snatching a full bottle of scotch off the tray, Goldenplover settled into an armchair in a neutral zone of the room. "Let's get this started, shall we?"

With a murmur of agreement, the parties separated into factions. Lady Stang-Helion moved to Blackwood's side. Miss Pankhurst took a seat on the opposing divan. Tim joined her. Vandenberg disappeared behind the curtain for a time, then emerged with Miss Nightingale on his arm, whom he stationed beside his wife, standing guard over them. After inhaling a deep, centering breath—which happened to elongate his already impressive stature and widen his already broad shoulders—Hiero paraded over to center stage.

"My dear ladies and gentlemen, I regret to inform you that there will be no séance tonight."

"Bash," Blackwood growled. "I might have known."

"I daresay you did," Goldenplover challenged, "and yet you came."

"It must come to an end," Vandenberg insisted. "For all our sakes. The robberies were bad enough, but murder—"

"Oh, no! Is your fang gone as well, Val?" Lady Stang-Helion asked.

"Of course not," Blackwood sneered. "He's got them all."

"That is a lie!" Vandenberg lunged forward; Landgravine Vandenberg caught his arm. "And from the likes of you!"

Goldenplover cleared his throat. "We all know who the collector is here."

"Take care," Blackwood warned in his reedy voice.

Silence fell, sharp and swift as an axe. Staggered by this demonstration of power, Tim made a quick study of all the faces in the room. To a one they blazed with murderous anger.

Twin prongs of hopelessness and despair clamped around his heart. Unless everyone was guilty—an intriguing but unlikely possibility—he needed a full confession to support the evidence of the notebook. If they couldn't link Small and Croke to anyone but Blackwood, who had the weakest motive for stealing the fangs now that they could prove a long history of blackmail and intimidation through other means, a murderer would go free. Tim's only chance of avoiding dismissal, no matter how remote, was to deliver the culprit to Quayle along with Blackwood.

And somehow convince Superintendent Quayle of Hiero's innocuousness. As he lay in the sanctuary of his lover's arms the previous night, Tim had confronted the one thought he had been avoiding all this time: if he didn't exonerate Hiero in Quayle's eyes, Quayle would find another means of investigating him. The witch hunt wouldn't end with Tim's career. While Tim held a certain amount of faith in Hiero's ability to wiggle his way out of dangerous situations, he believed far more zealously in the indefatigability of Scotland Yard. If they wanted Hiero's head on a spike, they would have it.

Even if they had already spent their last night together, Tim would sink to the bottom of the social abyss before he let that happen.

"Ah, dear Stephen." Hiero poured every last ounce of condescension into his smile. "Very smart. You've hit on our theme for the evening." Though a Greek chorus of scowls sought to censure him, Hiero relished their attention as if it were flattery. "Let's be done with squabbling for the moment. There's a murderer to bring to justice, after all. Or have you already forgotten poor Whicher, the man whose spirit we're here to summon?"

A sob escaped Miss Nightingale. "Let him be. He's at peace."

"What's this, my dear? Have you communicated with him?" Lady Stang-Helion asked.

Miss Nightingale dabbed her swollen eyes with her handkerchief. "If only."

Tim caught the gleam in Hiero's eyes, saw him war with the temptation to out her as a fraud. But if he knew anything about him—and, indeed, this was one of the only things Tim knew about him—it was that he had an enviable sense of compassion.

"My dear lady, I will be the only one communicating with those beyond the pale," Hiero insisted to Lady Stang-Helion. "Fortunately such tricksy spirits are all present and accounted for in this room."

She let out a dry laugh. "Do you now claim to be a medium, Mr. Bash?"

"Mmm..." He once again played an unseen piano his fingers. "More of a fortune-teller, I'd say. As to your earlier question, Landgrave Vandenberg entrusted the final fang into my care prior to this evening. Not even my manservant knows of its location, so anyone looking to complete their set will have to go through me."

"And thus betray their guilt," Blackwood said. "Brilliant."

"How kind of you to agree." Hiero took a moment to regard each member of the party in turn, his animated features firming into a look of genuine seriousness. "Before I present my conclusions to you, all but one of whom will be the judges of this affair, I will allow the murderer this opportunity to come forth and confess. As Lord Blackwood handily pointed out, much will be revealed here tonight. Secrets that would make most men blanch. After weeks of arduous investigation, my team and I know all. If you confess now, these secrets will go with us to our graves. If there is someone you are seeking to protect, they will be protected. This is your one and only chance to behave with honor. I suggest you take it.

His audience held their collective breath, shot each other suspicious glances. But to Tim's dismay, no one uttered a word.

"Please, Bash." Blackwood's reptilian grin made Tim's skin crawl. "Do go on."

"Yes," Goldenplover interjected. "Be so good as to confirm for us what many already know."

Chatter broke out across the room. Landgravine Vandenberg wheezed out some invective against Blackwood. Hiero, like any skilled conduction, waited until he had their undivided attention.

"From the first the theft of the fangs struck me as peculiar. The thieves wanted their presence to be known, waited until a well-attended séance to strike. They could have spirited the fangs away in the dead of night or on a quiet afternoon. But they chose to let the world know of their crimes, to sneer at the four hunters who had brought the Scavo lions down by stealing out their prized possessions from right under their noses. Thus the first question we as investigators had to ask ourselves was this: Was there a direct link between the events in Scavo and the robberies, or did the thieves merely want us to conclude such a link existed?

"Such a fertile exercise yielded a bounty of motives. The death of Lady Stang-Helion's husband, for one. Or Denys Finch. Or your headman Chiwi, for another. The supernatural aspect—was someone in the village or in the group of hunters seeking retribution for some unknown wrong? Do the thieves believe that the fangs protect those they were given to and were they attempting to remove that protection by stealing them? Or was something far more nefarious and, dare I say, necromantic at play, the fangs required for some dark magic ritual?

"All decent theories. All utter rubbish."

His last words hung in the air, waiting to be pierced by any objections. Tim surveyed the audience, but no one twitched, flinched, or batted an eye. Indeed Landgravine Vandenberg appeared to be asleep. Their sangfroid would have been admirable were it not so misplaced.

Hiero pointed to the far wall, snapped his fingers. Mr. Han melted out of the shadows; the party gasped. Tim focused on Blackwood, watching the skin of his face tighten as Mr. Han slipped the notebook out of his inside jacket pocket and placed it in Hiero's outstretched hand. Tim knew the exact moment he tapped the red cover and tucked it against his chest like a cherished child, as Blackwood's cinder-black eyes flamed like coals.

"Secrets," Hiero proclaimed. "Rather like vermin. Try as you might to exterminate them, they keep scurrying back, lured by the scent of fresh meat. There's only one way to be rid of them: distraction. Direct their focus toward something more enticing. Easier prey. The secrets in this book, for instance, are of direst importance to those who would conceal... Oh, a lesser familial relation, say." Tim noted Miss Nightingale's shoulders stiffened. "Or certain private-hours proclivities." Goldie snorted. "Or proof that an accidental death wasn't quite so accidental." Lady Stang-Helion withdrew her hand from the arm of Blackwood's chair and tucked it in her lap. "Or the most galling secret of all: that the secret-keeper's hounds have slipped the leash and have set upon their former master."

Blackwood cleared his throat, an oddly musical sound. "You will give that to me."

"What, this?" Hiero pet the notebook, the devil in his eyes. "Certainly."

He tossed it in the air. Hiero had a fop's aim; it crashed through a vase of white roses, bounced off an ottoman, and landed some-where at Blackwood's feet. He let out a snarling sigh but didn't bend to retrieve it.

Instead he asked, "Useless now, I take it?"

"Entirely."

Blackwood nodded. "What do you want?"

"I should think that rather obvious."

"Say it loud and say it plain, then, great consulting detective. Unveil the killer's identity. Make your case. Tell me, once and for all, which of those nearest and dearest to me conspired to wrest my empire away. I am, as they say, all ears."

Hiero confronted that brimstone glare with considerable

aplomb. He scoffed, crossed his arms over his chest, and stared back tauntingly. Rather than evoke the image of two stags locking horns, Tim's mind set upon those clever birds who picked the teeth of crocodiles.

One snap and they were done for.

"Well?" Blackwood demanded, voice cracking.

Hiero leaned in Tim and Callie's direction. "Well?" Tim shook his head. Callie made a moue. Hiero shut his eyes, mouthed a silent curse, and shifted back into character.

"Ah, yes, Mr. Kipling. The most recent convert to the cult of Bash." Blackwood almost cackled as he reclined back in his chair, fixing those beady eyes on Tim. "Curious that out of all the gadflies and sycophants that gather at our soirees, you should be the one to bear witness to our public shame."

"You were the one to introduce him to the group, weren't you, Stephen?" Goldenplover pointedly inquired. "He was, if I recall, your man."

"Quite. But is he still, I wonder?"

Tim stood to face his accuser and immediately regretted it. He should have known such a pithy thing as height gave him no advantage over a conniver like Blackwood.

"I am, and have ever been, DI Timothy Stoker. The Yard's man, if anyone's."

A choir of exclamations sang from the ladies.

"And what, pray tell, is your remit, DI Stoker?"

"To investigate me." Tim felt Hiero fall in at his side and could have kissed him for it. "Which he has done most thoroughly, I assure you."

"At my behest," Blackwood hissed.

"On the orders of Superintendent Julian Quayle, sir. The Yard thanks you for your efforts in facilitating my entree into Society and will happily receive my copy of the deciphered notebook upon the conclusion of this affair."

"Unless…"

"I'm not sure I understand your meaning, my lord."

"Come now, Stoker. Everyone can be bought. Name your price."

Hiero clapped his hands. "I'm afraid your credit has run out. With everyone, if I'm not mistaken. But if there are any others who care to make an offer, bidding will open shortly. A small price to pay, wouldn't you say? A confession for a notebook?" Tim thought he'd be confronted by a pack of hungry eyes. Instead they gawped like guppies. "We'll give the last of the guests a few more minutes, shall we?"

As if on cue, Silas Croke kicked in the door. With no more grace than a penguin, he waddled over to Blackwood and pressed a gun to his temple. His half-toothed grin and round, squished nose further undermined his air of menace.

"I'll take those odds," Abraham Small declared as he sauntered through the door, rifle aimed at Hiero. His gang of masked thugs fanned out behind him, their weapons trained on every member of the party. The largest one seized hold of Mr. Han, slamming him against the wall and cuffing his hands behind his back.

"Now see here!" Tim turned to Small, all too aware of the uselessness of his truncheon. "You will unhand that man. He's a servant and no part of this."

Small laughed. "Bruises don't lie, Stoker. And my mates here haven't forgotten how many you dealt out." He gestured to the thug closest to Tim. "Do him too."

For the second time in a fortnight, Tim found himself pinned to the floor by a large black boot, his head smarting and his wrists bound. Still conscious, of course, but to no advantage. He did see Small swoop down and pluck the notebook off the ground.

"What is the meaning of this?" Blackwood thundered, all pretense of composure gone.

Small's shoes stalked into view as he moved to the center of the room. Hiero wasn't the only showman about, Tim thought.

"We've come to take Mr. Bash here up on his offer, my lord. What was it? A confession for a notebook?" If Tim craned his neck, he could just see Small sidle up to Hiero. "You know, the one you said you didn't have."

Hiero's smile was as mischievous as ever. "I lied."

"So you did."

"I could be lying still."

"So you might. An awful big risk to take in such hoity-toity company."

"No risk, no reward."

"I did hear you were something of a gambling man."

"Oh?" Hiero raised a mocking eyebrow. "Why? Do you care to raise the stakes, Mr. Very Tall Small?"

"I rather think they are high enough," Goldenplover grumbled. "Say your piece and be done with it."

"Starting with why we should trust a traitor like you," Blackwood seconded.

"Oh, that's rich, that is." Small whirled around, gunshot eyes trained on his former master. "'Come work for me,' this one says. 'I'll give you the keys to the kingdom.' Only he don't say that he'll dangle them over our noses till we come to heel, feeding us scraps while he gets the best cuts. But we do owe you a bit of thanks, *my lord*. If you hadn't taught us your wicked ways, we could've never used 'em against you."

Vandenberg gasped. "You're the thieves."

"Aye," Small chuckled, wrenching his stare off Blackwood to challenge this newest accuser. "Do you know me, my lord? Know my face, remember my name? Ever looked at me the way you are now, like I'm actually *in the room* with you? Not part of the furniture?" Small scoffed, addressed them all. "Nah. I reckon not one of you can. But we've all met before. You hired me to protect you, and I'm like a stranger to you. You didn't trust me, you trusted your money to keep me quiet, keep me begging, keep me faithful. Never dreaming of wanting more for myself. Well, I want more!"

His gaze swept the room and landed on Miss Nightingale. "I used to think that with your airs and manners and refinement, maybe you were better than me, a mush-headed rozzer. But when I finally got close, I saw that you were just as crooked and mean and ruthless. And if you can be that way, then why can't we?"

"'Look like th' innocent flower. But be the serpent under 't,'" Hiero quoted.

"Aye, that." Small veered back to Blackwood. "This fool opened the door, and we rushed in. And none of you were the wiser. You even hired this doughbake Bash to suss us out, and he's so thick he's calling for a confession!" Croke sniggered. "And so you have it. We took your fangs, and we'll have the last one before we go." Small stretched his hand toward Hiero, palm up. "I'll take that notebook now, Bash. The decrypted version, if you please."

Tim didn't have to see the rest of the room to know all eyes were on Hiero, who appeared decidedly unruffled by Small's accusations and demands.

"You can't possibly think I was thick enough to bring a smoking gun to the scene of a crime."

"The only crime here is what will be done to you all if you don't have it."

"Oh. Well, then, that is rather unfortunate." Hiero flounced over to the spot vacated by Tim—forcing him to scratch his chin on the carpet as he shifted his view—and perched on the edge of the cushion, eyes turned up like an avid schoolboy. "What was your plan? Did you bring another lion?"

"Curse you, Bash! This is no time for games!" Vandenberg burst out. A thug jabbed him in the neck, and he collapsed to a chorus of shouts. No one, however, dared move to attend him.

"Consequences." Small strolled around the room. "You taught me those, didn't you, my lord? 'To every action there is a consequence.' Many a good man sacrificed for his mistakes, or those of another. You never bothered to learn who was responsible, did you? As long as there was someone to blame." Tim imagined he could hear the tympani of a dozen panicked heartbeats, including his own, whenever Small paused. "No mercy. To answer your question, Bash, that's our guiding rule." Momentarily blinded by the glint of his knife, Tim didn't see him slip behind Miss Pankhurst until it was at her throat. "Now where is the key?"

Rather than answer, Hiero took Callie's hand in his own. He gazed with undisguised affection at her proud, determined face.

"Are you well, my dear?"

"Perfectly."

"No harm will come to you."

"Not a promise I would make," Small sneered.

"I know it," Miss Pankhurst affirmed. "I know you."

"So you do." With that Hiero stood, walked across the room— giving Tim the world's worst case of carpet burn as he struggled to keep eyes on him—and replaced Vandenberg behind Miss Nightingale.

A twirl of his hand revealed Callie's pistol, which he aimed point-blank at her skull.

"Who," he purred in a voice which even now was like a lick up Tim's prick, "is your accomplice?"

Shouts of outrage erupted. Tim wrestled against the boot that pinned him, desperate to improve his view, to see the expression on Small's face. A kick to the kidney stilled him, and in the ensuing silence, he chased after the logic that had led Hiero to make such an unexpected move against Small. For why should Small care if Miss Nightingale lived or died, unless...

Then he remembered the confidence man who had christened himself Hieronymus Bash was not a creature of logic, but of instinct. A gambler of the highest order, yes, which meant he only wagered when reasonably certain of the outcome. Some tell, some turn of phrase or gesture or look of Small's must have given the game away:

he and Nightingale were lovers. Or else Hiero risked all their lives on some flight of fancy which, if the thugs didn't slaughter them all, Tim would see him pay for. And not in the nice way.

"Where is the key?!" Small choked out.

The reemergence of the glint in Hiero's eye told all.

"Your accomplice. Make your full confession."

"Silas Croke and many others. Ask his lordship for a full account. Though I doubt he remembers the name of a single one."

"But you do, don't you?" Tim muttered and was crushed by the boot's full weight. "Let me up!"

"Do as he says, won't you?" Hiero suavely ordered. "Since we're all gentlemen here."

Small growled but commanded, "Do it!"

Tim swallowed a smile as two thugs hoisted him up and threw him back beside Miss Pankhurst. The power in the room shifted; perhaps he could nudge it further in their direction.

"The names of all those good men. Lord Blackwood's consequences. You know them all. You bore witness. There's value in that."

"Not as much value as what's in those boxes," Croke interjected. "Won't spare us the noose, neither."

"It won't, at that," Small said in a quiet voice, as if reminding himself. He fixed Tim with a sinister stare. "Ain't nothing worse than a dirty copper, is there, DI Stoker?"

Hiero cleared his throat. "Not terribly germane to the matter at hand, gentlemen. Now if you care to refocus your efforts on our standoff, I'll ask one final time for the name of your accomplice, Very Tall DS—"

"Stop it!"

"No." Hiero cinched his free arm around Miss Nightingale's throat and shoved the pistol into her hair. "The name."

"The key!" Small bellowed, cutting a thin line across Callie's jugular, just enough for blood to trickle out.

"Abraham." Miss Nightingale looked up at Hiero, put a hand on his arm. With a satisfied smirk, he moved it to her shoulder. The pistol remained in place. "He knows."

"Dahlia!" Vandenberg bleated, staggering to his feet.

"What?!" Lady Stang-Helion fanned herself furiously. "But you... you can't possibly..."

"Explain yourself this instant," Landgravine Vandenberg rasped, moving to distance herself.

Miss Nightingale cackled, regarding them all with a contemptuous glare. Her face had undergone a galling transformation from demure, dovelike softness to the rapacious grandeur of a villainess. It was, Tim thought, her most compelling performance thus far.

"How shall I put this in terms you might understand, my dear cousins and patrons? Alas I cannot. For you have never known a moment's deprivation, or discomfort, or loss, or misery. You have never been shunned by society. You have never gone hungry. You have not lived a day without servants to wait upon your every whim, with a banquet's worth of vittles to fatten you and a house that would comfortably fit a dozen families under its eaves. You have not toiled the day away at some exhausting employment, only to be beaten at the end for not doing the work of ten. You have never begged for a crumb of what others have gorged themselves on. You fools who spend fortunes contacting spirits but have not a minute to spare for those starving to death."

She attempted to rise, to take the stage, but Hiero shoved her back down.

"Quite a neat little speech for a murderess. But I daresay our friend Small here is no Robin Hood, and you are rather miscast as Maid Marian. Or am I mistaken? Do you intend to donate your bags of gold to the poor you spoke so eloquently of?"

"What gold is this?" Goldenplover inquired as if they were at a cocktail party. "I thought you spoke of secrets."

"Oh, didn't I say? Where did I leave off..." Hiero bit his lip, muttered to himself as he mentally reviewed the finer points of his summation. Tim grunted. Loudly. "Ah, yes, dear Kip. Would you do me the honor of continuing? I'm a bit—" He gestured toward Miss Nightingale with his free hand. "—indisposed at the moment."

"If I must."

"Do."

"As you wish."

Hiero had the temerity to wink at him. Tim might have been reassured by this if he had any confidence he was a cog in a larger clockwork scheme of Hiero's. But the mechanism beneath those velvety locks did not run on steam like most, but on fairy dust, as likely to produce a flamingo as an escape plan.

"In the course of our investigation, we discovered Lord Blackwood had been stealing precious items and family heirlooms not just from the people in this room, but from dozens of the great families. He hired DS Small, DC Croke, and other policemen to steal the items for him. He hoards these treasures in a labyrinthine vault, where they are protected by a pride of lions. The notebook, which is encoded, details which treasure belongs to which lord or which lady. Without the notebook, it will be impossible to determine the true value of many of the items, some of which have their own rich history, or to blackmail those whose secrets are contained there in the form of documents and such."

"My word!" Lady Stang-Helion exclaimed. "Did you say lions?"

"So I did. Two of which found their way into your ballroom, my lady." Tim locked eyes on Miss Nightingale. "Did you intend all along for your brother to die, or was that merely a fortunate turn of events?"

"If you knew of the abuses I suffered at his hands—"

"Oh, spare us the soliloquy." Hiero huffed. "Amateurs. Do continue, Kip. You were doing quite well."

Goldenplover snorted. "You might consider engaging him as a permanent translator of the flowery nonsense you spout."

"You wound me."

Blindsided by a blow to the head, Tim thumped down onto his knees.

"I'll do the wounding here!" Small snarled. "If you know so much about our dealings, Stoker, then tell me, where is the key?!"

Mouth full of blood and legs screaming, Tim rounded on him.

"Do you think we're so thick as to have brought it with us?"

"What of your promise?" Miss Nightingale demanded. "I've made my confession."

"And what a pretty one it was." Hiero patted her on the shoulder. "From where I stand, our part of the bargain is fulfilled. Your lover, if I may be so bold, has the notebook."

"Useless," Small seethed. "The lot of you."

"Just like the information it contains," Tim reminded him. "Even if you could decipher it, it's hardly of any value to you now."

"Mr. Stoker," Miss Pankhurst warned.

"Every person in this room knows of your plans. The jewels can be fenced, but the documents are worthless without vulnerable people to blackmail, and we will shout of your guilt to the rooftops."

Miss Pankhurst grunted. "Hiero! Someone! Stop him!"

"Why you'd be better off..." Tim's mouth hung open mid-sentence, robbed of breath as he finally let their present predicament play out to its logical conclusion.

"Now you're catching on." With a fiendish smirk, Small cut another shallow slit across Miss Pankhurst 's neck, garlanding her décolletage with crimson buds.

"Ah-ah." Hiero yanked Miss Nightingale by the hair, jabbing his pistol's muzzle into the soft under her jaw. "Don't lose your head now, Very Ta—"

"Shut it!"

"It appears," a voice like brittle ice interrupted, "that we are at something of an impasse." His fingers steepled under his chin, his eyes sharp as flint, Blackwood could have been Satan's consigliere.

"Bash, you cannot bluff your way out of this room alive, even if you give up the key. Small, kill as many of us as you like, but your lady love will not survive the night. I see only one way out of this quandary of yours. Do you?"

"And what is that?"

"Me." Slowly so that Croke and his shotgun could follow him, Blackwood stood. "Did you forget? I know the key. Which I am willing to exchange for our lives." He stepped out of the circle of furniture, toward the door. "Together we will go to the vault. Leave some of your... associates here for an hour or so, enough time for our journey. Once there I will give you the key to the notebook's code. You may do with me as you wish."

"Stephen, no!" Lady Stang-Helion gasped.

"Dearest Tommy." A look of remorse wrinkled his features. "It's the only way." They firmed into an inscrutable mask anew, raised against Small like a haplite's shield. "Well?"

Small's dull pebble eyes skipped between opponents, each thought plunking into its proper slot on the abacus of his mind. The moment stretched on as if a string drawn out by one of the Fates. Soon enough their patience stretched just as thin. The men ground their teeth, the ladies wrung their hands. The thugs began to slouch their stance, their vigilance wavering. Tim took stock of all the members of his team: Miss Pankhurst, rigid and ready; Mr. Han, shackled but steely; Hiero, exasperated and... well, rather bored. His troops were hobbled, but hardy—if only there was some way to marshal them.

Hiero forcefully cleared his throat. "Well, DS—"

"No."

"Very—"

"No!"

"Tall—"

"Enough!"

"Small. How will you make your escape? Lives are in the balance."

"I'd shoot you, for a start."

"Now that's hardly sporting. Besides..." Hiero shot him in the arm. "Me first."

Chaos erupted. Miss Pankhurst wrenched the knife out of Small's grip, stabbed him in the thigh. Mr. Han, who had somehow found his way across the room, strangled Croke with the chain that bound his hands. Goldenplover and Vandenberg launched themselves into the fray. Tim rolled onto his back, kicked out at the thug above him, swung his shackles under his feet. He sprang up, punch ready.

Twining his fingers, he whipped his combined fists around like a wrecking ball. He bashed in one nose, two, smashed a thug in the gut. He snatched a red-faced Croke's rifle from his very hands, stamped the butt down on an enemy foot. Swinging the gun like a cricket bat, Tim wrong-footed two thugs who knocked each other out. Mr. Han deposited Croke atop them once he'd finally fainted away. A blur of movement, and Mr. Han had uncuffed himself. He set to work on Tim's shackles with a hairpin.

Just as he heard that telltale click, Tim spied Blackwood hauling Small toward the door. He pocketed the cuffs and gave chase.

Chapter 16

A shriek split the air. Hiero stepped gingerly aside as Callie yanked Miss Nightingale back by the collar. A twist of the cloth garroted her. She lunged for Callie's wig, all trace of the delicate Dahlia gone. Callie whipped her back into her chair, lashing her limbs with curtain ties. Goldie and Val saw to the last of the thugs, piling them in a great muscular heap beneath the window—a sight that under different circumstances might have proved alluring. Han instructed the servants to usher Landgravine Vandenberg to her room before the police arrived. Lady Stang-Helion remained in her chair, head bowed, trembling.

Hiero swirled the whiskey in his tumbler, contemplated the wreckage their little scene had caused. *Not,* he thought, *as disastrous as the encounter with the lion.* A near thing, though. He downed his three fingers in one go, wandered back to the liquor cabinet. He fished a second—and only—intact tumbler from the flood of shattered bottles soaking in crème de menthe, refreshed both glasses, and turned to lead Kip in a celebratory toast.

Only Kip, Blackwood, and Small were nowhere to be found.

Hiero let out a measured sigh. How typical of his righteous lover to cart the culprits off to gaol without even a fare-thee-well. Kip's dedication to duty was admirable, his social graces abysmal. Hiero would have to put him through the same finishing school that transformed him into the creature of grace and style who just solved the most high-profile case of his career. Already he could hear the clamor of the newshounds, the scritch of the sketch artists' charcoal. The applause of his peers as he made a cursory appearance at his club. The buzz of the patrons as he dined in the finest restaurants. The clang of—

Gunfire boomed. Han and Callie raced out the door, unarmed. With a groan, Hiero tossed his glass at the nearest footman and followed. Breaking out into the chill night, he hit the top step in time to see Blackwood shove a hobbled Kip into his carriage. Han leapt for the mudguard as they flew off but—in a rare miss—splashed into a puddle. He'd squeezed out his jacket by the time Hiero caught up, Callie cursing the length of her skirts on the bottom stair. As one they turned toward the Black Maria that had brought Small, Croke, and their gang of roughs to their fateful appointment and bolted.

Han had the driver well in hand before Hiero reached the side seat; he dodged the flailing man as he swung himself up.

"Don't you dare!" Callie barked as she waddled toward the back doors.

"We must, and we will." Han flicked the reins. Fortunately for her the horses didn't budge.

A leonine growl rumbled up from behind—such that Hiero feared they had an unexpected guest—until the back doors slammed with a jolt, kick-starting the horses, and off they went. A second clank startled Hiero, who shifted aside to see an un-mauled Callie peering through a sliding panel in the back cabin. She hissed at him.

"Head north."

"To Blackwood's menagerie, yes. Unless you've hit on some other destination?"

"No, he'll fly there. With every scrap of evidence and our two best witnesses. Neither of which are long for this world." Callie uttered an oath most fishwives would have blanched at. "How did it all go so wrong?"

"I missed." An acid flare seared up from his gut, his whiskey supper suddenly a flambé. Hiero imagined the terror in Kip's green eyes as the pride encircled him, his screams as their fangs gored his freckled skin. Remembered the clump of bone and viscera that young constable had been reduced to and nearly sicked up.

"Stuff and nonsense." A silk-gloved hand gripped his arm. "You're no murderer."

Hiero scoffed. "Truth be told, I only thought to avoid shooting the notebook. Trust a fiend like Small to carry it over his heart."

"I dare say Blackwood will follow his example from now on. If he hasn't destroyed it."

"He can't." Han lashed the reins. "It's his calling card. And this escapade will only enhance his reputation. Cross him and he'll feed you to his cats. He'll have the other half of London Society on its knees by sunrise."

"I can think of far better ways of passing the time. Especially—"

"Oh, do spare us," Callie chided. "A good man's life is at stake."

He glared at her, barely repressing a corrosive burp. "How well I know it." In a further fit of dyspepsia, Hiero remarked, "Forgive me for mentioning this, my dear, but I fear you're not dressed for the occasion. You will, of course, remain in the cab."

"And how do you mean to rescue them? Crush them with your wit?"

"A far sight better than strangling them with your skirts."

She gasped. "Have a care to remember who keeps you, Hak—"

A sharp, shrill whistle from Han silenced them both. Hiero swallowed back his latest barb, wincing as it scraped its way back down to his spleen.

"Apologies. I simply can't—"

"I know." She reached for his hand anew with her gloved one. He clung to her strong, steady grip as they raced through the gaslit streets. The link-boys' torches, dancing like fireflies at the height of summer, blinked out as they passed Marylebone Road and swerved onto Albany Street, circling the ominous blank of Regents Park. A bank of fog hovered just above the rooftops, a black pillow waiting to suffocate them all. A bubble of upset lodged itself under Hiero's sternum, twisting his lungs and robbing him of breath as the casket warehouses of Camden lined up into a graveyard that blight out the horizon. Somewhere amidst those hulking sarcophagi, Kip's fate was sealed.

An added blemish on a bleak landscape, Blackwood's fortress stood out by virtue of its isolation as if even the surrounding buildings shrank back in fear. Its saber-toothed gate had been left ajar—not quite a gaping maw waiting to snap down upon them, but enough to unsettle. Though no carriage waited in the courtyard beyond and not a glint of light illuminated the structure's slit windows, Hiero doubted they had beat Blackwood to his own endgame. The anvil-like edifice before them only looked impenetrable; hammer in the right spot and it too would collapse.

They abandoned the Maria before sneaking through the gates, planning for a quick escape they might never make. Hiero couldn't shake the sense of finality, couldn't stop hearing the click of the latch behind him, even though Han had chained one side of the fence back. Callie, having coopted a spare pair of uniform trousers, hurried him along, caught as ever between Han's haste and Hiero's prevarication. She surrendered the rifle she'd found to Han but snatched back her pistol. Unarmed and all too aware of his utter uselessness, Hiero gave himself twenty paces to fret, then, reminded he had at one time in his life defied steeper odds, steeled himself for the fight.

"Breadcrumbs," Han muttered, pausing before the entrance. The iron door swung from its hinges as if a giant had flipped it aside to search for stray villagers. Sickly green gas lamps ghosted down the corridor that led to the central cavern, at the end of which a whiter, starker light glowed. The stench assaulted them: the primitive trinity of piss, shit, and blood laced with terror. "He wants us to follow."

"And so we must." Callie strode forward, head high and pistol cocked, an Amazon by nature if not birth. Han and Hiero had to squeeze in to flank her. All three slowed as they neared the end of the passage. Hiero peered around its edge.

And clutched the coarse brick to keep himself from fainting.

Kip and Small were trapped in the lions' feeding area. Blackwood fussed with the ropes that would lift away one of the walls of the cage, unleashing the famished beasts behind. His carriage driver smoked—smoked!—on the far side, awaiting instruction. The starved, scruffy cats had caught the scent of prey. They prowled the divider, a chorus of low, ferocious purrs reverberating through the air.

Small pleaded with his former boss through the bars, his promises ever more delusional and desperate. Kip had retreated to the farthest corner, arms crossed, still as a statue. Hiero cocked an ear and listened for his thinking, trying to attune himself to the frequency of that genial mind. Even as his every instinct screamed there was no way out once Blackwood succeeded in lifting the wall.

Only one thing to be done, then. The one thing he did best.

Hiero strode out into view. Only a few steps in, he wished he'd had a servant fetch his cape before departing the Vandenbergs'. A touch of flair never hurt when disarming criminal masterminds, he always thought. As this one was too absorbed with unraveling a particularly pernicious knot to notice his arrival, Hiero took his time choosing his mark. Ignoring Han's frantic gestures and Callie's scramble to catch up, he licked a finger, held it in the air, wondering at the acoustics. He recalled them to be generally poor, as the bestial choir drowned out even the clearest conversation and the echo stifled idle chatter. Not ideal conditions, but he had acted in worse. A barn in the wilds of Herefordshire came to mind.

He permitted himself a glance—more of a flick of the eyes, really—in Kip's direction, but no more. He could not be swayed by emotion. Anger, fear, anxiety, desperation, these had no place on the stage. Fruitless to think of all the lazy mornings or lusty evenings lost to the swipe of a cat's claws, of the quests and quarrels and traded quips made quiet by the snap of a lion's jaws. Of the lovely, sinuous body of the very average man who had cocooned in his arms for the past few nights, as if such sanctuary had ever been denied him. Hiero looked for an instant, enough time for their eyes to lock. For everything and nothing to be said. For Kip's silent, screeching plea to stake him through the heart.

"Dear, dear Blackwood. Villainy is ever so much more complicated when you have to go it alone. Don't you agree?"

Blackwood glanced over his shoulder. "Ah, Bash. I did wonder."

"Yes, we had a spot of trouble at first, but you should consider the forces of righteousness corralled."

Blackwood appeared to smirk. "How unlike you to paint the circumstances in such monotone colors. Black and white—so common, so drab."

"Offering to add a splash of crimson, are you?"

A sharp laugh. "We'll make a clairvoyant of you yet." His bony fingers finally had their way with the knot, which loosened into a topsy coil. Blackwood threaded the rope through a lower pulley, then clamped the end onto a gathering wheel. Hiero was no mechanic but, by his estimation, Blackwood had only to yank the lever back in time with his driver on the opposite side, and the cage wall would rise. "Bit of a fool's errand you're on, wouldn't you say?"

"Oh?"

"Let me speak in words you'll understand, my gambling friend. I hold all the cards." He gripped the lever with an imperious fist. A snap of his fingers, and his driver did the same. Only then did Blackwood turn toward Hiero, arm at the ready. "There is no doubt I have conquered. What should concern you is how many unfortunate souls I squash as I scale to the summit."

"Something of a mixed metaphor, what? And here I always thought you such a cunning linguist. Why else would a lady of Thomasina Stang-Helion's gentle nature keep company with…" Hiero fluttered his fingers in Blackwood's direction. "The words 'tin whistle' do come to mind."

"Ah, I see. You're trying to bait me. It won't work."

"No?"

"No."

"Not even when I note that Miss Nightingale has every reason to sing, sing, sing. Especially if you make catnip of her lover."

"The word of a fallen woman over a lord. Now that I think on it, that *is* likely to sway the Home Secretary. He never could resist a skirt at Eton. Or since."

"As detailed in your notebook?"

"Why, yes. Fancy that."

It was Hiero's turn to smirk. "The one I tossed at you, but which you didn't pick up." With flourish he pointed to the ground. "Anger. Such a potent emotion. So... disarming." With a twist of his wrist, he plucked a second notebook out of thin air, displayed it with the panache of a magician's assistant. "What's the first rule of the antiquities trade? Pity we can't ask our friend, Mr. Kipling. No matter, I'll spoil it for you: authenticate."

Blackwood scoffed, the whine of a trumpet. "How do I know you're not deceiving me now?"

"I couldn't say."

"I've every reason to doubt you."

"And a vault of very valuable reasons to believe."

"Perhaps so." Blackwood pretended to consider his options, but the performance didn't convince. "Unless you're privy to my plan."

"Which is?"

"To kill you all."

Blackwood jerked the lever back, then a second to bar the exits. Across the way, Han clashed with the driver, who'd traded his cigarette for a flail. How positively medieval. Callie, pistol drawn, pushed Hiero aside and took aim. Blackwood stared her dead in the eye, marched forward until he was only a few feet away. Callie raised the pistol point-blank to his brow. He chuckled, the honk of a mangled oboe.

"So bold, Miss Pankhurst. And yet it is quite something to drop a man in cold blood. What was it you said about anger, Bash? It feeds you in the moment. Makes some ravenous. But others..."

"Appetite stirring, is it?" Hiero cursed himself for not steadying the quaver in his voice.

"Not in the slightest. The blood, you see, is never on my hands. I have my pride." He shot a coy glance at the cage. "I do wonder. Will you find your nerve before my kitties have snapped Mr. Stoker's neck?"

Tim didn't know whether to consider it a blessing or a curse when Hiero snuck into the warehouse, followed—in protest—by Mr. Han and Miss Pankhurst. But it was a distraction he didn't need. Bad enough he had bungled the investigation such that his gory spectacle of a death was imminent; now that spectacle had found its audience, and his humiliation would be complete.

Wrenching his eyes away before he cried out to Hiero like some dippy damsel in an overwrought novel, Tim instead called up all his faculties to find a way out of this death trap. He reexamined every inch of the cage, scrutinizing the details for that one slip, one weakness, one tactical error. The experience of deciphering the notebook had unlocked certain key aspects of Blackwood's character. If only he could harness these insights toward planning his escape, he might defy the odds.

Because it was impossible to forget whose blood caked the stone floor beneath him, whose bones had been kicked into the corner. The primal energy wafting off the hungry beasts gathered by the connecting wall hummed through the air like the surge before a lightning strike. The saliva that dripped from their fangs when they snarled; the stretch of their nostrils as they drank in the savory aroma of fresh, frightened prey. The screech of their claws as they dug at the bars. The undulation of their tawny hides as they flexed, preparing to run, to pounce. Only their eyes betrayed their innocence—eagerness as well, but mostly innocence. Their kill instinct was as natural as Tim's terror; they were as trapped as him. Only Blackwood had marked Tim as wildebeest, perverting the cycle of life as well as the course of justice.

The refrain of Hiero's confrontation with Blackwood, lively with innuendo, caught Tim's ear, but did little to drown out the alarm clanging through his head. At least DS Small's bleating had quieted with Hiero's arrival. He now lay slumped against the bars, his right side drenched with blood, looking as green as the entryway lamps. Tim wished he could pity him, but Small was no better than the boodlers he nabbed, thumbing his nose at the laws he should have been enforcing. How a man of such purpose could be so dishonest in his dealings while a hornswoggler like Bash had such an inbred sense of honor...

Hiero could have taken the glory and run. He had Miss Nightingale's confession and could have claimed he let Blackwood deal with Small since the detective sergeant was in his lordship's employ while committing the thefts. Tim's disappearance he could have shrugged off. Instead he begged for Tim's life the only way he knew how, by trying to brazen their way out. The least Tim could do was keep up his part and prevent himself from being mauled.

A lioness crashed against the connective wall, snapping him back to reality. Ignoring the near-choking pound of his heart, Tim scanned the cage anew. Though the cats' low growls quivered his knees and Small's whimpers prickled his conscience, he forced his brain to focus on his predicament. Seconds flowed quick as the sweat down his face and back, but Tim searched on, when suddenly...

The clank of the lever. The shriek of metal on metal. Slowly, as if Blackwood couldn't resist one last taunt, the connecting wall began to lift.

Tim staggered back, fought to steel himself, but his resolve sank with his stomach. Those glinting fangs, those impatient hisses. He thought of Hobbs, just a boy trying to do his duty, now no more than a stain on the floor. He thought of his mother and father in their final moments and wished he possessed their bravery. He thought of Hiero's hot, silk-covered form at his back, and thanked the Fates for smiling on him, even for just one night. He looked up to the ceiling, searched for a wisp of fog, a shimmer of moonlight, some final image on which to fix his gaze before...

There.

Small slammed into him. Tim staggered, recovered in time to duck. The detective sergeant swung, dizzy with weakness, missed. Tim scarpered to the far wall. He leapt onto the side of the cage, climbed as fast as he could, shucking off his boots as he went. He caught a whiff of blood, realized Small had marked him, and shed his jacket. Just as he reached for the top, Small snagged his trouser cuff.

"Stoker!" he slurred. "Take me with you! Take..." He dodged Tim's kick, clamped hold of his other leg. Tim's biceps strained under the weight of two men. "Don't you think you're any better than me! I did what any many would do, took back what should have been mine. You blighter, Stoker! Come back here! Come—"

A titanic force yanked Tim back. Small screeched, an inhuman sound. Tim clung to the metal bar with the very tips of his fingers, his knuckles straining, his wrists near dislocating, his joints stretched to their limit. Just as his left index slipped, Small howled, released him. Tim hauled himself up, out of paw's reach. He blocked out the squelch and crack of Small's wiry body, the savagery of his final screams.

The cage ceiling stretched out before him, a long grid not unlike the *tabula recta,* with enough hand and foot grips to last him, if his muscles could hold. There was no pile of boxes for the lions to leap from, but he would not discount the intelligence of starving predators. A chance—his only chance—lay in slipping through the space left at the far end by the removed connective wall. If the wall should be replaced, he would be trapped. Either his strength would give out, or the lions would find a way to make him fall.

Tim pulled himself up tight against the cage ceiling, rested his weight on his legs so his arms might recover some. He didn't dare look outward at how his friends fared; he didn't dare look down at the drooling, snarling pride.

He looked inward at the man he'd become since all this madness began, and judged himself worth saving.

Hiero yelped. All he could do, really, when witnessing a scene of such riot and chaos. The lions unleashed; Tim racing up the back of the cage; Small a hairsbreadth from his heels. Han and the nimble driver battling on the far side, mere blips of motion amidst a screen of snarling cats. Callie still as a statue in the foreground; Blackwood opposite, his pickaxe taunts chipping at her resolve. And Hiero, both hands clapped over his mouth to prevent further exclamation, watching the three-ring circus unfold. He didn't know whether to reach for a bag of roasted nuts or run screaming.

With a shaking hand, he dug for his flask. He fiddled with the cap as Abraham Small howled his last, threw his head back, and poured the scalding spirits down his throat as he listened for the second, eviscerating shriek to rend the night air. Hiero waited till the last trickle splashed his tongue, then stared at the empty spout, wishing like Juliet for the help of a friendly drop.

None came. Nothing from the cage either, if you forgave the snap and squish of lions tearing a man apart. Chains rattled in the distance, but the grunting had ceased. A peek toward Callie revealed a slight smirk to her lips. Another more tentative glance at the cage showed...

Hope. Hiero hadn't the slightest idea what to do to help Kip escape. Which suited him quite well. The best laid plans, he always said, though he never could remember the rest. He tossed the flask over his shoulder, snatched up his spare.

This he proffered before Blackwood like a waiter a particularly fine Chateau Corton Grand Cru. "Tipple?"

"What have you got in there? An entire cellar?"

"Wouldn't you like to know."

"I'll confess to a passing curiosity."

"Ah, but surely one must strike..." A twirl of his wrist, and the notebook replaced the flask. A second and he fanned out empty hands. "... before the opportunity's lost."

"If that's your motto..." Blackwood diverted his eyes toward the ongoing drama in the cage beside them. "... you'd best not blink."

Ignoring the urge to watch Kip's progress across the top of the cage, Hiero nearly missed Callie's lunge forward. She bashed Blackwood on the side of the head with the butt of her pistol, kneed him in the groin. He doubled over; she shoved him hard onto his back. Hiero dove forward, let his slippery fingers loose upon Blackwood's pockets. Callie pinned Blackwood's neck down with her boot as he tooted his protest like a departing train. Hiero picked himself a pipe, a pocket watch, two handkerchiefs, a billfold, and some lozenges before hitting on the real notebook.

He smacked Blackwood on the arse and hopped to his feet as someone began pounding on the warehouse door.

"Abraham!" Miss Nightingale's raw voice wailed. "Abraham, please!"

Unclench, slide, secure.

Unclench, slide, secure.

Tim muttered this mantra as he climbed across the cage's ceiling, bit by bit, rung by rung. He locked his stare on each of his limbs as he loosed them, moved, and hooked them into a new position, not daring to deviate until certain they would hold. Refusing, on pain of death, to look ahead or measure his progress. He blocked out the muscle spasms, the pound of his heart, the pump of his pulse in his ears. He held his breath through endless seconds of paralysis, overpowered his exhaustion through sheer force of will.

He would live. Though he scorched all thought of survival from his mind—a flicker of distraction could lead to a fall—every aching, cramping, flaring inch of him burned for it.

The beasts tracked his every move. Their rancid breath, teeming with Small's blood, clogged his sinuses. He drank it like ambrosia. Every frustrated growl played like a symphony, the soundtrack to his most operatic achievement. This time Tim would not cower behind the crates while some traitor's wolf pack set upon his parents. The lure of release, of a swift if feral end, tempted him whenever his wrists cracked, his knees juddered, his shoulders snapped, but he kept on.

Unclench, slide, secure. Steady on, no stopping.

The rungs quivered, then shook. Tim threaded his arms through, knotted them tight. He pressed the side of his face against the grate, his body to the bars. The quaking started at once, tremors that tore fault lines through his muscles and hammered at his joints. He extended his gaze beyond the cage, toward Hiero, but it blurred with tears.

A nightmare choir of roars deafened him. The bars he barely held vibrated with the cats' ferocity; his muscles convulsed in answer. Tim swallowed hard against the bilge of terror and sorrow that surged up his throat. He would live, he would live, he would live...

The rattle of a chain startled him, more so when it snaked around his torso and cinched him in. A second wove around his posterior while a third caught his knees. Tim relaxed enough to hear the clink of a familiar set of steel-tipped boots. To his great surprise and unexpected relief, Mr. Han covered Tim's hands with his own, warming him with a brotherly comfort.

"Got you well trussed, Mr. Stoker. You can let go."

He gently pried Tim's fingers off, held fast as he lowered him into his metal basket. The chains held, and Tim sagged his entire weight back, unable to stop himself from weeping with relief. He couldn't unhook his legs without upsetting the fine balance of chains and clamps, but he embraced this awkwardness as he would Mr. Han when returned to solid ground.

"You rest awhile." Han appeared through the grate above him, assaying one of his rare smiles. "Might still have to slip you through the gap, but take the time to gather your strength while I rig something up."

"What of Blackwood?"

"That situation's... fluid."

"See to them first."

"And interrupt Miss Pankhurst? Not on your life."

Tim managed a weak chuckle. "Which I now owe to you."

Han shrugged. "I've no use for it. Best devote it to someone who does."

With that he raced off to deal with the rabid beasts below, a chore Tim wished on no worthier man. Though part of his mind listened to the drama still unfolding around him, he shut his eyes and attempted to slow his breaths.

He would live.

"Abraham! Let me in!"

Her pounding had become a frantic knock, her pleading more

shrill as the seconds passed. Hiero imagined her slumped against the door, a thousand fateful scenarios whirling through her mind like a never-ending carousel as she beat her fists raw. He sat on Blackwood's legs, considered their options as they waited for Han to fetch the shackles.

"Not very practical, is she?" Callie's boot was still having its way with Blackwood's windpipe. "There must be another way in, but she'll never find it bleating like Little Bo Peep."

"Ah, but she's lost more than sheep, and I daresay she knows it."

"Could be a ruse. We did leave her with a small army of toughs."

"True. An oversight, that."

"We'll know for next time."

"Quite." Hiero turned to face her, enjoying Blackwood's curses and groans. "What shall we do?"

"I fear we must let her in."

He glanced at the lion cage, where the cats fought over the last scraps of Small's carcass, and shuddered. He pointedly ignored the area above, where Kip, though cradled by chains, hung limp, too close to a clever fang or ready claw for comfort.

"Is that wise? She may have conspired to blackmail the aristocracy, but surely no one deserves to see their lover reduced to... that." He twiddled his fingers in the cage's direction, then pressed them to his chest.

"Are you suggesting that in her feminine state, she is too delicate to confront the realities of what her conniving has wrought?"

At that even Blackwood wheezed out a chuckle.

"No, nothing of the sort. Merely that—" Han appeared, startling him. Hiero hopped to his feet, inspected the shackles, and nodded. He sauntered around to Blackwood's head while Callie kicked their prisoner onto his stomach, leaning over to catch those steely eyes. "Really rather good of you to keep these lying around."

"Go to the devil."

"Now, now. Best behavior, Stephen. Your cats are still a bit peckish. And I don't think they'd let a little thing like nobility get in the way of a good snack, do you?"

"Ask your accomplice. The detective the Yard sent to spy on you." Hiero batted his eyelashes but was otherwise unmoved. "He may wish he'd let himself be mauled once his superiors are through with him."

Hiero laughed. "Accusations. They're like axes, wouldn't you say? Any fool can hurl them around, but it takes the weight and skill of hard evidence to cleave someone in two."

"Not if you aim for the head," Blackwood snarled.

Hiero watched as Han rolled him onto his back so Callie could bind his legs. With a magician's flair, Hiero unfurled his scarlet handkerchief and stuffed it in Blackwood's mouth. Not far enough to stifle his cackle of triumph, alas.

"Go fetch our Kip," he instructed Han, more for his own comfort than out of any reluctance on Han's part. "We'll require him shortly." Hiero moved to second Callie just as the volume of the "Abrahams" and the intensity of Miss Nightingale's knocks increased anew. He veered her toward the door, unable to bear witness to the last act of Kip's rescue lest the beasts earn themselves a second supper. "Now turning to our escape. What are your thoughts?"

"Much as it pains me to malign a fellow lioness... She's hardly a threat on her own."

"But is she alone?"

"She must be. Unless..."

Hiero sighed, longing—just for a moment—for the days when their biggest challenge was locating Countess Davenham's lost poodle. Then a cry of relief erupted somewhere behind them, and he shut his eyes, whispering his thanks to the Fates he did not believe in.

Resisting the urge to spin around and race to the side of the cage, arms outstretched, ready to receive his shaken and sore, but still breathing, lover, Hiero concentrated on the problem at hand.

"Only one way to find out."

He marched over to the control panel, selected a lever, and pulled with all his might. This unleashed a swarm of uniformed policemen and one very loutish-looking Superintendent Quayle.

Tim hobbled over to where Quayle and Hiero circled each other like a bull and its matador. Though his body felt like it had been trampled in the streets of Pamplona, the sight of his governor righted his posture, readied his aching muscles, revived his addled mind. Evidence wanted presenting, messes wanted tidying. He may be on the verge of losing his badge, his reputation, and his good name, but he would not succumb to his worries and injuries when a case needed closing. For if Blackwood and Nightingale slipped the noose after all this, Tim would feed himself to the lions.

"Stoker! What the blazes—" Even Quayle had the good sense to start at the sight of him. He must have been a portrait of failure: trembling arms, hair akimbo, a limp to his step, tear-streaked cheeks, and blood-stained clothing. At least he couldn't claim Tim hadn't suffered for his results, even if they fell short of the intended mark.

He kept his gaze fixed on Quayle's hulking frame as he lurched forward. Tim knew even a glance at Hiero would seal his fate. Perhaps it was fancy, but he imagined an amber light flaring in his dark eyes at the sight of him. Hiero's face wouldn't soften—he never gave that much away—but it would shine, pride and relief and celebration radiating from his handsome visage. A clap of his hands, a curl of his lips, and Tim wouldn't be able to take another step before hurling himself into his arms.

But Hiero wasn't his to keep. He never had been. Tim should be instructing his fellow officers to clap him in irons along with Blackwood and Nightingale—by Quayle's gritted teeth and glowering brow, he would relish this very order, even from an inferior. But Tim's gift to the mesmerist who had him under so deep he couldn't tell right from wrong was freedom. An effortless concession that cost an impossible price. Quayle's arrival had turned the hourglass with a few grains of sand left to spill. Their time together was already over; the countdown to Tim's dismissal only just begun.

"Sir." Tim fell in before Superintendent Quayle, straightened as best he could. "Thank you for responding to my letter. All the evidence is in order, and I'm prepared to make my report."

Quayle snorted. "Someone better explain this..."

"Menagerie?" Hiero suggested.

"Not a peep out of you!"

"Guv." Tim attempted to draw his attention, but Quayle's stare could have staked a lesser man where he stood. Hiero clasped his hands together as if addressing a favored baroness. "The lions belong to Blackwood. He's killed two men that we know of, both police officers, and tried to kill me. He's been stealing from his friends—"

"I can read, can't I? Where's DS Small?"

Tim stammered, gestured toward the lions.

Quayle nodded. "Croke we have. Who was the third accomplice?"

"Miss Dahlia Nightingale, aka Astrid Vandenberg."

This earned him a raised eyebrow. Quayle called over his head, "Watson, cage that bird! She's dirty!" He locked his stare back on Tim. "Now where's this notebook?"

"I believe this is what you're looking for." Hiero unfurled the little red book from one of his hidden pockets with his usual panache.

Quayle yanked it out of his hands, bent it open, flicked a few pages. "You sure those docs you sent match this?"

Tim nodded. "To the letter, sir. It's a win, just like you asked."

"I'll be the judge of that." Superintendent Quayle gave him a final once-over, clicked his tongue. "Get yourself seen to, then get back here and clean up this mess. I want everything orderly on this. Not a foot wrong. Get the witnesses' details. Nail them for appointments at the Yard, starting tomorrow, and send 'em home. Full report on the night's activities, 9:00 a.m., my office, sharpish. Got it?"

"I do, sir."

Quayle surveyed the scene inside the warehouse with wary eyes, sighed. "Bloody madness."

Tim watched him stomp off, dread lodged like a stone in his gut. He crossed his arms to stop them from quaking, slacked his muscles to spare their screaming. The twenty or so feet to the exit stretched out like an oasis to a desert traveler, sliding farther back with every forward step he took. There would be no lush green sanctuary at the end of his journey, no headlines or accolades or commendations. A win in name only, one Tim couldn't even claim for his own.

A hand fell on his arm. He jerked away. "Not here."

Hiero followed him down the nausea-green hallway, out into the smoggy night. The bank of fog had descended, thick with smoke from the nearby railroad, only a marginal improvement on the charnel house they'd broke from. Tim nevertheless gulped down lungfuls of the sooty air. A few constables busied themselves with securing the gate. Every so often an arriving carriage would sail out of the brume, but otherwise the courtyard took on the desolate landscape of a remote planet or the isolated confines of a padded cell.

The Black Maria loomed tomblike in the near distance. Tim managed two thirds of the way before his knees collapsed. A pair of surprisingly solid arms broke his fall, juggled with his lax torso and limbs until they secured their hold, then hauled him into the Maria's cab. Hiero refashioned Miss Pankhurst's discarded dress as both pillow and blanket, tucking Tim into a corner so he could rest without sleep threatening. Not that he'd dare doze off with Hiero's conjurer's hands working their magic on his stiff shoulders, alternating massage with pets to his head, arms, and back.

Though he craved further care, Tim wrestled with wilding emotions. The urge to gather their misfit crew and flee to the countryside warred with his righteous streak. He, an officer sworn, married to his duty above all else. And what did he know about the enigma who nursed him now? His gentleness, his kindness, his sexual and spiritual ministrations could all have been in service to his agenda: convincing Tim to forget the true goal of his investigation and instead solve Hiero's case.

Just as he had done.

Even as he leaned into every stroke, met every caress, gave himself over to his miraculous hands, Tim remembered one of his mother's earliest lessons: two things can be true at once. A person can flirt and flatter with genuine interest and still pick your pocket. Hiero could enjoy Tim's companionship and wish him well, all the while working to protect his eccentric little family. Tim could give in to his desires and surrender his reason for a time and still return to his duties in the end.

He stilled the hands at his shoulders, pulled Hiero down beside him. With a glance at the back door—open onto a swath of dense fog not even a bat could see through—he reclined his head against Hiero's chest and wove his arms around his waist. Hiero curled his sleek body around him, not unlike a lioness with her cub. Tim held tight until he felt the sting of tears behind his eyes. He gave Hiero a final squeeze and carefully slid out of his embrace.

"Thank you." The glint in his black eyes somehow caught what little light misted in through the fog, guiding Tim in like a beacon. "No matter what transpires, I've rediscovered a lost part of myself because of you. I won't forget it."

Hiero feigned a cough. "Forgive me, but I've caught the distinct whiff of finality in the air."

"You've a nose for many things, Mr. Bash. Even sincerity."

"You've delivered him three thieves and a murderer. One deceased, but even so. Not to mention a conspiracy to defraud the wealthiest members of society and a veritable treasure trove of riches the Yard will no doubt be handsomely rewarded for—"

"But not the man he asked for. If anything I've assured that his reputation and celebrity will grow."

The white of Hiero's grin prompted one of his own. "You think so?"

Tim laughed. "I've every assurance that once word gets out of your efforts to reunite your peers with their most prized possessions, you'll be the talk of the town."

"A lad can dream." Hiero sighed. "But you. Will they really sack you for delivering... what did you call it? A win."

Tim considered this. "More likely I'll be banished to H Division and demoted to constable. Street patrol and the like."

"*Street patrol?* A mind like yours rousting drunks and breaking up brawls? Outrageous!"

"But preferable to looking for work as a disgraced officer. When you're dismissed without cause, there's always suspicion. I've seen better men ruined."

Hiero growled low in his throat. "It galls me that after our triumph, you'll have to beg for scraps. From that knuckle-dragger Quayle, no less."

"After your triumph, Mr. Bash." Tim managed a hint of a smile. "And well-deserved it was." After a second glance at the door, Tim cupped his comely face, pressed a soft, solitary kiss to Hiero's mustachioed lips. "You're a kind man, whoever you are. Mind you don't forget it."

With a lingering glance, Tim rallied his strength for the long night to come and set out into the gray.

Chapter 17

The clang of a gong blasted Hiero awake. Startled upright, the silk of his robe sailed across the slippery leather of the couch; he capsized onto the floor. This, alas, did nothing to anchor his swimming head. He lolled it to the side, the coarse fibers of the carpet scraping like barnacles at his face. A cutlass of sunlight pierced through his bleary vision, blinding him. His body creaked and groaned like an old ship kept seaworthy by spit and hope. The echo of the gong ricocheted around his skull, destroying what wits he had left after the previous night's indulgence.

A storm cloud loomed over him, then crack! Smack! A lightning strike of slaps centered his reality. Winchlike arms hoisted him up into his favorite armchair, poured a bitter tonic down his throat. Hiero gagged, gasped, glared at his captor, contemplating mutiny. Han the Merciless shoved a cup of water into his hands, pointed at the decanter, and promptly left.

With a roll of his eyes and a begrudging sigh, Hiero downed the entire glass. Then another. As he sipped his third, he admired the detritus of his past few nights. A collection of empty bottles a publican would envy clogged the center and end tables, the mantel, the far side of the desk, and the windowsill. His rolling papers fanned out over the far end of the couch, sprigs of tobacco dusting the pillows. A small mountain of newspapers, headlines shouting his praises, sprouted from the kindling box. The business end of the study had been preserved like an archeological site, not a scrap of Kip's notes or a scratch on the chalkboard erased. One of his jackets lay slumped over a pile of books as if taking a long-overdue nap.

Seven days had passed since the night of the final séance. Seven days and not a word from Kip. Hiero's nightly libations had spilled into his days, his victory lap into a vigil. Ridiculous to miss a man he barely knew, but then he was ridiculous. A ranker. A trickster. A lush. Ludicrous he should lust after one of the most upstanding and dedicated officers of the Yard, who'd been charged with declaiming him, no less. He always mourned their concluded cases—the endless stillness after the frantic rush disoriented him—but never a paramour.

He gazed up at the portrait of Apollo in younger years, long before Hiero burst into his life, and sighed. "Oh, my darling... What have I done?"

"Fat lot of nothing for the better part of a week," Callie declared, barging in with a breakfast tray. She kicked some bottles onto the carpet, then set it on the table. "That's the first and last time I wait on you, so you'd best eat up."

Hiero ignored the heaping bowl of Macau-style kippers and noodles in favor of the coffee pot. The aroma wafting from the cup was rich with sense memories, of homes both cherished and reviled, of the history of his people, of a past he could not bring himself to regret, no matter the scars he bore. Could a man like Kip ever understand the serpentine turns of the path he'd followed to this family of misfits? Could he accept Hiero's choices for what they had been, the snakes whose venom were least likely to kill him when he thrust his hand into their nests? Hiero may have molted skin after skin in order to survive, but at his core, he was who he had always been and would always be: someone who dared, consequences be damned.

"Aldridge is readying the hunting lodge. We're due a spell in the country." Callie parked herself on the ottoman, cradled her bowl, and dug in. She'd eschewed her bewigged finery for a laboratory smock and jodhpurs, and, by the flush of her brow, had been boiling up a chemical brew while Han manned the cooker. "Might be best, at least until we cause less of a sensation. Dinner at Lady Bonham's turned into a scene out of the Inquisition."

"How ghastly."

Callie smirked behind her chopsticks. "I'd have thought you eager to do the rounds, bask in the glory. They're not clamoring for me to recount it."

"In time."

Hiero, who hadn't torn his eyes from his dear, departed Apollo, imagined his proud expression turned scornful. He felt a second pair of eyes burning a hole in his temple but refused to drop the pretense. Instead he searched around the discarded bottles for a trace of amber. Finding one, he fished it out of a lopsided pile and spiked his coffee.

A clatter of chopsticks heralded Callie's ire. "Do you care to make yourself presentable, or shall I have Han haul you down to the wash bin and scrub you like a hog?"

"I beg your pardon?"

.   "We're to receive a call. In an hour. I'd prefer not to make your excuses, but I will if we have to scrape you off the floor."

Hiero hated the flicker of hope that lit in his chest, wanted to stamp it out with his palm. But almost against his will, he found himself asking: "A call? Arranged? By card or note?"

"I promise to tell you if you promise to dress. And behave. Like someone who doesn't dwell in a sewer."

"You have my word of honor."

Callie scoffed. "A pittance for a prize. Very well." But even she couldn't repress a smile at the thought of their guest. "We're to be the very first to receive Lady Odile de Volanges, newly arrived from the salons of Paris."

Hiero barked a laugh and hastened to finish his coffee.

An hour later the chime of a far more melodious clock sounded in time with the knock on the door. Hiero had made himself more than presentable in a brocaded smoking jacket with velour cuffs, collar, and trousers, and waited by the drawing room window. He watched Lady Odile mount the front steps, swathed in a blue more regal than the Queen's, and blinked away tears. To haunt the theater pubs and molly houses bedecked in the fairer sex's finery was a common risk among their kind. To achieve so seamless a transformation that one could walk in full daylight undetected and unsuspected was a peerless act of courage.

It had gone unsaid between them that Goldie had long desired to embrace such a life. Of all the souls Hiero had known who struggled in that way, Goldie was by far the most determined. But how to make such a choice without losing everything in one's life, tempting ruin or, worse, risking imprisonment? Especially when one had wealth, ambition, family, friends... Therein lay the rub.

But if the razing of the Belgrave Spiritualists' Society helped Lady Odile rise from the ashes, all the better, in Hiero's view.

"My dear!" He rushed to take her hands the second she entered the drawing room. "What a delight! How wonderful of you to do us such an honor."

Callie beamed as she gestured her toward the divan. "I'll have you know Lady de Volanges is quite sought after. All the ladies at table last night buzzed with intrigue at the mere mention of you, my lady."

"Better than shrieking in terror," Odile quipped. She perched herself on the edge of the cushion, then invited Callie to join her. She inhaled a long, shaky breath, unfurling her fan and batting up a gale. "I've had a flood of invitations, but I'm still testing the waters."

"Your legend will only grow if you don't show yourself," Hiero warned, claiming his favorite armchair. "You know how those magpies are."

"Too well. I'm contemplating an escape to the continent. A nuptial voyage, to be precise."

Hiero gaped. "Nuptials?"

"Forgive him, my lady. He's not heard the news, having spent the better part of a week trapped in a bottle." Callie straightened in her seat, the keenest pupil in the class. "After that dreadful business last weekend, Commodore Goldenplover decided he couldn't live without his Odile a moment longer. He raced to France to be by her side, and they eloped."

Lady Odile closed her fan and grabbed it with both hands. "A rushed but romantic affair, to be sure. After testifying at Lord Blackwood's trial, Abyndon and I will set off for Africa. Which brings us to the reason for my call."

"Oh?"

"The name of your seamstress, Miss Pankhurst, would be a godsend. I've heard she's discreet and doesn't mind fashioning a few... unconventional items."

"Of course!" Callie sprung up. "I'll send her a note posthaste."

Once she'd swished up the stairs, Lady Odile confronted Hiero with a stare that had commanded far hardier men. "As for you... I confess to being more than a little displeased."

"Join the queue." Hiero waggled his fingers in the direction of an imaginary line of objectors. "Though I would visit the powder room before taking your spot, as I expect it will be a long wait."

"Don't be vulgar."

"It's rather my specialty."

"I thought that was spinning a tale out of whole cloth."

Hiero gave this due consideration. "You may be right."

"I am on many counts." Odile sighed. "I've come, of course, to settle our business. Though I had rather hoped you would come to me of your own accord."

"Elopement not enough of a distraction, so your thoughts turned to me? How touching."

Lady Odile stamped her foot. Hiero started. He felt the strange urge to stand at attention, but his spine wobbled, weak as jelly.

"I've decided, after several visits to Scotland Yard, to award your fee to DI Stoker."

Further cowed by the mention of Kip, Hiero nodded. "Fitting."

"You've no objection?"

"None at all."

"Do you care to know what I observed whilst at the Yard?"

Hiero clasped his hands in his lap to keep them from conducting as he spoke. Lady Odile, he determined, would not take well to having her emotions underscored. Neither would he, at that.

"So long as he remains in their employ, it is not for me to judge."

"And you are satisfied with this outcome?"

"I am accepting. I've no choice but to accept."

"That's very unlike you."

"I've... evolved. I've migrated to another island and lost my ability to fly, like Darwin's birds."

"I see. Because in my experience, you are not one to let things lie. You poke, you prod. You flatter. You cajole. You draw our attention away just long enough to have your way, but you never, ever abandon a friend."

Hiero shook his head. "You have the wrong end of it. He took his leave from me."

"Ah." But Lady Odile wasn't daunted for long. "And you accept this?"

"I'm not his keeper."

"Not yet..."

"You're one to talk, marrying yourself."

Lady Odile chuckled. "Worse. I'm to be my own murderer."

"Ha! And you call me vulgar." Whereas some would but dip their toe into the murky waters of such a pronouncement, Hiero drove right in. "Do explain."

"Sometime during our trip to the dark continent, my sweet Abyndon will fall sick and die. After an appropriate period of mourning, I will return a widow and take up my London life with a heavy heart."

"Genius. Black is so unflattering."

"Indeed." A heaviness she had not yet cast off tempered Odile's smile, but Hiero had every confidence she would shed it in time. "Perhaps I might coerce you down for the funeral. After this business with the lions, you must be curious."

"Ah, but you know what they say about curiosity and cats."

"When has that ever stopped you before?"

"Quite."

"You could steal away with your young man. Things are much... freer there, if you've coin enough in your pocket."

Hiero shook his head. "Kip isn't like us. He only takes what he needs, no matter what's given. He was made for the Yard, for detection. Our little group may play at it, but he... he is good. He is loyal. A counterweight to all the evils of the world. Without men like him, the whole sphere threatens to spin out of control, subject to the whims of tyrants like Blackwood."

"Who was, in the end, engaged in his own twisted form of mating dance. And they call me perverse..."

"There is no word for your magnificence, and I pray there never will be."

Odile scoffed. "Flattery, as I said." She extricated a silver cigarette case from her bag and pulled out a thin hand-rolled specimen before offering one to him. When he reached out, she clapped it shut on his hand. "Coward!"

Hiero recoiled, aghast. "My dear—"

"You, whose dependents multiply quicker than a warren of rabbits, can't finagle a way to be of use to a man who..." She continued sotto voce. "I have on good authority has saved your life and shared your bed. You who was fished out of the gutter by one of the truest seamen around and bequeathed a trove of treasure cannot see your way around helping a lover in kind?"

"He is his own man."

"And so were you when Apollo first invited you in as a lodger and companion. I would say you are one still despite all evidence to the contrary." The strike of her match resounded like cannon shot, the glow of the flame alluring in its warmth until Odile puffed it out. "But perhaps the truth lies, as ever, in what remains unsaid. You've praised his work as a detective. Has he come too close to finding you out? Is that why you abandoned him?"

Hiero grunted. "You can hardly find fault in self-preservation."

"Fault, no. Hypocrisy, yes."

"His mission to unmask me is the only reason Kip and I became acquainted."

"I meant my own." Her eyes sought out a distant shore, somewhere in the sea of memory. "Your every argument is an echo of the time when I debated inviting Chiwi here, to London, to live in my home and act as my companion. His life there was so complete, and he was content. Our affair was an interruption, or so I wanted to believe. The truth was I feared he would not accept me when I revealed myself to him. Not just as a woman, but..." She shut her eyes, exhaled a shuddery breath. "He might have lived, had I been less of a coward. Certainly we would have shared something... wonderful. Or more wonderful, at any rate. I denied myself for so long, out of guilt, out of shame, out of... I would not hesitate to kill a man—did not hesitate, when in battle—but I could not wager on the man I loved."

Swallowing down a sudden tightness in his throat, Hiero moved to join her on the divan, cradling her hand in his.

"Hieronymus, don't poison what might flower at the root. Take the lesson from me. Even a man with many faces has only one life to live."

Tim eyed the door to Superintendent Julian Quayle's office like an innocent man the gallows. A half-hour early for their scheduled meeting, his hair trimmed and his shoes polished, armored in the gunmetal-gray suit and shield-silver waistcoat Hiero had bought him, he straddled the stool opposite the office door. His notes on the case had been transcribed into a neat black book similar to Lord Blackwood's, clamped under his arm like a joust. He sat straight and tall in the saddle, appearing ready for anything that charged at him...

A mask. A good one, he hoped. He had, after all, learned from the best. A week of sleepless nights—on the nights he managed to scrape together a few hours to return to his rooms—had left him brittle and uncertain. Were it not for the very real evidence he held, and the fire-breathing earl locked in their holding cell, he might have thought the past month a dream. Spirit writing and séances. Stolen fangs and man-eating lions. Colonels tarted up in ladies' finery and pageboys with dainty airs. A Chinese man with the plumy vowels of a duke.

An actor who played him like a fiddle.

For the past week, Quayle had treated him no better than a dustman sent to sweep up a royal mess. Tim had been glad of it. The details of detective work were the altar in his church, and he threw himself upon them with zealous dedication. Already he had confirmed the theft of fifty items in Blackwood's notebook, with signed statements from the victims and vows to testify at trial. Already a dozen officers at C, D, and E divisions had volunteered information about their off-hours jobs for Small and Croke. The sheer number of them created quite a quandary for Commissioner Winterbourne, with the press howling for an internal investigation and the pundits crying scandal. Tim had interviewed each member of the Belgrave Spiritualists' Society at length, as well as Miss Nightingale, who confessed to spare her life. He meticulously documented her course from fallen minor noble to celebrated medium. He accounted for every penny of Small and Croke's wasted wealth—

gambling debts and spending sprees tempted them into business for themselves. He cleared the obstacles Quayle would have set for him before Quayle had erected them, all while keeping himself to himself.

Only the work would prove his worth. Only the work would set him apart, make him indispensable. Only the work would save him from what fresh hell Quayle unleashed next. For no matter how loud the headlines screamed, Tim had failed to deliver on his promise. His recent success hadn't blinded his superiors, only bought him time. There was also some question as to whom that success was down to: Tim or the target of his investigation, the notorious Mr. Bash, more popular with the aristocracy than ere before.

Reading headline after headline about this figment of the journalists' collective imaginations had dulled Tim's mind to the truth. Or what version of the truth Hiero had presented to Tim, a bowl of cream to a stray, starving cat. Day after day, lapping it down, Tim had grown too fat with satisfaction to take advantage of being in Hiero's house, bed, inner circle. Too gluttonous to remember what left him so skeletal and ravenous: the soul-deep hunger to solve his parents' murder. He had risked their legacy on a blancmange of a man—his instincts wiggly, his intentions saccharin, his logic gelatinous.

A phantom presence prickled his spine as if Hiero's sleek frame still pressed hotly to his back. A ghostly mustache tickled across his lips. Like the memory of a severed limb, Tim felt Hiero's absence from his life as a series of impressions, sensations too otherworldly to be real. But as with the wiliest of spirits, Hiero himself slipped in and out of view. Little wonder Tim hadn't been able to summon up anything useful from him. Perhaps after all this time, all this dissimulation, Hiero didn't even recognize himself.

Tim shook his head, straightened. He could ill afford such distractions mere minutes from begging for his career. He veered his mind down a darker corridor: a trail of bloody handprints, a gory tangle of hair, his father's mouth frozen in a scream, his mother's...

"Stoker!"

He stood, stared the door down. Unbidden, his defiant mind supplied, *I go, and it is done. The bell invites me. Hear it not, Duncan, for it is a knell that summons thee to heaven... or to hell.*

Tim cursed himself a fool, marched in to meet his fate.

At first he thought the room empty. Spartan in design, with a spotless desk, meticulous files, not much in the way of personal mementos, and a giant map of London stretching the length of the far wall, on its surface, Quayle's office concealed nothing. But Tim read fine print the way some men scoped headlines, his eyes drawn to the near-overflowing wastebin, the edge of an open drawer just visible over the desktop, and the glint of an empty glass on the windowsill. What he mistook for an overloaded coat rack was, in fact, Superintendent Quayle, dirty-blond hair tamed and darkened by a slick of pomade, his undertaker's coat so long it skirted his heels.

All evidence pointed to a recent visit by Commissioner Winterbourne, an event Tim imagined displeased Quayle even more than him. The silk glove that enveloped Quayle's blunt rock, Hugh Winterbourne knew when to deploy Quayle's brutish talents and when to order him back. And little wonder Quayle scowled at the mullioned window like an ape the bars of its cage, given he resented any interference in his command and harbored no love for the upper classes. Winterbourne had been the one to insist Quayle keep Tim on; it was possible he acted as his champion now. While Quayle sought efficiency and obedience from his officers, Winterbourne turned a blind eye to their methods, so long as they produced results. Tim took Quayle's brooding as a sign that, though still in a prison of his own making, he'd 'scaped the noose.

"Sit, Stoker."

"I'd rather stand, sir."

Quayle punched a knuckle into one of the squares of glass, turned. He lumbered over to the desk and kicked back his chair. "Sit."

Tim fell into one of the rickety seats. Quayle clunked a pair of meaty fists onto his desktop, leaning forward until Tim feared he would swing over it. Instead his beady black eyes, so different from Hiero's dark star eyes, zeroed in on their target: his notebook.

"Well?"

"Sir?"

"Make your report."

Fingers gnarled with tension, he flipped to the first page without so much as a tremble. Tim held in a breath as he wet his parched lips, then launched into his update. He let the details, the tiny scraps of information he had pieced back together like a shattered vase, collate and cohere into a clear portrait of the crime. With the occasional pause to allow Quayle to reason out some minor discovery on his own, Tim spun the straw of facts and fair assumptions into one golden conclusion: the solving of this case was a triumph for the Yard.

His recitation complete, he shut the notebook and slid it onto the desk. He prayed Quayle, as Lord High Executioner, would see it as an offering, an appeasement. For what god would toss back such a bountiful sacrifice? What deity would be so churlish as to strike him down for drawing praise and doing good?

Ah, but the monkey god was an avatar of the destroyer of worlds, and Kali would ever have her vengeance.

"A fine mess and no mistake. But we've come out smelling roses, and I know that's down to you. Your work on this... I don't know any other officer could have done it. I won't deny it."

"A win, then?"

"Not quite." He shifted his weight back and forth on his arms as he considered Tim. "Not for you."

"Sir..."

Quayle held up a hand. "It's impressive work. And you have your defenders. A lot of mucky mucks have written a lot of letters, and I read 'em all. Even those I didn't understand half of—those poncey gits with their 'heretos' and their 'wherefores.' But that don't change the fact that you got in deep with an enemy of this department."

For several minutes he let the words spread between them like sick up on the desk. Tim couldn't swallow back his own upset long enough to form a response.

"Trust, Stoker. When our back's against the wall, that's all we got against the mob. Your little black book sews up this case neat and tidy, but it's the testimonies that bind it together. I have to trust they aren't coerced. I have to trust you came about your information honestly. I have to trust that when I assign you a case—"

"Understood." Tim gritted his teeth against the rise of bile in his throat. "What's the verdict?"

"Trouble." Quayle looked fit to spit. "I've been ordered not to sack you. And *my* orders aren't up to interpretation."

"A transfer, then?"

Quayle grunted. "If only. Can't be seen to be rid of you, and you'll get promoted over my dead body. Or yours, comes to that."

"A demotion? Back to the streets?"

"If I did, those rag-hounds'd have their snouts so far up my Aris, I'd be smelling for two."

Tim nodded. "Then I'd say we're at something of an impasse, sir."

"And I'd agree." His gunpowder eyes bore all the way to the back of his skull. "If I were an agreeable man. But I'm not, am I?"

"Sir..."

"Am I, DI Stoker?"

Tim opened his mouth to reply, thought better of it.

"The toffs and the swells who pull my strings forget I'm still the one who plucks yours. And you don't play to my tune. Never have. Never will. So I want you to have a good, long think about your future here."

A cold spike of fear stabbed Tim in the chest. "You want me to resign."

Quayle straightened, said nothing. His pinprick eyes fixed on him, emotionless. He crossed his arms, waiting on Tim's decision.

Tim stared back, at first incredulous, then disbelieving, then…

Defiant. He again felt the tickle of mustachioed lips at his ear, pouring in their mischief and mirth. Reminding him of who he was. Who he had become, in the company of a man they wanted him to hand over, trussed like a Christmas goose. Tim had faced down a pack of lions not once, but twice, and lived. Broken a Vigenère cipher. Delivered three criminals to justice, earned hundreds of pounds in reward for the Yard. Distracted the press from their string of recent bungles. Got them a win. By the letter of the law, he had failed in his duty, but he would not sign away the rest of his life.

He rose to his feet, jaw set, gaze steady, arms relaxed but ready at his sides. He lifted his chin as he met Quayle's commanding stare with one of his own, matching him in might if not in height. With eager tongue, he savored his words before unleashing them, relishing their power, their precision, until finally he could cage them no longer. Tim opened his mouth, and—

The door crashed open. Before they could whip their heads around, a hand gloved in tangerine silk tossed a white handkerchief between them. Tim watched as it sailed through the air, then fluttered down to the desk, landing in a puff underscored by Quayle's oath. He locked his eyes on the monogrammed *HB* as the scent of spiced musk and strong coffee invaded his senses. For a time he couldn't bring himself to bear witness to the travesty about to take place. The sound of protesting voices being slammed out by a door he heard as a drum of war.

"Mr. Bash, this is a private meeting," Quayle barked. "Get out!"

"And here I thought I'd simply mislaid my invitation." Hiero clicked his tongue as he perched himself on the edge of the desk in too-close quarters to Quayle. "Superintendent, I regret to inform you that I'm here to report an injustice."

"We have sergeants for that."

"I'm sure you do, and they would no doubt scribble down every last detail for an extra shilling or two, but this concern, my concern... Well, it concerns you."

"Does it now?"

Tim heard the growl under Quayle's tone and sighed. "Please. Leave us."

"But I've only just got here. It's rather..." Hiero clasped his hands together to keep them from waving about. "'Official' is the word, I suppose."

Quayle snorted, the sound of a bull preparing to gore. "'Authority, rather, is the order of the day. Mine over yours. As I said, get out."

"A boyhood dream of mine," Hiero continued as if no one had spoken, "to stand proud before a field of men and lead them to the charge. No temperament for it, alas. Too..."

"Artistic," Tim offered.

"Buffoonish," Quayle countered.

"... curious. The world holds so many marvels; I cannot fathom why men would want to waste their time fighting over petty rivalries."

Quayle had turned the color of a boiled quince. "Holds its share of horrors. That's why."

"Precisely, sir. Precisely. Why, that's the very reason my little cabal took up our great endeavor: to right a few of the wrongs committed in this great city of ours. Surely you cannot argue with such an ambition."

"On the contrary, Mr. Bash, I—"

"Of course, we've had our stumbles along the way. This most recent case, as you may have noted, was rather like a pound cake. It started life as a sticky little mess, then baked itself into quite the cinderblock. Mixed-metaphorically speaking. Though not if you've ever had pound cake. You see what I mean?"

"I do not, nor do I care to."

"Oh, you are a bit of a curmudgeon, Superintendent Quayle, if I may observe. I shall speak plain..."

"I doubt it."

Hiero chuckled. Tim didn't think he imagined the undercurrent of menace. "I see my reputation precedes me. Very well. I will attempt to speak in a language a blunt and righteous man such as yourself understands." Hiero rose to his full height, which Tim discovered outmatched Quayle by several inches. With pantherlike intent, he prowled around Quayle, stepping a toe inside his socially acceptable perimeter and staring point-blank into his gun-sight eyes. "The DI will be the last man you send our way. Oh, I know you won't stop. But neither will I. I'm a detective, Superintendent Quayle, though I may not have the shield to show it. I'll suffer no more insults to my character. I'll suss out every spy you send. I'll sup with your superiors until I have them eating out of my hand. I'll have your badge and honor and—"

"Hiero," Tim pleaded. "Don't."

"—before I'm done with you, and if you doubt it, read the papers. I'm the hero of the day."

"Sirs," Tim appealed to them, "I do not want this. I did not ask for it."

Quayle glared at Hiero, murder in his eyes. But he held his tongue, nodding for him to continue.

"I see no need to toddle down such an ominous and obstacle-laden road, do you? And where would it lead us, pistols at dawn and the like? No, it won't do." Hiero strolled around the office, a lecturer warming to his topic. "Where others see rivalry, I see opportunity. And in the very clever and very worthy DI Kipling—"

"Stoker."

"—whathaveyou, I see not an arrow, but an olive branch." Hiero halted, positioning himself in such a way that he addressed them both but looked directly at Tim. Who could not, despite a manful struggle, pry his eyes away. What a strange and glorious creature stood before him. How had he ever thought himself up to the task of taming him? "My team and I will continue our good work. With your blessing, the DI will act as consultant and liaison, making certain we do not overstep and keeping you abreast of our investigations. The result will be a happy marriage between our consulting agency and your efforts here at the Yard."

Hiero clapped his hands together as if the very act would make it so.

"No." Tim intervened before the pensive silence could stretch out further. "Absolutely not. It's very"—he stammered, struggling for clarity and control—"kind of you, Mr. Bash. You have my gratitude and my admiration, but my place is here. I am a sworn officer of the Metropolitan Police, and I'll accept whatever punishment Superintendent Quayle judges to be fair."

The silence, ever persistent, burrowed its way around them. Tim knew to say any more would be unwise—Quayle, bushy brows furrowed and leathery lips frowned, looked even more the primate than usual and as likely to pummel as ponder. Hiero kept twinkling at Tim with his starry eyes, an entire galaxy of light contained in those twin orbs.

Tim felt tethered to two wild stallions set off in opposing directions. The darkest part of him, the craven, libidinous thing that wanted nothing more than to crawl into Hiero's bed forever, slithered its way up from his groin, coiling around his heart. But that noble organ pounded with ten times its normal strength, a vibrant tattoo steering him down a far more righteous path: penance for his mistakes. He conjured up the bloody handprints, the gory trail, the sight of his butchered parents drowning in the multitudinous seas incarnadine...

"Hold, Stoker." Superintendent Quayle's words startled Tim out of his reverie into an atmosphere that unnerved him. He could have punched the smirk off Quayle's face, it was so unwelcome. "There may be some merit to Mr. Bash's proposal."

"Sir, you cannot—"

Quayle halted him with a look. "I don't care for people who try to have one over on me, Mr. Bash. But I'll tell you what I do admire: loyalty. It's a cold day in hell when a man like you sticks his nose out for one of us. Mixed-metaphorically speaking. What's in it for you?"

"I should think that obvious, Superintendent."

"Enlighten me."

"The opportunity to keep satisfying my... curiosity."

"About?"

"The world. Criminal acts. Violent acts. Thievery and despera-tion. The inscrutable at the heart of every man."

Quayle scoffed. "You might not like the answer."

"I daresay not. My search continues, regardless."

"Your timing's nothing to sniff at either." Quayle considered Tim and Hiero in turn. A glint in his beady eyes signaled the exact moment Tim lost. "All cases will be cleared by me before you start investigating them. DI Stoker has final say on everything. Any conflict of interest with the Yard, you beg off. You nick anyone, you deliver them here. At the end of each case, you'll turn over all the evidence. Including the rewards. You'll tell the press that the police helped you every step of the way, and you are working with our permission. Need help? You ask us first. If you learn anything that might help one of our cases, you tell us straightaway. I can change my mind about this arrangement of ours at any time. I can dissolve your partnership and continue to investigate you. If you commit a crime working for us... well, God help you. Those are my terms."

Hiero's eyes went supernova. "Agreed."

With reluctance Quayle proffered a hand, which Hiero clasped in a surprisingly firm grip. The shake sealed Tim's fate.

"Get him out of here," Quayle ordered—to either of them, or both.

Dizzy with shock and heavy with despair, Tim stumbled out into the corridor. The echo of his former colleagues' bustle and laughter buzzed out from the common areas, swarming him as he fled to the side exit, burst out into the street. He gulped down long draughts of air, but the smoky brume only clogged his lungs, making him cough. An ashy grime coated his teeth and tongue—the taste of London and failure.

An arm linked with his own. Tim stared down at the tangerine-silk glove that curled so elegantly around his wrist, wanting to stroke it, needing to pull away. Forever tantalized by the mystery man who now kept the key to his shackles.

"You've ruined me."

"I've done nothing of the sort."

"I was already the subject of ridicule; now I'll be a laughingstock. No better than one of those barkers that accompanies sideshow magicians—"

"Bite your tongue. An honest living, that."

"Not if you're a detective!"

Tim wrenched away from him, racing off down a side street toward the Thames. He'd decide between here and there whether to hurl himself into the river. He didn't slow when he heard the footfalls behind him, smirked at the panting breaths, the grunts of annoyance.

He hadn't burned off even a quarter of his ire when he darted down an alley, hated himself for weakening at Hiero's whimpered "Stop!"

A lonely courtyard ringed by shuttered windows reignited his anger. "I had one ambition. One! And you've dashed it with your... your wheedling and your trickery and always your chatter, chatter, chatter! You *talk* people into submission, that's what you do. Converse me away from my instincts and reason and into..." Tim gave his head a violent shake. "Why couldn't you just leave me be!"

Hiero huffed. "And what good would that have done you?"

"I'd still have a career! A reputation!"

"A pittance for a prince such as you."

"Don't do that!" Tim's head swelled so hot he feared it might explode. "Don't flatter me when you've just smashed my life to pieces!"

"And they say I have a flair for the dramatic." Hiero regarded him so softly Tim had to turn away. "Your talents are wasted at the Yard. I think you know this."

Tim swallowed hard, admitted, "I do. But it was the only way."

"We will find another. Together."

"You don't even know what I'm talking about."

"Gregory and Amaranthe Stoker. April seventeenth, 1858." Tim spun around to find Hiero right beside him. "You're not the only one who can play detective."

"I see Mr. Han was thorough."

"Touché." Hiero brushed a lock of hair off his brow, stroked down the side of his face. Despite himself Tim leaned into the touch. "Have you truly had such a bad time of it with us? I'd thought you were rather... well, inspired."

"There's too much at stake for me." Tim tried to shake him off, but Hiero closed the distance between them. His breath licked at Tim's temple, ghosted over his cheek. "Too much distraction in your world. Too much exposure."

Hiero chuckled, pressed a cool kiss to his hot skin. "One of the unexpected prices of freedom."

Tim shut his eyes, drank in his spiked-coffee scent, as intoxicating as ever. His arms shook, his tongue scraped, no better than a drunkard with a fresh bottle within reach. The urge to press himself against his sleek, sensual body came on like a fever. When he felt the telltale tickle of Hiero's mustache, he turned his head, caught his mouth. For a heady minute, Tim indulged, thieving Hiero's affections like the bandits they were. There in the daylight, a few paces off a crowded street, he gave into the utopian vision of his future for a moment, embracing passion and endless possibility.

When Hiero latched an arm around his waist and nudged him

toward the shelter of a nearby alcove, Tim stole a final kiss, then slipped out of his embrace.

"And too high a cost for one of my humble means."

Hiero, to his credit, didn't pursue him a second time. Instead a smile so wicked it would have the Sphinx stripped bare and spread curled his lips. "As luck would have it, you've come into some money. Not an extravagant sum, by any means, but enough to fund, say, a private investigation into certain personal affairs."

Tim stiffened. "I won't take a penny from you."

"You are not. I swear it. In whatever language you require to accept the truth."

"I'm fluent in five, and that's not nearly enough."

"Are you? Fascinating. Well, know this. The gentleman in question will take great offense if you refuse him. He's not long for this world."

"I won't be some rake's lapdog. Or worse."

"What you will be, my dear Kip, is at leisure. At liberty to keep your own hours, take on your own cases, right the wrongs you see fit, chase down the very villains that have evaded you for years. By the heavens, man, where is your sense of adventure? Turn your logical mind away from what's done and let yourself imagine, for once, what might be!"

Tim inhaled a breath to object but caught it before it escaped. Retreating to the sanctuary of his most rational mind, he considered the offer from every conceivable angle. The years of drudgery he would return to if demoted by Quayle or, worse, sacked. All the promises he had made to himself in the aftermath of his life's great tragedy. The risks inherent to Hiero's proposal. The fluidity of his relationship with the truth. The mystery of his origins and the magnetism of their mutual attraction. Want versus need versus desire verses duty...

He started when Hiero stilled his ever-busy hands long enough to cup his face. Tim gazed up into his black-pearl eyes as if they held the secrets of the universe.

"I see you." A tinge of sadness softened Hiero's smile. "The wonder you are. The great man you'll become. Other more sultry visions of our future. They ripple out in all directions from this moment. There's beauty in that, and symmetry and possibility. If only..." A sigh. "But there's no need for haste. Think on what I've said. When you've made your decision, you'll know where to find me."

Hiero traced his thumb across Tim's bottom lip but did not dare a kiss. A final, aching look and he flew off, through the courtyard to a hidden archway on the far side.

"And where is that?" Tim called out despite himself.

He paused by one of the crumbling pillars, glanced back. "My dear Kip. You're the detective."

As Hiero disappeared into the fog, Tim fought the urge to flee, to follow him, to fall to the ground and cry out his heart.

Epilogue

$\mathcal{A}$t the knock on his dressing room door, Hiero inhaled deeply, downed the last of his flask, and rose from his fainting couch. Doffing his robe and donning his cape, he hummed a little ditty whose lyrics would scandalize even the saltiest molly house matron as he checked his makeup in the mirror. A change in the program had forced him to improvise—some admiral with more influence than taste requested a soliloquy from Coriolanus, or perhaps Goldie wanted a proper send-off. Regardless, the right side of his face looked as if he'd already been hit with a tomato by an irate punter. Not his specialty, gore. His cosmetic talents lay in hiding in plain sight, not flaying himself open for all to see.

A second briefer knock found him prostrating himself in front of his muses. Divided in his devotion between Melpomene and Thalia, Hiero paid suitable homage to both, chanting their praises— a bit of Aeschylus never hurt—and kissing their feet. Quite literally since both their skirts parted to expose a single sandaled foot. A common motif in all of Han's sculptures and, Hiero suspected, something of a fetish.

At his new shrine to Aphrodite, he lit a candle. While it never hurt to flatter the goddess of love, Hiero needed more than a little of her grace to shine down on him tonight. As he quit his cocoon and followed the stage manager into the wings, he found himself overcome by an altogether unfamiliar sensation: anxiety. Not since his first appearance as Erskine's apprentice had his throat been cinched by an invisible noose, his stomach roaring as if he'd swallowed a bear, and his bowels... Well, the less said, the better. And all because of the possibility of an empty chair.

Taking his position between the side curtains, Hiero measured his breaths out evenly, finding solace in the familiar sounds and smells of the theater. The greasepaint and the gaslights. The hubbub of the crowd. The rustle of the ropes. The wisps of smoke that made him long for one of his roll-ups. The creak of the curtains as they parted. The tension in the air as the audience quieted and he stepped out, heavy footed, stern, commanding. Sword at the ready.

Some other person within him—for he contained multitudes— launched into his speech. The actor in him, perhaps, or the mimic. The one who aspired to greatness but so often fell short. With his usual flair for distraction, Hiero fought the urge to glance over at the box to his left, the one where he often glimpsed Apollo's ghost, still cheering and championing him. Hiero waived payment for his performance if the theater owner agreed to reserve the box for him. Except for tonight when Apollo must finally cede his chair to Hiero's most expected, and most cherished, guest in some time.

If, of course, Kip deigned to show himself.

Hiero had dropped clues aplenty, so many even a clod like Croke could have puzzled them out, given enough time. But three nights had come and gone, and still Apollo's chair sat empty. Three career-best performances wasted on the Gaiety's fickle crowd; three bottles of Glenlivet drained in their aftermath. Three times he almost repaired to their hunting lodge, for no man so plain and rigid and do-goodly and bright and daring and altogether maddening as Kip ever dared resist Hiero's temptation before. He knew how to bait a hook, even if he threw them back in the end. The thought that his rod would be left to slump, limp and lifeless, by the water's edge while such a prize fish swam rings beneath it didn't bear contemplation.

He would not look. Not tonight. Not ever again. Leave Kip to seek him out, hat in hand, on his knees, prostrate before his dressing room door. Hiero would devote himself to his carers and dependents. Take up croquet. Sup more often at his club. Have an entire suit fashioned out of seashells and wear it to the Marchioness of Bathurst's annual naval widows' luncheon. Lecture at Oxford on the history of prestidigitation. Sit for a portrait dressed as Napoleon. Invite the Queen for tea. His life brimmed with possibility and potential. He couldn't abide hesitation or indecision, had no tolerance for worrywarts like Timothy Kipling Stoker. Life, after all, was for the daring.

Hiero slipped back into himself just in time to bellow, "He that depends upon your favors swims with fins of lead and hews down oaks with rushes. Hang ye! Trust ye?" Shakespeare always had the right of it when it came to betrayal and cowardice. And maddening police detectives. Perhaps he'd persuade that peacock Irving the public clamored for his Benedick and himself take on the dual role of Dogberry/Don John, playing both sides of villainy, bumbling and mercenary. He'd write the libretto himself: "Oh, I am as pretty a piece of flesh as any in Messina..."

The telltale click of a curtain being drawn. A blur of movement. A face as pale as a moon drew his eyes to the left. Flighty as a hummingbird at the best of times, Hiero couldn't help himself. He looked. He saw. He smiled. The climactic lines of Coriolanus's speech sank unspoken into his tongue. The audience, confused, took up a tentative applause.

Hiero didn't care. Green eyes the color of the first buds of spring, of endless lush fields, of ferns and moss and everything fecund, like the rich earth in which the seeds of their new alliance had been sown, gazed down upon him. Perhaps not as adoringly as Hiero might have wished, but with intrigue. Expectation. A glimmer of something deeper.

Hiero straightened his posture, resumed his speech. Every word of it directed to that box to the left, from which the most cherished ghost of his past had recently been evicted. To that freckled moon. To those forest-green eyes. To his audience of one.

The End

STOKER AND BASH WILL RETURN

Acknowledgements

This book would not have been possible without the discerning eye and indefatigable enthusiasm of my editor, Nancy-Anne Davies, or the insights of an incredible group of betas, Karen Wellsbury, Liv Rancourt, Day's Lee, and Judie Troyansky. Cocktails are on me, ladies! My cover artist, the Lady Tiferet, worked magic of her own and accomplished quite the feat of prestidigitation in finding a cover model for Hiero. Mila May helped breathe life into my character descriptions with her fantastic promotional drawings, and Robin Patterson designed a beautiful flyer and proto-cover. And heartfelt thanks to Aleks Voinov for paving the self-pub way.

The list of incredible historians doing wonderful, detailed work on the Victorian Era and other periods is too long to mention, but I was particularly helped by books/websites by Liza Pickard, Lee Jackson, Ross Gilfillan, Alan Moss, Chris Payne, and Fern Riddell, and the plentiful resources at the V&A and British Library. Any mistakes I made while transforming their sterling facts into fiction are entirely my own. I am particularly indebted to Agatha Christie, Douglas Adams, Christopher Fowler, Joss Whedon, John Logan, and many more writers of great detectives and trickster princes in mystery and paranormal fiction.

A quick note on historical accuracy. In a very few places, I deliberately changed some historical details for dramatic effect—most notably the burlesque Hiero performs in at The Gaiety. It was not a satire of Robin Hood, but of *Don Giovanni,* the opera by Mozart. Likewise the inspiration for the mystery plot stems from my fascination with the story of The Ghost and The Darkness, two man-eating lions who did indeed terrorize an African village in 1898 (and who are now on display in Chicago's Field Museum of Natural History). I changed the time period and most of the details, but the real story is well worth investigating.

Share Your Experience

If you enjoyed this book, please consider leaving a review on the site where you purchased it, or on GoodReads.

Thank you for your support of independent authors!

Books by Selina Kray

Like Stars

Campania (coming in Fall 2017)

About the Author

Selina Kray is the nom de plume of an author and English editor. Professionally she has covered all the artsy-fartsy bases, having worked in a bookstore, at a cinema, in children's television, and in television distribution, up to her latest incarnation as a subtitle editor and grammar nerd (though she may have always been a grammar nerd). A self-proclaimed geek and pop culture junkie who sometimes manages to pry herself away from the review sites and gossip blogs to write fiction of her own, she is a voracious consumer of art with both a capital and lowercase A.

Selina's aim is to write genre-spanning romances with intricate plots, complex characters, and lots of heart. Whether she has achieved this goal is for you, gentle readers, to decide. At present she is hard at work on future novels at home in Montreal, Quebec, with her wee corgi serving as both foot warmer and in-house critic.

If you're interested in receiving Selina's newsletter and being the first to know when new books are released, plus getting sneak peeks at upcoming novels, please sign up at her website: www.selinakray.net

Find Selina online:
Twitter: @selinakray
Facebook: facebook.com/people/Selina-Kray/100009929464776
Google+: plus.google.com/104484914913249635905
GoodReads: goodreads.com/author/show/9853715.Selina_Kray
Email: selinakray@hotmail.ca
Website: www.selinakray.net